THE PERFECT VICTIM

Lee Ann felt herself falling, but he helped her land on the soft mattress. The room seemed to turn at odd angles. For the first time, she was worried, twisting her head around to see where he was standing. Her heart started to pound.

He chuckled and said, "Lay down. This'll be fun."

His powerful hand pulled her flat onto the bed, then jerked her arms over her head. A pinch around her wrists made her squirm to look over her shoulders. Now her stomach had a block of ice in it as she realized the guy had handcuffed her to some kind of hook in the wall. Fear washed over her, making her head spin faster.

She tried kicking her legs, but they felt like cement as he secured her ankles with another set of steel cuffs.

Now he sat on the edge of the bed, writing in a small, blue journal. His eyes focused on the precise movements of his pen.

"What are you doing?" She couldn't form the question in her mind.

He smiled. "Just a few notes. All has to do with my pharmaceutical work. I think I gave you just the right amount of Oxy and 200 milligrams of Anafranil, but I want to see what happens."

Panic surged up her throat. "Right amount for what?"

"We're gonna see how long I can keep you here quiet and happy and with me . . ."

THE
PERFECT
WOMAN

JAMES
ANDRUS

PINNACLE BOOKS
KENSINGTON PUBLISHING CORP.
www.kensingtonbooks.com

To my agent, Meg Ruley. She never gives up.

PINNACLE BOOKS are published by

Kensington Publishing Corp.
119 West 40th Street
New York, NY 10018

All Kensington titles, imprints, and distributed lines are available at special quantity discounts for bulk purchases for sales promotions, premiums, fund-raising, educational, or institutional use. Special book excerpts or customized printings can also be created to fit specific needs. For details, write or phone the office of the Kensington special sales manager: Kensington Publishing Corp., 119 West 40th Street, New York, NY 10018, attn: Special Sales Department; phone 1-800-221-2647.

ISBN-13: 978-0-7860-2215-1
ISBN-10: 0-7860-2215-9

First printing: April 2010

10 9 8 7 6 5 4 3 2 1

Printed in the United States of America

One

Lee Ann Moffit sprawled across the slick leather couch with a brown stain on the middle cushion and let her head slip onto the guy's broad shoulder. Why not? It was a clean house, and he'd been nice to her all evening. He bought her a fried shrimp dinner at Popeye's (the big shrimp dinner, not the snack meal), gave her a couple of Vicodin to keep her sane, and now he sat quietly with her as she drank a Rolling Rock and watched some cheap rip-off of *America's Next Top Model*. It had been awhile since she was someplace she could watch TV this time of night, especially a show like this. One of the few fantasies she still held was being a supermodel on the cover of *Sports Illustrated*. Everyone at Sandalwood High had told her she was pretty enough to model. She was convinced of it too until she scraped together three hundred bucks for a "photo-shoot." She believed the tubby, bald photographer when he said she could be a star. It wasn't until she found out what kind of star he meant that her dreams came crashing down.

Now she realized that at an even five feet she was too short to be a model, even if God had given her good cheekbones and an athletic body. Her high school career had been as successful as her attempt at modeling. Aside from playing lacrosse, she didn't accomplish a whole lot in school. She was nice to people and loved kids, so why was it so important to find France on a map or know that President Reagan didn't free the slaves?

She had fights with her mom and new stepdad that she now understood were useless. It was just her way of showing she was growing up. Her stepdad wasn't that bad of a guy. Even her new stepbrother and sister didn't seem so annoying. Lee Ann had to prove she was independent and knew what was best, so she moved out (her mom called it running away) at fifteen. She'd been on her own for a few months when she was found dancing at a strip club off the interstate and sent back home.

Then, at sixteen, she moved out for good. Or so she thought. It was frustrating six months later when the same cop found her, bought her lunch, then took her back home to live. She even knew the cop a little. She had played lacrosse in the same league as his daughter, and that embarrassed her mom.

The third time was the charm. She was close enough to eighteen that her mom didn't even bother calling the cops. She'd moved out and was on her own. Now, Lee Ann didn't like where she had ended up.

It felt like her luck was changing. The right guy might give her the chance to turn things around. Lee Ann was working two different jobs. During the day she was a clerk at a copy/printing place. She liked the word "clerk," and that's what she told people when they asked what she did for a living. It was nice to have a legitimate job. A couple of nights a week she still worked as a dancer. The money was too good to ignore, and she no longer looked at it like a lifetime job, what most people called a career.

She didn't have a drug habit like a lot of the dancers at the Bare Belly Club. She only used prescription drugs, because they were safe. A few painkillers a day, some Oxy when she had the cash, and then the Lunesta to sleep. It all helped and kept her drug-free. That was important to her. She always bought her "safe" prescription drugs from the same two guys. One was a friend of hers named Malachi and the other guy, Ernie, was a sweet college kid who made sure she only took pills that wouldn't hurt her long term. He always stressed that she couldn't get addicted to pills; that's why he sold them instead of crack.

Now, in this pleasant house she felt a thick arm wrap around her bare shoulder. This guy was quiet but smart, really smart. His whole house was wired with cool electronics and he used a few words she had never even heard. He was some kind of teacher in college and seemed just that brainy. The guy also worked at a pharmacy, and that's what interested her. If she got a good hookup in a pharmacy and introduced him to Malachi, things might get better for her. She told Mal she'd met a pharmacy worker, but he told her to play it cool for a few weeks before asking him about supplying some pharmaceuticals or "Farm Aids."

This guy was built too, with a hard strap across his shoulders and biceps she couldn't fit both hands around. She knew how much dedication it took to put on muscle like that. Her old manager, Jamais, who now went by his real name, Franklin, had the same kind of build, only a little taller.

"You okay, Lee Ann? Can I get you anything?"

She purred and gave him a peck on the cheek.

He held out his hand with a couple of Oxycontin pills.

She just nodded and he set them on the coffee table, then used the bottom of his glass to mash them into a light powder. A black cat scurried past when he started to grind the pills.

The guy said, "That's Mr. Whiskers IV. He's a little skittish."

Lee Ann smiled, scooped up the powder, then licked her hand to take in every grain of it. She gulped her beer to wash away the bitter taste.

The room already had a hazy quality to it, and she felt a slight whirl. This was some good shit. She reached for the green Rolling Rock bottle again and knocked it onto the throw rug on top of the hard, cold terrazzo.

"I am so sorry." She meant it, but the words sounded slurred. She hoped she hadn't frightened the cat even more.

He shrugged. "Don't worry about it." He stroked her face, then added, "You wanna go into the bedroom?"

She didn't really, but he'd been so nice. "Maybe just to lay down for a few minutes. This stuff is really hitting me."

He stood and helped her to her feet. Earlier she'd stepped off the path to the front door and her left foot slipped out of her shoe into the decorative sand. Lee Ann was afraid she had twisted her ankle, but now with the Oxy in her system she couldn't tell. Since then she'd carried the shoes around the house with her. Now she discarded the clogs with three-inch heels next to the old couch and allowed him to lead her through the small house. She tripped twice on funky little steps between rooms. It was weird that each room was on a different level. She stumbled once more as they stepped through a doorway near the front of the house.

She paused as he flipped on the overhead light. The room was bare except for a mattress on the floor. Her knees buckled and she lost her balance, but he steadied her. What a gentleman.

An empty duffel bag lay on the terrazzo floor next to the bed.

Lee Ann said, "I've never had Oxy hit me like this before."

"That's because it's not just Oxycontin."

She stared at him, but her eyes couldn't focus well. She felt herself falling, but he helped her land on the soft mattress. In an instant he had slipped off her tank top and was working the hook on the back of her bra.

Before she could protest, her breasts swung free as the room seemed to turn at odd angles. For the first time, she was worried, twisting her head around to see where he was standing. Her heart started to pound.

He chuckled and said, "Lay down. This'll be fun."

His powerful hand pulled her flat onto the bed, then jerked her arms over her head. A pinch around her wrists made her squirm to look over her shoulders. Now her stomach had a block of ice in it as she realized the guy had handcuffed her to some kind of hook in the wall. Fear washed over her, making her head spin faster, like the whirly-wheel at the fair.

She lost track of where he had gone. Her jeans were unsnapped and roughly yanked off along with her favorite pair of panties. She tried kicking her legs, but they felt like cement as he secured her ankles with another set of steel cuffs. Lee Ann thought she might vomit from fear.

Now he sat on the edge of the bed, writing in a small blue journal. His eyes focused on the precise movements of his pen.

"What are you doing?" She couldn't form the question in her mind.

He smiled, revealing strong, healthy teeth. "Just a few notes. All has to do with my pharmaceutical work. I think I gave you just the right amount of Oxy and 200 milligrams of Anafranil, but I want to see what happens."

Panic surged up her throat. "Right amount for what?"

"We're gonna see how long I can keep you here quiet and happy and with me."

Detective John Stallings scanned the front of the shitty old lime-green motel, nasty parking lot, and the alley that led to the beach behind it. The low clouds and light drizzle gave the whole image the perfect accent of grime, gray, and grit. Typical Jacksonville.

A behemoth in a cheap jacket standing in the front of the building was his main concern. Just some gun-toting crack dealer from Springfield hoping to stake out a new zone over here. He was a mountain of "show" muscle, all chest and biceps, probably an ex-jock who used his gym time to look scary but not necessarily to stay in shape. All street cops could tell the difference. Probably scared the damn hotel owner into silence and set up a stash in one of the rooms upstairs. That's why a lanky kid in a Patriots hoodie was at the base of the stairs. If they moved in too quick the whole place would know the po-po were on-site.

Hidden a couple of blocks north with his black Impala in front of them, Stallings twisted his six-foot frame to stretch a kink out of his back, then looked down at his partner and said, "I just see the two ass-holes. The one that looks like a Jaguars lineman out front could cause some shit." He had a good sense of danger. At least danger to himself. After sixteen years with the Jacksonville Sheriff's Office he trusted his judgment when it came to tactical operations. It had taken a few too many beatings, a knife wound, and a bullet in the leg to teach him that, but no one acquired knowledge without suffering or work. Sister Mary had taught him that his first day in kindergarten.

Patty Levine nodded at his assessment, then said, "We should get narcotics in here for these two, then check out room 2-B." Her blond hair hung in a loose braid down her muscular back. Stallings thought she looked like a cheerleader who would kick your ass. And he had seen her do it on several occasions.

"No time for the street team. If she's up in the room, we gotta move right now." He didn't want to get his younger, more ambitious partner in the shithouse with the agency, but this was what kept him going. Finding a young girl who had run away with some middle-aged jack-off gave him the will to move in the morning and fall asleep at night. At least on the nights he slept at all. Unlike most of his fellow detectives he needed work to give him a break from home once in a while. And he needed lucky tips like this one to feel like he was doing all he could for these kids. God knows he hoped some cop somewhere was doing all he could for his Jeanie.

Stallings had asked to be assigned to the missing persons unit. First time they had ever had a detective transfer in. Usually it was just a way for a patrolman to make detective, then move on to the more interesting narcotics or high-profile homicide. For Stallings it was logical, after everything that had happened, to work in crimes/persons and handle missing persons. Even if the other detectives called it the "runaway roundup," he didn't care. It meant something. It also gave him the schedule to see his family more, to coach soccer, and to help Lauren with her homework. Maybe he could correct the mistakes he'd made with Jeanie. He knew his partner, Patty, wanted to try robbery or homicide if she got the chance, but this was the only unit that made sense to him now.

They had the run of the county, and way out here in Jacksonville Beach, fifteen miles east of their main office, he had the freedom to make choices and do the right thing no matter what policy said.

Patty saw his mind drift and smiled at him. "What is it you like to say? Is today the day?"

"C'mon, I know you went through the academy ten years after I did, but they had to still be preaching it. 'Is today the day that changes the rest of your life?' " He glanced back across the two blocks to the monstrous crack dealer, with a neck like a spare tire, in front of the hotel. When he was sure no one had moved, Stallings turned his attention back to Patty. "It's a way to stay focused on the job. I've said it before every assignment, and it keeps me alert."

Patty said, "What if I don't want a change today? What if, and I know this sounds crazy to you, we call for backup before we tangle with a drug dealer who looks like a brown Incredible Hulk in a cheap vinyl jacket?"

Stallings let out a quick laugh. Patty was a great partner: smart, tough, and knew when to crack a joke or two. It had been hard to be around him the past few years, but she never complained or let him down. He hoped he could return the favor. But right now he was on a mission. Keeping his eyes on the mountain of dark flesh and the young lookout at the base of the stairs,

Stallings untucked his shirt to cover his Glock and gold badge clipped on his belt.

Patty flipped over the cover of the battered gray metal notebook case she carried everywhere that stored all aspects of their work and her life, including her schedule, to-do lists, her family's birthdays, and a complete schedule of the University of Florida's sports teams games. She slid out a small photograph of a fourteen-year-old girl with bright orange hair holding a small black dog.

Stallings glanced at the photo. "I saw her picture before. If there's a girl in that room she's coming with us. I don't care who she is."

"And if there's a man with her? We got no PC or warrant. Just a shaky tip."

"Jail is the least of that creep's concerns if he's in a hotel with an underaged girl." He looked down the empty street again. They'd have to walk down there, because the Impala the county issued him was too obvious. "Can you handle the guy by the stairs?"

Patty gave him a sly smile. "No sweat."

Stallings never had to worry about Patty having his back. She could kick just about anyone's ass and moved like a leopard in a fight. Her looks sometimes lulled men into thinking she wasn't a threat. They were always wrong. He gave no more thought to the smaller thug by the stairs.

He was about to start walking when he saw someone at the base of the stairs of the little hotel. Stallings paused, then slowly ducked back into his car and retrieved a small set of Bushnell binoculars with the logo for the Ponte Vedra Inn and Club on the side. He surveyed the area under slightly more magnification and then said, "Shit, hold on."

"What is it?" Patty held a closed ASP expandable baton in her small hand.

"A family is gettin' ready for a trip to the pool. Looks like an Asian family with three little kids." He checked again and saw one small girl holding a bright pink plastic tube as her mother bent to adjust her tiny suit.

"Who'd go swimming in this weather?"

"Let's wait a minute. I don't want to ruin these kids' vacation if this is the only place their parents could afford."

Finally, after several minutes of waiting, the little troupe moved down the walkway toward the pool at the rear of the building, and Stallings watched as Patty slipped down onto the beach across the street to approach from another direction.

Stallings crossed the two-lane road and then started strolling toward the hotel and the giant sentry out front. He didn't hurry; that way Patty had time to set up. He also didn't want this monster to have any reason to suspect that Five-0 was in the area. This wasn't downtown; he probably expected a more polite police force. That assumption would be shattered in the next minute.

Stallings wasn't cocky. He knew he could be the one on the wrong end of a fist or a cheap pistol, but he had surprise on his side. He focused on the academy mantra: "Is this the day that changes my life?" It really was something he'd said his whole career. The hell of it was now he really did need a change. He needed a miracle to get back all he had lost.

There were cops he knew who were quick to mix it up with a suspect. They liked the thrill and violence. Violence accomplished a goal, whether it was an arrest or a lesson; physical aggression was just another tool in a good cop's bag of tricks. If you took it too far you had to be prepared to explain yourself. He could admit, at least to himself, that he enjoyed confrontation with the right thug. Bullies, pimps, and predators often didn't understand anything but a good thumping. And sometimes he didn't know how to deal with them except with a good thumping.

A Ping-Pong ball bounced around inside his stomach as he got closer to the hotel. He drifted to the inside of the sidewalk so the bulky dealer wouldn't see him until he was at the next building. His heart picked up a few beats as he nudged his pistol under his shirt and hoped he didn't have to use it. Through this entire ritual of checking his gear and his attitude he didn't lose sight of the mission: save the girl. He knew if he could grab her before anything serious happened up in the room, he might not have to look for her as a runaway later. That was the key, identifying a problem early and acting. He only wished he'd been that smart for his own daughter's sake.

Now he was near the hotel and visible. A small smile crept across his face when he saw Patty step up next to the skinny lookout near the stairs. The dumbass didn't even know she was behind him. Patty was letting him focus totally on the giant man leaning on the battered and rusting chain-link fence. He was younger than Stallings, maybe thirty-five, and taller by at least five inches. The monster had to go six-five and over two-fifty without as much fat as Stallings had originally thought.

Stallings gave him a casual nod as he came closer but kept looking down the street like his destination was another cheap-ass hotel or maybe one of the ancient, beat-up condos that mostly housed aging snowbirds. That little maneuver allowed him to walk right past the man without telegraphing his intentions. Just in front of the giant man, he spun and threw an elbow under a prominent chin, then a knee into the side of his leg. The man crumpled as Stallings's knee connected with the common peroneal nerve.

Stallings turned toward the stairway as the surprised lookout stood, prepared to rocket up the stairs and sound the alarm. Instead, Patty popped open her ASP with a flick of her wrist and tripped him as he started to take flight. She had a size-six Rockport boot on his chest before he knew what had happened. The twenty-eight-year-old detective looked like a big game hunter posing with an unfortunate antelope.

Stallings wasted no time with his man on the street, thumping his head against a metal fence post, then reaching to his waistband to retrieve a Taurus nine-millimeter from the dazed man.

The dealer gasped, "I ain't holding. You got nothing on me."

"I got this gun, you dumb shit." He tucked the cheap pistol in his belt, then shook the man by the collar to make sure he had his full attention. "This is just a warning. Leave this hotel alone and head back over to Phoenix Avenue or this shit will happen to you every fucking day." He wrapped his hand in the front of the crack dealer's shirt and jerked the man's face up to him. "Are we clear?"

The crack dealer's shiny head bobbed as he caught his breath and tried to regain some composure. The thug may have weighed more than 250 pounds, but right now he was looking up into blue eyes that conveyed the threat of violent injury better than any pistol ever made by Smith & Wesson.

Patty led the other young man over, tugging him by his ear, then thrusting him into his cohort. She said to them both, "Give up your cell phones." Her voice left no room for argument.

"What?" asked the skinny lookout.

She snapped her fingers. "Phones, hotshot. Then you can scurry off." She paused and added, "If you behave." She took the BlackBerries from the men, then casually dropped them onto the asphalt and crushed them under the heel of her boot.

There was no protest.

A few minutes later, Stallings and Patty were on the stairs ready to go into room 2-B. They had allowed the dealer to call his partner in the stash room to clear out. Stallings thought it was a good idea so they wouldn't bother the hotel owner later. He knew the dopers had flushed a good part of their profits before they had piled into a tricked-out Escalade and fled back to Jacksonville proper. He didn't give a shit about the dope.

Patty leaned in close and said, "If there's a man with her up there you can't hurt him."

He just stared at her.

"That's not Jeanie up there. Nothing you do will change the past. We're cops, not vigilantes. We need to hear the whole story."

"Whole story! If there's an adult male with a fourteen-year-old up there it's a crime. He can't even try the Roman Polanski excuse. Those days are past." He dialed it down before his voice carried up the stairs and across the open hallway. Patty had a point. She always did. But in cases like this she really didn't understand. He would save the girl, but if he got the chance to teach this pervert a lesson he'd do it for every father in the country.

As they eased up the stairs, Patty stooped down and picked up two towels in front of 2-A. She just looked at him and smiled, then motioned him to the side of the door with a nod of her head.

He knew she was street-smart, so he stepped to the far side of the door to 2-B, where he'd been told the girl was staying, and let his partner do her thing. She stood directly in front of the door so anyone inside would see her standing there, holding towels like a hotel employee, then knocked on the door firmly.

From inside he heard shuffling, then a man's voice said, "What? Who is it?"

Patty calmly added a slight, Latin-flared accent and called back, "I got towels and a new TV remote for you."

There was a pause. Patty turned and whispered, "No man will turn down a new remote."

Sure enough the door moved with a chain keeping it from opening all the way. Once the man got a look at Patty by herself, he shut the door, removed the chain, and then opened it wide with a predatory grin still on his round face.

Stallings stepped from around the corner and shoved the man hard, back into the room.

"What the hell?" shouted the man as he steadied himself against the cheap dresser. He wore only a stained, white towel around his waist and looked like he was in his early thirties. His chubby body and touch of gray made it hard for Stallings to guess his exact age other than it was old enough to get his ass kicked.

He looked around the room quickly, but didn't see anyone else. He nodded for Patty to check the bathroom as he stepped up next to the startled occupant.

Stallings smiled and said, "Nice day, huh?"

"What the hell is going on?"

"C'mon, you're not an idiot." He lifted his shirt, exposing the gun and badge. "You know why we're here."

An old trick, but one that worked. Usually people started jabbering about what they were doing. Not this guy. He clammed up immediately.

Patty tried the door then knocked softly. "Hello?"

No answer.

The man in the towel said, "I don't know why you're here. Why don't you explain yourself, Officer?"

"It's Detective, and I'd rather have your guest explain it."

Patty jiggled the doorknob again and tried to force the door.

The man said, "I have no idea what you're talking about. You just violated my civil rights."

Stallings kept his cool and started to ease toward Patty. If this guy was alone he had some ass-kissing to do and he wanted Patty out before the guy got her name at least. He stood next to Patty and tried the door. He thought he heard a faint noise from the other side and slammed his shoulder into the old, hollow wooden door. It popped past the lock and opened into the empty bathroom. Uh-oh.

He stepped inside and then over to the tiny open window. Glancing out he saw a young girl, wrapped in a towel, on the lower roof of the office below.

Patty slid in next to him and they both said, "Shit." Then they sprang into action. But once he had gotten back to the main room he froze, because it was empty too. He turned and said, "You get the girl, and I'll go after the man."

Patty darted out of the room at least knowing the last location of the runaway. Stallings shot down the closest stairway into the trash-strewn parking lot. Nothing. His head swiveled in every direction as he dashed toward the street. He looked in both directions on the main street but only saw a few pedestrians and a couple of cars. The panic of a parent who'd lost their child at the mall built inside him. He didn't want this scared runaway to screw up her life. He raced back toward the hotel and down the hallway between the one-story office and two-story hotel. As he crossed a doorway to the covered parking area he slammed into someone like two trucks on a highway.

Stallings dropped backward onto the ground, already apologizing and trying to see who he'd run into. Then he froze as a smile washed over him. On the ground next to him was the pudgy man from upstairs, his towel unwrapped and blood dripping from his cut lip.

Stallings sprang to a crouch, but the man didn't move. He stood slowly, making sure none of his middle-aged bones were broken, then looked down at the unconscious man.

From the end of the hallway Patty called out.

He looked up and breathed a sigh of relief when he saw her with the girl, unharmed and crying like she had just found her older sister. Patty wrapped an arm around her and said, "Let's go get you some clothes." She had worked in the unit long enough to realize how confused this girl was and the fear of being caught with an older man. It was not the typical detective's assignment. Not cut and dried, guilty or innocent, but layered like a counselor's job, with several sides to every story. For every kid that ran from abuse and neglect there was another who left for reasons no one could ever explain.

A few minutes later, Stallings sat with the motel manager, a neat Pakistani man with a name tag that said WOODY. He had asked for all the registration slips from the hotel and Woody had pleasantly complied.

He waited while the little Asian family, who had rushed in from the pool after the excitement, checked at the desk to make sure everything was all right.

Stallings stood next to the manager like another employee and said to the father, "We're sorry for the inconvenience. We'll be happy to give you your room free for three nights."

This caused Woody to turn and stare at him in shock.

The Asian man beamed and thanked them as he turned with his kids in tow and headed out the door. The little girl turned and smiled at Stallings, who returned it. That felt good.

Now Stallings looked at the manager and said, "Relax, I'll pay for the room."

Woody said, "Forget it. Chasing away the drug dealers will help me more than milking that guy for a few nights. Besides I charge sixteen dollars a day to park." He winked at Stallings, but saw the look on the detective's face and tore up the parking card as well.

"How long have those jerk-offs been bothering you?"

"Maybe a month now. They came over two days a week, threw some cash at me and said they'd burn the place down if I called the cops."

Stallings nodded as he went through the registration slips Woody had provided.

Patty sat in the car out front with the girl leaning on the hood, sobbing softly. The creep, who had checked in under the name "Joe Smith," sat in the backseat in cuffs, still only wearing a towel.

Stallings thumbed through the flimsy sheets of paper, then paused, reached into his shirt pocket, popped out the cheap reading glasses he had picked up at Walmart, and resumed his search with more clarity. He had resisted the glasses until last year, when his arms no longer reached the distance he needed. His youngest daughter, Lauren, told him the glasses made him look smart, so he didn't mind. He doubted many smart people had scarred eyebrows from fistfights or a knife wound just under their left armpit, but he liked the illusion anyway.

After he had established a signed slip as the only record for Mr. Smith, Stallings handed the registration slips back, thanked the manager, and started to turn away when he caught a whiff of something that stopped him. He turned and said, "What's that smell?"

Woody shrugged and said, "I've been smelling it too. But I checked. No gas leaks. Nothing unusual."

Stallings stepped one way then the other, trying to find the source of the odor, following it toward a narrow hallway with several closets. "What's in here?"

The manager stepped from behind the desk, looking like an adolescent next to the taller, beefier Stallings. "All storage."

"What kind of storage?"

"Beach chairs, suitcases, lost and found."

Stallings stood in one spot to let the smell drift to him, then took a few steps to one side. Finally he said, "Open the middle door."

The manager fumbled with a ring of more than fifty keys and opened the solid wood door. The stench slapped Stallings in the face.

The manager said, "You've got a good nose. I couldn't tell where it was coming from."

Now Stallings was more precise, careful not to touch the door as he flicked on the light in the long, crowded storage room. He looked down one wall and back the other until his eyes fell on a thick, black duffel bag shoved in next to the wall on the dusty cement floor. He nudged it with his finger, then stepped closer, the manager following him into the cramped room.

"Where'd this bag come from?"

The manager shrugged. "I think the other clerk slid it in here when someone forgot it in the lobby yesterday. He mentioned there was a heavy suitcase left here."

Stallings studied the small lock on the bag, dug in his front pocket for a Leatherman tool, and used the needle-nose pliers to rip it off the bag. The manager, mesmerized by the action, didn't protest.

Stallings hesitated with his fingers on the zipper, then yanked the tiny handle down the track of the zipper about ten inches until he saw the pale, pretty face of a young woman.

"Oh, no, no, no, this is a dreadful thing," said the manager, his accent becoming much more pronounced. Then he was quick to add, "She wasn't a guest. This isn't our fault. I don't know who she is."

Stallings sighed. "I do. Her name is Lee Ann Moffit."

This was a day that would change his life.

Two

Patty Levine had just handed off the runaway girl to a county social worker, who was taking her to a shelter until they worked out something with the parents. The second she looked up from her metal notebook and saw John Stallings, Patty knew that something had happened. Stallings's handsome face was usually a mask of calm during times of stress. His curly brown hair framed his blue eyes and made him look like a stylish doctor who had played rough sports as a younger man. He rarely showed any reaction, preferring, like any good cop, to keep people guessing, but now he was leaning out the front door of the motel motioning her to come in and she knew something bad had happened. She could tell their day had swung off the ordinary track. The Xanax she had sneaked at lunch kept her reactions smooth, but she popped another just to be on the safe side and swallowed it dry. She was careful never to allow any nervous tension to show at work. As one of the few female detectives, Patty felt as if she had to set an example and be twice as tough as any male cop. That only led to more stress. She didn't drink like a lot of the cops, so this was her answer to dealing with the job. It was a decent rationalization that worked most of the time.

"What's wrong?" she asked as she hurried toward him, her hand dropping toward the Beretta on her hip. Her Rockport boots were a little clunky, but she could hustle in them and no street thug in Arlington gave her shit once he felt her boot buried in his ribs or stuck up his ass.

Stallings leaned toward her, keeping his voice low. "We got a body zipped in a suitcase in one of the storage rooms." He conveyed concern but not panic. She liked his professionalism.

"Is it related to the dopers we let go?"

"No, it's one of the runaways I used to deal with. Lee Ann Moffitt."

She saw it in his face and heard it in his voice. This poor guy didn't need something like this right now. Not after his own daughter had disappeared.

"I'm calling it directly into our homicide unit."

"Stall, this is Jacksonville Beach. They should catch this homicide."

He looked up at her, his expression certain and direct. "I have to be involved in this case. I'm calling the Sheriff's Office."

She knew not to suggest any other course of action.

The store on Edgewood Avenue was his favorite to work in. The clinics and hospitals sent all the people who needed cheap prescriptions to this store or the one in central Jax. Both stores were in areas with a lot of homeless and street people, the safest group to look for test subjects. If they disappeared no one noticed for a long time, and if the body was found, there wasn't a family screaming for the police to solve the crime. But he had to use his brain and be patient to find just the right one. This was still new to him.

Right now there were no customers in the pharmacy area and he was using the free time to straighten up. He grabbed a commercial container of Vytorin and tucked it back onto the narrow shelf where the big sellers were stored. The whole time his eyes scanned the area picking up information he might be able to use in the future. That was the way his mind worked. It had earned him a 4.0 at the University of North Florida and a master's degree eighteen months later from the University of Florida. That had been a rough year and a half, driving back and forth to Gainesville three days a week to cram in classes from early in the day until late afternoon. He still had to help his mother every evening and never felt like he was part of the "Gator Nation." Just like he never felt like one of the group at the pharmacy.

He picked up an information flyer on a new muscle relaxer to see how it interacted with serotonin reuptake inhibitors. He'd seen the big commercial container of them in the back but hadn't noticed any prescriptions come across the counter yet. He tucked the flyer into his back pocket so he could study it better at home. He knew no one here was going to bother to read it.

The tubby old pharmacist looked down from his perch to a young, well-dressed woman who he guessed was a "Chi-Chi," which was the store slang for paying customer from the phrase "cash in hand with insurance." He didn't know how they got the longer "Chi-Chi" from that, but everyone used it to be cool. Besides, "Chi-Chis" weren't something they saw very often in the small pharmacy. The woman listened as the old pharmacist used his condescending tone almost as much as he did on the free clinic patients.

"Look, sweetheart," said the man in the coffee-stained white smock. "This is a twenty-five milligram tablet. That's low for Elavil, but you should start seeing the effects in a couple of days. Okay?"

He stepped closer to the pharmacist and tapped the flabby man on the shoulder.

The older pharmacist turned and glared at him. "What the fuck is it, Billy? Can't you see I'm busy?" His red face almost glowed.

Although it was a slightly lower tone than the pharmacist's normal voice, William Dremmel cringed, knowing the customer could hear him just like the cashier and anyone else in the rear half of the store.

Dremmel cleared his throat and whispered. "That blouse makes me think this woman might be pregnant."

"So?"

"Elavil can't be used by women in their first trimester."

The pharmacist turned his ruddy face to look at the woman, then looked back at Dremmel. "She's probably just fat."

The woman looked past the pharmacist and said to Dremmel, "What did you say about pregnancy?"

The pharmacist said, "Don't worry about what he says. He's just a stock boy." He turned to Dremmel and said, "Get back to cleaning up."

Dremmel hesitated, but the woman turned and marched out of the store, so he had accomplished his goal. The pharmacist wouldn't complain about losing a customer, because he'd eventually realize Dremmel was right. This wasn't the first time Dremmel had kept him from making a potentially fatal error. He'd go back to cleaning up, but the psychological wound that porky pharmacist had inflicted sapped his energy. When would the other employees see this was just a part-time job for him? It meant nothing. If the community college would let him put his mother on the insurance, he wouldn't worry about the little extra cash and cheap prescriptions he got from here. It sounded better to be a science teacher than a clerk at a second-rate, family-run, nine-store chain of pharmacies. But he'd been there ten years, since he graduated from UNF. At thirty-two he felt he should have more responsibility. At the community college he was considered young for a professor, even a part-time, contract instructor who usually ran the lab classes.

He slinked back to the stock area and finished straightening up.

The cashier, Lori, strolled past him and whispered, "He's just a dumb old fart." She smiled and winked. Her brown skin set off her white teeth in the most complementary way. She also stood in perfect contrast to his pale complexion and wispy, blond hair. Rogaine had helped him but not as much as he wanted. Lori added, "That lady is lucky you were around."

That made Dremmel smile too. Lori had taken one of his classes on Earth Science last year and knew his real profession. She was lithe and graceful at five foot seven, just about his height. She said she was twenty-three, but he had gotten into the company records and saw she was really thirty-one. Women and their vanity made him shake his head. It was this little secret he had that made him feel superior. He loved finding out information and hoarding it for himself. Secret things that took effort to find on a computer or by following a woman around. The only thing he had found that was better than hoarding the secrets was telling the woman everything he knew about her when she couldn't do anything about it.

He was still high from his last "girlfriend," who he had finally discovered couldn't last a full three days with all the different drugs he had pumped into her. She'd seemed hardier than that with her good biceps and healthy hair. He had traveled all the way to Jax Beach to drop her off. He knew how things worked. The Sheriff's Office found the first body in their jurisdiction, now the Jax Beach police would be responsible for Lee Ann. That would screw things up, and he'd take his time to find just the right girl to take as his next "girlfriend."

He couldn't resist putting the bodies in luggage as a nod to the cops that only one person was doing this. It wasn't smart, but he recognized that and accepted it for the little grin it gave him from time to time. He was careful and knew they wouldn't find anything that led to him. Still, he had a procedure for the girls and their disposal, and showing off to the cops wasn't part of the equation. It was just something he felt like doing. So he kept looking for the right woman.

Lori wouldn't do because they worked together; she had family that would report her missing, plus she didn't ever look down on him. That seemed so rare in a woman. Certainly his mother had pushed his father until he snapped. Man, had that fucked up his life.

He thought about his first victim. She hadn't reacted well to his Xanax and Percocet cocktail, just fizzling out and never really regaining anything close to consciousness, lying on the little bed like a lump. Her name was Tawny Wallace, and she had striking green eyes but not much of a figure—just a straight board with square shoulders. Her face was extraordinary, with delicate, precise features, high cheekbones, and clear skin. He'd found her at the community college but she wasn't in either of his classes. That would have been a stupid mistake, and he didn't make mistakes. She'd just asked his opinion of a schedule, and they started talking. No one had any idea they had even met. She was perfect from that perspective.

Tawny told him about her family in Bunnell, an aunt and uncle she had lived with after her mom died of breast cancer when she was fourteen. Her mother's sister had done all she could, but her uncle was an alcoholic who ran the house like his unit in the Marines. He hadn't just retired from the service, they had asked him to leave because he was so tough. She'd moved out as soon as she turned eighteen and hadn't spoken to her aunt or uncle in three months. Dremmel had been subtle but asked who she did talk to on a regular basis. The answer had sealed her fate: no one.

After he took her to eat at Pollo Loco, a fast-food Latin chicken place, she had agreed to come home with him to watch his DVD of *Sleepless in Seattle*, her favorite flick. She didn't even make it to the Empire State Building scene. Instead she had dropped unconscious on his couch, and the thrill to him was indescribable. To finally have a pretty girl at his absolute mercy. No comments about how much money he made or why he lived with his mother. Just blissful, beautiful silence. Then, after silence and lethargy became boring, he realized he might need to work on his drug combinations. He had access to anything he wanted. No one would ever know unless they started losing whole bottles of pills. His needs were substantially under the threshold where anyone would ever notice.

The planning he'd put into his scheme was meticulous and flawless and gave him confidence to know there was no way he could ever be caught. His years of study and natural intelligence would make it impossible for the cops to tie him to any deaths no matter how far he took it, even if he left each body in an identical American Tourister or duffel bag. He had his own methods to avoid detection beyond the simple steps of rubber gloves and a hairnet when he was dealing with the bodies. He had been careful to purchase the bags at a variety of locations using only cash. Thinking like that made him untouchable and above the law.

The experience of holding poor, unconscious, flat-chested Tawny Wallace as she slipped from steady breathing to a slower and slower respiration until the life drained right out of her young body had changed William Dremmel forever. For the better. He now had a task to occupy his considerable intellect and needs.

He now had goals, and all he needed were subjects.

The cops had found Tawny in a Samsonite Jumbo Suiter more than a month ago. He had watched them take the bag after a quick survey of the area. The detective in charge, a well-built guy in a suit, rushed the crime scene people along, and they were out of the shopping center before much of a crowd had gathered. He thought that was just the way things worked in real life instead of TV.

He wondered if he would ever hear anything about Lee Ann. She'd been a good girlfriend. She'd be hard to replace

Lead Homicide Detective Tony Mazzetti adjusted his Joseph Abboud silk tie before stepping into the crappy little motel's lobby. He had waited a few minutes after his lieutenant had verbally knocked the shit out of the Jax Beach assistant chief to ensure the Sheriff's Office investigated this case. He wasn't sure why the L.T. wanted it so badly. All she had said to him was, "Check out this body and tell me how you want to handle it." It was an odd way to phrase a command. Usually the L.T. just said, "Keep me informed." That was cool with him. Lieutenant Hester hadn't worked many homicides as a detective and never told him how to do his job. She just wanted to stay up to date. That's all any good boss wanted.

He knew that jerk John Stallings had found the body, and Mazzetti didn't trust that guy. Not the way his daughter's disappearance was handled. Mazzetti never thought the circumstances or the way Stallings reported it were probed enough by the Sheriff's Office, or as most cops just called it, the S.O. The whole fucking S.O. looked for the missing girl, but no one seemed to care about the conflicting stories or odd time line. Mazzetti could deal with him like he could any lucky schlub who seemed to stumble into one decent case after another. If Mazzetti had that kind of luck on the job he'd be a major by now.

Mazzetti knew the importance of making an entrance. It gave the troops someone to look up to and let them know who was in charge. It made him feel like a prince walking into a royal court. He'd come a long way from skinny Anthony Mazzetti with legs like toothpicks and asthma that made him wheeze like an old vacuum cleaner. He decided a long time ago he'd overcome the puny body God had given him and excel at everything he did so no one could ever say shit about the way he looked and breathed.

Now Mazzetti took in the lobby as he nodded to the various crime scene investigators, making them feel special and not just like nerds here to get in the way. Two uniformed Jax Beach cops had secured the perimeter, and he was pleased to see one of them was smart enough to start a log of who had entered the scene. The Indian hotel manager sat quietly behind the main counter, hypnotized by the activity as if he were watching an episode of *Law and Order*. All these little hotels were owned by dot-heads named Patel or Singh. All the politically correct types down here called them middle easterners. Mazzetti didn't buy into shit like that.

When Tony Mazzetti got accepted to Flagler College in St. Augustine, he never considered he'd go into police work; he just wanted to live in Florida for a while. As a kid he dreamed about it, but the idea of a cop running on stick figure legs made him cry up in his room until his P.E. coach, Mr. Shepard, introduced him to weight training. Once in school he never thought he'd stay down here in this fake, Southern shithole. Quiet St. Augustine was a far cry from his native Brooklyn, and Jacksonville hadn't been any improvement. But he had gotten hooked on the idea of being a cop, and the Jacksonville S.O., despite being stuck in the middle of this swamp of rednecks, was a good, well-paid department. And Mazzetti knew he was the smartest of the entire detective corps, East or West zone.

Mazzetti had risen through the ranks at the Sheriff's Office by taking every assignment he'd ever been given seriously. Whether it was community relations as a patrolman in the upscale tract of Mandarin or narcotics in the downtown slums or crack-devastated Justina Street, Tony Mazzetti treated every case like it was the biggest one he ever handled. Until it was cleared. He cleared ten burglaries on one guy caught in a similar crime. He once closed out five robberies with one mope holding a gun in the same neighborhood. He was a master of clearance rate and the only way to do that was to work hard and use your head. When the national average for solving burglaries was 25 percent he was clearing simple B&Es at almost 80 percent.

Sure he liked arresting the actual perpetrator of a crime. It was satisfying every time he put a killer behind bars. But he didn't want any unsolved cases either. That was why he drove the forensic people so hard on a scene. He wanted nothing left to chance. He was known as the "King of Homicide." A royal title that befitted him. Royalty at thirty-eight, not bad.

Now, after assessing the room, Mazzetti cleared his throat and called out in his fast, sharp Brooklyn accent, "All right, folks, we got everything in place, let's get to work." He looked at the photographer. "Wally, start your survey out here. Tina, do a video from the outside all the way up to the storage room door." He paused to see who moved first. "We're gonna need fibers from the room and body, and"—he looked at the hotel manager—"I'm gonna want to talk to you personally." He couldn't count the number of things he'd ask this little guy; Security video, strange guests, records for everyone checking in the last two weeks, access to the storage room, who the other clerk was. The list went on, and he wouldn't miss any of it.

Satisfied he'd made the appropriate impression with the crime scene geeks, Mazzetti strutted toward the door marked off with bright yellow crime scene tape, slipping on a pair of surgical gloves without losing a step, waiting to see what they had before donning a full white biohazard suit. He pushed the door inward, then froze when he saw the small, feminine face staring up from the opening in the zippered duffel bag. The L.T. had said it was a body in the storage room of the hotel, not one inside a suitcase in the storage room. This changed everything. Immediately Mazzetti realized the implications for the case of a body they'd found in a suitcase last month. The brass had kept that one quiet, and now Mazzetti saw how badly he'd screwed up by clearing the case as an overdose. This body made it obvious he had written off the last case too quickly. A screwup that could haunt him. This could potentially change his career if he didn't handle it right. Holy shit, this was why the lieutenant asked how he wanted to handle it.

Mazzetti stepped out of the room to catch his breath. Knowing all eyes were on him, the senior homicide detective reached for a notepad as he returned to the lobby and took his time flipping through the pages. The first six sheets were notes on an article about the British defeat at Yorktown. At this moment his writing hobby seemed much more promising than his career as a homicide detective.

He had to get his shit together and start these humps moving on the scene. He stood up and carefully said, "I want fibers from that duffel bag too." Mazzetti gulped a breath, clapped his hands. "C'mon, people, let's get moving."

Mazzetti hoped this wasn't the last time he got to handle a scene like this.

Three

William Dremmel sat in a booth at a little sports bar named the Fountain of Youth, ignoring his dry burger and greasy fries as he daydreamed about his former girl-friend, Lee Ann. That was one fine girl. Not to mention how far she advanced his research. He felt as if he were on the brink of discovering the perfect combination of drugs to hold a woman in stasis indefinitely. Just the thought of it made him smile. Then he heard a voice say, "You doin' okay?"

The waitress' bright, pretty smile made his troubles melt away as he gazed at the young woman for a moment, soaking up the light she gave off, or at least the light he saw. He could always spot the right woman.

"Just thinking about everything I have to do." He smiled, knowing his Ralph Lauren shirt, a size too small for him, showed off his biceps.

She smiled again, her white teeth and pink gums radiating health. He'd never see a girl like her in his pharmacy. As he studied her, he saw no physical attributes that would throw off his dosages.

She said, "Well, I'm right here if you want more to drink or something else off the menu."

William glanced around the quiet bar area to make sure no one noticed him talking to her. "What's your name?"

"Stacey. What's yours?"

"William. How long have you worked here?"

"About two weeks."

He leaned toward her slightly and said, "Why don't you tell me about yourself?" He already saw the important stuff, like she was only five foot one, clean, curvy, and pretty.

She glanced at her other occupied table, saw the elderly couple happily chatting over their New England clam chowders, and took the stool next to him.

Her voice had a youthful tinge of excitement. "I just moved down here from Ohio and fell in love with the ocean. I've been going over there every day."

"Which beach?"

"Neptune Beach."

He nodded, "I like that one too. How do your parents feel about you living all the way down here? How do they know you're okay?"

She looked down, her face clouded for a moment. "That's one of the reasons I stayed. They're way too protective and I mean, I *am* twenty-one. I call them once a week, but if they knew exactly where I was they'd be down here bugging me to come home."

"You're here all alone?"

"I had my girlfriend Marcie with me, but she's homesick and is gonna move back this weekend." She paused, then added, "But I'm staying for the sun and beach."

He processed the information, careful not to say too much yet. He didn't want her blabbing to Marcie. Instead, he decided to wait until Monday to really start working her. She was definite girlfriend material as well as a perfect research specimen.

John Stallings had seen it all in the course of his career, and like all major crime scenes, this one spiraled into an organized chaos quickly. Of course in the early days of his career they didn't worry so much about the high-tech biohazard suits and other protection from blood-borne pathogens. Now there was a separate class on it for his refresher training every year. A new cute crime scene tech carefully sketched out the lobby for future use in court. He noticed the young, uniformed, Jax Beach cop stare at the pretty crime scene tech's face. As she concentrated on her work, her tongue stuck out the side of her mouth like it held her lips in place. A tall, skeletal photographer named Wally, wearing a full biohazard suit, snapped digital photos near the storage room. Stallings knew the majority of photos were of Lee Ann Moffit in the bag. He knew the enterprising crime scene photographer moonlighted shooting weddings and birthdays, because he had once seen him at his cousin's wedding using a slick digital with a "JSO" property sticker on the side. The photographer's secret was safe.

This was the first time Stallings had ever looked at a corpse of someone he knew. The young woman had played lacrosse in the same league as Jeanie four years ago, and when Stallings had found her as a runaway he had bonded with the girl's mother. It wasn't too long after Jeanie had disappeared, and it felt satisfying to use his experience to help someone else.

He missed those warm Sunday afternoon games, when problems seemed so far away. He'd sit in a folding chair while Lauren and Charlie romped around the edges of the field and Jeanie drove for a score. Lacrosse was a good outlet for his oldest child's determination and energy. Maria called it stubbornness. That was about the time Jeanie started showing how entrenched she could be. The threat of punishment had little effect on her. Privileges like TV and telephone meant nothing to her. She would sit out groundings silently. After his own childhood, Stallings would never have considered physical punishment.

He still searched for her, or even a hint of her. He had to keep his efforts quiet, because he could never be assigned to his own family's case. But he knew a boatload of other missing persons cops around the country, and they all tried to help. They ran down silly leads he heard on the streets, checked regularly in homeless hangouts, and had her photo up in every police station from Miami to Seattle. Stallings even watched every documentary on runaways in the slight chance he might notice Jeanie in the background of one of the scenes. He had been more overt just after she disappeared but quickly realized he was alienating investigators and screwing up the search more than helping. What was he expected to do? He was a father.

But those warm Sunday lacrosse games and the terror of Jeanie's disappearance were a long time ago. Stallings's main interest now was getting involved in this homicide case. Not like a lapdog or some rookie errand boy, but as a real part of the investigative team. The regular homicide detectives got the real assignments. He'd given up his slot in the unit and now had to find a way to worm his way back in. He knew to get ingrained in the case right now so he couldn't be denied when he asked to work it with homicide.

Patty had written the probable-cause affidavit for the

creep now only known as "Joe Smith" who had checked in with the girl. He'd used every tired excuse Stallings had heard before. "I thought she was eighteen. It was consensual. She doesn't look like a little girl." Fuck him and all the predators that look for these girls that get turned around or have to leave home for some reason. This wasn't even his own personal bias, it was the common view of cops who saw it day in and day out. Just the thought of a middle-aged guy and a thirteen- or fourteen-year-old made him sick to his stomach as he thought about Jeanie and where she might be.

The public had shown an odd interest in predators with the TV show where a reporter lured them into stings. Somehow the show didn't convey the true creepiness of these lowlifes. People even laughed at the antics of some of the numb nuts on the show: one man stripping down in the kitchen, another returning even after being stung already. Stallings saw no humor in it. This was an epidemic as far as he was concerned, and he wished justice could be both harsher and swifter on these pusbags.

Looking out into the lobby, Stallings saw the lead detective, Tony Mazzetti, standing on a chair to be seen and heard by everyone. He stated a few obvious concerns, in his Brooklyn buzz saw of an accent. He didn't want anyone inside the tape that didn't sign the log. So what? He wanted the crime scene guys to take their time with the bag and the room. Anyone would've known that. Finally, no one could talk to the media. That meant no one except him. In fact, that was really why he was on the chair in his fancy suit and monogrammed shirt; he was giving the TV cameras a chance to shoot some interesting B-roll before he got sweaty and had to take off his expensive coat. He was such a media hound the other homicide guys called him the "King of Homicide." Everyone got a nickname. But this jackass didn't realize everyone was goofing on him with his title. His tailored suits and time in the gym building his arms and chest made him look like an extra in a Martin Scorsese film each time he shoved his way in front of a camera.

Mazzetti was a good detective even if Stallings hated to admit it. He was good for the opposite reason that Stallings was. He didn't care about people. They were either victims or perps or witnesses, not mothers or sisters or uncles. Guys like Mazzetti looked at the family of homicide victims as not much more than a bundle of DNA to supply samples so some lab tech could advance a case. It wasn't even like the bullshit that TV shows peddled. All the DNA evidence in the world didn't help in a murder if you didn't have a suspect. Most cases were broken by detectives who knew how to interview and could sift facts from crap in an instant. Mazzetti could interview, interpret what lab reports might mean to a case, and get his face in the newspaper, but he didn't know shit about life. He had no idea what it felt like to lose a loved one or see what one act of violence could do to a whole family. Mazzetti was out to solve the case, no doubt about it, but he missed out on the real value of it, the satisfaction a cop could find by knowing that someone might rest a little easier because of what they did. He was the kind of cop who kept score and rubbed it in people's faces. He was a glory hound.

Stallings knew this asshole would resist assistance on a homicide, and his history with the well-dressed detective wouldn't help. But Stallings could work a room and knew there had to be a way to slip in on the case. Mazzetti just had to think it was his idea, or someone above him in the chain.

Briefly, Stallings considered what would happen to his family if he got involved in homicide again. Although his wife didn't openly blame his long hours for Jeanie's disappearance, he felt her contempt in between rehab stops or when sorrow just overtook her. He didn't like the idea of missing Charlie's soccer practices either, but he knew himself, and this wasn't something he could forget about and move on. Now, more than ever, crimes against young women hit him like a truck. He settled down at a table knowing that sooner or later Mazzetti would have to come to him. The question was whether to let the detective in on his plans to join the case or wait until after he could call in a few favors.

Ten minutes later Stallings watched Mazzetti strut toward him, saying, "Another lucky break for Detective Stallings."

Stallings knew his big arrest of serial killer Carl Cernick years earlier bugged the King of Homicide, so he didn't bother to take the bait.

Stallings said, "Just good police work, Tony." That would bug Mazzetti more than anything else. He hated that Stallings was a local celebrity because of the case.

"You got anything to add, other than you smelled her, then checked the duffel bag?" He rolled his brown eyes to indicate that it wasn't really police work that led Stallings to the body.

Stallings had a lot to add, but for now he said, "I'll write up a report on it. I know her."

"What? How?" The cool detective couldn't hide his surprise. He tried to cover it by smoothing his thin mustache, then pulling the cuffs of his expensive shirt.

"First, I knew her from my daughter's lacrosse

league a few years ago." He had to take a second to swallow, then said, "She was a runaway after that, and I found her." He paused and added, "Twice." He kept his eyes on the dapper detective, looking for any hint of what he was thinking. Mazzetti ignored the work going on behind him as he locked gazes with Stallings.

Finally Mazzetti said, "So the last time you saw her was working the 'runaway roundup'?"

Stallings nodded, still trying to get a fix on what this guy was thinking.

"She a hooker?"

Stallings resisted the urge to punch him. "She did what she had to, but I had heard she was clean the last few months. She even had a job at a copy place." He purposely didn't offer more.

"You know her boyfriends or anything?"

He shook his head. "No, I hadn't seen her in a while. She turned eighteen last year, and her mom stopped filing the missing persons reports."

"You talk to the mother since?" Mazzetti managed to make it sound like an accusation.

Stallings waited as Mazzetti stopped to take some notes. There was a rough sketch of the floor with a few dimensions, list of potential witnesses, and five lines of scribbled words. When the homicide detective looked up again Stallings knew what he was going to ask. It was perfect for his goal.

"You wanna make notification?"

Stallings didn't want to seem eager. No cop wanted to tell the family one of their kids was just found dead, especially if the parent couldn't add anything to a death investigation. Every cop learned that two areas could get you in real trouble real fast: death notifications and missing kids. You never put off either task.

Finally, after making Mazzetti twist in the wind a

while, he said, "Yeah, I could tell Lee Ann's mom. Probably better coming from me anyway."

Mazzetti relaxed slightly, sucked in a breath, and said, "Thanks, Stall. I'll be busy here for a long time anyway."

"Who's helping you on this?"

Mazzetti looked over his shoulder at the crime scene techs and a couple of detectives, then turned back to Stallings. "Don't you worry about it. Homicide has got this covered. You can make notification, but remember to tell me if the mom can add anything." He stood up.

Stallings nodded to Patty and stood up too. The start of a migraine blossomed somewhere deep inside his brain. It was getting late and he felt the need to check in at the house. God knows what could happen if he were too late. That's why he preferred working the seven to three shift; sometimes he'd go 10-8, or in-service, on the radio right from his house and could manage to be home before either of the kids rolled in from school. Today wouldn't be one of those days.

Mazzetti said, "Go find those runaways." His stupid way of making a joke. It was childish, but so were a lot of cops.

"Tony, you don't need to be a dick. I like the assignment."

The homicide detective looked away, stroking his trimmed mustache, "That what happens when your homicide career is based on one lucky grab?"

Stallings smiled. "That may be true, but I'm still the only one in the room with a medal of valor." He didn't wait to see the effect of his response.

Four

John Stallings pulled his county-issued Impala into the driveway of his Cedar Hills home, southwest of the city, took three long, deep breaths, secured his pistol in a metal box under the driver's seat of the car, then consciously put on his "home face." This was the same ritual he had completed after a day at work for many years. It sunk in that he needed two separate personalities when his three-year-old daughter had called someone a "jerk-off." It wasn't even funny to him now thinking back on it.

His comfortable, two-story house was ten minutes from his mom's house if he needed her or his sister, Helen, to come by and help out with the kids, or on occasion with his wife, Maria. They both lived in the house that he grew up in. His dad had spent the final eights years of his career in the Navy at Mayport and grabbed the house a block from the St. Johns River from a chaplain who was getting shipped out to San Diego. The old man had been a hard-ass who wouldn't listen when everyone said he was losing sight of what was important. After Stallings had left for his baseball scholarship at the University of South Florida, his mother made a stand and the old drunken bully moved out. As far as Stallings was concerned it was seventeen years too late. He'd seen his father twice in twenty years. Once at his uncle's funeral and once when the asshole was in the drunk tank at the city jail. At least he had had enough class not to ask for any help when he saw his son in his new blue JSO uniform with a patch that said BOLD NEW CITY OF THE SOUTH on his shoulder.

Stallings helped the old man anyway. He got one of the booking officers to lose his paperwork, and the senior Stallings never had to answer for the drunken punch he threw at some other rummy at a bar off Arlington Avenue.

Stallings had stuck out the beatings and drunken fits, but his older sister, Helen, made her escape at fourteen only to show up a couple years later. She never talked about her time away from the family, but the fact that she still lived quietly with their mom at forty-three spoke volumes about what had happened to her on the street. She never drank, smoked, used drugs, or even dated. He knew she felt guilty about Jeanie's disappearance, like it was some kind of genetic code that had passed to her niece. Secretly, Stallings himself wondered if somehow his sister had influenced events. Either way it was just one more fucked-up aspect of his personal life that he had to keep a lid on for the sake of the family.

The late afternoon sun peeked between low clouds as he prepared to enter his other world. He slid out of the car, nodded to his neighbor like he always did, and headed into the house, hoping for the best, but prepared for the worst. Like he always did.

He let out a quick sigh of relief when he saw Lauren helping Charlie with his homework as soon as he walked in the door. His eight-year-old son's dark hair hung down in front of his face as he looked at the page and listened to his thirteen-year-old sister. Looking at them made any of the shit he saw during the day seem petty and filled him with a sense of purpose like nothing else. He never did understand how parents couldn't do everything in their power to make the best life possible for their kids.

His daughter looked up. "Hey, Dad. You're late today."

"Sorry guys, got hung up at work."

Charlie looked up and grinned. "Hey, Dad."

Stallings walked over and ruffled the boy's hair. "Hey there, Charlie-boy."

"How's the homework going?"

"It's so easy tonight a firefighter could do it." He smiled at the proper use of the joke.

Stallings laughed out loud. Like most cops he had a slight pang of jealousy toward firefighters. Everyone loved firefighters, because they didn't write speeding tickets or arrest people. Cops joked about how their brother public servants got to work out and sleep on duty, and every firefighter he knew had a second business. So jokes at firefighters' expense were common.

Charlie smiled and said, "Can we kick?"

He hesitated. Kicking the soccer ball with his son was one of the things that kept him sane. He had preferred baseball, at least he had some talent there, but his son loved the soccer field, so Stallings adjusted to the new generation's sport of choice. The athletic boy could already outrun him. "I have to head back out in a little bit, pal. We might need to kick twice as long tomorrow."

"Gotta catch a bad guy?"

Stallings laughed out loud, amazed at how his son

had a way of pulling him out of a funk. "No, nothing so exciting. I have to talk to the lieutenant, then see a lady about something. I should be back before bedtime." He caught the look on Lauren's face and shook his head slightly so she knew not to worry. This was business, nothing to do with Mom.

He kissed his daughter on the forehead and looked up at the bookcase holding family photos. Every time he walked in the room he looked up at the last photo with all five of them in it. His oldest daughter, Jeanie, smiled back at him, and he closed his eyes for a quick prayer that she was safe. The support groups all said it was important to remember a missing child and have positive feelings about him or her. Stallings did his best.

Now, three years later, he tried to focus on the family as best he could and these two seemed happy. It had taken counseling, anger, frustration, and time. His quiet search continued as he worked closely with the National Missing Children's Clearinghouse in Washington. They were a smart group that did good work even if most people were ignorant of their efforts. He had computer databases at work he checked once a month or so. Unidentified bodies of young females, a mental patient who wouldn't speak, usually called Jane Doe by the facility, bulletins about any possible connection to his daughter, but nothing had panned out. He needed to show the kids that he had not given up on Jeanie.

He knew that if his wife wasn't out here in the living room, she was on the computer or phone, and he found her in the bedroom, where she tapped away at a black Dell keyboard.

He took a deep breath and felt able to face Maria.

"Hey, dear." He always stayed upbeat until it was clear he couldn't anymore.

She glanced up from an instant message she was composing. "Just finishing up. This poor woman from St. Joe, Missouri, has a daughter who's been missing eight months. I'm just giving her a few ideas for support."

He leaned down to kiss her forehead. It was also a way to sniff her breath

She hit Send and looked up. Her dark oval eyes and high cheekbones made her look as fresh as she did on their wedding day in Las Vegas on her twentieth birthday. They had eloped without fanfare to hide the fact that she was pregnant from her Orthodox Cuban parents. By the time Jeanie came along the goodwill of the baby had distracted Maria's father from the math.

After Stallings's failed baseball and academic career at USF, Maria had seemed like the only thing in his life that was worthwhile. He searched everyday for that old feeling.

Maria said, "How was your day?"

"Not so good."

She glanced back at the screen. "I have to answer this e-mail. Hold on." She plunked back in the swivel chair.

Stallings didn't mind. It looked like another night of peace, and he could go back out to work without distraction for a couple of hours. But he wanted to see the kids before they went to bed. That would keep him going.

Rita Hester pressed the unlock button on her key chain and heard the familiar double beep of her blue

Crown Vic parked in the detective bureau lieutenant's spot outside the main sheriff's building on East Bay Street. Everyone knew the three-story building as the Police Memorial Building or PMB for short. The wind was just right for her to smell the coffee from the Maxwell House plant a few blocks away. That beat the shit out of the breeze carrying the acrid, rancid odor of the paper mills as it had for years. Even though the community and industry had worked hard to ease the effects of the paper mills, and the locals quickly got used to the stench, the wrong breeze would smack you in the face and make tourists gag. No one missed the mill's departure as part of the city's identity. Unfortunately that was just about the only thing visitors remembered from trips to the "bold new city of the south" when the mill poured out the foul-smelling byproducts of paper production. She knew that the sulfur used in the process was part of the odor equation, but later learned it was also the cooking out of the lignins and sugars in the wood. She was just glad it was gone.

From her car she could look up onto the second floor and see "The Land That Time Forgot," as the detectives called it. The detective bureau, with its mismatched carpets, scuffed walls, and ancient equipment, was always the last unit to get upgrades. The public saw the patrol cars and marveled at the computers to get information to the patrolmen but never dealt with detectives. No one seemed to care if there was money in the budget for them. Rita never really cared until the detective bureau fell under her command. She hadn't bothered to actually move into the bureau, deciding instead to keep her office next to the clean lab facilities, but she fought to get any scrap she could for the detectives. Just outfitting them with laptops was a monumental task but she had accomplished it. Sure, they were leftover computers from the training division, but they worked, and it was better than nothing.

As she slid the key into the lock, she sensed someone approaching her. Even in the safety of the Sheriff's Office lot, her twenty years of police work made her reach for her purse and the small Glock model 27 inside. The nine years she spent on patrol taught her to automatically reach to her right hip, where she carried her duty weapon, but as she worked her way through the D-Bureau and up the command structure she had made it a point to retrain herself to reach for her purse.

Then she heard someone say, "Rita, got a minute?"

She relaxed as she realized it was her old road patrol zone partner John Stallings.

"Stall, what chu doin' out so late? Mazzetti keep you on that scene all this time?"

He hesitated.

Normally, in her rushed existence, Rita would bark out a command to "get to the point," but she let Stallings have a moment. Not just for the sake of their time on the road together, but because of the way his daughter's disappearance had affected him. Everyone at the S.O. whispered about the way it was reported, his slow recovery, and speculation his assignment to missing persons was a way to protect him. They didn't realize he wanted to be there and was doing a bang-up job in the unit.

Finally Stallings said, "I gotta ask a favor."

"What's that, Stall? I'll do whatever I can."

"I gotta get assigned to the homicide of the dead girl I found over on Jax Beach."

"Why, Stall? That just doesn't make any sense."

"It's a feeling I have. If we don't find the guy who did that to her, he'll strike again."

That comment froze her. Did he know already? Was

he that smart? She gathered her thoughts and said, "What would Maria and the kids do if you started on a case like this? You could be on it for weeks with barely enough time to eat and sleep."

"They'd understand. Especially because Maria knew Lee Ann Moffit."

"That's another problem, Stall. You knew the victim."

"That's not a problem, it's a benefit. I never really talked to her or the family when she played lacrosse. Mainly, I knew her professionally, no conflict there. I also know who she hung out with and the circles where she traveled. Those kids would never talk to an asshole like Mazzetti." He paused and added. "I'm on my way over to make notification to the family now. Mazzetti needed a hand and I already knew them." He looked at her with those blue eyes and added, "Rita, something is telling me I need to be in this case. Maybe I'm still fucked up over Jeanie, maybe it's something else, but I have to be involved."

Rita thought about telling him the whole story, but decided to wait until they could all sit down together. She considered the veteran detective's request. Stallings was a passionate cop who sometimes did things she didn't approve of. Well, didn't approve of now, as an administrator. When they were on patrol together she supported his offbeat, sometimes unlawful actions to solve a crime by any means available. Some guys could operate like that, knowing how far to take a particular situation and then how to smooth it out afterward. Stallings was the best at that. At least he used to be.

She nodded and said, "Okay, Stall. I may regret this, but I'll have you assigned. We could use a guy like you on this case. But Mazzetti is still the lead."

He smiled. "Thanks, Rita." Then he paused, looked

up at her again, and said, "Any way we could bring my partner, Patty, in on this too? She wants the experience."

"She can't go around with you on this. I got plans for that girl, and getting a beef for being with you when you crack someone's head won't help her on the sergeant's board."

"You're still the best."

She wanted to hug him, but it wasn't appropriate in her current position. She liked him. Everyone did. More importantly, she could use him. It never hurt to have a scapegoat if everything went to hell on a case that was already screwed up

Tony Mazzetti sat in his car for a few minutes to get away from the constant noise and activity of the crime scene. He needed to make some notes and start his "book" that would document every activity related to the case. The so-called murder book was necessary, because even a simple homicide like one gang member shooting another in front of seventeen witnesses typically didn't go to trial until two years after the incident. Even Mazzetti's razor-sharp mind couldn't keep facts straight that long. Not with dozens of homicides in the interim.

He'd have help on this one. The only question was how much help. Right now he and the lieutenant were the only ones familiar with the bigger picture connected to this girl's death. By this time tomorrow or maybe the day after everyone in the department would know, and he was pretty sure he'd be blamed for the fuck-up. The fact that that asshole John Stallings found the body wouldn't help anything. It would only remind everyone of the jerk's lucky grab a few years ago.

Mazzetti shook his head in the silence of his brand-new Crown Vic, the royal carriage of police vehicles. No one had any idea how busy a homicide detective was on a big case like this one. Not only would he be investigating leads, but he'd have to manage other detectives, keep the Book, update command staff, be the spokesman for the media (which he actually liked quite a bit), and deal with all the crazies who would wander in with tips that he'd have to follow up so some smart-ass defense attorney couldn't bring it up in court as a possible defense.

This was a lonely and thankless job. Thank God he'd make a fortune in overtime.

Streetlights came on and TV sets glowed in most windows of the upscale neighborhood off St. John's Bluff Road, in the eastern patrol zone of JSO, as John Stallings took a few minutes to gather his thoughts. Patrol zone 2 covered Arlington Road all the way to the beach, and even though it had a lot of miles, it wasn't the busiest zone in the Sheriff's Office. The acres of slash pines and scrub brush differed from the tall, sturdier looking Southern pines along the interstate. When he'd offered to notify Lee Ann Moffit's family of her death it was a way to weasel onto the case. Now, with the job at hand, he didn't like the idea of using the poor dead girl's family as an excuse to get something he wanted. It bothered him so much that he had sent Patty home for the night, telling her he'd be more comfortable talking to the family alone. Patty had resisted, but he put on his sad puppy face and she relented with a minimum of fuss.

Stallings eased out of his Impala, smoothing his shirt to his chest. This sucked.

On his way up the long driveway he passed a Mercedes convertible with the top down and a Range Rover with a huge gash in the side. The lights inside the house cast a glow onto the entrance that allowed him to dodge a bicycle on its side with a tricycle positioned like a bull over a fallen matador. He hoped the accident wasn't as bad as it looked. He knew the younger kids belonged to the stepfather who had entered Lee Ann's life about the time she started running away.

He mashed a lighted doorbell button, then followed it with a double rap on the door. Out of habit he stepped back and to the side, away from the door or anything that could potentially be shot through it.

After a few seconds he could hear a woman's voice, and the door opened inward. Lee Ann Moffit's mother, Jackie, swayed as she tried to focus her vision enough to see who the hell was knocking on her door at this hour.

Seeing Stallings, her harsh expression eased, revealing the attractive woman he'd met when Lee Ann ran away. She still had on the dressy blazer that identified her as a major dealer in the real estate market. A cigarette was wedged between her fingers. "Detective John Stallings. What are you doing so far east?" She stepped aside and waved him inside in a long drunken curtsy.

He nodded and said, "How are you, Jackie?"

"I'm here. What about you? How's your wife holding up?"

Stallings paused, uncertain how to answer the question. He knew he'd disclosed too much of his private life to this pretty woman. The shared circumstances had caused him to let go with Jackie Moffit. Jeanie had not been gone too long, he was new to the missing persons unit, and he'd known the Moffitt family slightly through lacrosse. Now he realized he might have shared too much with Jackie when Lee Ann had run away the first time, explaining how his wife was having a hard time coping with their own situation. At the time, he thought he was helping her. But it was to help him too. Sharing an experience like a missing child helped people feel they weren't alone and was a major source of comfort for most people. But most people didn't have a profession like his. Now he knew he had no frame of reference to help this poor woman whom he was about to tell her oldest daughter was dead. All he could do was promise himself he'd do whatever it took to catch the person who killed her.

Suddenly the migraine made him squeeze his eyes shut as flashes of pain shot through his brain. The distracted Jackie didn't notice as she searched for a place to lay down her cigarette.

When she turned to face him Stallings said, "You better sit down, Jackie. I'm afraid I have some bad news for you."

Five

Patty Levine picked at a Lean Cuisine lasagna as she watched the late local news. The first story was, of course, the body Stallings had found earlier in the day. Tony Mazzetti stood in front of cameras to explain that the Sheriff's Office had taken the homicide investigation and managed to talk about very few actual facts of the case. Jacksonville Beach was the official jurisdiction where the body was found, and Patty wondered why the Sheriff's Office had decided to take on more work, but in the end it wasn't her concern. Her job was finding missing persons, usually kids, and it was important. And she got to wear a detective's shield. But two years at the same thing was getting old. It wasn't like there were a bunch of volunteers to come into the missing persons unit. Pretty much it was her and John Stallings, and it looked like that's how it was going to stay.

She looked across the room at her kitchen counter, where she had six prescription bottles lined up in a row, then glanced at the clock in her DVR to see if it was time to throw down a few Ambien. She'd taken the last

Xanax about four in the afternoon and didn't like the drug effects to overlap too strongly. Luckily, she hadn't needed any Percocet this evening for her chronic hip pain. The years of gymnastics had taken their toll on her young body. When someone commented that she'd been a cheerleader, Patty dropped into her speech about the rigors of gymnastics, one of the toughest sports in the world and recognized by the Olympic committee. She only gave the speech to someone one time; the second time they faced physical confrontation. Cheerleading was fun and games, gymnastics was a sport, which was why she needed the drugs to mask any physical problems. Everyone knew she was as tough as any male cop, and she didn't intend to let a little hip pain slow her down. No one at the office realized she often had a throbbing ache in her hip or that she was a serious insomniac or that she felt anxious for no reason. And no one ever would. She liked her image.

Right now she needed sleep, and Ambien was the only thing that gave her any chance at that. She exceeded the dosage because the twelve milligrams just didn't cut it anymore.

Her cat, Cornelia, butted a hard, furry head against her leg, then jumped up onto the low couch. Patty, still looking at the TV, said to Cornelia, "That Tony Mazzetti is a sharp dresser. He looks good on the tube."

She tossed the plastic container of her dinner and rinsed off the fork; this routine had kept her from using her dishwasher for the last three months. Ready to watch something lighter with Cornelia, she paused at the counter and threw down two Ambien, way more than the usual dosage, knowing the onset would be more than twenty minutes, if at all. Her cell phone, next to the parade of pills, started to ring. She recognized the number as one from the sheriff's main office.

She flipped it open. "Patty Levine."

A sharp, fast male's voice said, "Report to homicide at oh eight hundred. Got it?"

"Yeah, I got it. Who's this?" But the phone went dead before she got an answer. A wave of excitement swept through her. She had just gotten called to the major leagues.

William Dremmel felt the familiar rush as he learned more about the lovely young waitress, Stacey Hines. He had casually strolled behind the restaurant where she worked and found a beat-up Ford Escort with Ohio tags. From there it was an easy step to access a hacker's Web site he knew and run the tag through the Ohio motor vehicles bureau and come up with Stacey's full name and date of birth. Now he'd find out everything about her before he visited her again next week. It made him feel like an all-knowing god.

The hacker's site he was on was set up by one of his former students who appreciated his Natural Science professor's ability to see things other than academics. He'd bonded with the little group of social misfits who felt out of place at the community college. They had the grades to go to any state school, but not the drive or, in some cases, the money. They reminded him of himself at that age: lonely, smart, awkward. He enjoyed showing them ways to beat the system. Dremmel had used his knowledge of computers to show the young man how to tap into a number of different computer data banks and then the hacker took it the rest of the way. Now Dremmel used this site as a way to search things quickly and quietly. No one could trace any of his queries back to him.

The Toshiba notebook computer sat on the small

oak desk that had been in his bedroom as a child, in this same one-story redbrick house in Grove Park. The quiet neighborhood on the west side of the city was the perfect place for his experiments. The houses had a little space between them, most of the residents were too old to be nosy, and he could be on the interstate or heading east in a matter of minutes.

One-third of the house had been constructed as a "mother-in-law" suite with a large bedroom, sitting room, and its own bathroom. A small, covered courtyard separated the two sections of the house. His grandmother had lived in that side of the house until he was seven, about the time of the accident. That part of the house had level floors, even with the kitchen both sides shared. His father had never bothered to change the odd, multilevel floor of this part of the house, and now Dremmel was glad he didn't. Those little five-inch steps made it almost impossible for anyone in a wheelchair to get around. Thank God.

In the last few years the oak desk sat in his "darkroom," which he had quickly converted to a normal room since his last girlfriend had moved out. The small mattress was back in the garage on the top shelf of a storage rack. The eyebolts from the reinforced wall sat on his workbench. Matching end tables perfectly covered the holes where the sturdy eyebolts screwed into the wall and held his girlfriends securely. The photographic equipment and developing chemicals were out of the closet and set up again so if someone were to wander in the room they wouldn't think it was anything other than an amateur photography studio. That explained the bricked-up windows.

Now he quietly made notes about Stacey Hines, who was twenty-one, five foot two inches tall, had electricity in her name, but not cable TV, and had not yet been listed as an employee of the Fountain of Youth sports bar/restaurant where he had chatted with her earlier in the evening.

The intercom wired to the other section of the house buzzed and he heard his mother. Sound echoed over the terrazzo floors and bare walls like a cave. He could tell by the crackle of the intercom and the volume that she had the intercom right next to her mouth.

"William? Are you home? William."

He waited, hoping she might drop back into sleep.

"William, I'm hungry." Her voice was cultured, calm, with a hint of a southern accent she usually put on, especially if she was around people, which he had discouraged for some time now.

He sighed, hit the intercom, and said, "Give me a few minutes, Mom." He scooted out of the wooden chair and padded toward the kitchen, knowing exactly what would shut her up—a can of Campbell's chicken gumbo. He let the soup plop into a large green bowl, sprinkled in a little garlic powder, then mashed 50 milligrams of Molindone and stirred it into the soup. He had found that the tranquilizer/antipsychotic had several beneficial effects, but mainly it calmed her down enough that he could deal with her and keep her clean. He added an Ambien to the soup for good measure. It should give his mom enough time to eat before she dozed off until the morning when he left for work. He popped the bowl into the microwave as Mr. Whiskers IV bumped his leg.

He squatted down, his heavily muscled legs straining his jeans, and stroked the black cat. So far he had tested a few pharmaceutical theories on Mr. Whiskers IV, nothing like the ones the original Mr. Whiskers and the two that followed had endured. In the ten years he'd worked at the pharmacy, Dremmel had learned more about drug interaction and sedation than any standard textbook or drug study could ever teach him. He was smarter than any pharmacist. Legitimate drug companies weren't prepared to do the things he'd done to test the effects of sedatives and narcotics. He had kept Mr. Whiskers II asleep but alive for more than three weeks. That was a good drug trial.

Now his goal was to replicate that kind of effect on something a little larger. His test subjects were all between 100 and 120 pounds, within five years of the same age, and around five feet tall. He had decided on shorter women, because he didn't know if taller subjects with less fat would metabolize the drugs the same way. He preferred them to be attractive, but that had no scientific bearing.

From the intercom he heard, "William, is my dinner ready?"

He mashed another Ambien, pulled the soup from the microwave ten seconds early, scooped the powder into the bowl, and mixed it as he hurried through the short gap between the sections of the house into the room on the far side of the courtyard. He padded past the sitting room, then down the hallway, and paused at his mother's open door.

He eased in the room and forced a smile. His mother lay on top of the bedspread, her wheelchair next to the bed. She was in a bright yellow dress that covered most of her thin, discolored legs. From the waist up she was still an attractive, fifty-five-year-old woman with no gray in her brown hair. Looking at her sitting at a dinner table no one would be able to tell what she had been through or what she had put her son through. She was still trim, and her face showed few wrinkles or other signs of age. But her expression was a different story. She looked confused and detached from her surroundings.

The car accident that had killed his father and crippled his mother was a turning point in young William Dremmel's life. It had certainly changed his relationship with his mother.

She reached out silently with her long fingers for the bowl of soup. Almost the identical meal she had every night.

Dremmel turned to leave, but she said, "Sit down a minute. I haven't seen you today."

He plopped into the padded folding chair next to her messy queen-size bed, where half-finished crossword puzzles littered the comforter.

"Are you alone tonight?"

He nodded.

"No date?"

"Lee Ann and I broke up."

His mother frowned. "I wanted to meet her too."

"You would've liked her."

"What was she like?"

He couldn't contain his smile when he answered. "She was real quiet."

Six

It was early, too damn early for a meeting, but this was what he wanted. At least he thought this was what he wanted. Shit.

Detective John Stallings sat in front of the lieutenant's desk with his mouth shut and his eyes on the senior officer in the room. He didn't like the idea of Tony Mazzetti and a young female homicide detective sitting out of his line of sight, but that's how it shook out when he walked into Lieutenant Hester's plush office with a view of a new condo going up across the street. One of the detective sergeants sat next to him. The regular homicide sergeant, a stand-up guy named McAfee, had just retired, and this was a nervous temporary admin sergeant from computer crime. Rita Hester stepped from behind her wide oak desk and sat on it directly in front of Stallings, folded her considerable arms, and leveled a gaze at him.

"This is what you wanted, Stall. You're on the case. In fact, we're setting up a task force to find this killer."

"A task force for a single homicide? Why the fire-power?"

The lieutenant's eyes flicked over to the sergeant, then back to Stallings. "It may not be so simple." Her voice steady and calm.

"How so?"

"This is the second victim in a suitcase in thirty-five days."

"What? I never even heard about the other one."

The fact that no one in the room said anything told Stallings that someone had fucked up. From behind him, Mazzetti chimed in. "We thought the first one was an overdose. No big deal. You know how it is."

Stallings didn't bother turning to face him. "You claimed a body inside a suitcase was an accidental overdose? No, Tony, I don't have any idea how something like that is. I know that helps the clearance rate, but it sure fucks up everything else."

The pudgy computer crime sergeant turned and said, "Stall, she was naked with no ID. We honestly thought she had overdosed in a drug house and someone decided to dispose of her in the bag. There was no sign of trauma, and she had Oxycontin in her system. A lot of it."

"What about Lee Ann Moffit?"

"We're waiting on the toxicology, but it looks like the exact same thing."

Stallings started to stand. "Are you fucking kidding me? We gotta get on this before this asshole kills someone else."

The lieutenant held up her hand. "Not so fast, Stall."

He eased back down into the chair, waiting to hear that other shoe that always seemed to drop. But after hearing that the same killer had struck twice he doubted she could say anything that would be more fucked up than that.

The lieutenant considered her words, then nodded. Her pretty face hid the fact that on the street she was known as the "Brown Bomber" for her devastating strikes with her baton. "You're on the case, but this is Mazzetti's show. You're gonna look at leads related to the runaway culture and use your contacts there. You will assist Detective Mazzetti on leads as he sees fit. You will not give Mazzetti any shit in front of the other detectives. And you will keep your mouth shut about the how the first homicide was initially handled."

"You mean how it was fucked up?"

"I mean that if I have to waste time explaining how to act for one more second you can go back to the 'runaway roundup' and we'll somehow manage to carry on without your help." She stared him down. "Do you understand everything I just said?"

Stallings swallowed hard. "Yes, ma'am, I understand." It was hard to argue with a good cop.

The lieutenant cracked a brief smile. "Good to hear."

Now that all issues were settled, Stallings leaned forward in his chair to leave, but as he started to stand up the lieutenant placed a hand on his shoulder to have him wait.

Mazzetti hesitated when he saw Stallings was sticking around, but a glare from the lieutenant chased him out the door.

The lieutenant waited a moment as the door clicked closed, then looked down at Stallings. "We need to talk privately for a minute. Just Stall and Rita, not detective and big-black-bitch-who-can-bust-him-back-to-patrol-if-she-needs-to."

She was still funny. "Sure, Rita, anything you need."

"The girl you found with the predator yesterday. I

know you popped a crack dealer from Houston Street and then sent him on his way with no official action. But just like every other time you kicked someone's ass, you said or did something that kept it quiet. You've never had a serious complaint against you. You get results. That's what we need on this case—results."

"So you want me to break the rules?"

"I want you to find this killer. Talk to all your snitches, scare the street dealers, I don't care. Mazzetti will do most of the investigative work, find where the luggage was bought, see if some pharmacy is missing Oxycontin, find forensic links between victims. But you're going to be doing your thing too."

"What about following the book?"

"We will follow the book. But John Stallings is going to be John Stallings no matter what any book says. That's what I need."

Stallings wasn't certain, but it felt like the first time anyone in command had ever told him it was time to kick ass and take names.

Seven

By the time John Stallings marched into the homicide squad bay in the detective bureau, Patty had already grabbed her computer and the metal pad case where she stored everything. The dented and scratched case said a lot about Stallings's partner; she was practical, didn't care what others thought, and was tough as nails, just like the case. The back of it had the indentation of a smart-ass pimp's forehead for suggesting Patty would be a good addition to his stable. Luckily the man didn't want his reputation to suffer because a petite, pretty, female cop had knocked him unconscious, and he never said a word about it. But everyone knew after that not to smart off to the diminutive detective from Crimes/Persons.

Stallings trudged down the hall nodding to several of the detectives already in place. Tony Mazzetti intercepted him at the doorway.

"There's a dress code here, Stall. This is homicide." His smirk would've earned him a punch on the street.

His trimmed mustache and perfect hair moved in unison as he broke into a full smile.

Stallings gave him a smile as he shook his head. "A suit like you? Too hot outside." He started to push past.

"C'mon, Stall, we got an image. Your pullover and the whole exposed badge and gun on the belt thing doesn't fit in." He straightened Stallings's collar. "Maybe just a shirt and tie would be okay."

Stallings stared at him. "Where do I sit, asshole?"

Mazzetti just pointed to a desk stuffed all the way inside the old, unused holding cell that was a remnant of the building before the jail was built next door with booking areas and interview rooms. A gray computer monitor took up an entire side of the desk.

He ignored the ancient, lingering urine smell and then scooted the desk out into the squad bay, careful to balance the gigantic monitor as he did. He didn't look up to see who was laughing or who was in on the little joke. When he sat at the desk with his files on top, he noticed most of the detectives were watching him. There was another joke on its way. He opened the bottom drawer to put his files in order and saw it immediately. Sand. All the drawers were filled with fine, white sand. Someone had carted up bags of the stuff to dump in his desk.

He knew how to play it off. He'd pulled the same prank on rookies coming in the bureau before. Stallings rolled back his chair, left the files where they were, and headed out the door.

On his way he looked over at Mazzetti. "I got a lead on the case. I'll call you if I make an arrest." He knew the vague hint at a break in the case would eat at the lead detective.

A smile crept across his face as he walked out of the

D-bureau. Behind him he heard Mazzetti calling, but he kept walking right into the open elevator door. What timing!

Patty Levine wasted no time grabbing the two thin case files on the previously unrelated deaths and started to do her thing. She was an organizer, a task-oriented, detailed, precise investigator who often found things in records that other detectives missed. She'd located more than one runaway by painstakingly looking through e-mail records the family had provided, then determining who might hold the key to the missing child's whereabouts. She'd used bank records to help uncover a drug suspect when she was pulled out of patrol for a temporary duty assignment, or TDY, in vice and narcotics.

It was that kind of investigation that fit her pack rat mentality. It also fed into her mildly compulsive personality. It made her a standout cop in a profession where men liked to stand out.

Now she looked at the reports, the early lab results, and the pile of photographs, to see if the connection was obvious beyond both victims being found inside luggage. Immediately she saw it. Both dead women, more like girls, were short. As a gymnast, Patty had been small for her age until a growth spurt shot her to a towering five foot five. She had still managed a scholarship to the University of Florida for her ability on the open floor exercises but she just didn't have the drive to go any further. The pressure of the competitions had also worn on her. Her second year was the first time she learned about the relief the right pharmaceutical could provide. After she suffered back spasms, a doctor prescribed the muscle relaxer diazepam, under the name of Valium, and the effect on her anxiety was stronger than the effect on her tight back. She lost her fear of competition but also lost any edge she had, which, added to her height, meant she quickly fell off the list of potential champions. The photos of the dead girls reminded her of teammates.

Just thinking about her past and competitions made her reach into her knockoff Coach purse for her tiny travel carrier of Xanax. She popped one and swallowed it dry, her eyes dancing around the crowded squad bay quickly to make sure no one noticed.

She'd seen Stallings come in and set up shop at a nasty old desk on the inside of the bay. The whole room looked like a set out of a 1960s TV police show with thin, ratty carpet running down the center of the room and cheap linoleum near the old holding cells that were now filled with ancient files and rotting boxes of records. Why was the sheriff punishing the detectives in Crimes/Persons when the rest of the building looked like a modern, clean, efficient office complex? Patty didn't get it.

Focusing again, Patty laid out the photos of the two dead women and stared down at them, wondering how something like this really affected John Stallings. Although he didn't talk much about his missing daughter, he had to wonder if Jeanie's photo was on some cop's desk, dead, discolored, and unidentified. She hadn't known Stallings three years ago when his daughter's disappearance was a major news story and the S.O. did everything possible to find her. She had heard the rumors that the girl had been gone quite a while when they finally reported it, and some of the officers, the ones who didn't really know Stall, speculated that there was something fishy about it. She knew it was all bull-shit, and she knew that one of the things that drove a guy like Stallings was his sorrow over losing Jeanie.

A voice snapped her out of her tunnel vision.

"I'm glad you got assigned to the case." It was Tony Mazzetti, and the cute smile seemed at odds with his reputation or even the way his Brooklyn accent changed from funny to harsh.

Most people raised in the South didn't view an obvious accent from north of Maryland as friendly and inviting. She smiled back. "Thanks."

"You'll see how things run pretty quick, but keep an eye out for practical jokes. The guys pull 'em on everyone who joins us."

She let out a laugh and said, "Doesn't every unit?"

He nodded, his brown eyes focused and clear. She'd seen him directing most of the detectives and looking over at the material that was starting to flow into the bureau. Mazzetti had pulled all the reports of drug thefts for the past three months, the missing persons reports for young women, any reports of assaults where a man approached a young woman and tried to get her to leave a public place with him. She was fascinated at how much raw data had to be sifted and how this one guy seemed to be doing it all.

She gestured to the photos on her desk. "I'm just getting familiar with the case and looking for a pattern."

"We'll have a meeting later with specific assignments. Then you'll have plenty to do."

"Will I be working with my partner, Stallings?"

His face darkened. "No, he's been told to run some specific leads alone. We have a mountain of things that need to be done. I doubt we'll see much of the master detective."

Just by the phrase "master detective," Patty sensed there was a bigger problem than she thought between John Stallings and Tony Mazzetti.

William Dremmel drove over the Fuller Warren Bridge to his Tuesday morning biology lab class at the community college. He bumped along in his tan Nissan Quest. It gave him the appearance of a family man, but the missing middle seats gave him plenty of storage room, and the minivan never seemed to have any mechanical problems. It was as invisible a vehicle as there was. No one noticed a bland minivan tooling along at the speed limit. In a sense the van was like him, unnoticed by almost everyone. It could hold a suitcase or a pallet of decorative sand from Home Depot with equal ease. Easy to vacuum out and wash down, it was the perfect vehicle for him.

At the school he automatically set up the frog sections so students could prepare slides for the microscope. He was distracted by the image of the cute Stacey Hines, the waitress from Ohio who didn't want to go back. The hours he'd spent on the computer discovering the little mysteries of the girl had been so satisfying that he'd experienced a near-constant erection since he first learned just how alone the young woman really was. Soon, after her roommate had returned to Ohio, he would step in and show her the attention she deserved. Just the idea of her living so quietly in his special darkroom made him grin from ear to ear.

He'd done some research on men who had been successful in endeavors similar to his own. Ted Bundy had escaped detection several times by cleaning his VW bug with chlorine on a regular basis. Of course forensics were a lot less sophisticated in the 1970s, but the theory was sound. Bundy went on to become a legend of American killers.

Dremmel knew that few people learned the lessons of today from studying history. That was what he tried to get across to his students; by studying the past you can avoid the same mistakes again. No one followed this concept: not presidents, not generals, and apparently not serial killers.

He'd been reading up on Jacksonville's most recent serial killers. One of the killers, Paul Durousseau, had broken a simple rule: don't let anyone see you with a victim. As a taxi driver, Durousseau had access to a number of victims, but one concerned family tracked their missing daughter to him. Jovanna Jefferson's body had been found in early 2003, and the fact that she had ridden in his cab was the break the Sheriff's Office needed to direct their attention to the former soldier. It was his troubled time in the army and violent disputes with his wife that convinced the detectives he was their man.

Dremmel had no criminal record. There was hardly any record of him at all, anywhere. He was truly the invisible man, and he had something else Mr. Durousseau didn't: brains. He could outwit anyone looking into the disappearance of a couple of petite girls. Hell, he hadn't even heard anything about Tawny Wallace since he dumped her over in Springfield. It was as if she had never existed.

The other local killer he had read about was Carl Cernick. The crazy Czech upholsterer had strangled four women over nine months when a cop named Stallings, who at the time was investigating some other crime, had found him. That was a huge element of luck, but Cernick could've survived it if he'd been prepared with a story and nothing to link him to the victims. Instead he had kept mementos, in this case, a finger from one of the victims. But that had more to do with being a psychotic than it did with being smart. Dremmel would avoid that problem, because he knew he wasn't crazy.

He was a scientist.

Tony Mazzetti had tried to focus on assigning duties to the other detectives, but he kept wondering what John Stallings was doing and if he was more than just lucky. Stallings's capture of Carl Cernick had seemed like the luckiest break any cop had ever had. That was the kind of arrest Mazzetti had always dreamed about making. Glory, news coverage, citation. Damn it, Stallings even got the medal of valor for making the arrest by himself. That's the kind of thing that Mazzetti needed.

He knew these rednecks didn't necessarily appreciate a New Yorker in their midst. But no one, not the lowest crime scene weenie, all the way up to and including the all-powerful sheriff, could say he wasn't a great detective. No one had his clearance rates. No one spent more time keeping his shit straight. All he needed was a big, flashy arrest like the one Stallings had made. With something like that no one would care if he was from New York or a goddamn Arab. He'd just be the best fucking detective anyone knew.

He decided to test Stallings right away on his willingness to be a team player. He had the secretary call everyone involved in the case to be at a meeting right after lunch in the homicide squad bay. That way he could see what the detective was up to, show him who was in charge, and set the right example for all the lesser detectives who'd been sent to help on this case.

Eight

John Stallings knew the town pretty well. The city of Jacksonville was traditionally good to visitors. It was essentially a Southern town both geographically and culturally. But it had a severe inferiority complex. The industry wasn't large enough to support the town alone. Tourism wasn't nearly as strong here as in South Florida, and the climate made it a lot more like Georgia than Florida. Jacksonville wanted to be a shining star in the Sunshine State, but felt more like a traffic tie-up on the way to Disney World.

The city dumped tax dollars into image control, hosting the Super Bowl, promoting the Jaguars and the annual Florida-Georgia game at the Alltel Stadium, which used to be called the Gator Bowl, but no one wanted to talk about the homeless and runaways who had to pretty much fend for themselves. *Business Week* magazine listed J-Ville as one of the saddest cities in America based on stats like cloudy skies, crime and suicide rates, and unemployment.

John Stallings had spent a few hours checking some

of the places that attracted runaways. It wasn't like the old movies or stupid TV shows where everything happened at the bus station. Hell, the Greyhound terminal in Jacksonville on Pearl Street was relatively clean and comfortable, and it took people to other places. Teens who had left home were either gone or had come to Jacksonville from somewhere else. Finding runaways while at a transit point was like finding supermodels at the deli.

Teens who lived out on the street had hangouts. There was an old, abandoned hospital that homeless people found ways into and used as a shelter. Houses that offered some security either by an understanding adult or sometimes quietly by some foundation that figured having the teens safe was better than letting them loose on the streets, where they always ran into trouble. These safe houses may not contact parents or get the kids back home, but they were better than nothing. There was a place called the Trinity Rescue Mission that did a good job of looking after the homeless.

Years ago Stallings viewed them as an impediment to investigations, a group who thought they were above the law. He believed that teens should be dragged home if found and these safe houses were sending the wrong message. Part of that was hearing his father complain about Helen while she was gone and believing that she was better off with the family. Now he had the opposite sentiment and even tried to throw a little cash their way when he could. It was funny how his view of the world had evolved in the last few years.

Stallings had learned what it took for a sixteen-year-old to fend for herself and where she might do it. He also learned that it took a long time to build up trust with this subculture and shuddered at the thought of that idiot Mazzetti blundering into it thinking he could use his size and commanding voice to scare people into talking to the cops.

But Stallings knew better than to ignore the call to a meeting on the case just after lunch. Most meetings were useless and just a way for someone to show they could call a meeting to tell other cops things they already knew. Stallings had to admit that in this case he was interested in what they already knew and who was going to do the legwork.

Rita Hester had told him his role, but he wondered if they would abuse Patty. She was a sharp and tough detective, but also junior in the D-bureau. Patty's looks could be deceiving, and he hoped the macho homicide dicks didn't stick her on menial, worthless tasks. He wanted her to see if this was the kind of work she was interested in, and if she wanted to move on from missing persons, he'd support her. He was her partner; that was his job.

At the top of the staircase leading to the "D-bureau" or detective bureau, a tall road patrol sergeant named Rick Ellis stopped him.

"Stall, what's shakin'?"

Stallings shook the bearlike hand and said, "I'm up in homicide for a little while."

"I haven't seen so many guys up in the Land That Time Forgot since Cernick was on the loose."

Stallings looked down, not sure what to say. He didn't know how public the task force was yet.

Ellis's eyes popped larger. "Jesus, don't tell me we got us another serial killer." A good cop read between the lines, and Ellis was a damn good cop.

"I don't know exactly what's going on yet, Rick."

"Days like this I'm glad to be working traffic and patrol. Let me know if I need to pass something on to my troops."

"I promise."

As they started to head in opposite directions the uniformed sergeant said, "You look good, Stall. I'm glad to see you're back in the game."

Stallings sat at his desk, writing down a few phone numbers as Tony Mazzetti prepared to address the group of detectives by looking down at a few pages of notes. Someone had already cleaned the sand out of his drawers and his few personal belongings were arranged on the desk next to the computer that looked like something out of the *Flintstones*. It resembled a stained, off-white boulder with a rounded, green screen. He never had a lot of things to move around whenever he changed units at the S.O.—a photo of the whole family from a trip to Six Flags four years ago, an old-style Rolodex with business cards and little notes crammed into it, and a penholder with a soccer ball that was a thank-you from Charlie's team he coached last fall. It said, "Coach John. You Rock." It might have been his most cherished possession.

The low ceilings and stained fiber panels that hung between dim fluorescent lights made Mazzetti's clean, crisp suit look impressive. The other eleven detectives took life in the Land That Time Forgot more casually. Patty and the other two female detectives had on jeans and professional blouses. One of them, Christina Hogrebe, or "Hoagie," as she was commonly known, wore a pullover with the JSO badge and her name embroidered on the left chest.

The male detectives seemed to pattern themselves after Mazzetti, only with less taste and cash to throw into their wardrobes. Short-sleeve shirts with cheap polyester ties were the average, with Stallings at the low end of the scale in a simple polo shirt. What he needed to do on the case didn't involve undercover or trying to impress anyone with his clothing.

Mazzetti began, "We've got a lot of forensics and lab work to decipher. So far we've found some black cat hair that may match on both victims. There are other factors that might tie the victims together."

Someone called out, "Like what?"

"Their size, for one thing. Both women were five feet give or take an inch and a little over a hundred pounds. That may mean a lot." His dark eyes scanned the room to see if anyone had any theories to throw out there. "I think it might mean this guy has his own height complex. That may be how he targets his victims. The fact that both victims were found stuffed inside some kind of luggage is also a detail that connects them."

A lean, hard-nosed guy named Luis Martinez, pulled in from auto theft, said, "What's with the first victim? I didn't even realize we had another homicide like it."

Mazzetti fumbled. "I-I," he paused, took a moment, then said, "we were handling it quietly." He cut his eyes to the silent Rita Hester sitting at the rear of the main group of detectives, but she didn't offer any help. "That's not important anymore. What's vital is that we're all on the same sheet of music and hit these leads hard."

Stallings chuckled quietly, knowing the subject of how Detective Perfect screwed up would not go away. If anything, as the case wore on it would become more of a concern and subject to scrutiny.

Mazzetti looked down at his notes. "Right now we're just gonna call this a homicide case. No nicknames or operations."

Martinez said, "C'mon, Tony, I already had a perfect name for the investigation."

Mazzetti sighed, "Okay, Luis, I'll bite. What do you want to call it?"

"Son of Samsonite."

The laughter around the squad bay was typical of cops who were exposed to the worst of society everyday. They could make jokes at horrific crime scenes, laugh at car accidents, and basically ignore things that would drive the average person insane, but for Stallings that shit had gone by the wayside a few years ago. He wanted to hit the street and find who had killed these girls. He wanted to start right this fucking minute, before the killer had a chance to strike again. He didn't have time for jokes anymore.

He raised his hand and said, "Tony, now that we know about the linked deaths, what are we gonna do about it?"

"Good, at least someone is ready to get out there." He looked down and started writing a few comments on his note pages. "We gotta see if we can identify someone named 'Jamais.' Moffit had his name tattooed on her upper right shoulder." He pointed at a few detectives. "You guys are gonna fan out through the city." He turned to another pair of detectives. "You two are going to check tattoo parlors to see if anyone local drew it." After a few more assignments he looked at Patty Levine. "I need you to see if you can track down the manufacturer of the luggage to see if there is any way to get an angle on it that way.

"We've got a mountain of other things. Each of you has a photo of the first victim. We're putting a drawing of her out to the media today. We gotta find a name to go with the body." They often used the drawings of photographs to spare showing a dead body on TV, especially if there was a family out there that was unaware of the death. He clapped his hands. "Let's get to work."

Stallings stood up from his desk and grabbed his beat-up pad folio. Mazzetti stepped right over to him. In a quiet voice that made his slow speech more labored, he said, "No bullshit, Stall. You need to keep me filled in on anything you come up with."

"Do you want to catch this guy as fast as possible?"

Mazzetti nodded and said, "More than anything."

"Then I'll keep you completely filled in."

Nine

John Stallings didn't usually work after sunset, at least for the Sheriff's Office. He worked at providing his kids with a comfortable place to grow up. He worked at keeping the pressure off Maria so she could stay sober if not completely sane. He coached soccer, drove Lauren and her friends to gymnastics, and generally lived the life he had taken for granted years before.

But tonight he was on the street with a real purpose.

The analyst in the detective bureau had tried searching for anyone named Jamais arrested for procurement in the last five years but came up dry. This was a long shot like most leads on a big case, but it was real, and Stallings knew he wouldn't be able to sleep if he didn't make an effort to find this guy and see what he had to say.

The other detectives were searching for Jamais as if it were a competition, and they all seemed to play by the same rules, looking in the same kinds of places, talking to the same kind of people in the same stupid, cop way. It was more like talking *at* someone. There wasn't one working girl on Arlington Avenue who would admit to knowing Jamais to one of the homicide guys if they didn't have a reason to. And no one had a reason to give up someone to the cops. Not in J-ville or any other town with a street community. Talking to the cops was bad for business and bad for your health. That was why Stallings decided to go at this in a slightly different way, only talking to people he already knew—specifically former runaways who had reached eighteen and still lived on the street.

He headed into the Springfield area because he happened to know that Lee Ann Moffit had hung in the central Jacksonville neighborhood a lot. One of the times he found her she'd been in a house on North Liberty Street.

Prostitutes walking the streets were not as obvious as when he started on patrol as a green twenty-three-year-old. Back in those days of unbridled enthusiasm and endless energy he'd arrest prostitutes and their clients parked in the rear of Publix shopping centers or in dark, quiet parks. Slowly he started to prioritize his duties, and prostitution usually didn't rank up there with robberies or drive-by shootings in his daily professional life. But Stallings, like most cops, had a particular distaste for pimps. The popular stereotype of a flamboyant, benevolent manager could not be further from the truth. The world of street prostitution is filled with violence and mistrust. Pimps essentially enslave women, usually young women, and use threats of all kinds to keep the girls out working and giving them the lion's share of the money.

Rolling into the lot of a shopping plaza that shut down at sunset, he waited like all lonely and desperate men did who were looking for a woman. He knew that parked here in the innocuous, unmarked Impala he'd probably have a lead on this Jamais in a few hours. This was an area where Stallings had spent a lot of time. He'd know someone on the prowl.

The activity on the street, which might not be obvious to the average driver, blinked like a neon sign to cops. The three men sitting on a bus bench were selling crack to a specific group that knew who they were and what they were doing. An undercover couldn't buy from them because the dealers wouldn't know them. A man sitting in a car across the lot was looking for a prostitute. A young man on a park bench across the street was available for sex. It was a parallel universe to normal life that most people chose to ignore and Stallings liked to avoid at this stage in his career. He didn't want to think that his oldest daughter might be part of this subculture in some other city.

After fifteen minutes of sitting in the car with the windows down, he had ignored two different women because he didn't know them. They were older than the crowd he had caught as runaways and he didn't want to broadcast what he was doing if the likelihood of success wasn't good.

Finally a young woman approached the car slowly, high heels slowing her progress over the uneven asphalt, sounding like an old telegraph, tapping out an uncertain message. She leaned into his open window and said, "Hey there . . ." Then stood up, "Oh shit, Stall."

Stallings eased out of the car so the girl wouldn't start running in those high heels and break her leg.

"Don't worry, Tabitha. I'm looking for someone. You're not done for the night yet."

She placed her hand over her large fake breasts and smiled. "You scared the shit out of me. I thought you were a real cop."

Stallings smiled at the comment. Many of the young people Stallings looked for in missing persons got to know him as a person, not just a cop. He always talked to them before bringing them into a shelter or back to their parents. It was as much for him and his efforts to understand his own Jeanie as it was to help the kids. But they realized he was doing what he thought was best for them and they told their friends. After three years in the missing persons unit, he had a network in the city unlike any other cop. He may not have been able to work drug cases with informants like this, but he damn sure could find anyone that was in the city whether they wanted to be found or not.

Stallings said, "What're you doin' out here anyway? I thought you were dancing over near Fernandina."

"I lost the gig and can't renew my adult entertainment license yet."

"Why not?"

She hesitated.

"I won't do anything, just curious."

She nodded and said, "I got paper on me."

"What for?"

"Possession, failure to appear."

"Why didn't you go to court, Tabby? You're smarter than that."

"Just got caught up in things. I'm gonna take care of it, I swear."

He shook his head. "I'm out here because I'm looking for someone."

"Who?"

"All I have is a name—Jamais."

She thought about it, her pretty face running through the database of names and aliases she'd learned while living in Jacksonville. Finally she shook her head. "Doesn't ring a bell."

He made a note, then looked back at the young woman and noticed the makeup covering a mark on her neck. "What's that from?"

She looked at the ground.

"Tabby, I've known you since you were sixteen. Tell me what happened."

"I was light on the take Monday night. My manager wasn't too happy about it."

"Who's your manager?"

She looked up at him. "It's nothing, really."

"Who is it?"

"Davey Lambert."

Stallings knew the name and could picture the atypical pimp. He wasn't known for his rough stuff and had some kind of computer sideline. He combined the two professions to become the wealthy king of Internet prostitution.

"Why's Davey got you out on the street? I thought he only worked online?"

"He had trouble with someone and they knocked Davey off-line for a while."

"Knocked him off-line? How?"

"Smashed up all his computers, tried to burn down that house he owns over on Beaver Street. He always thought it was funny selling pussy from a house on a street named Beaver." She still had an engaging smile.

"Hysterical."

"He ain't so bad."

Stallings looked at her. "C'mon, Tabby. You were light, so he choked you."

"I'm tellin' you, Stall, it wasn't nothin'."

"Where's he now?"

"Why?"

"Because I'm gonna kick his ass."

She smiled. "And you won't tell him it was me?"

"You know better than that."

She hesitated but not for long. Her smile spread at the thought of her pimp meeting up with someone like Stallings. "He's at the house now trying to get the computers up and running. And he's plenty pissed off. That's why this happened." She pointed to her discolored neck.

Stallings smiled, handed her half the cash in his pocket, and said, "Take the night off, Tabby. Your manager is going on vacation."

William Dremmel stopped at a Wendy's off Beaver Street after the pharmacy closed at nine. It had been a quiet night, and he'd spent the last three hours organizing one of the storerooms and tossing the newspapers and magazines that the vendors didn't pick up after the periodicals were out of date. He liked that kind of work because it gave him a chance to acquire different pharmaceuticals for his experiments. No one noticed while he rooted around in the rear with crushed cardboard boxes. He could easily open a commercial tube of Percocet and Oxycontin while he was in the secure controlled-substance area because the fat pharmacist never bothered to lock up like he should.

He also got his pick of three-month-old magazines, so tonight he grabbed two copies of *Muscle and Fitness* and a *Playboy* that featured the "Girls of the Southeast Conference."

Now he lingered over a Wendy's spicy chicken sandwich hoping his mother would be fast asleep by the time he got home. Sitting in the grubby fast-food joint, watching the diverse parade of humanity stroll through, gave Dremmel a sense of his own accomplishments.

These poor slobs would never get the chance for a decent education or to advance science like him.

Outside the wide glass window he watched a roach scurry along the metal frame. This was not the part of town where the nicer restaurants stayed open long or the young business crowds gathered for a drink after work. This was the kind of area he would find a test subject some day. But it was someone inside that caught his attention. One of the workers had slipped out from the back with a burger and fries, eating quietly in the corner. She looked up and caught him staring. Even in the frumpy uniform he saw her perfect, small frame and cute, wide face. She had brown eyes with thick brows, and her hair had six or seven different colors dyed into it. On one side were patches of blue and pink and the other had white, red, and yellow. A rat-tail–like length in the back was pure black.

Instead of looking away when she saw him or ignoring him like most women would, she smiled, displaying the line of bright, if not completely straight, teeth. Dimples formed at each corner of her mouth. Then she said, "You work over at the pharmacy, right?"

Dremmel was surprised and just nodded. "I work at different branches on different days." How had this girl slipped into his store and he not have noticed her?

She picked up her tray and ambled over to him, plopping in the other seat at the tiny tabletop. "I've seen you behind the counter a couple of times when I'm checking out up front."

"So you've never come back to the pharmacy section."

"Never had to, yet."

She shot him a smile that showed a lot of intelligence and something else. Maybe a brashness he wasn't used to. His thoughts of Stacey Hines faded for a brief moment as he looked into this girl's face.

She said, "I'm Trina."

"I'm, uh, Bill."

"You don't sound so sure."

He forced a smile. "I'm sure." Dremmel let his gaze turn toward the window and watched a black Impala slow down and pull into the lot.

Trina leaned across the table toward him and whispered, "So, Bill, can you get any drug you want?"

It was a question that threw all his carefully laid plans for Stacey Hines into a holding pattern.

Ten

John Stallings pulled his county-issued black Impala into the Wendy's parking lot. His stomach had been rumbling for more than an hour, but he wasn't sure the effect a Wendy's burger would have on him. This stretch of Beaver Street had only a few restaurants, and Wendy's was the best choice of the bunch.

He pulled into an empty spot near the big bay window and glanced inside to see how busy the place was at this hour. One man stood in line and a few people sat at tables in the main dining area.

A girl in the window right in front of him munched on a sandwich as her head bobbed in response to a question from her companion. Her multicolored hair swayed in every direction as she nodded. She smiled and her whole face lit up, reminding Stallings exactly why he was out here at this hour. He felt guilty detouring off the main case to seek retribution on a pimp for hurting one of his girls. But in the big scheme of things Stallings really felt he was on this job to help people, and those he felt were most at risk were younger women working the streets in some way. Spending a few minutes scaring a pimp would help some women but wouldn't necessarily stop the killer.

Looking back up into the Wendy's, Stallings watched the young lady finish her sandwich. The concrete pillar blocked his view of the other person at the table, but from her gestures and posture he guessed it was a young man.

Moments like this made him wonder what it would have been like to see Jeanie in social situations. Dating, bringing boys by the house, growing up in front of his eyes. He knew not to dwell on those kinds of ideas, because they would crush him if he let them. He appreciated the smile on the girl's face and then decided if he was going to take a few minutes away from the case to frighten a pimp, he better skip dinner to make up for it.

Besides, hunger put him in a nastier mood to deal with Davey Lambert, the pimp who went too far.

Patty Levine had lost track of time as she made call after call into every time zone in the country and pored over online catalogs of luggage and duffel bags. She had no idea how many companies made similar looking bags and that the number of outlets was in the thousands. She had narrowed the initial focus of stores that sold large bags to a small geographic area of Jacksonville and the surrounding area. She had a small map and marked from the Georgia border south to Flagler Beach and from the coast inland to Macclenny off Interstate 10. She liked this kind of work but more importantly realized no one else would put as much energy into it and might miss something.

Just as she felt her stomach growl someone said, "You're here late."

She turned to see Tony Mazzetti leaning in the doorway. His tie was loosened and his sleeves were rolled up almost to his toned biceps. This was the most casual she'd ever seen him.

She scooted her chair all the way around to see him. "You should talk."

He smiled and said, "I'm used to it. I'm a homicide detective."

She let out a snort, even though she tried to control that sort of thing in front of good-looking men. "C'mon, Tony, don't give me that shit. We're all detectives." To her surprise he gave her a cute, sly smile. Maybe he wasn't the asshole everyone thought he was.

"Really, you can pick that stuff up in the morning. You should get some rest. See your family."

"First, I can outlast you or any other homicide dick, and second, I have an automatic feeder for my cat. My responsibilities at home are met for the evening."

Mazzetti set his intense, dark eyes on her and said, "In that case, fill me in on what you've found so far."

John Stallings cruised the area near the house Tabitha had told him about. His stomach rumbled with hunger, but he was glad he'd skipped a Wendy's burger. The house on Beaver Street was what Stall would consider a "sleeper" and proved just how crafty this Davey Lambert really was. But to a cop who had worked the street and paid attention, little things gave it away. It was a lot like when a cop tried to go undercover as a street person, but their shoes always gave them away. Cops could wear old, unwashed shirts from the Salvation Army, ripped off-brand jeans, lay next to the smelliest pile of trash this side of the Mississippi, but they loved their good running shoes. A pair of expensive Nike Air Pegasus or Asics Air Cumulus shoes would tip off street people as fast as driving up in a patrol car. This house was a lot like that.

Set off the road, it gave the impression of being run-down, with high weeds in the unkempt front yard, paint flaking off the cheap siding, and a front door with the screen drooping down from one corner like a puppy's ear.

Stallings noticed the run-down house also had a new, interlocking roof that could withstand a category-five hurricane and still not leak a drop inside. The reinforced storm windows were tinted tempered glass, and the door behind the screen was reinforced to discourage home invasions and withstand storm winds whipping off the Atlantic.

A surveillance system of linked cameras covered the front door all the way to the end of the driveway and a trip line ran along each side of the yard. A dark green H3 Hummer was partially hidden behind the house. Someone had invested a lot of cash to keep this house safe, dry, and very low key.

Stallings didn't try to hide his approach; he didn't have time. He needed information, but he also needed to let this asshole know it wasn't cool to choke women. It would only take him a few minutes out of his way. He whispered to himself, "Is this the day that changes my life?" He checked his pistol in a sturdy polymer holster on his right hip, then headed for the front door.

As he started up the five wooden stairs to the porch, the inner door opened and a white guy wearing a bathrobe, with thinning blond hair, a goatee, and glasses stood in the doorway with the fake rickety screen door between them. He had the look of a college professor in his midthirties and was about six foot one with a little beef on him.

Stallings said, "You Davey?"

"Yep," was all the man got out before Stallings threw a straight right punch through the screen and into Davey's face, knocking the clunky man backward into the house.

Stallings didn't hesitate to jerk the screen door open and follow the dizzy man into the house.

Davey was on his back trying to sit up when Stallings offered him a hand. Davey accepted without thinking and as he rose to his feet, Stallings head-butted him, knocking him into a sitting position on a small, expensive leather couch against the wall.

"What the hell, man," cried out Davey, checking his nose for blood. "This is very uncool. You don't know the fucking week I've had." He took a moment, then said in a quieter voice, "Who the hell are you?"

Stallings calmly sat down across from him in a leather chair. "My name is John Stallings, and I'm a detective with JSO." He crossed his legs like he was doing a TV talk show.

Davey said, "You're Stall? I don't work with under-aged girls or runaways. I swear it, man." The pattern of the screen was embedded into his face where Stallings had punched him. It already looked like it might bruise in that odd, woven pattern. "Why'd you punch me?"

"I don't like pimps."

"I don't like cops, but I don't go around smacking them."

Stallings was sure he'd never met the man but was happy to know he had that kind of reputation on the street.

The pimp said, "Tabby told me all about you and what you did over on North Broad Street last year when they had a sixteen-year-old girl working there." Davey shuddered. "I run a different, respectable opera-tion, mainly over the Internet."

"But you got girls walking the streets right now."

"I have to so I can make the bills. Some asshole knocked me off-line for a few days."

Stallings turned his head and looked in to the larger living room and saw six computers in various states of disassembly. He stood up to take a closer look. Davey followed him in.

"You're not busting me for prostitution, are you? I thought you had better things to worry about."

Stallings turned and made a fist. "This is an unofficial visit to make sure you don't mistreat any of your employees again."

Davey held up his hands in surrender. "I know I've been a dick this week. It's a reaction to having my home dissed and shit trashed. I swear it won't happen again." He looked around the room at smashed computers and lines ripped from the wall. "This cat from over near Springfield accused me of violating the first law of pimping."

"You stole one of his girls?"

"He thought I did. I never even heard of no one named Lee Ann, and I told him just that. He and his buddies still wrecked the place." He pointed to a corner that was singed black where a fire had started.

Stallings placed a hand on his forearms to shut him up. "Whoa, whoa, did you say 'Lee Ann'?"

"Yeah, he went off on me about her."

"Lee Ann Moffitt?"

"Man, we don't use no last names, you know that. This dude said she worked for him part time and since she worked part time at a Kinko's near here and he saw me in there, he thought I stole her."

Now Stallings knew that fate or karma or whatever you wanted to call it had brought him to this nerdy pimp's house. "What's the name of the guy who did all this?"

"Franklin Hall."

"Describe him to me."

"Black gentleman, he could be governor of California with arms as big as my legs and short hair. Always acts pissed off." He looked at Stallings. "A little like you."

"Where would I find Mr. Hall?"

"Shit, man, I don't know. He doesn't check in with me." Davey snapped his fingers. "He's a freak for breakfast. Eats it every meal. Eggs, bacon, pancakes. He's probably at some Denny's or IHOP. Guy like that usually runs his business from a booth where no one bothers him."

"What's he drive?"

"Full-sized Hummer. Jet black."

Stallings looked at Davey. "Are Hummers the new Cadillacs for pimps?"

"They show some class and power. And I can drive around three or four girls at a time for parties and special events."

Stallings headed for the door, then turned. "Remember what I said. No more rough stuff."

"I understand, sir. I swear it won't happen again."

Stallings turned, satisfied he had made the world a little safer for at least a couple of girls. You had to pick your fights and measure your wins carefully in this business, and he had just been rewarded with a lucky lead on the only suspect they had right now.

He looked up at the dark Jacksonville sky and whispered, "Thank you."

* * *

William Dremmel opened the door to his house as quietly as possible, hoping with all his heart that mother was asleep. Sound asleep. He should have realized when the woozy girl, Trina, flopped down onto the path next to the walkway in a fit of laughter that silence would not be accomplished without pharmaceutical help. He shushed her as best he could as he helped her to her feet. She was absolute dead weight as he yanked her arm.

Then, after he was inside, he heard the table next to the door rattle and Trina burst out in a laugh that sounded like a tractor-trailer horn.

"Sorry," she said like they were at a bowling alley.

He raised his finger to his lips and gave her a quick "Shush," then held still and listened to see if his mother would call out. He peeked to ensure the door between the sections of the house was secured. Silence.

"Why? You got roommates?" Her harsh whisper grated on him.

He handed her another Oxy, hoping that might mellow her out some. So far the drug had shown little effect on Trina, who had told him she was a runaway from Cleveland and her folks had no idea where she was. After hearing that vital information, Dremmel's mind started churning and solving problems one after another.

First, he made sure no one from Wendy's saw her sitting with him. Then he was careful to meet her on the street, giving her some bullshit story about how he had to go back to the pharmacy to score her some Oxy. She wanted to come, but he said there would still be someone there. He arranged to meet her a block from the pharmacy and told her not to say anything to anyone. She'd promised and explained she was finished at Wendy's for the night anyway. He had watched her leave from down the street to make certain she didn't stop and talk to anyone inside Wendy's.

She had just waved good-bye and walked out alone, a big satchel over her shoulder. He knew she didn't have a car and she'd been carrying around her essentials to spend the night wherever she could. Sometimes at a runaway "safe house," sometimes with friends, and sometimes with men she met and slept with for a few bucks and a comfortable bed for the night. Dremmel knew the runaway culture like a cop would. He listened to them in the pharmacy, read everything about runaways he could find, and wasn't afraid to ask questions of the youths that were sent to the pharmacy from the free clinics.

Now that he had her at his house, with no witnesses, knowing she had no one expecting her, and an obvious taste for pharmaceuticals, he had his next set of obstacles. Mainly he had to keep his mother quiet and unconscious, then lay down the bed in his "darkroom" as well as set the hooks in the wall and get out the restraints. He figured he'd be able to accomplish that after this girl passed out from all the Oxy he had fed her.

He locked the front door, and when he turned around Trina was already wobbling unsteadily down the single step down into the sunken living room. She held out her stubby arms like she was one of the freaking Flying Wallendas on a high wire as she balanced on her platform Crocs. Now Dremmel had to consider drug interactions, because this girl obviously had her own supply she'd hit before meeting him.

"Wow, nice big screen." She let her tiny fingers dance across the top of the forty-two-inch Samsung. Her head swiveled, taking in the whole room, multicolored hair flipping in every direction. "Cool couch," she said, flopping down onto it. Without preamble, she slipped off her sleeveless shirt and then popped off an industrial-strength bra to expose large, fleshy, lopsided boobs. Her skin was creamy and consistent like she didn't get out into the sun much, with only the occasional youthful pimple to blemish such a perfect picture.

The sight knocked him speechless.

She wiggled her shoulders, making her breasts sway in wide arcs. "That must be worth some more Oxy." She had an impish smile.

"Yeah," he smiled. "Sure." But as he stared, transfixed at the topless girl, he was overwhelmed. A panic rose in his throat. These situations were much easier when the female was lashed to the wall or comatose. He tried to swallow the basketball in his throat, then forced his eyes up to look in her face.

Trina said, "You'll be amazed at what it takes to get my pants off. Hope you bring that pharmacy home with you at night." Her tiny hands reached up to cover her bare breasts. The pose made his legs go weak.

At that moment he didn't care if his mother rolled in on them. This girl was perfect. Just a bit loud.

Eleven

Patty Levine had spent a few minutes scratching Cornelia's neck, feeling the low rumble of her purr, watched the ten o'clock news to see what they threw up on the homicide. She was surprised to see that it was only a sketch of the first victim, and the S.O. spokesman made it sound more like an accidental death. She figured they wanted to avoid the spectacle of the news covering a serial killer as long as possible without actually lying to the reporters. With all the cutbacks in the newsrooms it didn't feel as if reporters pushed for the "real" story like they used to. People could talk about the erosion of constitutional rights, but revenue shortfalls had done more to curtail freedom of the press than any government action ever could.

There was a short interview with Tony Mazzetti, who looked good as always in a suit that showed off his sculpted shoulders and strained ever so slightly when he bent his arms. Seeing him on her flat screen frustrated Patty again. Earlier, she'd thought he was flirting with her, asking if she was attached, but when she gave him the obvious opening he just wanted to know where she was on finding out about the luggage. Did he really only live for homicide investigations the way some of the officers said? Something told her there was a lot more to Tony Mazzetti than good taste in clothes.

She'd spent a full twelve hours at her desk working, skipping lunch, blowing off the gym, eating her usual TV dinner. She was still going over in her head possible avenues she could pursue to figure out if the bags used to hold the bodies could lead them to the killer. This was the kind of challenge she'd been searching for in police work.

She turned off the tube after the story on the victim ran, then padded into the kitchen and made a quick assessment of what pills needed to be taken now. It was late, her back wasn't sore, and she didn't feel anxious, so that left only Ambien to let her sleep soundly. She shook out two 12-milligram pills and tossed them in her mouth, then chased them with some orange juice right from the plastic jug. As she replaced the container she looked over at Cornelia, who was staring at her from the counter.

"That's right, it's my house, so I can drink directly from the jug if I want." She sighed, reached over, and rubbed the yellow cat's chin, then added, "It's not like anyone would mind."

It was now officially late for a veteran cop like John Stallings. He'd just called home to see if Maria and the kids were okay. Lauren had told him that Mom and Charlie were asleep, and she was finishing homework. As he was about to shut his cell phone Lauren said, "Be careful, Dad."

He smiled, and all he could say was "Love you, girl."

Stallings focused back on work and recalled he was in Jacksonville Heights when he had picked up Lee Ann Moffit once. People in the sex trade tended to stay in one area where they had contacts, knew the clientele, and knew when a stranger was around. It helped to avoid arrests, designate an area where the competition would think twice before entering, and gave pimps several places to set up shop and be available if one of their girls needed help or, more often, if they needed to find one of their girls to explain how the business arrangement worked.

Stallings was a little disappointed to hear Lee Ann might have still been hooking in addition to her legit job. But it had to be hard to make it on minimum wage. He wasn't in the business of judging. He had left that behind a while ago. Right now he wanted to find Franklin Hall and see what he knew about Lee Ann. And maybe convey some of the downside of being a man who preyed on women.

He'd been past a Denny's, two local diners, even the shabby McDonald's, but the closest vehicle to a Hummer he saw was a black Expedition. Jacksonville wasn't like Miami, no matter how hard it tried. High-end vehicles weren't as common unless you were talking about old people in Lincolns or Cadillacs. A Hummer would be easy to spot if it was out on the road. Then, as he turned onto 103rd Street he saw the unique shape of an International House of Pancakes with the shiny blue roof marking the spot where even cops hesitated to stop.

He spotted the obnoxious-looking vehicle that, to him, was the epitome of conspicuous consumption, taking up two spaces on the side of the building. This was the second break he'd had in the last hour. Now the question entered his mind of whether he should call backup. But who? Patty? Mazzetti? It was late, and this could be a dead end or he may not want a witness to know how he went about getting information. He hated wasting a detective's time as much as he hated getting his ass kicked by overgrown pimps. Then he noticed someone leaving the restaurant and by his size realized it must be the pimp known as Franklin Hall.

Fate had made the decision for him

William Dremmel had concluded that even though she was pretty, topless, and apparently willing, this girl Trina was the most obnoxious person he had ever met.

She had stomped around the house, poking her nose into rooms and saying things like, "What's the little ramp for in the kitchen?" or "Is that the same room you used since you were eight?" The one that cut into him the most was, "Why don't you have your own house by now?"

Trina showed no self-consciousness about her semi-nakedness and didn't appear to be cold either. He was fascinated that her left breast looked a full cup size larger than her right. His experience with naked women, at least conscious naked women, was limited, but she looked good. Too bad she wasn't a mute. That would make her perfect.

As the time wore on, her voice had a scratchier quality to it and the effects of the Oxycontin seemed to fade in and out as she would become manic and abrasive, then sweet and listless. She finally flopped back onto the leather couch, her breasts bouncing as she did, and he hoped this might be Trina's final display of energy and she would soon start to drift off. Dremmel had slipped out to the garage to grab some of the things he needed, then set the mattress on the floor of the dark-room. When she asked him about it, he said he was getting her bed ready. She smiled at the thoughtfulness of her host, but still did annoying things like chase Mr. Whiskers IV around the house, complaining about how cats don't respect human authority. He had no idea what that meant but was ready to move on to the next phase of his plan.

He'd brought in a plate with cheese, a few strips of leftover steak, and a knife and fork, then set it on the coffee table in front of her. She had to be hungry with all the talking she'd done, plus he had mashed 100 milligrams of Seconal into one of the patties of fancy aged cheese. He knew the strong sedative could over whelm her in combination with the Oxy, but at this point it was a risk he'd take. The pills were also the handiest in the kitchen, and he was starting to rush things to get her secured before something bad happened like his mom waking up. The kitchen counter was a mess, and the bright red capsule halves were still by the sink. He had other reasons to use the Seconal. Mostly he was amazed that this chick was still up and functioning, so he didn't want to risk that she had built up a tolerance to something common like Ambien or Lunesta. The Seconal was harder to come by, but packed a wallop, so he was ready to carry her into the darkroom/lab whenever she nodded off.

Trina had been topless so long that it held less fasci-nation for him. He wondered what she'd be like when he hooked her up in the lab, secured and on a steady diet of sedatives. She was a little heavy for his average subject and that accounted for her exceptional curves. She was also a few years younger than the others, but he was certain he could extrapolate any data he got from the drug trial.

He sat across from her in a heavy bamboo chair his uncle had bought in Korea, trying not to show his concern, but one leg bobbed up and down in rhythm to an unknown song. Finally he said, "Why don't you eat something?"

"Why? You get off seeing chicks eat?" Her speech was slightly slurred, and she had a woozy quality to her movements. Her childlike hand snatched up a strip of the skirt steak he had grilled the day before, then she bit off a chunk, her lips smacking loudly as she chewed.

She picked up the fork and prodded the small cheese wedge designed to knock her unconscious. She looked up at Dremmel. "Got any beer, Billy?"

He hesitated, calculating the effect of alcohol in combination with everything else she'd ingested. He needed her alive to gain any benefit. "Yeah, I think I have some Bud out in the garage refrigerator." What would it take to get her to eat the damn cheese?

She cocked her head, dipping her multicolored mane onto her pale, bare shoulder. "What are you waiting for? Go get it."

Dremmel remained motionless in the chair wondering what to do.

Trina said, "You might get my pants off if I get a beer in the next thirty seconds." She hiccupped the last part of the sentence.

"Just get a little more food in your stomach so you don't get sick."

"What're you, my dad?" She snorted and giggled, then added, "You could be if you fuck me. That's why I'm down in this shitty city anyway." Then she started to sob.

Dremmel had no experience with comforting distraught women. His instinct was to ignore the whole unpleasantness, but he knew she expected some reaction from him—even if he just faked it. He eased onto the couch next to her and placed his arm around her shoulder, not knowing what else to do. It took several minutes for her to regain any composure until she took a napkin and blew her nose like a goose honking.

Without speaking, she reached down and picked up the spiked cheese, then stopped in front of her mouth like she was inspecting it. He waited patiently. At least while she cried over her father's shameful behavior she wasn't asking annoying questions in too loud of a tone. The sobs seemed to subside, but she still had the cheese in her hand. Then he heard something much worse than this girl's voice.

From the intercom in the kitchen his mother's voice screeched, "William, are you home? William, I need you."

His stomach tightened as Trina's head snapped up and she sniffled to end her crying jag, held on to the cheese wedge, and said, "Wow, who is that? She sounds like something out of a horror movie."

Dremmel thought, *you have no idea*.

This was not working out the way he wanted it to.

Twelve

John Stallings parked his Impala behind the Hummer, blocking it in place. There was no way he wanted to be in any kind of car chase. He'd leave that to the show-offs and actors on TV. He lost sight of the pimp but knew he'd run into him shortly.

Before he even saw Franklin Hall come around the building, he heard the pimp shout, "Who parked that piece of shit behind my Hummer?"

A smile creased Stallings's face at the thought of his coming confrontation. He hated psychobabble, but had put up with it for the last few years in counseling with the kids and Maria. All the issues the family had revolved around Jeanie, but he had attended a lot of AA and NA meetings with Maria too. The one term he had picked up that he felt was accurate was "anger issues." He was about to explore some of those issues and possibly find an outlet for his pent-up frustration. The best part about it was that he knew, no matter what, this asshole pimp deserved whatever was about to happen to him. That made him keep smiling as he stepped out of his car and stood to face the taller, muscular man. Traffic was light, and the IHOP staff couldn't see them from inside. This was perfect except he needed to get the big man's attention quickly.

"John Stallings, Sheriff's Office."

"I ain't done nothing, so you can speak to me through my attorney. His name is Scott Richardson, and he will eat you up and spit up out." Hall had the rough Southern street accent so common in the area.

Stallings didn't acknowledge the man. Instead he popped out his ASP expandable baton, and knocked out one of the Humvee's taillights with an easy backhand swing.

"Oh shit! Is you crazy?"

Stallings laughed and said, "Is you Franklin Hall?"

The man just stared at him.

Then Stallings whacked the rear tailgate, leaving a dent and flecked paint.

Franklin took a big step toward him, so Stallings changed his stance, swung the ASP, and caught the muscle-head mid-thigh, sending him to the ground like a redwood cut at an angle.

"Franklin, we gotta talk. I only need a minute." He squatted next to the groaning man.

The man cut his yellow eyes up to Stallings but didn't speak. He held his bruised thigh with both hands like everyone hit with an ASP did until they realized it didn't help at all. Only time and maybe some ice sped the healing after meeting the business end of a weapon like that.

Stallings pulled out his photo of Lee Ann Moffit on the coroner's table. "Who's this?"

Franklin flicked his gauzy eyes to the photo, then

froze. A hand came off his leg to hold the photo and study it. He sat up on the asphalt and mumbled, "Goddamn, baby, I thought you just run off."

Stallings watched the injured pimp and sensed real sorrow from him. The traffic sounds of the night echoed in his ear as he allowed this nasty excuse for a person a few moments to grieve. Franklin showed no sign of wanting to give back the photo, as if he knew this would be the last time he'd ever see Lee Ann.

He looked up at Stallings. "Goddamn, what happened to her?"

"Was hoping you could tell us." Stallings could sense this guy was troubled by the photo of Lee Ann on the autopsy table. That was unlike most pimps. One thing Stallings had learned was that not everyone was what you expected. It made him take a moment to view the muscular pimp in a new light and perhaps give the man the benefit of the doubt.

Franklin said, "I thought she'd found a better business deal and had changed managers."

"When's the last time you saw her?"

The pimp was still reeling but attempting to provide accurate information. After looking off in space and taking a few seconds, he said, "Don't know, maybe a week ago." The pimp had his hands out behind him on the asphalt, his hazy eyes moist. "She was a good girl. Never hurt nobody."

Stallings stood up and offered a hand to Franklin. It took some effort to hoist the muscle-bound pimp to his feet.

"Franklin, you know you gotta come in and talk to the lead detective on this."

"I didn't kill her."

"I believe you, but we got a ton of questions." Stallings was shocked at the sympathy he had developed for the pimp in a few minutes' time. He was almost sorry he had struck him with the ASP. There was a chance that Stallings was developing something he lacked as a rookie: a sense of empathy. He wasn't altogether certain he liked it.

Franklin said, "Can't go to talk to nobody." He struggled on his feet as he turned to run.

Stallings didn't move. He had seen this before. The pain had eased up for a moment, but the leg still wouldn't support him. The stout pimp took three steps, then went down to his knee.

"Like I said, Franklin. We're going to talk to someone. Right now."

"Can't I just talk to you right here?" Now he sounded like a sullen little kid.

"You can, but there's another detective who'll need to speak to you, and that's gotta be back at the Police Memorial Building."

The muscular pimp scooted back to lean on the tire of the big Hummer. He shook his head. "Poor Lee Ann. She was almost completely clean."

Stallings looked at him. "What do you men 'almost' clean? What was she using, and where'd she get it?"

"She was using what all the young girls like today— prescription drugs like Vicodin or Oxy. They think it's safer and cheaper than anything else."

"They think Vicodin is safe?"

"Yeah, I know, when we was kids we all smoked pot. Everyone said it would kill us and turn us into lazy bums. That's what my mama would say, 'You smoking weed, you nothin' but a lazy bum.' " He let a slight smile spread on his wide face. "You believe that shit. Turns out pot is safe compared to everything else."

"Where'd Lee Ann get the prescription stuff?"

"She had a couple of sources. All the girls tend to

use one or two different guys because they're safe. A couple street dealers downtown. They all go to them."

"Got a name?"

"They all white dudes. No brother would be caught dead selling shit like that. There's guys named Chuck and Ernie, then there's a little dude named 'Peep' or some shit like that."

"Peep Morans?"

"That's the dude. You know him?"

Stallings frowned and couldn't hide his real feelings for the man known as Peep Morans. All he said was, "Yeah, I know him."

Dremmel froze for a moment. Sweat started to drip from his forehead.

"William." Her tone was back to her preferred, calmer southern hostess voice but it still filled the whole house, belching out of three separate intercoms, bouncing off the terrazzo floors and echoing in the halls.

His eyes cut from the courtyard door to Trina, until she said, "Who the hell is that and where is she calling from?"

He cleared his throat and said, "It's my mother on the other side of the house. She's not well."

"Are you going to see what she wants?" Finally she popped the whole pie-shaped pat of cheese into her mouth and started smacking her lips.

He motioned her to stay put, turned, and hurried into the kitchen, through the courtyard, down to his mother's bedroom, bursting in the door without his customary knock, then shutting it tight behind him. His pulse was galloping over 120, and he was starting to see spots in his vision. Was this a stroke? He'd have a hard time explaining a few things to the paramedics and cops when they showed. His legs went weak, and he slipped onto the folding chair next to the bed, shoving the magazines off onto the floor.

His mother turned her pretty face toward him and grasped his hand in her own delicate hand. "Are you well, William? You look odd." Her eyes had a bright, lucid look to them as she sat up in her bed. "I was about to get into my chariot and venture into your side of the house."

Dremmel tried to control his breathing, flinching slightly at the touch of her hand. "I'm fine, Mother. I was in the middle of something when you started screaming. What do you need?"

"I just hadn't seen you, son. I was afraid you might not come home. What are you in the middle of?"

"I have a lot of work to do. Papers from school."

"I wish those people at the college recognized how hard you work." Her voice sounded clear and light for a change. He almost wished he didn't have to force her back to sleep. Lucidity was a rare quality for his mother anymore. Mostly because of him.

"You need some rest, Mother. You look tired."

She drifted off for a moment, then asked, "Can I watch TV with you for a while?"

He shook his head. "Tomorrow night. I have to get busy on my work again." He wanted to say 'experiment,' but historians didn't do experiments and he didn't want to explain his personal pharmaceutical work, especially since she was the most successful test subject to date. He dimmed the light next to her bed and pulled up the flowery comforter. "I'll get you some milk so you can fall back to sleep, okay?"

She smoothed the floral patterned gown over her chest and stomach, then smiled at him like a mother looking at her newborn baby. He patted the comforter, feeling her surprisingly firm stomach.

"I'll be back soon. You stay quiet."

She nodded and shut her eyes.

He looked down and had to admire how attractive his mother looked with her mouth and eyes closed. It reminded him of the month immediately after the accident when his grandmother would take him to see her in the hospital. It was the first time in his life he had realized his own mother was pretty. When she wasn't barking at him to sit up straight, clean his room, or fetch her a drink she was a lot more fun to be around.

He slipped out of the room, quietly closing the bedroom door behind him, then turned into the courtyard to the rest of the house. As he entered the kitchen he froze at the sight of Trina standing, still topless, her magnificent cockeyed breasts drawing his attention, her tiny hand open with the two bright red capsule halves of the Seconal in her palm.

She snarled, "I thought that cheese tasted funny. What the fuck is this all about?"

William Dremmel's heart started to race again as a new film of sweat built up on his forehead.

Thirteen

Patty Levine felt a little woozy after answering the phone call from John Stallings saying he had Lee Ann Moffit's pimp at the D-Bureau. She'd been called out to a scene a couple of times in the past after taking a sleeping pill and knew the drill. First she went straight into her bathroom and stuck a finger down her throat until she vomited. It wasn't dainty or subtle, but it usually worked. Then she showered real quick, got dressed, and drank a Red Bull on her way into the office. The sugar and caffeine seemed to counteract any of the Ambien that had dissolved in her system and kept her awake, if a little jittery, for as long as she needed to be. Every time it happened she renewed her vow to lay off the sleeping pills, but she never lasted for long. A night or two of tossing and turning and she was back to her kitchen counter looking for whatever she had that would make her nod off.

Now she sat with Stallings as the interview with Franklin Hall concluded. She was surprised Stallings had done the proper thing and brought in the suspect for Mazzetti to interview. That was the way things were supposed to happen, the lead detective calling the shots on something like that, but she hadn't expected her partner to play by those rules. She had noticed the bulky pimp walking with a slight limp when they had taken a break for him to use the bathroom. She expected that from Stallings.

She and Stallings had watched the interview over a closed-circuit TV that also videotaped everything that went on in the small room with only three chairs. The newest homicide detective, Christina "Hoagie" Hogrebe, sat in on the interview. Mazzetti had said it was because he wanted a female perspective on the guy's demeanor, but Patty knew it was a jab at Stallings. If Patty had to admit it, she felt a stab of jealousy too. The beautiful detective was already in homicide, a year younger than her, and she had earned it by good, smart police work. But Stall had found the guy, and he was a senior detective.

Stallings had already gotten most of Franklin's story on the ride to the S.O. and the wait for Mazzetti to return to the office. Patty listened as Mazzetti laid out the same questions they all would've asked and assessed the pimp carefully on each answer. Like any team used to interviewing, Mazzetti kept good eye contact and developed rapport while Hoagie took notes and developed more questions for later. They were pros, and it showed.

The story was logical, and Franklin Hall didn't seem to be hiding anything. He admitted to making a living as a pimp, to smashing Davey Lambert's computers because he thought the brainy computer-pimp had stolen one of his girls, and that Lee Ann Moffit worked for him. She had recently tried a real job and was only working one or two nights a week for special clients that called Franklin and asked for her. The dark-skinned pimp had not hesitated to provide every name and number of those clients. There was no honor in the profession when someone turned up dead—the loser-pimp privilege didn't apply.

Franklin also revealed that he used to be called "Jamais" and had each of his girls tattoo his name in the same place on their backs.

On the small screen, Patty heard Tony Mazzetti ask, "Why were you called Jamais?"

"Because Franklin isn't the scariest pimp name in the world. I just made up Jamais and liked the sound of it."

"Why'd you stop using it?"

"Jamais Cook down in Daytona came up with a couple of his boys and explained copyright to me."

Mazzetti smiled and said, "How'd he get the lesson across?"

Franklin Hall lifted his shirt, displaying perfect abs and wide, chiseled shoulders. He turned in his seat and showed Mazzetti a jagged swath of scar tissue on his upper right shoulder.

Mazzetti winced.

Hoagie calmly said, "Let me guess, you had 'Jamais' tattooed on your own shoulder too."

The pimp nodded.

She said, "How'd they cut it off?"

"Straight razor."

Mazzetti was the one cringing, but Hoagie just nodded and made a note. Patty liked that this younger detective didn't waver. She asked, "Take long?"

"Only a second or two. The man was fast. Real fast. But it got infected, and I was out of action a week." He slipped the shirt back on. "I got the message and decided Franklin was an okay name as long as I stayed big and buff and didn't take no shit."

Hoagie said, "Except from Jamais Cook."

Patty smiled at her shot and poise.

Franklin Hall bowed his head and mumbled, "Yeah, 'cept for him."

They finished up, taking a few more notes, then Tony Mazzetti emerged from the small interview room shaking his head. He looked over at them, shook his head some more, and marched in the other direction.

Stallings said, "What's up his ass?"

"He's probably pissed you brought in such a good lead. Made him look like an administrator."

"But I did bring him in. I'm a team player. Sort of."

"I noticed the pimp limping when he got up to stretch his legs."

"So?"

"So, you can't keep beating people for information."

"Why not? It's worked pretty well so far. Some instant street justice keeps everyone on their toes."

She looked at him. "For me. For my sanity, please be a little more careful. Think about the consequences of your actions. Think about how much Maria and the kids need you."

"You don't need to worry about me."

"Franklin is pretty big, Stall. You could've gotten hurt by yourself."

"So now I'm an old man?"

Patty snickered. "No, you've been an old man for a while. Now you're acting like a rookie."

Rita Hester stepped out of an office, wiping her eyes as she walked. "Stall, you couldn't have found this guy during the day? I'm too old to be out this late."

"Sorry, Rita. I just lucked into finding him."

From behind the sleepy lieutenant, Mazzetti said, "I believe you're lucky. Luckiest son-of-a-bitch in the whole S.O."

Stallings smiled.

Patty knew he thought it was more fun not to bite and let Mr. Type-A personality stew in his envy.

Rita Hester said, "You were a little rough on him, Stall. You really want to risk a fight like that at this point in your career?"

"To catch this killer, you bet. I hope everyone here is willing to take some risks."

Mazzetti stepped into the conversation. "That was a hotshot move, Stall. You wanna be the one in the spotlight, don't you?"

He smiled, shaking his head. "I don't even want to be the one around the spotlight, Mazzetti. I just wanna find this killer."

Mazzetti looked at Patty. "Maybe you can talk some sense into this guy."

"Believe me Tony, I've tried."

As Mazzetti stomped off, Stallings turned to his partner, "You called him Tony. You getting friendly with the enemy?"

She hoped he didn't notice her face flush.

Stallings eased in his front door about two and was surprised to see Maria asleep in the recliner in front of the TV. Before he woke her, Stallings leaned down to smell the drink with a puddle of condensation around it. Ginger ale. He tasted it to be sure. Just ginger ale.

He gently shook her shoulder. "Hey, beautiful, let's go to bed."

Her eyes fluttered open. "Are you just getting home?"

He nodded.

"What time is it?"

"Two."

"Why were you working so late?"

He knew it wasn't the right time to explain his new assignment, especially that it was his choice. Tomorrow would be a better time. "Just have a few things happening. Let's get some rest." He took her hand and helped her up, happy to see her sober, safe, and with a smile on her elegant face. She kissed him lightly on his cheek, and his heart raced like it always did around her.

After trying to fall asleep for more than an hour, Stallings flipped for the twentieth time trying to get comfortable. It was an anxiety that surged through him and he didn't know if it was from his case, his constant worry about the kids, sorrow for Jeanie, or the feeling that Maria was about to drop off the deep end any day. He never wanted to have to visit her during a "spa treatment" again.

He eased out of the king-size bed and made a quick circuit through the house, a habit he had only developed in the last few years. He found it calmed him and helped him sleep. He checked the front and rear doors, a few random windows, then looked in on Charlie, who snored away in a steady rhythm, then on his precious Lauren. He stood by her door, which she always kept slightly ajar, and gazed at her flawless face. Her room was a typical adolescent's with an iPod in a charger next to a cell phone and computer. Her science textbook lay open on the small desk near her bed.

He searched both the kids' computers on a regular basis, because he knew the predators that lurked on the Internet and how often runaways were lured from their homes by these creeps. He never kept his snooping a secret from the kids and explained his concerns openly, just like he explained drug use with them. Charlie never cared, but Lauren was getting to the age where she resented little intrusions like that. He knew he'd never be complacent again; she'd just have to get used to it.

Satisfied everything was secure, Stallings headed back to his bed, but still couldn't shake the anxiety. He knew the only answer would be in finding Lee Ann Moffit's killer.

Dremmel's mind spun as he tried to buy time. Trina was clearly smarter than he'd given her credit for, and she was more resistant to the Oxy and Seconal than he thought possible. He'd read in one of the medical journals that continued use of most pharmaceuticals created a tolerance in the user even if the big drug companies claimed it didn't. This girl was a walking, jabbering contradiction to the notion that continued drug use didn't build tolerance. She had enough chemicals in her body that she should be snoring loudly in his lab by now.

If he bought enough time and calmed her down, maybe the drugs would start to hit her. He just needed a few minutes to get her into the lab, secure her, and then he could breathe a little easier.

He said, "I, er, I was worried about you and wanted you to get some rest. You'll have your own bedroom even."

She flung the empty Seconal capsule halves at him and screeched, "Bullshit. You're a fucking perv." A small fist blasted him in his right eye, snapping his head back. A trickle of blood ran down the side of his face. Trina turned, stomped into the living room, and started gathering her bra and blouse. "I'm outta here."

He stood, silent, feeling the sticky blood from the small cut and the lights still dancing in front of his right eye. Test subjects weren't supposed to act this way. He said, "No, wait. I can explain." As much as he didn't want to lose her as a potential test subject, he really didn't want her as a potential witness. He rushed after her, a lump in his throat and his stomach so tight he thought he might vomit. "Please just hold on a minute."

Trina looked up at him with her clothes in her hand, brown eyes angry but showing no sign of the sedative about to kick in.

He was on alert for another blow to the face, so he paused outside her short arm's range and studied her face as it darkened. All that emotion wasn't just because of him. This girl brought a whole stack of issues to the table. Certainly not as complex and debilitating as his own problems, but she definitely needed help. That fire, the rage shocked him. This was valuable information in itself; natural adrenaline could overcome even a sedative as strong as Seconal. He watched her carefully as she shuffled back and forth in front of the low coffee table, like she was deciding on a course of action.

Finally she said, "No, no way. I'm gone."

"Where? How will you get there?" He fought to hide the panic in his voice.

"Don't know, but I'm not staying in this nuthouse."

Then he knew she was lucid. She had identified his house for what it was—an asylum. He knew he had to act.

Trina spread her blouse on the couch and started to lift her arms through the straps of her bra.

Dremmel dropped to one knee, took a firm hold on the thin but sharp knife he had brought out with the cheese, and looked up at the half-naked girl from his crouched position.

Her arms were straight up now and her bra was just slipping over her hands when he struck upward with the knife, between and slightly below her breasts. The blade slid just under her sternum, the bone providing a guide for the steel through her soft tissue into her heart and lungs. He felt her flesh close in around his fist clutching the handle of the knife and knew all those years of studying anatomy had just paid off with a perfectly placed blow.

He stood up and withdrew the knife in the same motion, leaving a surprisingly slim, neat slit in her abdomen.

Trina dropped the bra to the floor and stared at him as blood finally started to dribble, then pour out of the wound. "Oh God, oh God." She clutched her upper stomach, covering the hole, causing blood to seep between her petite fingers. Then she started to scream. "You're crazy. Oh God, you're crazy." She had tremendous volume not only for a small person but for one with a knife hole almost directly in the middle of her body.

Dremmel looked down at the blade to make sure it was as long as he had thought. Blood dripped from its pointy end all the way down to the sandy-colored wooden handle. That should've killed her.

Trina reached out with her right hand like she needed help, then, in an instant, grabbed at his left ear. She raked her dull nails across his face as she stumbled back, knocking her can of beer from the coffee table onto the hard terrazzo floor, then steadied herself on the big-screen LCD TV. Now she looked up at him with an air of defiance.

Dremmel flinched at the blood getting on the most expensive item in the house, felt his face where the scratches started to sting, then moved toward her with the knife still in his hand.

"Don't come near me, you freak," shrieked Trina, trying to back away more. At last her legs gave out and she plopped onto the cold floor, blood now spurting between her fingers. She rolled over and got up on her hands and knees, then started crawling away from him like an infant.

He had to stop her screaming. It dug into his brain like a power drill and made his ears ache. It sounded so loud that he was afraid his neighbors might hear it, let alone his mother. He knew he was panicked, but he also realized this had to stop.

As she crawled, she started muttering to herself. "I'm sorry, I'm sorry. Oh God, I'm sorry."

Dremmel wondered what she was sorry for and to whom she was apologizing as he looked down at her exposed back. A tattoo he hadn't noticed sprang up from below her belt line. A fancy, symmetrical design with no words. Her colorful hair drooped to her right side and he saw her round, meaty neck. Now he knew what to do. He changed his grip on the knife, squatted down next to the terrified girl, and then drove the blade down through the center of her neck. He put his weight behind the blow and felt the resistance as the blade bounced off vertebrae and sliced through her windpipe. The tip of the knife popped out the little indentation in the front of her throat as she collapsed flat onto the ground without another sound or movement.

Dremmel took a deep breath and fell back against the wall. Trina's lifeless eyes stared directly at him as more blood seeped out of the stomach wound onto the hard terrazzo floor.

"Shit," he muttered. He had lost a perfectly good test subject, and now he had this mess to clean up.

One thought cheered him slightly. He could focus on Stacey Hines in a few days, and he doubted she would act like this girl.

Fourteen

John Stallings felt rested after a day off. He'd spent Saturday talking to various prescription drug dealers in the downtown area and looking for Peep Morans without success, but he would keep the little shit on his radar until he found him. The other dealers would've given up anyone to keep from losing their freedom. Stallings had only used the threat of arrest to scare each of the bloodsuckers, but they had all been specific about who they dealt to, and none of them recognized the photos of either of the girls.

Stallings spent Sunday with the kids, shooting hoops with both of them, kicking the soccer ball with Charlie, and watching in stunned silence as Lauren displayed her gymnastic talent at flipping, tumbling, and stopping his heart all at the same time. Patty Levine had gotten her interested in the sport, and the girl had shown a real knack for it. He wasn't sure he was happy about it considering the danger in some of the stunts, but she was happy, even if a backflip took two days and three hours off his life.

Now, at seven in the morning on a Monday, he thought his early entrance would give him a jump on any leads they might have developed on his brief time off. Rita Hester had ordered a general shutdown of the investigation for the mental well-being of the detectives involved. That was the kind of thing an administrator did—assign two people to cover leads for one day while everyone else, including Tony Mazzetti, recharged their batteries. It made sense, but the Rita Hester he knew as a regular officer would've bitched and moaned as much as he did when he was told to take a day off.

Now, he had to give her credit. He did feel better and energized, and he still wanted this guy so badly his stomach had burned the whole day he was off trying to be the father he never had. Even Maria had interacted with the family, briefly leaving her computer to watch Lauren's tumbling display.

He'd barely made it through the door when he noticed Patty Levine hunched over something on her desk.

"You're in early," he said, slowing at her desk.

"Catalogs, catalogs, catalogs." She slapped a pile on the side of her desk. "The search for luggage never ends."

"You are dedicated. I like that. Anything new?"

"I'm not sure. Mazzetti and the L.T. have been huddling in the conference room for the last ten minutes." She looked down the main squad bay of the Land That Time Forgot to the only room big enough for a table and ten chairs. By default it became the conference room.

"Ten minutes. What time did you guys get here? I thought I was early."

"They were here when I walked in at six-thirty."

Stallings nodded and padded on toward his desk. He

had his own notes to go over and see where he should look next. First he'd like to find Peep Morans and see where that led. Then he would carefully canvass the city neighborhood by neighborhood, talking to former runaways he knew. Once they figured out he wasn't trying to find new runaways, they opened up and helped him as best they could. So far it hadn't led to anything significant. But Jacksonville was a big city. In fact, it was the biggest in square miles in the entire United States thanks to some consolidation of government in the sixties when the city and county merged.

He intended to try a couple of unofficial safe houses in the north part of town. He'd work his way out to the outlying communities as he needed to, but he felt he'd find a lead closer to the center of J-Ville.

As he was starting to look up info about Peep Morans on the ancient computer at the edge of his scarred, stained desk, Rita Hester popped her head out of the conference room and motioned him in.

Stallings felt the other detectives watching him as he slowly walked down the center of the room, his shoes sliding on the cheap, thin carpet. Every cop wants to know what's going on and who knows what, that's part of their curious nature. They couldn't hide their jealousy that Stallings was about to find out something they didn't already know.

Involuntarily, he straightened his shirt and adjusted the pistol he wore exposed on his belt just to annoy Tony Mazzetti. He stepped into the conference room and saw Mazzetti sitting at the lone, long table with photographs of the first victim spread out in front of him.

"Sit down, Stall," Rita Hester nodded to the seat across from Mazzetti.

"What's up?"

Mazzetti wiped his bloodshot eyes—apparently he hadn't taken yesterday off—and said, "I think we've identified the first victim. A tip from the TV sketch. We need you to drive down to Bunnell and talk to her aunt to make positive ID."

"Why me? I thought you guys wanted me talking to runaways."

Mazzetti looked at him and said slowly and flatly, "You're good at talking to people. This will be a death notification, and God knows what could happen."

The lieutenant added, "Take Patty with you. It'll be good experience. I'll turn you loose on the city later in the day. The pimps could use a break." She smiled, but he heard the subtle warning: Don't take things too far.

William Dremmel had spent the weekend getting his life back in order. Now, as he sat at his Walmart pressboard desk, crammed in what used to be a utility closet at the community college, he felt like things might be back on track. He had no students scheduled to meet with him today, and that was just as well. His right eye had turned from a dark blue to a splotchy yellow from Trina's well-placed punch. All he had to do was get through today and tomorrow at the school; then he'd have a few days for his face to heal up. The scratches on the left side of his face were mere red lines now, barely visible. He had a good story made up about playing basketball if anyone asked.

He pulled out the thick textbook he used to teach his Biology One class in case someone wandered in his office, but the second book was what he was really studying. It was a compilation of white papers on prescription drugs published by Johns Hopkins University. He also had his own journal out, making notations on his findings so far. He really needed to figure out the right drug combination, available in the pharmacy, that allowed more conscious thought and wakefulness but less activity. He wanted a more listless subject who could still be awake much of the time. Once he had them in the right stasis, he could work on the formula for a maintenance dosage.

Young, wild-looking Trina was a real disappointment. Not only had she behaved like a spoiled child, cost him a night's worth of sleep, and wrecked his plans for a decent test run, he had a lot of cleaning up to do. He had mopped the floor in the living room, where it looked like she had lost a gallon of blood. Then he wiped down the floor, TV, and table surfaces with Clorox to cover any specks of blood he had missed.

He stuffed Trina into an expandable nylon suitcase with no manufacturer's name in it. He'd paid cash for the black suitcase at the giant flea market down in Daytona. In case there were any prints on it, he'd sprayed the inside and outside with WD-40. Of course he wore surgical gloves when he loaded the bodies, but he was so flustered after Trina's fit that he wanted to make certain he didn't slip up.

That night he drove her to a wooded area next to a park and left her about a hundred yards into the dark, spooky forest. His biggest concern was someone noticing the van, but he had made a calculation comparing driving during the day when people were out, or driving at night when there would be fewer vehicles to notice. He decided night was the right time and tried to stay calm as he parked, then dragged the bag through the sand and pine needles until he felt it was safe to leave her. He knew she'd be found but not for a while. Then she'd have to be identified. He thought he was in the clear on Trina even though she added nothing to his research.

Stacey Hines would fill the gap, and he wouldn't rush her. He'd done his research. Her car was still parked at the little apartment she rented. Tonight he'd have an early dinner at the restaurant where she worked and see if her roommate had, in fact, left for Ohio and if young Staccy liked the idea of someone to confide in.

In his journal he started a whole new page that had Stacey's name and vital statistics at the top.

John Stallings sat on the plastic-covered couch with Patty Levine next to him, both caught in that horrible, endless silence that always seemed to come after notifying someone that a loved one had died.

They had driven to the little town of Bunnell, about an hour south of downtown Jacksonville, and found the house, really more of a compound of trailers, of the aunt of the first victim, Tawny Wallace. She was a pleasant, tired-looking woman of fifty who lived on the three-acre lot with her retired Marine husband. Now she sat across from them quietly wiping tears from her pretty blue eyes while her husband had said he needed a beer, stood up, and disappeared into another room. The aunt and uncle had already identified the dead girl from two photographs from the medical examiner's office, so now there was no doubt what had happened to their missing niece.

Patty reached across and placed her hand on the aunt's and said, "Is there anything we can do for you?"

The woman looked up sniffling and shaking her head. "No, no, we hadn't heard anything from Tawny in a while, and I was worried something had happened." She looked up into the detectives' faces. "We had her since her mom died of breast cancer when she was fourteen. Earl wanted to try and, um, correct, some of the habits she'd been raised with. They just never got along well."

Stallings waited with his official questions to just let this poor woman speak. Patty showed her competence as a cop and a decent human being by talking to the woman as a person and not just a witness. She knew cops who used the term "citizen" instead of person missed out on a lot of the rewards of being a cop. He appreciated her professionalism as well as her humanity.

He looked around the walls of the clean, orderly living room. A Marine poster on one wall read, "USMC, Providing enemies of America the opportunity to die for their countries since 1775." On the opposite wall another framed poster read, "Patriotic dissent is a luxury provided by men better than they." The guy loved the Corps, and that usually meant he was a decent guy but not necessarily someone who could relate to a teenager.

Then he noticed the recycling bin near the kitchen door filled to overflowing with empty cans of Busch, and Stallings made a snap judgment about Tawny's uncle Earl, which wasn't favorable. He knew from his own experience being raised by a strict Navy man who drank that life was probably not much fun for her around this desperate little town. Especially if Earl thought he could "correct" the habits of a fourteen-year-old girl who had just lost her mother.

Just then the retired Marine stalked back into the room and sat, with his back straight as a board, next to his grieving wife. A can of Busch was in his left hand and another piece of the puzzle fell into place for Stallings. The man made no effort to comfort his wife.

Stallings just stared at the man in his late fifties and all he could picture was his father on a Saturday afternoon, shitfaced, after he had screamed at his sister for some inane issue, feeling bad for Helen and terrified of his father at the same time. Anger rose inside Stallings as Uncle Earl appeared unfazed by the news of his niece's death. He just took another sip of his beer and sat silently.

Stallings felt his right fist ball as the idea of clobbering this jackass flashed through his brain with a stronger signal every second. He felt his heartbeat in his neck and knew his face had turned beet red.

Tawny's aunt continued to sniffle into a Kleenex over a missed opportunity to do the right thing because this asshole had no more idea how to handle a teenager than he knew how to do brain surgery. To him life was good guys and bad guys and knowing how to work an artillery piece or fire an M-16 could solve any problem. Most military men could separate their personal and professional lives. They were good fathers who missed their kids. Uncle wasn't one of those guys.

Stallings took a deep breath hoping to relieve the growing desire to show this guy just how useless violence was to solve domestic situations by kicking his ass.

Patty, sensing a problem, reached across him and patted the aunt on the arm. "Do you think you could answer a few questions for us?"

The woman nodded quietly, but Uncle Earl still held that look of annoyed satisfaction, like he knew the girl wouldn't amount to anything. Asshole.

Since he couldn't do anything to stop creeps like this from driving teenaged girls from their homes, he felt the need to at least stop a killer like the one who killed her. His own daughter could be out on a street somewhere. He might have inadvertently driven her off. He hated to even consider that, but it was still possible. The emotions from his childhood flooded back as he looked at Uncle Earl. The beatings his drunken father laid on him and his sister. The crazy demands made in the middle of a drinking jag that sometimes lasted an entire weekend. His father's dead certain attitude that serving in the Navy gave him the right to say and do anything he wanted to in his own house.

He had plenty of reasons to feel the way he did. He wanted this killer so badly he was starting to lose focus on other parts of his life. It wasn't just Lee Ann Moffit that drove him. It was his own daughter, Jeanie, and his sister Helen's secret trauma from running away from their bullying, drunken father.

Now Stallings was just pissed off.

As they pulled away from the set of trailers, Patty looked over at Stallings behind the wheel of his Impala.

"You gonna tell me what that was all about?"

"What?"

"You and the uncle. You wanted to kill him. Why?"

"Look, Patty, I don't wanna talk about it. It's just that all any parent or guardian should want to do is make a better life for their kids. There's just too much that could go wrong with life, so you gotta be a good parent. If you think about it, raising a kid is scarier than police work. And that asshole back there did not help that poor girl."

"How can you know that?"

"I lived it."

He had more to say on the subject, since she'd gotten

him started, when his phone rang. He dug it out of his front pocket and barked, "Stallings," still with an edge to his voice.

He heard Rita Hester say, "Stall, we got another body."

Fifteen

Stallings heard Patty say, "Holy shit, look at the news trucks. How'd they get here so fast?"

His throat went dry at the sight of the media vehicles. This wouldn't help the investigation, and he knew from experience that it could make some of the detectives crazy and competitive for attention. The whole idea of a goat-fuck like this made his anxiety over finding Peep Morans move to the back of his mind.

"Someone probably put it out over the radio and it was a slow news day. What else are they gonna cover? The missile frigate docked at Mayport?"

"You think they've linked the bodies yet?"

"If they haven't, they will, or someone'll leak it." Stallings pulled the Impala into the lot across from the wooded park. Yellow crime scene tape blocked the entrance and patrol units were parked at the corners of the woods to discourage anyone interested in a closer look. For now the reporters were behaving, crammed together in the designated media area roped off near the main road. Two helicopters circled overhead, giving the scene more of a Francis Ford Coppola feel.

He could see Rita Hester and Tony Mazzetti talking to a group of the task force detectives within the crime scene tape. It was a staged move to give the media some decent video and make the Sheriff's Office look like they were throwing a lot of effort into the problem. Keep the soccer moms calm and give the realtors something good to say about the area. They used phrases like, "Our police force is outstanding and jumps on any problem that arises."

Stallings was already in a bad mood from his encounter with Tawny Wallace's Uncle Earl. His own childhood memories didn't help things today. He had a job to do and had to move past his own issues. The idea that this creep had killed again made him realize how he'd blown his desire to stop the asshole before some other poor girl paid the price. Now this scene looked like a zoo, some family would be heartbroken, and Stallings felt like shit.

Patty looked around like a kid at the fair. "Wow, you ever see anything like this?"

"Yeah," was all he said as he ducked under the tape and nodded to a patrolman, who almost saluted the senior detective. It reminded him of the circus he had endured after capturing Carl Cernick. Even his family got dragged into it as reporters hounded him for information.

Mazzetti looked up and motioned the two detectives over to his group. "I was about to go over what we've got so far." He waited as they all crowded in, so he didn't broadcast sensitive information across the crime scene to the media outside the tape. "We've got a young, white female, nude, in a suitcase."

Stallings felt himself sag. He had hoped, by some wild chance, that maybe, just maybe, this wasn't their killer.

Mazzetti added, "This one's been stabbed."

Stallings head jerked up, but he didn't say anything because someone else said it for him. "A copycat killer?"

Mazzetti looked down and said, "Christ, I hope we don't end up with two of these creeps running around. The body is already over at the M.E.'s office, and they know what to look for. But I gotta say my first gut reaction is it's our man. She's short, barely five feet, same age range and method of disposal. The media hasn't caught on about the first two deaths. No chance someone just happened to kill a short woman and stuffed her in a suitcase."

Patty said, "Why the change in method of death? This is more violent than the others."

Mazzetti nodded. "That's what we been talkin' about. Right now I wouldn't want to guess. There are two visible wounds. One in the upper abdomen and one deep one all the way through the neck from back to front." He used his right hand on the rear of his neck to emphasize the angle of attack.

Stallings caught Patty processing the death and shuddering. All he could think was, *Welcome to homicide, kid*.

Mazzetti cleared his throat and stood a little taller. "The good news is that this girl might have gotten in a shot of her own."

"How's one punch good news?" asked one of the older detectives.

"There's a cut on her knuckles and some blood and skin under her fingernails. We got some decent DNA samples and maybe even some marks on the killer. At least for a few days." He sounded proud of the girl.

Stallings agreed. Maybe she was dead, but she gave them something to look for. He hoped whoever she was, they could identify her and bring some closure to her family.

They started to assemble teams to comb the woods for any possible evidence. Stallings knew how important tasks like this could be to a big case, but he still felt the urge to get out onto the street and turn up some kind of information that would end this quickly. He wanted the killer stopped. Making a case was secondary. His stomach growled, but he knew he couldn't eat.

Tony Mazzetti squatted to take a look at the pine needles on the edge of a trail where he believed the killer had dragged the body. Of course it had been trampled, but not too badly. After a jogger had noticed the suitcase and opened it, he turned on the afterburners back to the street and just happened to flag down a JSO cruiser. By the time the fat patrolman had crunched through the trail and then his sergeant and two other patrolmen who wanted to see what the fuss was all about, the scene had some contamination. Mazzetti shook his head.

It was a senior sergeant named Ellis who was smart enough to chase everyone out and wait for crime scene and homicide. Mazzetti thought the big sergeant was going to punch someone the way he was laying into the patrolmen for not being more careful. The Sheriff's Office needed more hardasses like that. Christ, it seemed like they had been hiring social workers for so long that no one knew how to do police work anymore.

As Mazzetti looked at some orange string or carpet fiber near the suitcase, he sensed someone behind him. Looking over his shoulder he saw the extremely cute Patty Levine gazing out toward the news crews.

Mazzetti said, "Like vultures around a dead antelope."

Patty jerked her head at the sound of his voice, her blond hair flipping like a model's at a photoshoot. "Huh?"

"The media types love juicy crime scenes."

"Yeah, I guess. I was just watching how all the cameras followed John as he walked across the lot. You think they realize he's the guy that caught Cernick?"

Mazzetti sprang to his feet and stepped closer to Patty for a better vantage point. Sure enough, three camera crews were following Stallings as he ignored them and made his way toward his car. *Son of a bitch*, Mazzetti almost said out loud. *That guy gets all the attention, and it's not right.* He'd worked too hard to let a lucky stiff like Stallings steal all the glory. He'd find this crazy-assed killer first if it took a twenty-four-hour-a-day effort.

He looked back at Patty to see if she noticed his aggravation and realized: she really was a knockout.

After he'd heard the news report, William Dremmel made a little detour to drive past the park where he had left poor, loud, obnoxious Trina two nights ago. He knew by the slow procession of traffic that there were other rubberneckers, and that would cover him well enough. He smiled at his realization that the old adage, "The killer always returns to the scene of the crime," was apparently true.

He could only see a couple of uniformed cops from the road, but he noticed the news vans parked along the edge of the woods and it made his smile broader. He didn't know why, but the whole idea of this much effort caused by his experiments made him feel special.

With a day's worth of reflection, he was starting to believe he'd learned something during the whole Trina fiasco. One thing that he needed to correct was his knowledge of the brain and anatomy of the spinal cord. He'd spent his academic career dissecting cats, frogs, and snakes but hadn't spent much time on human anatomy. The kind of labs and classes he taught revolved around basic biology, which treated humans as only one of the many species inhabiting the Earth. A very egalitarian, but not necessarily effective way to teach.

Although not as interesting or useful as holding a girl as she silently expired from one of his drug cocktails, Trina's sudden death held an interest of its own. The way his knife blow to her neck just shut off all brain function instantly gave him other ideas for future research. But that would happen after he perfected the drug regimen.

He drove his drab, common minivan past the scene, unnoticed by everyone, then proceeded to the restaurant where Stacey Hines worked. By now either her roommate had gone back to Ohio or he'd have to look for a new subject. He wasn't so desperate to risk being caught over a simple error like a roommate knowing his name or description.

Trina was a fluke, but he had gotten away with it. He'd worked hard to overcome his impulsiveness on the matter. Thank God his mother hadn't rolled into the kitchen, where she could see the living room. No excuse in the world would've explained the blood smeared across the floor. He was also lucky no one from the Wendy's had noticed them together.

He drove along, enjoying his feeling of power and satisfaction, then saw the little sports bar optimistically named The Fountain of Youth, even though the real fountain was supposed to be in St. Augustine, forty-five miles away. He turned a block early so he could come up from behind and see the lot where Stacey usually parked her ratty, rusted Ford Escort. He felt himself hold his breath as he took one corner, then another. He hadn't realized how much he wanted her to be there. When he turned onto the street he could see the little car wedged in next to an overflowing Dumpster.

Dremmel parked a block away and made it look like he was going into a clothing store, then slipped back out and hustled down the empty street to the sports bar. He caught himself a half a block away and slowed down, because he didn't want to seem too anxious even though Stacey was the only thing on his mind at the moment.

He paused inside the door and scanned the small restaurant. Two men sat at the bar watching a rerun of the Giants-Patriots Superbowl on the NFL channel. No one this side of Boston ever seemed to get tired of seeing the game over and over. Dremmel wasn't even a big sports fan and he knew the details of the legendary contest where basic football skills beat arrogance and entitlement. At least that was the most poetic way he'd heard it described.

A young couple sat on the same side of a booth, shared some fries, and snuggled. In the far corner, the beautiful Stacey Hines stood in front of a table occupied by one old man with a comb-over that made Rudy

Giuliani look like he had an Afro. He just watched her from a distance, her cute smile and lovely, graceful neck, the curves of her breasts and hips all contained in the little package that fit so nicely into his experiments.

He stepped in, nodded to the bartender, trying not to be too memorable. There was no other choice; he'd have to be incredibly lucky to catch her alone in the front of the restaurant. The first time had to have been a fluke. He wasn't sure how to get around a potential witness other than to be calm and play it slow. Dremmel just prayed the man didn't step out from the bar to take his order. He stole a glance at Stacey as she patted the old man on the shoulder, laughing with him as she took his order. Then he noticed the heavy man from the bar start to walk toward the open end of the counter. Was he coming to Dremmel to take his order? Jesus, no, prayed William Dremmel, as it seemed more and more obvious.

He looked back over at Stacey, who seemed to be finishing up her order. "C'mon, come on," he mumbled under his breath.

The heavy bartender cleared the end of the bar, glanced over at Dremmel, and nodded.

"Shit," whispered Dremmel.

The bartender leaned over the bar and said, "Stacey."

She turned and looked at the bartender as he pointed her in Dremmel's direction. She just nodded.

Maybe she doesn't even remember me, thought Dremmel. Then, as she started his way, a smile broke across her cute face. The smile had a crooked quality to it, dipping on the right side, but that just made her more attractive.

She said, "Hey, you came back. I knew you'd like our hamburgers."

He wanted to just jump in and ask if her roommate had really moved. It took all his concentration to say, "Yeah, it was great. How about the same thing?"

She paused and asked, "Which burger did you have?"

"I don't remember."

"How 'bout the blue cheese burger?"

"Perfect."

She made a note of his Diet Pepsi order and then looked down at him and smiled. "What happened to your eye?"

He hesitated for an instant and then said, "Basketball. Took an elbow."

"Looks like it was a rough game. Someone scratched you too."

"Same play. He was trying to keep me from falling."

"Does it hurt?"

"Not now."

"I'm glad you came back."

"Yeah, me too. Hey, didn't you say your roommate was moving?"

"Yeah, she left Saturday."

"You doing okay?"

"I guess. It's a little lonely. You know how it is."

He just nodded. He really did know exactly how it was. But maybe for not too much longer.

Sixteen

John Stallings had been home for less than five minutes when the news came on. Chicken with black beans and rice and a decorative ceramic bowl of steamed asparagus sat on the table, but no one had come into the dining room yet. The way he felt he couldn't eat anything, no matter how wonderful it smelled. The image of Tawny Wallace and her uncle stuck in his head and mixed with his guilt over the new victim. It was guys like Tawny's uncle and his own father that kept him from ever really drinking. Later tonight he planned to slip out to look for Peep Morans even if he was a long shot. He was meeting Mazzetti at the M.E.'s office in the morning to get a better idea of what happened to this new victim.

He paused in front of the forty-two-inch Samsung and watched as the news teaser came on. A long-range camera shot zoomed in, and the image was unexpected— his face at the crime scene. The announcer then said, "Is there a serial killer stalking the streets of Jacksonville?" The show's opening music and credits rolled by.

Stallings stood frozen in shock. Why did they care about him out of all the people at the scene today?

Charlie yelled into the kitchen, "Dad's on TV."

Stallings turned to shush the young boy, but it was too late. Maria was hurrying out of the kitchen and Lauren was rushing down the stairs.

Maria said, "Why, what happened?" There was an edge of panic in her voice.

"Just a case I'm working on."

Maria let out her breath and made Stallings realize she thought it might have something to do with Jeanie. She had almost turned to go back into the kitchen when the newscaster opened with, "Jacksonville homicide detective John Stallings has been called in to help on a possible serial killer who has emerged in recent months. The third body of a young woman was found in a park off Terrace Road in eastern Duval County earlier today. Reliable sources have told the Eleven News Team that all the bodies have been disposed of inside suitcases or duffel bags, earning this killer the nickname 'The Bag Man.' "

Stallings snatched up the remote and shut off the TV before Maria heard anything else that might upset her.

From the stairs Lauren said, "The Bag Man," out loud but to no one. It wasn't with a sense of cool, it was just a statement of a new fact. She was old enough to understand what could've happened to her sister and that killers like this prey on runaways and the isolated.

Maria turned to him and said, "When did you go back into homicide?" Her tone said it all. She may not have paid much attention, but she knew an assignment like that would keep him at work longer and more erratic hours. The idea of him feeling a compulsion to stop the killer would play no role in her resentment for losing him to the job again.

"It's temporary. Just for this case."

"Is this why you've been gone so much?"

He nodded, not bothering to explain that he'd been trying to tell her for days now, and she hadn't really acknowledged his odd schedule. Was she coming back to full reality and joining the family? He didn't care if it took anger for her to connect again, he just wanted her back with them.

She steadied herself on the back of the couch and he knew what she was thinking. He knew the look. She wanted something. Drugs, booze, she was reverting to old habits that had helped her cope with life. Now was not the time to pick a fight with her over why he needed to be working in homicide.

She looked up at him and said, "I need to make a call." She rushed past him and up the stairs, almost knocking Lauren out of her way.

Charlie said, "Where's Mom going? I'm hungry."

Lauren's face told Stallings she knew exactly who Mom was calling and that it could be a rough evening around the Stallings house.

This wasn't how he wanted her to find out about his assignment. Maria had blamed his long hours in homicide as a contributing factor to Jeanie's disappearance. She never used specific words like "kidnapping" or "runaway"; she always called it a "disappearance." She also looked for the first, most obvious excuse, which was his job. Now, after so much healing, he was worried the effect working homicide again might have on his wife. Maybe the AA sponsor she was calling right now would be able to talk her down. He knew his family needed him right now, but what they didn't realize is that he needed them even more.

He plopped down at the dinner table and tried to put

on a smile for the kids. Inside all he could do was imagine what it would be like to corner this Bag Man and work out his anger issues once and for all.

Tony Mazzetti stood alone in the shadows of the trees near where the body of the girl had been discovered that morning. It was after ten, and no one had been around for hours. In the spooky stillness of the park, broken only by the occasional car passing slowly on Terrace Road, Mazzetti tried to imagine the killer dragging the heavy suitcase across the pine needles in the dark. Did someone see him late? Did he do it in the middle of the night? What was he driving to transport her? These were the easier questions and the ones he preferred to ask himself. Other questions such as, was she scared before she died or was it a surprise? Did she have dreams for the future? Does her family realize she's missing yet? Those things could distract him from his duties on the case, so he tried to guide his thoughts away from issues like that. Instead, his mind had filed away things like the tangible evidence found at the scene. The orange string, the simple black suitcase that had to be twenty years old, the single footprint in the dirt that didn't belong to an arriving cop, the possible DNA material, and a host of other physical clues.

Mazzetti had to admit he didn't have the contacts or way with people that John Stallings did. He compensated by being thorough and putting in hours no one with a family could. When all was said and done he didn't have anything in his life but homicide and the recognition he got for his work.

For now that was enough for him.

* * *

John Stallings followed the medical examiner's comments, but his brain was hazy. That was the only way to explain it after staying up with Maria until the early morning hours, holding her as she swung through a spectrum of emotions that all led to a four-hour crying jag. He had even put off looking for Peep Morans, realizing how important this was. He tried to explain his new assignment and to put into words why he was doing it, even though he wasn't completely certain himself. He would've said anything to keep her safe and at home last night. He would've said almost anything to just make her happy again. Anything except, "I'll pull out of the Bag Man investigation." He was hooked, and he knew it.

Now a smart-looking woman about his age with rimless glasses and blue eyes that caught the overhead lights like a mirror explained what the autopsies of the three victims had found in common.

She stood erect like a Marine and looked at each person present directly in the eye, then moved on to the next. "The first two victims had similar levels of pharmaceutical drugs in their system. But this latest one had a lot more of everything, including marijuana, traces of ecstasy, and even Seconal."

"Who uses Seconal?" asked Mazzotti.

"Usually it's closely regulated. It's a heavy-duty sedative. Older patients with chronic problems might be prescribed it. But you don't see it in common street use. I'd say that the killer has access to a source and knows what he's doing. That's not the kind of drug you just try out."

"What about the stab wounds?"

"Very precise and with a great deal of power behind

them. The marks around the wounds indicate that the killer drove in the knife with enough force to damage the tissue around the wound with his hand."

Rita Hester looked at the M.E. and said, "Any theories?"

"On the knife? That's your department. I would say the wound to the neck was probably unnecessary. The one in the abdomen came up and damaged the heart. She was high, which warded off shock, so she probably moved around but she wouldn't have survived. I have no idea why he switched from drugs to a knife."

Stallings said, "I think he just screwed up. She started to scream, and he stabbed her. Killing them isn't his main objective. He's got some other plan or else he wouldn't go to the trouble of luring the girls away from where he meets them."

"That another lucky guess?" asked Mazzetti.

The lieutenant's hard look shut up Mazzetti and kept Stallings from making a comeback.

The M.E. nodded and said, "That makes sense, because the first two victims lived for some time with the drugs in their systems. I'd really try and find his drug source if possible."

Stallings listened and took a few notes, but the discussion was unsettling to him. Besides Mazzetti, the M.E., the chief forensic scientist, and Rita Hester were in the small room. Rita looked imposing in a brown pantsuit and her pistol on her belt by her hip with a badge exposed next to it. He didn't know if it was a subtle message to the M.E. that she was a working boss who was in charge or if she just decided to wear it like that.

Mazzetti looked at the forensic scientist, a stubby man everyone just called "Bud." "What do you guys have, Bud?"

He cleared his throat and somehow just that action telegraphed his Southern drawl. "It's too early on the DNA scrapings. We're rushing it, but it'll still be a week. We have a flake of skin from the wheel of the suitcase used in the first incident and the scrapings from this girl's fingernails. We might get lucky with a match."

"But there's nothing in CODIS?" CODIS was the FBI's database on DNA, the combined DNA index system. Like all police agencies the feds wanted a cool name for the toy.

"No, we checked. We're also hooked up with the FDLE on it. They have the best DNA database in the country. If the killer has been looked at and a sample turned in, they'll match it." He cleared his throat again, then took an old handkerchief from his tight rear pocket and wiped his lips. "We got a few things you might want to follow up on."

"Go on," said Mazzetti, the impatience evident in his voice.

"The killer is smart. He sprayed WD-40 on the inside of the suitcase so we couldn't lift any fingerprints if he left them. The only fiber evidence is the long orange string you found in the woods near where he left the body. We're going to see what we can figure out about it and let you know. Also, the last two victims had decorative sand on their bodies. The one from last week had a few grains on her feet like she stepped on a path barefoot, and the newest victim had a little ingrained in her elbow as if she fell. The sand matches and you might, with some help from a geologist, figure out where it came from."

Mazzetti looked at the squat man. "Anything else?"

"Cat hair, black cat hair was on all three victims."

"He's a smart killer, but he leaves cat hair on the victims? That seems sorta slipshod to me," said Mazzetti.

"Not really. Cat hair is insidious. It creeps into everything. Usually no one notices, but when we're combing through hair and searching armpits we tend to find everything."

Mazzetti said, "So we got a guy with a black cat and fancy walkway that likes to see girls die slowly on drugs, but is now about a violent stabbing too. Great, just fucking great."

The forensic scientist tossed an envelope onto the table next to him. "I had plenty of photos made up of each victim for your detectives in case they want to show them around or see if we're missing something when we compared them."

Stallings watched as Mazzetti pulled one photo of each victim out and stared at the three of them together. His stomach tightened when he saw the photo of the last, unidentified victim with colors dyed in her hair.

He said out loud, "I've seen her."

Everyone else turned their attention to Stallings.

"She was eating at a Wendy's the other night. I remember her hair."

Mazzetti said, "Which Wendy's?"

"Over on Beaver Street. I can go talk to them right now."

Mazzetti held up a hand and said, "Not so fast, hotshot. I'm on this one."

Suddenly it hit Stallings that the girl was eating with someone. He'd almost seen the Bag Man. Fuck! He'd been a few feet away from seeing this asshole's face. Stallings felt a little light-headed as the idea wrapped itself through his mind. He hadn't paid too much attention at the time, and Beaver is a busy street. What were the odds? But when he considered that both he and the killer were probably working the same areas of the city, the odds didn't seem so great. He knew Mazzetti realized it as soon as Stallings had spoken up.

Mazzetti said, "Go look for another lucky lead."

That was okay with Stallings. He needed something to occupy his mind and get the idea that he had let the killer slip by out of his head. He'd find his next witness today if he had to threaten every pimp and dealer in downtown Jacksonville. Someone would know where Peep Morans was hiding.

William Dremmel opened the store in Arlington so he could get in four hours before rushing over to the community college for his official office hours, then teach his Earth Science class. The one thing that cheered him about the change in routine was that Lori had also grabbed the early shift at the store. She was working from eight in the morning until close at nine that evening. He knew it was a tiring shift, but her graceful, slender body seemed to move with much less effort than most people.

"At least I have you to talk to for a few hours." She smiled after the comment, and it made his whole body swell. She was a really nice girl.

"I'd stay for the double shift, but I have to get over to the college."

"Did you see the police identified a victim of that killer as a student at your school?"

"No, I haven't seen that yet."

"There'll be a whole lot coming out about the killings. One of the cable channels is starting to pick up on it. That prosecutor lady from Atlanta might even come down here. Could you imagine a big star like that right here in J-Ville?"

"Yeah, she's big." At first he liked the idea of the attention, but he had to be careful that it didn't somehow interrupt his research. For the first time he wondered how it might affect potential subjects like Stacey Hines. Would she be worried about getting to know someone like him now that the whole world was learning about the Bag Man? He was a problem solver, and this was just one more hurdle to overcome. Then he had a great idea.

He turned to Lori, who was organizing the filled prescriptions and said, "You got a long shift today. Let me take you to a good lunch. You have a full hour break, and it's a little bit of a ride, but they have great burgers."

"Do they have fish too? Because I haven't been eating anything with legs."

"A vegetarian? I didn't know."

"I eat seafood too. I just saw a special on the Discovery Channel about slaughterhouses and decided I didn't need the bad karma."

"I saw fish on the menu, so you're safe."

"Wow, that's really nice of you, Billy." She turned and touched his arm. "You are a good guy." Her smile gave him ideas better left alone.

Seventeen

Peep Morans's real name was Walter Moranski and he'd lived in Jacksonville for nineteen of his thirty-nine years. He'd moved here from Detroit after a misunderstanding looked like it would turn into a rape charge. He thought a change of scenery and different name may throw off the cops long enough for the whole case to just fade away. He actually only shortened his last name; he got his nickname "Peep" for his unquenchable thirst to watch women urinate. Since he mostly lived on the streets, he knew women who lived on the streets and had no choice but to relieve themselves wherever they thought they had privacy. Peep had figured out where those spots were likely to be and set up covert vantage points all over the downtown area.

Sure he'd been caught over the years, that's how people knew to call him Peep, but he'd never been arrested for it. He had a rap sheet for minor drug violations and loitering but not for spying on women. During his first arrest in Jacksonville he gave the name of Walt Morans. He had a fake Georgia ID card in that name. Since he'd never been arrested or fingerprinted back home in Detroit, this was the only record of him. So now the whole world knew him as Peep Morans, and he liked it just fine.

He enjoyed Jacksonville, with its mild climate and friendly people. He liked being a small-time pharmaceutical drug salesman. He got most of his stash from a guy who could buy it wholesale from a relative in the pharmaceutical business and then marked it up accordingly. What he liked best about his specialized role in the drug market was that the cops didn't really care much about him. They focused on crack dealers and would thump them on a regular basis. Peep had been stopped with twenty or so pills and the cop would just make him throw them down the sewer rather than go to the trouble of determining what the chemical in the drug was or if he had a script for them. It was a sweet setup. For now Peep lived in a little apartment in Arlington that was nice enough to bring the kind of women he desired home. He ate okay and didn't worry too much about going to jail.

His clientele had changed over the years. For a while he catered to suburban moms who liked their Percocet and Vicodin without having to fake an injury for a doctor. Now young people liked the pharmaceuticals too. He adjusted his marketing plan and was doing fine as long as he got to see a lady pee every couple of days.

On this clear day he was waiting on a corner he'd staked out for himself near Union Street, a few blocks from the big Shands Medical Center, enjoying the sunshine and the cooler breeze off the Atlantic, when his world took a sudden turn for the worse.

As he leaned back on a decorative cement corner piece of an older office building, his eyes closed while he felt the sun warm his face, he heard a man's voice say, "Hello, Peep, how's business?"

Peep's eyes popped open to the scariest possible sight: JSO Detective John Stallings in his black Impala with the window down. He looked as calm as if he were ordering a McDonald's double cheeseburger from the drive-thru, but Peep knew that guy was no ordinary cop. He'd discovered that the hard way a couple of years ago, and that was why he felt like he might shit in his own pants and every fiber of his muscles told him to run as fast as he could. He'd rather be arrested than face this crazy fucker again.

He rolled to the side and started to run. No one knew the downtown like him, and he had plenty of hiding places. He'd gladly turn himself in at the jail if it meant he could avoid a confrontation with Stallings. He cut between buildings where the Impala couldn't fit, looking over his shoulder as he did. Peep didn't see the car or any sign of the detective. Just the thought of the tough cop made the arm that he broke three years ago start to ache. The first time he'd met Stallings he didn't know who he was but found out quickly when the detective learned that Peep was selling Vicodin to his wife. She had a secret habit, and Peep happily sold her ten pills. Then, a few days later, he sold her twenty. The next day this dude who was built for the cornerback position, lean and fast but strong, stepped up to him in the middle of the day right on the street. All he said was, "Sell to Maria Stallings again and this will happen to the other arm." Then he grabbed Peep's left arm, twisted it behind him, and slammed an elbow into it, snapping both of his forearm bones cleanly.

Then he spun Peep around and looked at him. "You know who I mean? Maria."

Peep knew the hot-looking Spanish chick. He nodded vigorously.

"You gonna sell to her again?"

He shook his head.

"I'm her husband. My name is John Stallings, and I'm a detective with JSO. You wanna complain, call it in. But I want you to know how serious I am. Are you convinced?"

Peep nodded his head as he fought the vomit wanting to spew out everywhere. He'd never had something hurt so bad it made him want to puke. Peep knew serious when he saw it, and this crazy dude was serious.

Over the last couple of years he'd heard more and more about Stallings. People either loved him or hated him. As long as you didn't mess with the runaways he treated you okay. Peep didn't bother runaways, but his history with the detective told him he was doing the right thing running until he wanted to puke from exhaustion instead of pain.

He made it to the edge of the Trinity Rescue Mission and started to slow down as he approached a little hutch in the bushes he used to spy on women across the street who couldn't work up the courage to enter the mission. He took one more look around, then ducked into the bushes, plopped onto the hard clay ground, and took a deep breath.

Just as he was thinking, *that was close*, he heard a man's voice almost next to him. He snapped his head to see John Stallings lounging in the corner of the wide space under the bushes.

Stallings made no move toward him but said, "You can run as fast as you want, Peep. All it means is that you'll be tired when I break your leg. Or you can sit still a moment and listen to what I have to say. I'm just looking for information."

Peep knew the man kept his word, and if he said he wasn't going to hurt him at that moment he felt pretty safe.

Peep managed to squeak out, "What do you wanna know?"

"Anyone buying a lot of Oxy or have any Seconal?"

"Why?"

"It's a homicide investigation."

"Thought you were in Missing Persons."

Stallings smiled and said, "It doesn't matter if I'm in sex crimes, I need the info, and you're gonna give it to me."

Peep knew the man well enough not to ask, "Or what?"

William Dremmel had a plan, but it required some luck. He'd driven Lori from the pharmacy to the Fountain of Youth sports bar at noon and made it in under fifteen minutes. He had to get her back to the store by one o'clock. The next lucky break was that Stacey Hines was working, and they were seated in her area. Unlike his other visits, the restaurant had a crowd today at lunch. Having Lori with him made it less likely people would single him out if the cops asked questions after he took Stacey as a test subject. He also hoped that allowing Stacey to see him with an attractive young black woman would ease her mind about him when it came time to ask her over to his house. He'd make it clear that they were just coworkers, but he knew how women thought, and seeing him with someone would give her the signal that he wasn't a lonely, creepy single guy even if that was the truth.

Now Stacey was walking toward them, a sway in her hips that made him smile. She saw him, and her face brightened until she noticed Lori. She still had a perky grin as she walked up and said, "Hey there."

"Hi, Stacey. I liked your food so much I brought my friend from work, Lori."

Lori just gave her a quick smile and nod.

Dremmel quickly picked up an odd vibe from his coworker. Had he misjudged their relationship?

Stacey leaned in closer to Dremmel. "So you two work at the community college together?"

He was happy she had bothered to remember the facts of his life. "No, at the pharmacy."

Lori had lost her smile and looked Stacey directly in the eye and said, "And I'm in a hurry. Could you just bring me a grouper sandwich?"

Stacey wrote it down and turned to Dremmel.

Maybe this hadn't worked out the way he had wanted. And now he looked at Lori in an entirely different light.

Earlier in the day Tony Mazzetti had been frustrated. He'd taken his usual partner, Christina "Hoagie" Hogrebc, with him to talk to the manager at the Beaver Street Wendy's. Not only could the guy identify the girl from the photo the M.E. had provided, he told Mazzetti she'd been an employee and hadn't shown back up to work. He didn't report her absence because he thought she just quit and didn't say anything.

Mazzetti had taken Detective Hogrebe with him because he wanted another permanent homicide detective to be in on what might be a huge break on the case. Stallings may have been lucky seeing the girl, but it would be the follow-up that helped the investigation. Instead, they found the girl had filled out the application using a fake name and social security number. She was trying to stay under someone's radar.

The application said she was Tina Marshall of Jacksonville, who was twenty-two years old, and provided the social security number of a girl who died at sixteen in 1977. The same number had been used on several employment applications at the store. The manager just needed warm bodies to work and didn't much care about references or backgrounds. He also didn't seem too surprised she'd been killed. He knew she stayed wherever she could each night. The manager pretty much felt it was none of his business. They had questioned him and everyone in the store about who she had eaten with the night she disappeared, but no one remembered her eating or talking to anyone. The one security camera hadn't worked in over a year, and trying to find her real name was a dead end.

Now, a few hours later, Tony Mazzetti felt much better, because he liked being in charge. It wasn't a power thing. He just liked getting things done, and no one knew how to cut through all the bullshit like him. The lieutenant had given him five detectives to head over to the community college and see what they could find out about the first victim, Tawny Wallace. He'd sent two of the auto theft guys to the registrar to see about her schedule and get a list of classmates. Two other detectives were interviewing her teachers and any friends they could find on campus to see if she associated with anyone in particular, and he had asked Patty Levine to come with him as he got a feel for the place and see if he could stumble across anything of value. It also gave him a chance to chat with her without that ass Stallings or any of the other dumb shits working temporarily up in the unit.

After a few minutes of wandering, Patty looked at him and said, "What are we looking for, Tony?"

"I'm trying to get a feel for the foot traffic through the different departments so when we start talking to witnesses we know our way around campus and know if it's reasonable that someone might notice a stranger." That was all true and he'd been doing exactly that, but this diversion to the science building gave him some time with her. He had a feeling that maybe Patty Levine could be good for him. It'd been a long time since he'd tried to hook up with a woman.

He held the glass door for Patty as they entered the long, wide science building.

Patty looked down and said, "Looks like they got a deal on part of a University of Florida rug."

Mazzetti noted the orange rug and nodded. All it would take was an equal length of blue carpet and it would look like a hall in Gainesville. They checked two offices, but there was no one around. The classes looked about half full and the building seemed to have regular traffic. Seeing the young girls in their tight blouses and capris made him think about his own age. When did college students start to look so young? He felt out of place and uneasy here.

Then a blond man in his early thirties nodded and smiled as he walked past and turned down a narrow corridor. Patty said, "I'll see if there's an office this way." She turned and walked the opposite direction.

Mazzetti nodded, then caught up to the blond man and said, "Excuse me."

The man turned. He was about five seven and built with thick shoulders and biceps that taxed his button-down shirt. "May I help you?"

"Are you a teacher in this department?"

"I am."

"My name is Tony Mazzetti," he said as he reached

back and pulled his badge and ID from his rear pocket. He'd done it so many times he had it timed to coincide with his saying, "From the Jacksonville Sheriff's Office."

The man stared at them and said, "What's this about?"

Mazzetti thought his tone was a little odd and paused before saying, "I couldn't find anyone in the office down the hall."

The man nodded and said, "We're a little short-handed and everyone has a class right now. Is there something I could help you with?"

"Not really anything specific. We identified a student as the victim in a homicide."

"Oh dear Lord."

"Tawny Wallace. Did you happen to know her?"

He thought about it, then slowly shook his head. "No, not off the top of my head. I only teach part time. This semester I have two classes, so I don't see everyone on a regular basis."

"Who would?"

"Professor Sporano is the head of the department. He practically lives here."

Mazzetti nodded as he wrote down the name. He liked seeing an Italian in charge. It seemed like that was the only way to keep things running smoothly down here in the South. Then he asked, "What do you teach?"

"I mostly run labs for biology and teach classes on natural and earth sciences."

Before he could ask anything relevant to the case, a bell rang and the classes let out. Crowds of young people and a surprising number of older ones flowed into the main hallway.

The man said, "Sorry, I have to go now."

Mazzetti said, "I understand." Then he looked at the man. "What happened to your eye?"

"Basketball."

"Rough game." It was a black eye turning to yellow.

"Especially here. The students don't cut me any slack." He smiled and turned toward his office.

Mazzetti called out. "I just need your name for my notes."

"Dremmel. William Dremmel."

Eighteen

John Stallings sat at his barren desk staring at his notes. He'd talked to four pharmaceutical drug pushers since noon. Three were converted crack dealers, and one, a little creep named Peep Morans, had dealt Vicodin to Maria when she had fallen off the wagon. None of them had any great leads but knew to keep their eyes open. Peep Morans had a series of hiding spots he used to spy on women, and Stallings had figured out where three of them were. When the pervert ran from him earlier in the day he didn't bother to chase him. Instead he drove to the hiding spot in the direction the dealer had run. The skeevy dealer had provided a few more names and areas where dealers pushed prescription drugs. That's how big cases tended to flow. One lead pointed a detective to three more until finally you had a break in the case. It could be tedious, but it was necessary, and in a case like this, where women were being killed, no one wanted to overlook a lead no matter how insignificant. Morans had mentioned a dealer named "Ernie" who hung out with the runaway population a lot and might have some info for Stallings. Ernie was now high on his list of priorities.

The squad bay was empty, as other detectives had their own leads and assignments. He heard someone come in through the back door and a moment later saw Patty Levine giggling at something Tony Mazzetti said. Patty giggling was not a sound Stallings was used to, and the fact that she found something that ass said funny was downright unnerving.

Both the detectives stopped midstride, like a cheating couple caught in public, when they noticed Stallings.

Mazzetti put on a politician's smile. "Stall, turn up anything?"

He just shook his head.

Patty looked from Mazzetti to Stallings and said, "I have to get my stuff together for tomorrow."

"Whaddya got tomorrow?" asked Stallings.

"Talking to a geologist at UF about the decorative sand found on the bodies."

Mazzetti said, "You look beat, Stall. You should go home and get some rest. We'll keep plugging away here."

Suddenly, as if by Mazzetti's suggestion, he did feel the weight of exhaustion wash over him. He'd been on a wide swing of emotions since yesterday morning, and maybe a little time with Charlie would put things in perspective. He just nodded and closed up his notepad, then walked right out of the Land That Time Forgot without a good-bye to anyone.

Fifteen minutes later he was still sitting in his car trying to get himself in the right frame of mind to go home. It wasn't like he didn't want to see them; he didn't want them to see him wound up in his job. Disconnected. That's how his father was even when he was sober. Drunk, he was too connected. Regardless,

Stallings had made a commitment not to show up at the house when his mind was still on work. Too many cops did that and ended up with fucked-up families and kids who spent more time in rehab than they did in school.

So he sat, with the engine idling, trying to figure out what had upset him so much. Initially he had thought it was his meeting with Peep Morans and the memories the parasite brought up for Stallings. The day he'd found Maria, passed out on the bathroom floor, and her admission on the way to the hospital of her serious habit. She mentioned a man named Peep from Union Street, and that night Stallings did a little off-the-books law enforcement. It wouldn't be the first time he failed to report crimes related to his wife. She needed protecting, and he was prepared to do it. That night, when he had the pusher from downtown cornered, he came as close as he ever had to killing someone out of anger. And it was because he had let his emotions and frustration carry him away. He hoped he knew a little more about himself now.

As he sat in the car he saw his friend Rick Ellis lumbering across the lot in his uniform. His gut was swaying as he walked, but he was still capable of inspiring respect just by his sheer size.

Stalling lowered the window and waved to the big sergeant, who turned his bulk like a giant cruise ship, easing toward Stallings's car.

"Hey, Stall, you guys holding up all right?"

"It's tiring. Big cases, big problems."

"That's why I like road patrol. No cases, no problems. And mine don't lead the news. The goddamn TV reporters are all over this one. Times like this I bet you wish you were just a flunky firefighter."

Stallings smiled and nodded. "The thought has crossed my mind now and then."

Ellis said, "What are you guys working on specifically?"

"Mazzetti was out at the community college today. We identified the first victim and she was a student there."

"No shit. Did he turn up anything?"

"Few friends, no real leads."

"What're you working on?"

"I'm checking in the homeless and runaway communities to see if anyone has noticed anything."

"Seems like that's a smart assignment. Those folks wouldn't talk to most cops."

"They're not saying much to me either."

"Something will break soon enough. I'm glad the bosses were smart enough to bring you in on something like this."

This is the kind of conversation Stallings needed right now. Just chatting with an old friend who had positive things to say.

After a few more minutes of conversation about the details of the Bag Man case they said their good-byes.

Feeling pretty good now, Stallings started to put the car in gear when he saw something that threw his whole mood off track; Mazzetti and Patty walked out the side door together and the body language said they weren't going out on a lead.

This was troubling.

It was dark out when William Dremmel parked his tan minivan about three blocks from the restaurant where young Stacey Hines worked. He could just see the restaurant's back door and had pulled a distributor wire on Stacey's beat-up Escort. In his simple but ingenious plan, he'd offer her a ride, explaining that he had a mechanic friend who would look at it tomorrow for free. That would work with a waitress who had just lost a roommate and was probably facing money troubles.

His idea to appear more appealing by showing off Lori still probably worked with Stacey, but it had unintended consequences. While driving her back to work, Lori laid a barrage of questions on him about his interest in Stacey. Lori was smart and immediately picked up on the fact that Dremmel was interested in the cute waitress. Of course she had no idea what kind of interest he had, but she saw the sparks.

What had confounded him was that he'd completely missed the fact that Lori might hold those kinds of feelings. If she was jealous, then she must view him as more than a friend. Now he'd have to watch how he acted around her at work.

His research was the most important thing. He'd come too far to let a personal relationship throw him off track. He focused all of his energy on Stacey now. Any time now she'd walk through the back door, find her car wouldn't crank, and he would start his van and ease into the situation that would move his research ahead and satisfy his obsession with the young woman. He knew all there was to know about her from his research. No medical treatment since she'd been in Florida. That may have been because she was still on her parent's insurance and she didn't want them to be able to track her down.

This was the right time. He couldn't risk the roommate telling her parents where she lived when she got back to Ohio. He could picture Stacey's father racing down and forcing his twenty-one-year-old daughter to return to the Midwest.

He froze when the back door did open a few inches. He started the van and turned the wheel so he could glide out onto the street, checking the mirrors to make sure the road was clear. The door opened enough for him to see Stacey's profile as she turned back and spoke to someone inside the kitchen.

His heart raced as a surge of excitement coursed through his body. An erection blossomed and his hands trembled with anticipation. He loved this feeling almost as much as the actual lab work where he could hold the girls and watch their bodies show the effects of the different drugs. Drugs that *he* had administered. No one else held that kind of power. No one else went as far in research. He wanted to pound the wheel to let off the building pressure.

Stacey stepped out of the door onto the low landing in front of her car.

William Dremmel pulled from the curb and started down the street toward his prize.

Patty Levine gazed up at Tony Mazzetti's dark, beautiful eyes. This was not the guy other people saw. Leaning against the wall next to her condo's front door, he had a boyish smile as they played the timeless game of who's going to say good-bye first. Normally the game, or any cute little ritual like it, would've made Patty sick to her stomach, but she so rarely had the chance to participate herself, she allowed the indulgence.

They had grabbed a quick dinner and did talk about the case. No cop could work on a case like this without letting it invade every part of his or her life. But unlike TV cops, real ones had lives off camera and couldn't work twenty-four hours a day. Especially Patty, who even now could feel the pain in her knee and back shoot up through her from standing in hard shoes all day. A couple of Percocets would knock it out.

She had declined alcohol at dinner as Mazzetti drank two glasses of moderately expensive pinot noir. She knew it gave him the impression that she was a health fanatic, but in reality she worried about how alcohol would interact with all the prescriptions she took, so she hadn't had a drink in more than six years. It added to her perception as an ex-jock around the Sheriff's Office.

Tony Mazzetti was no athletic slouch himself. He'd spent a lot of time in the gym, and it showed with his wide shoulders and the biceps she couldn't fit both hands around.

They danced around the good-bye to their impromptu date. She'd promised herself never to let the stress of a case push her too close to a coworker. With married John Stallings it was never really an issue. Besides, the senior detective treated her like a kid sister more than anything else, and she liked it that way. Now she'd been caught in the trap she'd seen too many female cops fall into. Was she interested in Mazzetti because he was an intelligent, funny, perceptive man or because there were no other options? Or was it the Bag Man case? Hell, she wished there was a pill she could take to figure this shit out. Instead she reached her hands around Mazzetti's muscular neck and laid a kiss on him like she hadn't had a real kiss in over a year. Which she hadn't.

The next move was all his.

Nineteen

William Dremmel eased the van down the street, rehearsing out loud the casual way he intended to approach Stacey. "Hey, what're you still doing here?" then, "Am I too late to eat?" He figured she'd laugh and tell him how her car wouldn't start. He'd be ready with, "I got a buddy who'll fix it for free. Can I give you a lift home?" It couldn't miss.

After he had her in the car he'd make an excuse to go home. He had his lab all set up with the bed in place, furniture in the closet, and the chains ready to go. He didn't want another disaster like Trina. But he did have a knife in his pocket and would from now on. It was just luck he had one available to use the way he did with Trina. His first priority was to avoid detection. If he was caught, his research ended. He didn't like losing a test subject, but it was better than the whole project going down the drain. Not to mention what might happen to him. He thought the authorities might frown on the way he'd been conducting research.

Now he looked out his spotless windshield and saw

Stacey still in profile at the door. He slowed down to a crawl to give her time to get out and to the car.

She stepped away from the door, then down the two steps to the ground, but the rear door was still open.

As Dremmel approached, he saw her hop into the small car and crank it as a large, round black man in an apron stood on the back stoop shaking his head. When the van was almost even with the rear parking lot, still moving slowly, the cook stepped to the car and bent to open the hood.

Dremmel didn't hesitate. He kept a steady speed right past them and hoped no one noticed. He'd have to figure another way to make his approach to Stacey Hines, and he knew he had to do it soon.

John Stallings sprawled on his comfortable microfiber couch with Lauren equally relaxed next to him, her head nestled on his arm. He took a sip of the cranberry juice he had been drinking all night. He had an occasional beer if he was away from the house without anyone from the family, but around the house it was strictly no alcohol. He and Lauren had been watching an ESPN replay of Jaguar highlights of the 2007 playoffs. He could watch David Gerrard scramble for a touchdown a hundred times and he wouldn't get tired of it. Lauren proclaimed a mild interest, but he knew that sometimes she just needed to spend time alone with her father. And he was glad of it. He needed time with the kids too. He wished time as a family was easier to come by and more rewarding for all of them, but that didn't happen much right now. Baby steps. That's what he kept telling himself.

He switched channels and caught a news update at the end of the hour on a local channel. The anchor said,

"JSO detectives invade the community college looking for leads in the death of Tawny Wallace." Video of the crime scene for the latest victim came on screen. "Veteran homicide detective John Stallings, known for his heroic capture of serial killer Carl Cernick, is heading the investigation of the so-called Bag Man, who is believed responsible for at least three deaths."

He snatched up the remote and switched off the TV.

Lauren leaned up, then turned to look at him in the face. "I didn't know you were in charge."

"I'm not. They say whatever sounds good to them. I'm more interested in how they got the information. Probably someone out at the community college called the TV station, but it's still gonna piss off the lieutenant."

"Why?"

"They wanted to keep the whole thing as low key as possible. Now that it's got media traction it'll cause us more grief."

"Is the killer really looking for runaways?"

He knew what she was thinking. It had darkened his own mind since he first saw the face of Lee Ann Moffit in the duffel bag. "We're not sure yet, but I promise we're doing everything we can to stop him." The same promise he'd made to Lee Ann and even to Jeanie as soon as he knew they had a killer like this on the loose.

She hugged him and said, "I worry about Jeanie."

"Me too, sweetheart, me too."

"I worry about you too. You have to be careful."

He was touched. Neither of the kids had ever expressed that kind of concern. Common among most cops' families was the idea that police work was just another job. The dangerous nature and risk were almost never acknowledged, let alone discussed openly. He could see the concern on her pretty face.

"I've got it easy, sweetheart. All I do is interview a

few people and hang out at my desk in the Land That Time Forgot."

She snickered. "You still call the office that?"

"They haven't done anything to make us stop. Even if they renovated the whole floor we'd still call it that because it's a good name that stuck."

Lauren's smile faded and she focused on her father. She turned her head and checked the room even though they were the only two awake in the house. "You still look for Jeanie, don't you?"

"I'll never give up." He thought about all the checks he made and cops he called on a regular basis. He really was looking for his oldest child while he tried to help others in the same boat. "I promise I do everything I can to keep the streets safe for her until she comes home."

She hugged him tightly and he felt the lump in his own throat cause a tear to run down his cheek.

Staccy Hines cried softly, sitting at the flimsy folding table she used in her "dining room," which was actually the corner of her living room with the kitchen occupying the opposite corner. She had a decent-sized bedroom, but now it held an empty bed.

She missed her roommate a lot more than she thought she would. By now Marcie was back in Ohio, but she hadn't called Stacey. The tiny apartment held only a turtle in an old aquarium with a few rocks, an inch of water, and a mound of mud for the turtle to rest on. She had found the turtle on the edge of a creek that ran off the St. Johns one Sunday afternoon when she and Marcie were exploring the area and stopped at a wooded park to hike. The heat had been refreshing back then. She still liked it and the fact that the beach was nice in the autumn as well as the summer.

Stacey hadn't called home yet this week, because she knew that if she talked to her folks they could probably convince her to come back. The way she felt right now, she might go on home anyway. She'd have to take a bus, because there was no way her car would ever make it and being stranded in Atlanta sounded ten times more scary than just lonely in Jacksonville.

She blew her nose into a paper towel, looked into the aquarium, and said, "Don't worry, Sidney. I'll set you free at the exact spot I found you if I go back." At the time Stacey found the turtle, she'd been worried for its safety, but in the three months she had kept him and fed him raw hamburger and turtle food from Walmart he had seemed to double in size. She didn't know what kind of turtle he was, but right now she felt like he was the only one who hadn't deserted her.

She did have a couple of friends at work. Don, the cook, had fixed her car this evening when it wouldn't start. He seemed concerned that the wires would be messed up for no reason, but she told him it was fine and drove back home. He was nice to her at work but not someone she could hang out with.

Tank, the bartender, was fair to her, but he was also the manager and didn't have any favorites. She doubted he even knew where she lived or if she lived alone. Then there was the nice guy who'd been in to eat a couple of times the last few days. Today he had a pretty, younger black girl with him but said she was just a coworker. That wasn't the vibe Stacey got from the woman, but he was clear about it. She liked him and wondered if he might ask her out.

She thought about William and how he was a little older than her but had a job, seemed nice, and took coworkers out to lunch. She hoped he'd come by the restaurant again soon.

* * *

John Stallings sat upright in front of the computer in the den at his house. The light of the Web site was all he used to navigate the keyboard. He'd been on three sites he visited regularly in an effort to calm his racing mind that he had covered everything that could be related to Jeanie for this month. It'd been his talk with Lauren that got him thinking, and once he got something in his head he knew he'd never sleep or eat or do anything useful until he had accomplished his goal. In this case, making sure there were no new unidentified bodies or unidentified medical patients that could, somehow, be his Jeanie.

He knew Tony Mazzetti had hit a dead end at the Wendy's where the last victim had worked. There was still more follow-up to do, but no one at the restaurant knew who she hung out with, and no one even realized she was such a heavy drug user. At least no one admitted knowing it.

Stallings couldn't just sit still, even this late at night. He usually went through official channels at work, but he had the addresses to several databases and knew how to find information even from his home computer.

The National Center for Missing and Exploited Children had the best resource dedicated exclusively to finding missing kids. Most children who were taken by an adult were taken by a noncustodial parent; the public tended to regard this as a lesser crime, but the parent who earned custody legally often didn't get a chance to see the child for years. Stallings felt for them.

The Web site had galleries of photos of teenagers who had either run away or been lured away and, sadly, either way they were gone. The parents were left without answers, frustrated with law enforcement, and felt a void that nothing else could fill in their lives. He'd experienced it all. Even with the support of the Sheriff's Office he felt like there had to be more they could've done.

Then there was the accusation that Stallings had hidden Jeanie's disappearance. That he had concealed vital information. He had, and he knew it. His actions didn't affect the search for her and protected what little he had left at the time.

His mind buzzed with the decisions he'd made on that lonely Friday night three years ago. Images of Charlie, too young to understand what was really going on, and Lauren, scared and looking for someone to cling to, and Maria. By that time Maria had already started to check out. And Jeanie's disappearance was a blow that knocked her into an abyss.

Stallings continued to click through galleries of missing kids, recognizing many from fliers or leads he had run over the years. He felt connected to all of them. Then he came to a screen and found his eyes frozen on a photo of a girl from Cleveland who'd been gone less than a year. Her dark hair was long and she wore cute rimless glasses. It was a yearbook shot, he could tell, provided by some family member while their world was crumbling.

The bright smile on her face gave no indication of fear or loneliness or any of the other things that might push a kid to listen to a stranger about the wonders of a far-off city. It was hard to tell in the photo, but she looked small. The description listed her height as 61 inches. Five foot one. Then it all clicked.

This was the victim they had just found in the park.

Twenty

Stallings didn't know why they were meeting in the lieutenant's office. He felt that the information he'd gotten from the National Center for Missing and Exploited Children needed to get out to the whole task force. Instead, he, Mazzetti, Lieutenant Hester, and the temporary homicide sergeant were sitting around Rita Hester's elegant dark oak conference table.

The printout of the newest victim from the National Center lay in the middle of the table. Her name was Trina Ester. She'd run away from home in Ohio ten months earlier and had made no contact with her family. She'd been a good student, involved in school, then, around the midway point of her junior year, she showed signs of drug use: lethargy, disconnection with her family, mood swings, slipping grades. Her mother's efforts to help her were met with defiance, and she made a choice to run for greener pastures. Stallings sadly knew that there was no such thing.

Mazzetti shook his head, "Can you believe this guy's fucking luck?"

The lieutenant scowled at him, then turned back to Stallings. "You did a great job identifying her, Stall. The analysts were going to start scouring the country today. We had them pretty bogged down with local leads from the community college yesterday. The media doesn't have the first clue about our resources and passes on that ignorance to the general public. They think we can snap our fingers for DNA or have enough people to cover every lead in a few minutes." She shook her head. "I wish we were allowed to punch those assholes at Channel Eleven."

Stallings just nodded, but sensed something else was going on in the room. They weren't just here because of his ID of the victim.

The lieutenant sighed and said, "Stall, you got any idea how the media knew we were at the community college?"

He shook his head and said, "My guess is someone out there called it in."

"That would be my guess too except that you were mentioned as the lead on this case. You by name." Her voice took a slight rise in volume at the end.

"What are you implying?"

"I'm not implying anything. I'm asking. Detective Stallings, did you have any contact with the media in reference to this case?"

"No." He knew not to elaborate. Just as he knew Rita Hester's code for him to keep his mouth shut was to start a sentence with his title. On the street she used to say, "Officer Stallings, did we take a two-hour lunch?" in front of a sergeant and he knew not to fess up. There were times to admit things and times to keep your mouth shut. Right now he had nothing to admit to but knew this inquiry was serious.

Mazzetti slapped the table. "Bullshit. This has your name written all over it."

Stallings ignored the excited detective and turned toward the lieutenant. "Is that all you needed me for?"

"You got any new leads?"

"I'm looking for a prescription drug dealer named Ernie."

"You'll keep Detective Mazzetti fully informed?"

"I have so far, haven't I, Tony?" He contained a smile.

"I guess."

The lieutenant said, "Can we support you in any way?" She gave him a slight smile to tell him she was enjoying torturing Tony Mazzetti a little.

"Yes, ma'am. Can I take Patty with me?"

Mazzetti sprang to his feet. "No, you fucking can't." His voice had more of an edge than usual.

The lieutenant said, "What Mazzetti means is that she's on another assignment. She's on her way to Gainesville to discuss some forensic aspects of the case."

Stallings nodded, not asking for another partner. If he couldn't have Patty he preferred to be left alone.

Patty Levine had driven her county-issued Ford Freestyle down 301 from I-10 to Gainesville earlier in the morning, saving a few extra minutes to have coffee with her gymnastics coach from her days on the team ten years ago. Unlike academic advisers in other areas, gymnastics coaches were never too disappointed you didn't find a job in the field. Any occupation where you always peak before your twentieth birthday is a dead end anyway. Coaches are usually happy to see their former athletes healthy and happy and in this case she would've liked Patty to be married and having children by now, but she hid the disappointment about as well as Patty's mother. It showed, but didn't hurt their relationship.

Patty was a success in a field where it could be hard for a woman to excel. That success gave her a satisfaction most people missed in life. She knew what her mom and others expected, but she'd start a family when she was ready. Right now she liked how she could focus on an investigation and make a name for herself at the S.O. When the time was right she'd focus on her personal life, and she knew she'd be just as good of a mother as she was a cop.

For a change Patty didn't openly flinch at the line of questions about her love life. She'd been on a date last night for the first time in months. She ate real food at a real restaurant. She'd even kissed a man she found attractive. There was some regret at ending the evening right there and sending the puppy dog–faced Tony Mazzetti home after a five-minute-long good-night kiss. He obviously wanted to stay but had been a gentleman and took a gracious exit. Patty noted that he hadn't called her yet today. His tough luck.

The chat with her former coach had brought up enough unpleasant memories of competitions that she took a Xanax with her second cup of coffee. The way things were going at work and at night, she didn't even think about weaning herself from the pills just now. She realized it took more and more Ambien to knock her out at night, and that concerned her, but she felt as if she had a handle on everything else.

After wandering around the campus she had known so well, she found Williamson Hall across Stadium

Road from Florida Field, known as the "Swamp" to every college football fan in the country. She'd spent many Saturday nights in the Swamp, her mood tied to the football team, like every other student caught up in the fall exercise in futility. No matter how much she cheered, win or lose, she discovered the Gators football record had very little impact on her life.

After asking several receptionists and students, Patty found the office of Jonas Fuller, one of the foremost experts on particles and commercial geological issues. Or as the detectives back at the office called him, "The sand guy." Now she sat across from him with the two vials containing a few specks of sand each that had been sent down here as soon as they were collected from the last victim Monday.

The fifty-five-year-old professor had the tough, weather-beaten look of a man who had spent his life in the hot tropical sun of some country rich in geologic history. She could almost picture him in an Indiana Jones hat with a bullwhip wrapped in a tight ring on his belt.

The lean older man smirked and said, "I don't think I've ever seen a cop that looks like you."

"I guess you've never been to Jacksonville and crossed my patrol zone."

He let out a laugh and stood up, showing his loose shirt and muscular forearms. "I usually do this kind of consulting for free. I like to work out fees in different ways." He eased to the end of the table. "I can say without a doubt that these two separate sources of the particles are from the same area. It's an ornamental sand produced in Racine, Wisconsin. I put all the manufacturing information in my report." He stepped around the corner of the table and crept up next to Patty, who remained silent and still in her chair.

She could smell his cologne and feel the heat of his body as he leaned his face down parallel to hers. "Now it's your job to find a way to get the report from me without costing your department a dime. Any ideas?"

Patty thought about this creep around freshmen coeds and what John Stallings would do to him. It made her shudder a little. She wasn't Stall and didn't always agree with his methods. She liked to teach people lessons another way.

She turned and said, "I'm not sure I catch your meaning, Grandpa. Do you mean like you want me to rub your bunions or help you trim the hair in your ears?" She could feel the heat from his face as it flushed red.

The professor stood, tried to compose himself, walked stiffly back to his side of the table opposite her, and said, "No, that's quite all right. Sorry for any misunderstanding." He slid across a three-page stapled report and added, "My bet would be the sand came from a big distributor like Home Depot or Lowe's."

Patty stood and smiled. "Thanks so much, Professor Fuller."

"No, it was my pleasure, really." He started to run his fingers through his long gray hair, then stopped short, realizing how Patty viewed him.

She said, "I'll make sure you're recognized for your work."

"Anything to assist the police."

Patty couldn't help it and started to laugh out loud as she walked through the door to the front of the building. She had another lead.

* * *

William Dremmel tried not to act any differently toward Lori while he sorted bottles of newly arrived pills, but she was clearly uncomfortable around him right now. He had made it through most of the morning when she finally appeared in the back like a ghost. No noise or warning.

"Have you asked your waitress friend out yet?"

He played dumb. "Who?"

"That cute little curvy thing at the sports bar."

"Oh, her. I like the food at the bar, but that's it. Why? Did you think I wanted to go out with her?"

"Don't treat me like an idiot, Billy. I can sense that kind of stuff. I always could. I know when people are made for each other. I know when married couples are gonna divorce. And I know you got a thing for Stacey the waitress."

"You even remembered her name. Good for you. But I have no intention of asking her out." He looked up at her and missed her usual smile. "Can you tell when *you've* met the right person?"

"No, it doesn't work on me. I've made more bad choices than President Bush. But I thought . . ."

"What'd you think?"

She turned. "I got someone at my register. I gotta go."

He felt relief at her sudden exit because his life was complicated enough without juggling a relationship with a conscious woman.

Twenty-one

Stallings threw a plain, blue Windbreaker on to cover his gun and badge on his hip. He could've concealed them better, but he wasn't undercover, just not advertising that he was a cop. This was where "Ernie" the prescription pusher was supposed to hang out as well as a good-sized group of street kids. In the light jacket's pocket he had photographs of the dead girls. This was his specialty: missing girls. He'd turn up something.

He parked his unmarked county Impala in the vast, crowded lot of the Gateway Shopping Center and started walking over to Carlton Street. Although most of the homeless people didn't hang out on the actual street, Stallings knew there were a number of camps in the bushes and brush just off the road as well as a couple of houses in the area that attracted street people for different reasons. He knew because he had entered several of them over the past two years looking for runaways.

A group of eight young people were gathered near

the road in front of a house known for its drug traffic and high occupancy. He heard the young man closest to him say, "Look out, it's a cop."

There was some movement, then a female voice said, "Don't worry, it's Detective Stall. He's looking for someone and it's none of us."

Stallings eased up to the crowd and smiled. "Hey, Sallie."

"Hey, Stall. Who you looking for?"

"All I got is a couple of photos." Some of the others had backed away from him. A tall, wiry youth had eased back to the house. Stallings took a moment to memorize his face and clothing. Anyone moving away from him like that needed a second look. It might even be Ernie, but he didn't want a dustup out here, so he let the youth leave. He pulled out the photographs of Trina Ester and Lee Ann Moffitt and gave them to Sallie to pass around the crowd. A request to look at the pictures coming from her was more productive than if he had sent them around. All he needed was someone who knew them and saw them get in a car.

After a few minutes and a decent examination by everyone, Sallie looked back up at him. The leathery skin around her eyes and neck showed how the sun had aged her the last couple of years. He had once thought she was a runaway; now the street dweller looked more like the mother of a runaway.

Sallie said, "Nope, none of us has seen either of them. These girls look a little older than your usual runaways."

"I'm helping out on another case. Someone killed these two. I don't want him to get the chance to hurt anyone else."

Someone muttered, "Bullshit."

Sallie got right in the pudgy young man's pimply

face. "Back off, Kyle. Stall says he's trying to help, he's trying to help."

"Thanks, Sallie." He looked toward the small, flat-roofed house. "Who's inside?"

"Just a few of the boys. They don't get out much."

"I better say 'hey' anyway." He had started toward the house when Sallie called to him.

"Darryl Paluk is in there."

He waved and nodded, appreciating the heads-up, but kept his steady pace to the front door. At the door he paused and mumbled, "Is this the day that changes my life?" Stallings knocked, then turned the handle and immediately opened the door and stepped in. The smell of pot smoke almost knocked him off his feet. The haze was so thick that sunlight coming in behind him barely made it to the nasty Oriental-style rug in the front room.

Darryl Paluk sprang up from a La-Z-Boy with surprising speed for such a muscular man. Then, as soon as he was standing, he relaxed.

"It's just Stall. You said a cop was out front."

Stallings looked over at the person Darryl was talking to. It was the same guy who'd slipped away. Stallings handed the photographs to Darryl, but kept his eyes on the young man. "You seen either of these girls?"

Darryl took the photos and studied them before handing them to a near-comatose Latin man sitting on the couch next to him.

Stallings pointed to the man he was interested in. "What's your name, son?"

"Me?"

"Yeah, you." He stepped closer.

"Ernie."

"Ernie what?"

Ernie stood up from the couch. "Why?"

Stallings looked at him. He wasn't used to queries like "why," and he didn't want to give up that Peep Morans had identified him.

Darryl shot Ernie a glare and said, "Chill out, man. He'd have already popped you if he was gonna."

Stallings nodded to the big, dark-skinned man. "How's the nose, anyway, Darryl?"

"Feels okay, but now I snore. You think if you hit me just the right way you'd set it back the way it was?"

"Hate to risk making it worse."

"I guess." The big man rubbed his nose. "Taught me to hide a runaway. Never do it again, I swear."

Stallings turned back to Ernie, but before he could say anything, the trim, young man bolted to the back of the small house.

By the time Stallings rushed to see where he was headed, all that pointed to the man's exit was the open rear door swaying in the breeze and more sunshine cutting through the smoke.

Tony Mazzetti fumed as he sorted through a stack of leads that had come into the office since the news had started covering the killings. His anger stemmed from that news coverage. Not that there was coverage, but that they said John Stallings was the lead on the case. Then to have that asshole deny it and the L.T. let him slide. No one ever called that guy on his bullshit. From kicking someone's ass on the road to the disappearance of his daughter, there were questions that hung over him like storm clouds, but no one ever came down on him. It couldn't be just that everyone liked him. Mazzetti knew he wasn't too well liked, but that's because he put the job first. Someone had to. But what kind of magic did Stallings have that kept him safe?

He took a moment to catch his breath. One of the problems was that he hadn't gone to the gym this morning. He had steam he hadn't blown off. Since he'd stopped using muscle-building supplements, he had hit the gym twice as hard. He didn't want anyone to notice him shrinking. He didn't want to end up looking like his uncle Vinnie, all hunched over and frail.

His mind was usually on work. This was a change. Everyone had problems. For the first time in a couple of years Mazzetti worried about one of his personal problems and he knew the role his sexual history had played in his predicament. His anger was only partly due to Stallings's grab for glory.

He snatched his cell phone from the holder on his shiny leather belt and flipped through until he saw Patty Levine's number. He felt a lift just looking at her name. Last night was the first night in a long time that he didn't want to be so exhausted all he could do was fall asleep. Holding Patty in his arms, feeling her hard, small body against his, even if it was only outside her door, made him forget about work for a few minutes and gave him a glimpse of what other guys search for so desperately.

But now he didn't want to look weak and annoying, so he set the phone back on the table. A few minutes later when it rang, he pounced, hoping that Patty had made the call to him. He could picture her on her way to UF to talk to the geologist. It may not be the lead that broke the case but neither would the stack of leads he held in his hands right now. Like any huge case with public interest they'd have to cover everything.

With so many real police stories on every channel from truTV to Bravo, juries expected all sorts of investigative tasks completed. It was no longer enough to follow the good leads. You had to follow up on the weak ones as well. Not only did a cop have to prove a suspect was guilty, but he had to prove no one else is guilty too. It had become a game of being able to say that no one suspect was looked at too hard until there was evidence. This was a catch-22, because it was hard to develop evidence without looking at a suspect really hard.

He slapped his hand onto the pile of lead sheets and sighed. No one was around the Land That Time Forgot right now because he had them out on all kinds of tips. No matter how fast things were rolling or how much praise he was getting from the bosses, he couldn't shake his jealousy, and he knew that's what it was, of John Stallings.

If only he could catch the guy passing on info to the media. Then he'd get the credit he deserved.

Stallings didn't chase people on foot anymore. He preferred to use his car and head them off like he had Peep Morans. It was unseemly for a detective of his age and experience to run. But it was more than that. It used to be suspects stopped when confronted by a police officer. Now people acted edgier. He didn't know if the street cops were tougher on people or the courts easier. Either way he hadn't had two people run from him in the same week in years.

He'd caught a glimpse of Ernie as he cut through the scraggly bushes in the rear of the house. It'd be a matter of time before Ernie returned to the house, but Stallings didn't have that kind of time.

He walked back to the shopping center and picked up his car, then headed east to the last remaining topless bar on the road. Pulling into the Venus Fly Trap, he parked directly in front of the door, then popped out as the top-heavy doorman rumbled off his stool to challenge him.

"This ain't no valet, Holmes." The giant black man stopped short and said, "Hey Detective, what're you doing here?"

"Relax, Terry," said Stallings, walking toward the door. "I'm not here for an underaged dancer. I'm looking for a guy that just ran from me."

The big man backed away and opened the door for him.

Stallings patted him on the arm and said, "Did a tall, thin fella come in here in the last ten minutes?"

"Yes sir. He's in there now."

"Thanks, Terry. Just wait here. I won't be too long."

The doorman nodded and quickly slipped back onto his stool by the front door.

Inside, Stallings paused a minute by the front door so his eyes could adjust to the dark room with lights above the two small stages. The bartender looked up and smiled. "Hey, Stall."

He nodded to the older, topless woman all the girls called "Auntie Lynn."

On stage an agile young lady held herself upside down on the pole. She saw him, smiled, and waved from her awkward angle. He could see three heads in the audience. Two were small Latin men, but the third looked around nervously. As soon as he saw Stallings, Ernie sprang up and headed for the rear of the building.

Stallings darted toward the exit to cut him off, but before he could reach the man, a large round tray flew from behind the bar and struck the fleeing man in the head, knocking him onto the hard cement floor.

Stallings stopped, looked over at the bar, and said, "Thanks, Auntie Lynn."

"If you were chasing him, he must be an asshole."

Twenty-two

Handcuffs bit into Ernie's wrists in the front seat of the county-issued Impala. Stallings wanted to be sure they were in a secluded, quiet place. This time of day Brentwood Park was perfect for an impromptu interview. He turned to face the younger man.

"Ernie, why'd you run?"

The man's eyes flicked back and forth as sweat beaded on his forehead. His greasy brown hair dipped between his eyes.

Stallings said, "I just want to talk. I don't care if you're holding. I need help on a case, and I want to know why you ran."

After a few seconds he said, "I'm holding."

"What are you holding?"

"Pills."

"What kind?"

The young man shrugged and said, "Every kind."

"Where?"

"My shoe, my pockets, a pouch under my shirt." He leaned back and wiggled his left foot. "Only this shoe."

Stallings bent down, slipped off the young man's smelly Top-Sider, and retrieved a plastic bag with sixty dark blue pills. He cut his eyes up to Ernie.

"Ambien."

Stallings reached carefully into the young man's front pockets and pulled out two more bags.

Ernie said, "Oxy and assorted painkillers like Perco-cets and Vicodin."

Stallings shook his head, then patted Ernie's midsec-tion until he felt the bag of pills. He reached under the shirt and pulled out the bag with odd-looking and un-evenly colored pills. "Okay Ernie, what the fuck are these?"

"Those are all combinations. I know a fella who can melt shit and recast it. Most of it is Oxy with Ambien mixed in. The kids think they're getting Oxy, but Am-bien is a lot cheaper, and once they fall asleep they don't care. When they wake up they only remember the short high they had first." He shrugged again. "Just good capitalistic business."

Without saying a word Stallings opened the car door, took the pills, and dumped them all down a storm drain on the curb. When he came back to the car, he said, "There, you satisfied I'm not trying to make a cheap drug case?"

The young man visibly relaxed.

"Do a lot of dealers mix the two drugs like you?"

"Every single pharmaceutical dealer in the city does it."

Then it made more sense to Stallings. Trina had been doing the same thing. The Bag Man had tried to drug her but she had built up a half-assed resistance from using this shitty, homemade Oxy-Ambien. The knife wounds were an emergency measure.

Then Ernie said, "I know the girl in the photograph."

"You saw the photo when Sallie passed it around?"

He nodded.

"Know the girl's name?"

"Lee Ann."

"Lee Ann Moffitt?"

"I try not to use last names."

"How'd you know her?"

He hesitated, then finally said, "She hung out with us sometimes. Nice girl. I think she worked at a copy place."

"You know if she had any boyfriends?"

The young man shook his head.

"She buy from anyone else?"

"Everyone does, that's why it's such a tough business."

"It's no picnic being a consumer either." He hoped Ernie understood his meaning.

The drug dealer snapped his fingers. "She did mention a guy she was close with who supplied her. I even saw him once. He picked her up from a little party."

"What'd he look like? What'd he drive? You remember a name?"

Ernie shook his head. "It's fuzzy in here." He tapped his temple. "I meet a lot of people and sometimes use my own stuff to keep mellow."

Stallings quizzed him a while longer until he realized he wouldn't get anywhere. The young man was cooperating as best he could. He gave the young drug dealer his cell phone number with the instructions to start looking for this mystery dealer and to call him if he found him.

Stallings felt that he might be getting closer as he started questioning the enterprising young drug dealer about anyone else who might be buying a lot of Oxy.

* * *

Tony Mazzetti had tagged along with Patty Levine to the Home Depot across I-95 near the PMB. He liked the way she thought and made decisions, both as a person and a cop. She'd tracked down the info on the report from the UF geologist, contacted the manufacturer, and discovered the sole distributor was the largest home-improvement chain in the country. That wouldn't narrow down things much, but it was a start. Now she just wanted to see how Home Depot maintained their inventory and if tracking the purchasers would be feasible.

Mazzetti liked how she had the huge manager of the store crammed in his minuscule office behind kitchen and bath remodeling going over possible lines of investigation while not scaring the guy into thinking she was a bully. This was the mark of a good cop. He realized he often came off as a bully even when he was trying to be pleasant.

Patty said, "You have to understand, Larry, that this is confidential and no one can know why we're looking at this line of sand."

He shook his massive bald head. His drawl was more central Georgia than Florida. It'd taken almost twenty years, but Mazzetti was finally getting his accents and drawls down here straight.

Larry, the manager, said, "Ma'am, I can't think of nothin' as important as catching this Bag Man. We'll help all we can and I won't say a word, I swear."

Patty flashed him that perfect smile and squeezed his arm to let him know he was part of the team. It was important to make people feel like they are working *with* the police instead of working *for* the police. Mazzetti didn't know if this guy cared about the investigation that much, but he wasn't about to let a little hottie like Patty be disappointed. The manager scrambled to find a sheet of paper so even the stupid cops could figure out how the process worked.

"Each store now," he started in a voice too high for his frame, "gets in a shipment of ten to fifty bags depending on how many the store sold in the previous month."

Mazzetti marveled at how much effort the man put into his impromptu lecture on the finer points of decorative sand distribution. He wished he had that kind of power over people, where they helped for reasons other than necessity. He just hoped avenues of investigation like this were kept quiet so the investigation could proceed unhindered.

He listened to more details about buying with credit cards or cash and how Patty could find out how many bags were sold and when. She really wanted to know who bought the sand.

"Only way to tell is if they used a credit card. Even then it'd take a good long while," said the manager. The he added, "Could be talking about a lot of people if we count all the stores in the area and go back a few months."

Mazzetti started trying to figure an answer for that. This was a piece of the puzzle that might yet fall into place.

John Stallings had never been comfortable in gatherings like this. Even though the concept of dinner meetings made sense, he didn't like missing meals with his family. But a squad dinner at the Law and Order Pub, less than a mile from the PMB, was a tradition most units kept, even if it was just the occasional meal to boost morale.

Tonight nine detectives and no management were spread along a long table in the rear of the pub that was generally frequented by cops. Right now the bar held only identified Sheriff's Office personnel so they could speak somewhat freely as each detective caught everyone else up to date on their aspect of the serial killer investigation.

Patty had explained how they might be able to track the purchasers of the sand found on two of the victims. She'd spent the afternoon at a Home Depot, and now, with her natural intelligence and inquisitiveness, she sounded like an expert on how products moved through the giant retailer.

Mazzetti looked down the table from his position at the end and said, "The question now is whether this is a good use of resources."

Stallings considered the reasonable question as all the other detectives looked to assess the pros and cons as well.

Luis Martinez, always one to move forward, shook his head. "Hell, no, we need to be banging our snitches' heads. Someone has seen something and is talking about it."

Mazzetti said, "That's a good point, Luis, and that's why we'll be offering a reward of fifty grand for info starting tonight."

Someone down the table whistled.

"This Home Depot lead is just another route." He was about to say something else when he noticed someone standing by the bathroom a few feet from the other end of the table. He recognized him. "Hey, Sarge, what's up?"

The big man in a blue plaid shirt gave a quick wave and said, "Didn't mean to interrupt. I was gonna say hey to Stall."

Stallings smiled at his friend Rick Ellis's reluctance

to approach the table. He spoke up and said, "Just a dinner meeting, Rick."

"I know y'all are busy so I'll move along. You guys gotta catch this asshole before the whole city gets spooked."

Mazzetti said, "I'm working on it."

Stallings wanted to correct him and say "we" were working on it but that was just Mazzetti. As much as he hated to admit it, the guy had run a decent case and kept everyone on task.

Mazzetti told everyone about Trina Ester working at the Wendy's, making the whole lead sound like something he developed, not that Stallings had seen her there.

Luis Martinez asked, "Why didn't they report her as missing?"

Mazzetti said, "Wendy's isn't like the S.O. The manager just thought she quit and didn't tell him. Happens more than half the time."

Martinez said, "So she didn't leave with anyone Saturday?"

"Nope. I even talked to a couple of the counter people who worked the same shift. She ate there and checked out around nine. No fanfare, just, 'good-bye, I'll see you tomorrow.' "

They paused in their meeting as the waiter brought over a tray of assorted hamburgers, sandwiches, sodas, and chips. Unlike the old days before Stallings had become a cop, there wasn't much drinking on duty anymore. He knew that he was headed back out onto the streets for a few hours after dinner and he didn't need the guilt or effects of a couple of beers.

He was pleased to see everyone else agreed. As he thought about that and looked down the table at Patty, he realized he'd never seen her drink.

That was a dedicated cop.

* * *

William Dremmel sat in his silent Nissan Quest with the driver's window down and the cool Atlantic breeze pushing the majority of bugs right past him. He was only a block from Stacey Hines's little apartment, which was attached to a larger, single-family house. The space that normally held her Escort was empty, and he was waiting for her to show. His plan this time was a little more direct. Grab her and take off. He had a variation of chloroform, which he had made himself and tested first on Mr. Whiskers IV, then on his mother. Neither knew what had happened and awoke an hour later. The cat looked a little dazed, and his mom complained of a headache until the next day, but he knew the stuff worked.

The rear of the van was empty except for a moving blanket and some heavy nylon rope, both items he could explain to any cop who might stop him. The tiny bottle of chloroform looked like a commercial nasal spray, which made it easy to spritz onto the washcloth he had to go over Stacey's lovely, delicate face. He'd prefer to talk to her for a while and interact, but his patience was wearing thin. He couldn't even concentrate on simple tasks anymore because she had filled up so much of his head.

Another lesson he'd learned recently had taught him to have a knife handy. His wasn't a large suspicious knife, just a folding Gerber with a sharp, serrated edge. He even knew the target now if he ever had to do it again: center chest and neck. Somehow he didn't have the impression that Stacey would ever have the bad manners to act like Trina did before he was forced to deal with her. But he was prepared and flexible. That was the key to success in any endeavor.

He checked his watch and saw it was just after eight

with no sign of her. She wasn't at the Fountain of Youth either. A pang of jealousy, like any boyfriend might have, popped up in him as he wondered what she might be doing. Did she have another man? Then a much worse thought had hit him—what if she had been lonely and moved back to Ohio?

Now his main urge was to enter her apartment through the back where no one would see him and see what was left around. He had to know if she had moved. He didn't think she could do it so quickly, but maybe he didn't know her like he thought he did. He knew all about her. Her checking account back in Ohio, her power consumption, her rent, and even the grocery store she shopped at, but maybe, just maybe, he didn't know her that well.

As he considered hopping out of the van and easing into her apartment he noticed some movement in his rearview mirror. He'd been so preoccupied with what Stacey could be doing that he'd gone soft on being aware of his surroundings. That was another key to avoiding detection. No one should be able to tell the cops they saw his van or give a description.

Now he saw that an elderly man was standing almost directly behind his van with a pipsqueak dog on a leash. Dremmel froze and waited to see what the man's movements would be. From the streetlight all he could make out was the stoop of age, a light jacket like old men used to play shuffleboard, a cane, and the leash. From his side mirror he saw the dog sniffing near the light pole directly behind his van. The dog had a tiny shirt that covered its chest and two front legs and its movements seemed jittery like all miniature dogs'.

Dremmel swallowed and consciously held still while the man lingered behind the van. He knew the old man had spotted him and wondered why he was just sitting there. Hell, old people like that, with nothing to do but walk their dogs, might even write down his tag, then he'd have to forget about Stacey. Nothing could happen to her if there was a record of his presence in her neighborhood.

Give up on Stacey? Not after all he had been through. He reached into his front pocket and felt the weight of his new Gerber knife. He pulled it out and used his thumb to pop open the vicious blade as his eyes cut back up to the mirror and saw the old man in the same spot.

He knew what he had to do.

Twenty-three

Patty Levine felt like a weight had been lifted from her as the last of the unmarked cars pulled away from the Law and Order Pub, leaving just her and Tony Mazzetti in the parking lot. They both knew that any attraction they felt for each other had to be kept low key for now. An office romance meant scrutiny, gossip, and sometimes jealousy. She didn't have time for any of that.

She looked up at Mazzetti now that they were alone in the lot. Still a little old-fashioned, she was waiting for him to make a move. If that failed, then she knew what to do.

He looked across the hood of her car and said, "You busy?"

Did he have an investigative task or was it a come-on? She had no idea how to read him, and that made it all the more exciting. She felt anxiety but no need to reach for Xanax. She liked this feeling and just smiled.

Tony Mazzetti said, "I was wondering if you might like to have a private drink with me?"

"Off duty?"

"Off duty."

"No police talk?"

"Not unless you're into that kind of thing."

She nodded and then, without any idea it would come out of her, "How about my condo? I have a bottle of wine that's been collecting dust for three years."

"Will you actually drink with me?" His eyes twinkled in the streetlights. She liked his cute expression. It was the opposite of his persona around the Sheriff's Office.

Patty considered the possibility of a drink. She'd taken her last Xanax on her way home from UF after the geologist came on to her. She hadn't felt anxious, but with habit, took one of the peach-colored pills about the same time she did every day. That was more than eight hours ago. Her back or hip didn't hurt, which meant there was no need for a pain pill. That left only Ambien. She needed her sleeping pill if she wanted any hope of dozing off. Based on her careful analysis, she finally answered him, "Sure, I'll have a glass of wine."

A grin slid across Tony Mazzetti's handsome face, lighting up his brown eyes. She liked the brash New Yorker and realized most everything he did for show was just an act. He was a history buff who liked to write. That was more like the real him. She was sure of it. Regardless, she was ready for some quiet time with him based on two important facts: he was really well built, and she hadn't slept with a man in almost a year. She needed a shot of confidence as well as a chance to get to know this guy better.

Mazzetti said, "I'll follow you."

She thought, I hope so.

* * *

William Dremmel had to commit himself to acting quickly. He already had his knife open and in his hand. He popped the automatic locks of the minivan and took a deep breath. This was something he'd never done before. He was about to assault the old man and planned to jab the knife into his abdomen and his throat, then shove him into the van and dump him God knew where.

The man's little dog yipped behind the van and that made Dremmel freeze for a second. What would he do with the dog? If he left it, the cops would know the owner was gone faster than if he took it. That was one more clue that could potentially point to him. Either option was unacceptable.

He thought about it and decided he couldn't kill the dog. Not with the knife anyhow. But maybe there was a way he could use the little dog in his research. It was a different metabolism than what he'd been working with. Unlike the girls or even Mr. Whiskers, the original or II and III, the little dog would present new opportunities.

Dremmel processed the decision, yanked the door handle, and slipped out onto the asphalt road. He turned and hurried to the rear of the van, ready to strike without warning. He couldn't afford to allow the man to scream.

As he cleared the rear bumper, the knife in his hand, but held low, he saw the man's face clearly in the light of the dim bulb suspended on the rough wooden pole. He froze and the man turned to look in his direction.

"Hello," said the man.

"Um, hello," answered Dremmel, now frozen in place a few feet from the elderly dog walker.

"Am I blocking you?" The man touched his dark glasses. "I know my way around but sometimes get in front of cars waiting to pull out. I'm sorry."

"No, no, I'm fine." Dremmel now realized the cane was not a walking aid but an indicator that the man was blind.

"I'm afraid Pico here is not much of a guide dog. But he's a good friend."

Dremmel squatted down and let the little Chihuahua scurry to him and sniff his hand. He patted the white dog, then reached under him to get a feel for his weight. "This is one tiny dog, mister."

"My daughter gave me little Pico Sanchez about three years ago, and I couldn't live without him now."

Dremmel made the snap decision that the man had no info he could give the cops and, reluctantly, that the dog was too small to provide any reliable or transferable research results.

He stood up and said, "Have a nice night."

"You too son, you too."

As Dremmel pulled away from the curb, leaving the old blind man with his useless little dog, he wondered where his Stacey could be and when he'd have her all to himself.

John Stallings had rushed home to make sure he could help both kids with their homework. The problem with that theory was that he'd have to understand their homework.

Charlie's wasn't that difficult, but as the TV show *Are You Smarter Than a Fifth Grader?* had taught everyone, there are things you learn that you forget. Most of Charlie's history quiz on the settling of Plymouth seemed familiar, but there was no way he'd know the

facts right off the top of his head. The name Miles
Standish and the Puritans were familiar, but reading the
little paragraphs taught him more than he thought he
ever knew about the settlement in what is now Massa-
chusetts. He never realized they left from Holland or
that the entire ship was not filled with people seeking
religious freedom. He never knew that the expedition
started off with two ships but one never left European
waters. Regardless, he made it sound like this was all
old news to him as he ran Charlie through the simple
fifteen-question quiz over and over.

Lauren's homework was another story. The algebra
didn't even seem familiar to him, and he couldn't
fake it.

Stallings looked at his thirteen-year-old and said, "Is
this the same math they taught when I was in school?"

"You mean back when you used slate tablets to add
up the figures?" Her smile did more to lift him than any
beer he had ever thought of.

"Yeah, we'd never even heard of calculators."

She looked at him and knitted her eyebrows but didn't
say anything.

He laughed out loud and said, "Yes we did, I'm not
that old."

The evening continued like that with Maria coming
out of the den for a good part of it. He'd noticed the
subtle shift in her appearances with the family. From near-
hermit status to a quick meal here and there, to spending more time at least in the same room with the family. Stallings would take it. He'd take whatever he could
get. This was the woman he'd been crazy in love with
almost twenty years ago and through all that they had
suffered his feelings for her hadn't changed. Sure he
got frustrated at her repeated stints in rehab and her
withdrawal from the family after Jeanie disappeared,

but she still had that magic quality to light up a room when she wanted to. He wanted to be around when she wanted to light up rooms again.

After the kids had gone to bed and he'd straightened the kitchen and house, he was surprised when Maria joined him on the couch for the ten o'clock news. She'd told him that she cleaned the kitchen every morning after making the kids breakfast, but he knew she rarely got up with the kids, never made them breakfast, and hadn't dragged a clean dish towel across any surface in the kitchen in a long time. But his mother had given him a little marital advice when he was young, and the smartest thing she'd said was, "As the husband you can be right or you can be happy, but you can't be both." Now he knew it was one of those times to keep his mouth shut. He was rewarded by Maria sitting next to him on the couch.

Of course the first story was about the serial killer. He cringed at the name Bag Man, but even the cops were using it now. Carl Cernick had gained the name "The Phantom" because there were so many false sightings of him. Six different men had been questioned because of the tips. The questioning was at the PMB, and the men were in custody no matter what they were told. Each time homicide was sure it was the right guy. Stallings was in the burglary unit at the time and paid little attention to the case. Until he solved it.

Now the newscaster opened with a line that made him take notice. The pretty young woman said, "Home Depot, the target of a new lead for the Bag Man investigation."

"How in the hell did that happen?" he muttered.

Maria turned to him. "What?"

"That was a confidential line of investigation. Tony Mazzetti is gonna be pissed." Stallings knew it was wrong, but he couldn't help but let a slight smile spread across his face.

Patty Levine lay on top of the sheets naked, computing how big of a dose of Ambien she would take. She took into account the two glasses of pinot noir she'd had a couple of hours earlier and the level of frustration that had risen in her since. She figured one canceled out the other.

She stared straight up into the dark, catching just a hint of streetlights through her blinds. Her chest rose and fell in a steady rhythm as she tried to control her anxiety and disappointment. She still had a muscular body and worked on it, but nothing like she did when she competed.

As she was about to get out of bed and pad to the bathroom she felt the whole mattress shift. She turned to face the muscular, naked form of Tony Mazzetti, who said for the ninth time, "I'm sorry. This has never happened before."

Twenty-four

John Stallings took three stairs at a time because he wanted to hear the drama inside the squad bay about the news leaks. Even though there were always leaks and it rarely affected a case, some detectives became irrational in their search for the tipster. It made for a fascinating few minutes after every newscast.

As he reached the second floor he saw Rick Ellis in uniform and ready for duty. Seeing the tall, middle-aged man made Stallings realize the truth behind the saying, "The uniform makes the man." Ellis looked like authority incarnate—the sergeant's stripes on his sleeve, the duty belt with a Glock model twenty-two on his hip. He looked like he knew his shit. The man was a cop's cop and everyone looked up to him, but the uniform made him seem almost superhuman.

Ellis smiled. "On your way to the Land That Time Forgot?"

"Yeah. I like an early start these days."

"I hear ya. When we were young all we wanted was afternoon shift so we could sleep late, now I can't sleep past six if I want to." He slapped Stallings on the back and headed down the stairs. "Gotta get on the road. Speeders are waiting." Then he stopped at the landing and turned to face the second floor again. "Hey Stall, call me if you guys need something on the Bag Man. You need to be careful out there. It's not like it used to be."

"Thanks, Rick, I'll keep you in mind for backup. I'd feel better with you around."

Ellis gave him a thumbs-up and then cantered down the remaining stairs.

Stallings hit the detective bureau door and was only a step in when he heard Mazzetti's voice boom, "Who the fuck keeps leaking our case?"

Stallings ignored him and settled right into his desk. He had leads to sort out and people to talk to. Leaks made no impact on him at all, except for entertainment purposes.

Patty eased over and plopped in a cracked plastic chair next to the desk. She said, "How's it goin'?"

"Not bad. You look tired. Something keep you up late?"

He noticed her eyes cut across the room to the ranting Mazzetti. That kind of behavior can freak out a newer detective.

Patty looked back to Stallings. "Nothing really kept me awake. I was just distracted and didn't sleep well. What do you make of the leaks?"

He shrugged. "Nothing new. Someone always has a hook at a TV station."

"But why?"

"Maybe a favorable story on them later, or meals, or even cash sometimes."

Patty sighed.

"What's wrong?"

"I need to go out on an action lead. Following up on suitcases and Home Depots has worn me out. Maybe I can ride with you today. See what we turn up?"

"Okay by me."

Before they could talk about it further, Lieutenant Hester walked up and said, "Patty, I need you for a while."

"Sure L.T. What's up?"

"Someone wants to talk to you about these news leaks."

"Why?" She thought about it and said, "Who wants to talk to me?"

"Internal Affairs."

As soon as William Dremmel entered the Fountain of Youth sports bar where Stacey Hines worked, he knew she wasn't there. A different waitress he hadn't seen before carried a tray of food to a young family in the area where Stacey usually worked. The waitress was a little older than Stacey, maybe twenty-five, and tall, with large, fake boobs positioned for the best possible tips.

He couldn't just turn around and leave. The bartender had seen him, and he didn't want to draw attention to himself. Sliding up to the far side of the bar, he took a stool and ordered a simple burger and Diet Coke. While he waited, he pretended to watch the TV above the bar. A sports show had footage of the University of Florida football team in its orange and blue that so many schools in the area copied. The carpet that led to his office was the same hue of orange. People in Jacksonville were crazy for the Gators.

The bartender brought back his soda and made no indication he remembered Dremmel from any of his previous visits.

After finishing his lunch and drinking three glasses of Diet Coke, Dremmel started to formulate the right question about Stacey without appearing too interested. Then he caught a break. The tall waitress leaned against the corner of the bar near him and asked the bartender, "What time does Stacey get in? I need to pick up Julie from day care by five."

The heavyset bartender didn't look up from polishing glasses and said, "She won't be here till six, but I'll cover for the hour. It's slow anyway."

"Thanks, Tank," said the waitress. "I could call her and see if she'll come in an hour early."

"Nah, it's no problem. She was going over to the beach, and I doubt she'd be ready in time."

The waitress nodded and turned to get over to a table.

Dremmel remembered his first conversation with the petite waitress from Ohio. She'd told him she liked Neptune Beach. It was the closest beach to her crappy little apartment.

A smile crept over his face. He knew where he was heading right now, and no one would be able to link him to her.

Stallings didn't think the news leaks were as humorous now that he'd spent an hour in I.A. answering questions about it. Everyone on the task force had been pulled up to the Internal Affairs office and grilled about their friends in the media and if they'd been talking about the case. The S.O. was serious about the security of the leads. The main thing that bothered Stallings was the amount of time taken away from the case to answer the questions. He wanted to be out stirring things up, and instead he'd been on the fourth floor talking to two young sergeants he hardly even know. He had nothing to hide. They knew his reputation—it was apparent in the deference they showed him.

One of the interrogators had been brand new in the homicide unit when Stallings had captured Cernick, and he mainly had questions about the arrest. Neither asked him any questions about Jeanie. At least they had some manners.

As he was getting ready to leave the I.A. office, he almost bumped into the senior investigator.

The tall, handsome detective with graying hair simply said, "Hey John."

Stallings didn't acknowledge him.

The detective said, "Why so rude?"

Stallings stopped, feeling the anger rise in him. "Listen, Ron."

"It's Ronald."

"Sorry, I forgot. Listen, Ronald, this is the second time you've held up an investigation that was important to me."

"I had nothing to do with this one. I told them you and I had history and that I shouldn't be involved. Besides, media links are small potatoes. Suspicious circumstances of a cop's missing kid is the kind of stuff I handle."

Stallings resisted the urge to punch Detective Ronald Bell right in his head. Instead he turned and forced himself to walk calmly out of the office knowing this wouldn't be the last time he ran into the senior I.A. man.

Ten minutes later, as Stallings sat at his desk, getting ready to leave, he heard a pissed-off Luis Martinez stomp through the squad bay bitching about I.A.

The ex-Marine shook his head and said, "I.A. isn't

anything like the Gestapo. At least you could reason with the Gestapo."

Christina Hogrebe laughed from her orderly desk in the "original" homicide section of the squad bay. "Did they rough you up, Luis?"

"Shit, you'd have thought one of us robbed a goddamn bank."

Hoagie said, "They didn't break you then? You still have your media contacts?" Her smile took any edge off the comments. She had a level head and hadn't gotten too wrapped up in the drama taking time away from the case. That was the sign of a good detective.

Mazzetti stalked out of the conference room, where he could hear the banter between cops. "You guys think this is funny? We got a traitor among us."

Hoagie said, "C'mon, Tony, I don't think anyone here is a traitor."

"Oh yeah, what do you call a glory hound that uses the media?"

From the rear of the squad bay someone said, "We call him Tony Mazzetti, Prince of Homicide."

The chorus of laughter made Mazzetti's face flush red. But before he could say anything, the secretary from the front office leaned in the door and said, "Stall, there's someone downstairs says they have info on the case and wants to talk to you."

"Me? Why me?"

"It's an elderly lady, and she says she'll only talk to the hero-cop that caught Cernick." She saw the expression on his face and added, "I swear to God that's what she said."

Stallings stood up as Mazzetti marched toward the door. "I'm going too. This is still my fucking case."

Stallings walked in silence with Mazzetti out of the Land That Time Forgot, down the main stairs, and into the lobby of the Police Memorial Building. He checked with a receptionist and found a small, frail-looking woman, wrapped up against Jacksonville's occasionally cold winds and frequently cold rain.

"Ma'am," started Stallings slowly. "I'm John Stallings. Can I help you?"

She turned in her seat, looked up and said, "Oh thank God. I didn't know who to talk to, but I've seen you on TV."

"What's the problem, ma'am?" He didn't want Mazzetti being rude to this lady, so he stepped in front of him as he spoke, then crouched down to eye level with the woman.

She appreciated the manners and looked over her shoulder at Mazzetti to see if he was going to bend down too. When he made no movement, other than one of impatience, she turned her full attention back to Stallings and said, "We have to hurry. He's got a girl in the house."

Stallings patted her arm softly and said, "Who has a girl?"

She didn't seem to hear. "A young girl. I know who he really is."

"Ma'am, who are you talking about."

She looked at him, then up to Mazzetti and said, "I know who the Bag Man is."

Twenty-five

John Stallings steadied himself as Tony Mazzetti pushed his Crown Vic around a corner too hard. He wasn't used to sitting in the backseat of a speeding police car, but there was no time to argue once they had the tip. The old lady had too many details for them not to take her seriously. She said the man lived alone with a cat, acted oddly, and she saw him usher a young girl she described as "petite" into the house a couple of hours earlier. She had also seen him with a small woman Saturday night, the night Trina Ester said goodbye to her coworkers for the last time.

Mazzetti had moved quickly and been decisive. Patty and Stallings jumped into the car with Mazzetti. Luis Martinez and Christina Hogrebe were in a county Crown Vic somewhere behind them.

Stallings's pulse had cranked up the moment he realized the lady might have a real tip and not the usual stuff that rolled across his desk during a case like this. Now with some time to think about stopping this creep he felt the rush of exhilaration he had as a rookie.

Mazzetti's phone rang, and Stallings caught his side of the conversation. The homicide detective's clipped voice saying, "Yeah, yeah, got it. No shit? Got it." Then he slammed the small phone shut.

Stallings couldn't wait. "What'd we got?"

"The guy was at the community college, which puts him near at least one victim, the Tawny Wallace chick." He looked over his shoulder at Stallings. "No arrests, but he's been questioned for loitering near a school. Could be our guy."

Stallings nodded, "Could be."

Patty remained silent up in the front passenger seat. Stallings had detected a strained vibe between her and Mazzetti earlier in the day but didn't want to stir anything up, so he decided to wait to ask her if everything was all right.

The handheld radio on the front seat crackled as Luis Martinez reached out for Mazzetti.

Mazzetti snatched up the radio and called out a little loudly, "Stay off the radio. Call me on the phone." The call was short, then Mazzetti tossed the phone on the seat.

"Luis thinks we need some uniformed cops. I'm trying to keep the media out of this by staying off the radio and not involving everyone and his brother."

Stallings said, "I could call up some uniform help on the phone quietly."

"Who?"

"Ellis and his traffic guys."

"That's perfect, Stall. He's a good guy and will keep his yap shut."

Stallings looked up Ellis on his contact list and was talking to him a few seconds later. "Rick, you said you could help if we needed something."

"You bet."

"We're headed over to the seven hundred block of Forrest Street, you close by?"

"The Forrest down south or off the Bridge?"

"Down south."

"See you in ten minutes on the next block."

"I'm with Mazzetti in his blue Crown Vic." He cut the connection and told Mazzetti not to worry.

The briefing was quick and to the point, just the way Stallings liked police work. The fear of endless lawsuits had slowed the process of investigation by several magnitudes. This was important enough that everyone was willing to move fast.

Then Mazzetti pulled him off to the side.

"Stall, I think we need to slow this train down. We got enough people to watch the house while someone gets a search warrant."

Stallings shook his head. "We got exigent circumstances. The witness says there's a girl inside."

"But we gotta make this case airtight. I'd rather err on the side of caution."

Stallings felt his blood rise. "And what do we tell that girl's mother if she's killed in the time it takes us to get a goddamn warrant?"

Mazzetti looked away, obviously weighing the options. Finally he looked at Stallings and said, "Okay, but if this is a fuck-up it's on you."

Stallings nodded. He didn't know why it would be his fault, but he knew he had to get this operation moving. They watched as three marked patrol cars rolled up and Sergeant Rick Ellis popped out with a shotgun in his hand.

The big uniformed sergeant grinned and bellowed, "Real police work. I love it."

* * *

A few minutes later the five detectives and three uniformed cops crowded around Mazzetti's car's hood looking at a rough sketch of the house in relation to the other houses on the block.

Mazzetti said, "We all stay off the radio. I don't want some reporter with a police scanner catching on to what's going on. We're gonna cover the back and hit the front. No one in the back comes inside. I don't want a cross fire and one of us getting hit." He looked at all the faces, spending an extra second on the two young uniformed guys he didn't know. "Everyone understand?"

Everyone nodded.

"All we got is a tip, but it may involve a young girl in the house. We know this guy was at the community college. No record, just a field ID card by one of the sex predator detectives a few years ago."

Ellis looked up and said, "Where do you want us?"

"Sarge, you, one of your guys and Stall will cover the back. Hoagie and one uniform will cover the front. Luis"—he pointed at a the biggest uniformed officer—"you and me and Patty will hit the door." He looked around. "Any questions?"

Stallings didn't like the idea of staying in the back, but there was nothing to argue. That was his assignment.

Ellis's radio beeped and a male voice asked for him by his radio number. When the big man answered the voice said, "What's going on out there? Brief me."

Mazzetti said, "Not over the radio."

Ellis clicked the broadcast button and said, "I'll call you, Captain. Stand by." He reached for his belt, then cursed and turned to Stallings. "Stall, let me use your phone. In the excitement I left mine in the car."

Stallings handed over his phone and turned back to

the hood of the car as Ellis walked off with the phone glued to his ear.

Mazzetti said, "You cool with this, Stall? We're going in without a warrant at your insistence."

He nodded. "It's the right thing to do."

Ten minutes later Stallings stood behind the small, single-family house with the two uniformed cops. They had crept into the yard with a few scraggly bushes and weeds instead of grass. No one had noticed the cops as they cut between neighbors' houses and now stood at each corner of the suspect's square house. Rick Ellis was right behind him on one side and a young patrolman on the other. Stallings looked down at his watch. Any second now the other team would hit the front. His heart pumped hard, forcing blood into his eardrums like thunder.

Stallings put his hand on the grip of his pistol, waiting for the expected pounding on the front door or, if things didn't go well, the sound of the door being knocked in. He tensed and waited. Still nothing, and it started to spook him. He drew his pistol, and Ellis, behind him, held his Remington shotgun up to his shoulder, then the officer on the other corner drew his service pistol. Stallings didn't know if they had their own gut feeling or if he had started the trend.

He crept around the corner, closer to the flimsy, cracked sliding glass door that looked like it had been cut into the back wall by a third grader. The cement was unpainted and slapped around the sides to fill in the gaps. There was a chunk of wall missing near the handle, and the track looked bent.

The first hard rap at the front door made Stallings jump and freeze in his position. Another hard knock echoed through the house, and he heard Mazzetti yell, "Police, open the door."

Stallings fought the urge to look in the glass door. Just his head in the door could distract the cops on the entry team not to mention the possibility of drawing fire from either a desperate killer or a cop.

He looked over his shoulder to make sure Ellis was in place and ready.

Then he heard shouting from the front.

Someone unlatched the slider from the inside and it creaked along its uneven tracks, wobbling like a tricycle with a crooked front wheel.

Stallings raised his gun as a teenage girl scampered out the rear with nothing but a floral pattern towel wrapped around her.

She turned and saw the gun, gasped, then froze right in front of the door, as the shouts inside the house grew more urgent. He heard, "Drop the gun." Then a single gunshot.

Instinctively he dove onto the girl to knock her out of the line of fire the door provided. They fell onto the sandy ground with a hollow thump. The uniformed cop moved past them with his pistol up to protect them in case someone came through the door.

Stallings rolled to the side, looked at the girl, guessing her age to be about thirteen. "Are you okay?"

She was shaking and nodded quickly.

"You're safe now. Everything is gonna be okay."

From inside he heard Patty call out, "Clear."

He stayed on the ground with the frightened girl as Ellis and his patrolman rushed inside.

It didn't sound like things had gone well, but looking at this young girl, Stallings couldn't care less if the case was made or not. She was safe. At least he still had his priorities straight.

Twenty-six

Stallings turned on the ground, still shielding the girl, then sprang into a low crouch with his pistol up. After a few seconds one of the young patrolmen leaned out and motioned Stallings inside.

Stallings stood and said in a low voice, "Stay with the girl."

As he stepped to the door a black cat darted out the open door and shot across the tiny yard toward the cover of a neighbor's hedge. He recalled the M.E.'s comment about cat hair being present on the victims' bodies. Things were adding up to look like this might be their man.

Inside, Patty was frantically performing CPR compressions on a man with a bullet hole in his chest. Patty had carefully placed her hands over the wound to make an effort to keep the blood from pumping out onto the grimy tile floor. Mazzetti kneeled over the man and attempted rescue breaths after every thirty compressions Patty completed.

It looked to Stallings as if all they had done was keep the guy alive long enough for his heart to pump a puddle of blood that had spread across the entire front room.

In the corner, Rick Ellis had his arm around Luis Martinez's shoulder. The big sergeant just nodded to Stallings letting him know it was okay. He knew better than to ask, "What happened?" Things would become clearer to him in the next few minutes. The important points were that the girl was safe, none of his team had been injured, and he was hoping this guy was the Bag Man and their problems were over.

Sirens began to tweak his ear from more than a mile away and from different directions. Stallings saw a pile of clothes that looked like the girl's from outside. He scooped them up and headed out the open slider. The uniformed cop stood next to her but obviously wanted nothing to do with her. She stood by the house holding the towel and squirming nervously.

He didn't want her to see the blood inside, so he led her around the front and then stood guard while she climbed in one of the police cars and got dressed. When she was ready he leaned in the window and started to chat with her.

"You okay, sweetheart?" He had patience. She'd tell him what he needed to know soon enough.

The girl nodded but started to sniffle.

"What's your name?"

"You're gonna call my parents."

"Someone will. You can't avoid that." He thought about it, then said, "I don't think you realize how much danger you were in."

"How?"

"That guy in there could be a killer."

"My boyfriend?"

"What?"

"My boyfriend."

"If he was your boyfriend why were you running out the back?"

"Because I'm underage, and I didn't want him to be in more trouble."

"More trouble? What kind of trouble was he in?"

"For the pot."

Stallings felt a lump in his stomach. "What pot?"

"The pot he's growing in the garage. Isn't that why you guys came to arrest him?"

Stallings didn't like the direction this interview was going at all.

Staccy Hines allowed the cool sea breeze to wash over her as she lounged in a low folding chair on the grass above the beach. The wind had been just a little stiff, and she had suffered the stings of the whipping grains of sand earlier, so she'd moved back up to her current spot. Now the Tess Gerritsen novel she'd been reading sat on the grass next to her, and she reminded herself why she wanted to stay in Jacksonville.

She hadn't called her family this week because she knew, as lonely as she was, they might talk her into coming home. It was the longest she'd ever gone without speaking to her mother. She worried about them and knew they worried about her, but this was the first time in her whole life she felt like she could make it on her own. She'd managed to find the apartment and had a decent job that paid her almost enough to live on. The little savings she had left would be gone by February, then she'd have to leave, but for now she just wanted to feel the ocean breeze, know that all she had to do was show up for work and try not to dwell on missing her family.

She sat up in the chair as two seagulls approached her cautiously. The bag of bread she always brought with her for the pigeons and seagulls was almost empty. She smiled, wondering if the seagulls recognized her from her other visits and the times she had fed them. No one else sitting on the grassy patch was being stalked by birds.

Stacey emptied out the bag so the few flecks left of whole-wheat bread sprinkled onto the ground. The birds pounced, pecking up every fragment; their little hip-hop dance made her smile.

Stacey looked to the side, near her car parked in the front of the small parking lot, and saw someone else feeding a trio of crackles or whatever the brown crow-like birds were really called. It was a man in jeans and a nice button-down shirt. He was even feeding them the same kind of bread she was. He cast it down in three separate piles so the birds didn't fight over it.

There was almost no one else on the beach or up here at the park. She stayed in her chair, but hoped the man would walk over toward her. She wanted to talk to someone and liked the idea that the man thought enough ahead to bring bread for the birds. After five minutes when he hadn't looked her way, she pushed up and out of her aluminum chair and headed toward him at a casual pace.

When she was a few feet away from him, Stacey said, "I was just feeding them too, but I ran out of bread."

The man turned slowly, and it was the nicest surprise of the day.

Stacey smiled. "Hello there, what're you doing out here?"

"I told you I liked Neptune Beach."

"You don't know how happy I am to see you. You like to be called William, right?"

He smiled too and said, "Right, William Dremmel, and you're Stacey."

Maybe her life was about to change here in Jacksonville.

Twenty-seven

John Stallings had been at the scene of many shoot-ings. Too damn many. Gangbangers shot from head to toe, a suicide where a man put the barrel of a .357 in his mouth, then turned slightly and blew out the side of his face and died in agony over the course of two hours as he bled to death. John Stallings had seen it all. He'd been involved in three shootings during his career where he fired his duty weapon. Once he hit the sus-pect in the arm, once he missed with four shots when a grocery store robber pointed a cheap Tecra nine mil at his head. The gun wouldn't fire, and after the spray of bullets from Stallings, the suspect dropped it and sur-rendered. He got a medal for that because the Sheriff's Office had gotten a lot of bad press about "trigger-happy" officers and they appreciated that Stallings didn't kill the guy like he meant to. Three months later the suspect choked a female jail deputy before his trial on the robbery. He was currently on death row at Raiford.

But the one that haunted him the most, the one time

he was truly afraid, involved a kid who was being held for a drug debt, and Stallings happened to spot the dealer with the kid. When he approached them the dealer scooped up the four-year-old and held a gun to the kid. Stallings tried to reason with the dealer, but when the dust settled, Stallings had fired one time and the bullet hit the dealer in the face. He still got a card from the kid every Christmas.

Today he was cooling his heels at the house they had believed the Bag Man owned. It now looked like the resident's name was Martin Zepher and he was not the Bag Man. He was an operator of a marijuana grow house and slept with a girl who was only fifteen. He was now dead. The girl was in child services because her dumb-ass mother knew of the relationship with Zepher and encouraged it since the dead pot grower supplied her with the best weed in town.

The mother was in custody on child endangerment, possession of marijuana, assault on a police officer for taking a swing at a female uniformed deputy, resisting arrest, and anything else the state's attorney wanted to file. It was not only to cover the shooting of her daughter's boyfriend; it was because of righteous indignation from the cops involved.

Stallings sat on a surprisingly comfortable and clean couch along with the uniformed guys who had come on the raid. Outside, crime scene trucks and unmarked JSO units clogged the yard. On the street, a house over, a Channel Eleven news crew with two cameras filmed all the activity at the house. They'd showed up before fire rescue even made it to the scene, but they had stayed out of the way. He wasn't worried about that as much as how this might slow down their hunt for the Bag Man.

Rita Hester, looking like a lieutenant in charge of

the detective bureau, in a green pantsuit with her gun and badge exposed on her hip, stalked through the house making sure everything was done by the book. Patty, Luis, and Mazzetti, who'd been in the room during the shooting, had gone down to the PMB to talk to I.A. about the incident.

The lieutenant paused in front of the couch to address Stallings and the others. She looked down at him like a child who was being punished and said, "You're goddamn lucky this guy was a criminal with an under-aged girl."

"Otherwise I would've been wrong to take a chance to catch the Bag Man?"

"Don't give me that shit, Stall. You know you could've done things a lot differently. If you got a warrant, the SWAT team would've done this."

"But I didn't know we had the time to wait when I made the decision." He knew not to get too snarky and didn't say anything else.

The lieutenant sighed for what seemed like a full minute, wiped her face with her bare hand, and said, "Martinez has a PBA attorney and is doing okay. We'll lose him on the case for at least ten days for the standard paid leave after a shooting. Mazzetti, Patty, and the uniformed guy are done for the day. I told everyone to meet at the Land That Time Forgot in the morning."

Rick Ellis and the other uniformed patrolman sprang off the couch and headed for the door. No cop wanted to be around a scene like this if they didn't have to be.

Stallings got up more slowly and was headed for the door when the lieutenant stepped over to him and said, "C'mon, Stall. What was the idea of rushing in here?"

He didn't want others to be blamed for his call. "It was the right thing to do."

"I think you're getting too tied up in this case. You're losing perspective."

"How do you figure that?"

"When's the last time you spent time with your own kids?"

Now he saw it was Rita talking to him and not the lieutenant. "There'll be time to see them as soon as we grab this asshole."

"What if it takes a year?"

"Then I'm afraid a lot of young girls are going to die in that time, and I'm not prepared to let that happen. Are you?"

William Dremmel had enjoyed sitting outside next to Stacey and just chatting for the last twenty minutes. The sun had poked out of the clouds and felt good on his pale skin. A party of seagulls now scurried around the bag of bread he'd dropped about ten feet away, and Stacey seemed calm and relaxed.

So far his plan had gone off without a hitch. He'd parked away from her little Ford Escort, then while she was still on the beach, he'd slipped his arm in her opened window, popped the hood, and pulled two spark plug wires, then put everything back the way it was. After he saw her feed the birds on the beach, he ran up to the Publix and picked up a loaf. He let her see him and not the other way around. This was a brilliant plan even for him.

Now he'd confirmed that she still lived alone, hadn't talked to her family in over a week, and basically was lonely. Welcome to the club.

Stacey said, "I can make it here, but I need more hours at the restaurant, or have to find a second job."

That gave him an idea. "You ever work with older people?"

"Tank the bartender is fifty-nine."

"No, I mean care for elderly patients."

She shook her head slowly. "No, why?"

"Could you do it?"

"Yeah, I like hanging out with my grandma."

He loved her midwestern accent and quaint notion of family. He couldn't see someone ever calling his mom "Grandma."

He gave her his earnest face. "I've been looking for someone to check on my mom on the days I'm at work late. You wouldn't have to do anything but talk to her and keep her company. I could pay fifty bucks a day for about two hours."

Stacey brightened just like he thought she might. "Really, you'd give me a try?"

"Sure, but you'd have to meet her first. That way you and she could see how well you get along."

"Sure, when can we meet?"

"How about today?"

She looked down at her Timex sports watch. "I have to work at six."

"That's no problem. I live in Grove Park. Shouldn't take long."

She immediately started gathering her stuff as Dremmel helped her with her chair. He packed it in her backseat as she cranked the little Escort. When it wouldn't start he had her pop the hood and pretended to evaluate the problem. In fact, all he did was make sure the spark plug wires were not connected but looked like they were.

He walked around to the driver's seat and leaned into the window. "Tell you what. I'll drive you to my mom's, then I'll get you to work. I have a buddy who could get this running in no time after he's off work. We'll have this to you before you get off work." He smiled and forced himself to stay calm.

She hesitated, then said, "I hate for you to waste your whole day."

"It's no waste if I find someone to help with Mom. Besides, you need a little support about now. If I was in Cincinnati, I bet your brother would help me."

"Yeah, I guess he would."

"I'll go get my van. I'll be right back."

She locked up the car and by the time she had her purse in her hand he pulled up in his minivan.

Stacey hopped in the passenger seat with a big grin.

She had no idea how close she was about to become with Dremmel and his mother.

Twenty-eight

Tony Mazzetti had a lot going on in his life. The serial killer case should've been the most important. The goddamn shooting should've been up there too. But somehow all he found himself thinking about was Patty Levine. If he closed his eyes he could picture her perfect, naked body, taut and tan. When she walked by, he smelled her perfume. All he could think about was Patty and his dick. Holy crap, what had happened last night? He thought he'd fixed the problem. That was his first chance in a long time to test it out and it should've worked. He used the mental tricks the psychologist had taught him and still it was a dud. And Patty seemed irritated by the whole adventure. He'd definitely picked up a weird vibe from her in the morning. Since Luis Martinez capped the pot dealer it was a different situation, but he worried about her early reaction to his failure to launch.

It was troubling, but who could he talk to? His mom supported him on everything, but her overriding goal in life was grandchildren. Lots of them. She'd tapered off on her inquiries the last few years, but he knew how she felt. He couldn't talk to any of the guys at work. Someone would leak it as surely as they leaked details on the Bag Man case. It would only be a matter of time before he was a laughingstock at the Sheriff's Office. No, this was an issue he had to deal with himself. He had to tell Patty the truth.

Now, Tony Mazzetti sat in the "hot seat" between the two internal affairs detectives. He knew both of them from their days in homicide. To be on the Sheriff's Office shooting investigation team or, as everyone called it, "the shoot squad," you had to have put in a few years in homicide. The shoot squad was housed in the Internal Affairs Unit on the third floor in surroundings that made Crimes/Persons look like a forgotten village in Somalia. The regular officers and detectives avoided the third floor as if it contained an infectious disease ward. No one wanted anything to do with the unit. It could be the route an ambitious detective took for promotion. It also gave the detectives a chance of promoting to sergeant without going back onto the road for a few years on midnights. In Mazzetti's opinion that was a shortcoming of most police forces. They put their smartest people in the detective bureau, encouraged them to try for sergeant, then, if they were successful, they threw them back out into road patrol to look after a bunch of rookies too scared to step out of their cruisers.

Taking the Internal Affairs or I.A. career route meant that sometimes you could get promoted in the same unit. Since there wasn't a long line of really competent people to join Internal Affairs, if the S.O. found someone bright, they could move up the ladder without risking uniformed duty.

The shooting squad looked at any officer-involved

shooting and tried to be impartial, even though more often than not they knew the cop involved in the incident. These two pricks were no different. They were jealous of Mazzetti's clearance rate and begging not to go back to patrol. If a boss had it in for any of the crimes/persons detectives, handing them up for something would go a long way toward securing a promotion.

The questions were pretty standard at first.

"Who gave the tip? Why no warrant? Did they know about the pot? Did they see a gun before Martinez shot?"

The senior of the two detectives leaned in close and said, "C'mon, Tony, you can tell me. Would you have shot?"

It was an old trick question designed to get someone to open up. Mazzetti looked at him and told the truth. "In a fucking heartbeat. That scumbag was going to shoot us." He thought about how Stallings worded the need to move without a warrant. "The girl's life was in danger too."

The detectives conferred for a few minutes, then the older one looked at him and said, "Who called the TV station?"

That was a new wrinkle, and he knew they thought it was him because he bitched about not getting enough attention, and the news had a long shot of him walking out of the house. What a time to get a little attention.

William Dremmel felt his pulse quicken as the clock edged closer to five. He'd told Stacey that he'd get her to work by six, which meant they'd have to leave by five to avoid her getting suspicious. She had a knapsack full of clothes and a pair of Skechers to wear.

Right at this moment she sat on his couch with a brownie she had taken one bite out of. She was small, but he doubted the combination of Valium and Nembutal would be enough to knock her completely unconscious unless she ate the whole thing. He'd been stalling her with the excuse that his mother was asleep but always awoke about four-thirty to clean up for dinner. In fact, he had fed his mom an extra one of her Seconals and watched as she slipped into a deep sleep.

He'd offered Stacey a variety of snacks and beer, which she refused. This was so much easier when the girls liked taking pills and capsules and expected to feel something from them. Stacey showed no interest in his efforts to introduce drugs into her system. She was also starting to show some impatience at not having met his mother yet and knowing she had to be at work.

Then she looked up at Dremmel and said, "Wow, the sun must've taken it out of me. I feel really tired. Do you have a Coke?"

He nodded absently from the kitchen, where he'd been waiting, and opened the refrigerator to grab a can of Coke. He was careful to only buy caffeine-free Coke since he rarely wanted someone with extra energy around the house. As he poured it, he found a bottle of Ambien he used for his mother's meals in the cabinet. He took one and used a spoon to mash the little blue pill, then scooped the fine dust into the drink. He let it dissolve completely while he pretended to straighten up the kitchen.

As he approached Stacey with the drink, he noticed her take another bite of the brownie. Excellent. But she looked more alert than he'd hoped. When he handed her the soda she took it and drank more than half immediately.

He sat down next to her on the couch, and she said, "I better get going."

He nodded. "Yeah, I guess. Sorry you didn't meet my mom." He stood slowly and said, "Let me just change so I don't feel so grubby when I eat."

"You're gonna eat at the Fountain of Youth?"

"Oh yeah. I probably would even if you weren't working."

"But isn't it kind of far for a good burger? I thought it was convenient to work."

"It is, but it's hard to find a good place to eat anymore." He smiled and wandered into the kitchen to get a look at her from a distance. She still looked alert. Then he saw her head bob. She drank some more Coke, and he felt confident his plan was working.

Just in case, he had his knife tucked in his front pocket. He'd even moved the TV back so it rested against the wall, out of the way, and he had Mr. Whiskers IV locked in his bedroom. He didn't want to repeat the same mistake, but he didn't want to act rashly either. He knew everything there was to know about Stacey Hines and needed her for his research. She didn't smoke, use drugs, had no medical conditions, and fit into his size parameters for a test subject.

She really could be the perfect woman.

Twenty-nine

John Stallings knew not to squirm in the hard wooden chair inside the third-floor office of Internal Affairs. He didn't know if the reason the chair was uncomfortable was to make people squirm or not. He just didn't want to give them the satisfaction.

There were two detectives questioning him about the circumstances of the raid and what he heard and saw concerning the actual shooting by Luis Martinez. Unfortunately, one of the detectives was Ronald Bell. The tall detective's suit had a distinguished, high-dollar look to it. So did Bell. Not just in his clothes, which were even nicer than Mazzetti's, but his whole demeanor. "Polished" was the word that came to mind. Neat, precise, cordial, and smooth.

Now Ronald Bell leaned toward Stallings with his monogrammed shirt rolled up his forearms and his Vineyard Vines tie loosened to give him the common-man look.

Stallings said, "Ron, I told you everything I saw. I

was around back with the girl when Luis saved everyone's life."

"Oh cut the shit, Stall. If you were out back, how do
you know he saved anyone's life?"

"Because he was there on official business and the
suspect had a gun. That could add up to a dead cop.
Would you prefer to have a dead cop? Luis did the
right thing."

The dapper detective grunted in frustration and
looked down at his notes. Stallings knew it was a ploy
to compose himself rather than search for the right
question. He felt a certain satisfaction annoying Bell.
He was the guy who had pressed Stallings with some
harsh questions after Jeanie had disappeared. The I.A.
flunky was just looking to get ahead and was acting as
a mouthpiece for someone higher up the ladder. It didn't
take the sting out of the inquiry as he grieved over the
loss of his daughter.

Stallings remembered when he finally snapped and
took a swing at the surprisingly agile detective. The
goof had asked, "Why call in a missing person at three
in the afternoon Saturday when no one had seen her
since noon on Friday?"

Now Stallings knew it was a legitimate question, but
at the time stress and the desire to have every swinging
dick out looking for her pushed him too far. To Bell's
credit he never said a word about the attempted battery.
But just the sight of the man brought up memories he'd
tried hard to suppress: the sheriff's tech unit searching
the home computer for e-mails and instant messages
that Jeanie might have sent; the crush of media; and,
worst of all, the questions he couldn't or wouldn't answer, like "Can we talk to your wife?"

He shuddered at the thought, then snapped back to

reality. As he did, he heard Bell's voice saying, "So you didn't think you needed a warrant or to use the SWAT team for the entry?"

Stallings shook his head; he was short of breath and didn't want to waste any speaking.

Bell paused, then said, "How'd that work out for you, Stall?"

Patty Levine had ignored the order to go home after the shooting and her I.A. interview. There hadn't been much to say about the incident. They had forcibly entered the house when no one answered the door but they had heard movement inside. They confronted the suspect, who had a pistol in his hand. Luis Martinez fired once, striking the man in the center of the chest. The suspect died. When you stripped away the issues of why they were there, why they had no warrant, how they developed the information, the situation was clear. It was a "shoot" situation. Martinez fired because he saw a threat to his life and the lives of others.

She had avoided Tony Mazzetti during the hectic day because she knew he already felt terrible about his failure to launch. She didn't know why it had happened but didn't feel like adding to the guy's guilt.

Right now Patty had records from Home Depot, tips from the general public, information from suitcase manufacturers, and the medical examiner reports on the three victims all on her desk. The killer's identity lay somewhere in the details of this pile of data, and she intended to find him.

John Stallings had the contacts with the street people, Mazzetti the drive to push everyone, and she felt like she had the eye for a detail that might break the whole thing wide open. At least that was her hope.

The task force members agreed that the killer had the ability to attract the victim without causing too much alarm. At least at the beginning of the encounter. The vicious knife wounds to Trina Ester showed that she had been frightened and the killer acted out of character. Patty sat and tried to figure out what he had done to spook her. Had he undressed? Tried to undress her? What caused the reaction?

The killer also seemed to fly under the radar, which made her think he might be a maintenance worker or someone else who fit into an area like a fixture and wouldn't arouse suspicion. That included such a range of people that she didn't waste time thinking about it. Except he also had access to prescription drugs. The drugstores had been canvassed to see if a large amount of Oxycontin was missing from anywhere and the search determined everyone was missing some. For a drug that helped so many with persistent pain and caused so much heartache for those who abused it, none of the stores seemed to pay attention to their inventory.

Finally Patty shoved some of the tip sheets aside and leaned back in her chair, pressing her palms into her eyes and feeling the events of the day start to drain her. It also gave her a moment to feel the regret of a missed opportunity bubble up in her again as she tried to consider what went wrong in bed the night before.

Then it hit her. In little fragments at first, then as a fully realized, crystal-clear vision: Tony Mazzetti was gay.

John Stallings kicked the slightly deflated soccer ball harder than he had intended as it flew up off the neatly cut grass of his front yard and whacked Charlie in the chest, rocking the young boy.

Charlie gave his dad a confused look, and Stallings raised his hands in apology.

The meeting in the Internal Affairs office had rattled him, and he knew it. The sight of Ronald Bell had sent him racing home to see his family and spend some time with the kids.

It wasn't just the shooting. A cop had a sense of his own mortality every time he stepped out the front door. A lot of their work was luck and fate as much as training. No, it was the face time with Bell that had brought back the memories of Jeanie's disappearance and his own issues with the suspicious I.A. investigator. It also reminded him of what the whole family had gone through, and he saw it as a testament to their strength that everyone was still together and functioning. Even Maria had come around in the past few months. After the loss, the allegations, and Maria's own issues, he'd never believed life could be good again.

But he still couldn't sit at home comfortably while he knew he had the power to stop the asshole roaming J-Ville and stuffing girls into bags. He knew that after kicking with Charlie and doing some stretches and conditioning with Lauren he'd be up on his computer organizing his schedule to interview the street people and search the city once again.

Charlie set the ball, stepped back, and, running toward the ball and swinging his spindly right leg, launched the ball at Stallings with a slight hook to it. The ball twisted like a knuckleball, cutting an erratic path through the air and striking Stallings directly in the solar plexus. His breath burped out of him in a fast swish and he felt his knees buckle as he went down first on a knee and then onto his back.

He concentrated on taking in first tiny breaths, then longer, more satisfying gulps of air.

Charlie appeared over him with a look of horror on his face.

Stallings held up a hand and waved him off, gasping, "I'm fine, I'm fine."

Charlie nodded and said, "That's what happens when you mess with Stall 2.0."

Even in pain a smile washed across Stallings's face as he reached up, grabbed the boy, and hugged him tight.

This was all he needed.

William Dremmel could see the apprehension building in Stacey as she fidgeted and glanced at the retro wall-mounted clock that looked like an Elvis LP record. He'd tried to buy some time to allow the drugs to kick in, but the whole scenario felt too much like the disaster with Trina. The difference was that he'd spent a lot of time learning everything about Stacey and had dreamed about the long months of her semiconscious activity, when he'd explain her whole life to her. He'd even planned how they'd spend the evenings watching TV shows on his computer from one of the broadcast sites and the different configurations for the chains to allow proper blood flow in her shapely limbs. The more he considered the plans he had made for young Stacey Hines, the less likely it became that he'd draw his knife and damage that beautiful skin of hers.

He was frozen with indecision when Stacey said, "I think we need to get moving now." There was a hint of a slur in her words, but they were forceful enough for him to realize time was up. Then an idea popped in his head fully formed and ready: blunt trauma. A blow to the head might do the trick if not delay his research for several days while she recovered. He didn't like the idea of overt violence on this precious girl, but he saw no alternative.

His eyes scanned the room frantically, finally settling on a lamp with a brass base resting on the end table on his side of the couch. Too hard, with sharp angles that might cut her scalp deeply. He didn't want another bloody scene that took all day to clean up.

Then he considered the leather TV remote holder that was sitting atop the coffee table in front of him. Too soft. Although it had some heft, he doubted the cardboard under the riveted leather would be sturdy enough to deliver a blow that would lay her out.

Then he noticed the thick plastic-covered coil he used to work out his forearms. It was a simple matter of leaning to the side, almost like he was going to stand up, and grasping it. When Stacey stood and turned toward the door he could swing it and catch her in the lower back of the head. It would certainly stun her if not knock her out completely.

He said, "Yeah, we probably should get going." Then he leaned across the couch and wrapped his fingers around the coil leaning next to the couch against the wall.

Next to him, Stacey rose to her feet, but he felt a shaky quality to her movement and noticed her waver slightly when she was finally upright.

He was standing with the coil in his hand when he noticed Stacey flail her arms in the air like she was surfing. She let loose with a "Wheeee!" as she turned to him and smiled with a whimsical quality that let him drop the coil, knowing one of the drugs had just hit pay dirt in her brain.

A smile crept across his face at the serene expression Stacey held as she barely maintained her balance.

The familiar and now vital thrill shot through his body as he realized his plans had worked and he was about to dramatically advance his research.

More important, he would be able to spend a lot of time with this beautiful young woman.

Thirty

John Stallings missed a presence like Luis Martinez in the Detective Bureau. He was currently on a paid leave of absence because he fired his weapon and killed someone in the line of duty. There was no stigma to this kind of leave. It was standard and required to avoid the tough-guy police mentality. Once you worked with someone you didn't realize all their qualities until they weren't around. Aside from being a good cop, Martinez could translate for detectives trying to communicate to people who spoke Spanish, he never complained, and he had a sense of humor that lifted the entire Bureau. Stallings hoped he wouldn't be too affected by the shooting. But you could never tell.

Shootings bothered everyone, whether they admitted it or not. That was one of the reasons Stallings had stopped watching most TV police shows years ago. No TV cops ever seemed to feel remorse for shooting. In real life that was the definition of a sociopath.

Patty Levine eased up to his desk. She looked tired, but Stallings knew she'd never admit to a problem.

That wasn't like her. This had been her first shooting, and it always took its toll on cops who shot or cops who witnessed the shooting.

Stallings said, "You okay?"

She shrugged.

He smiled and said, "It'll get worse around here. If we don't nab this guy in a week, we'll all have to readjust our lives."

"I had no idea it could be like this."

Before he could say anything to reassure her, like senior detectives were supposed to, an analyst rushed past them to Mazzetti and the L.T. in the conference room. They all knew what that meant.

An hour later, six detectives crammed in the conference room viewing the video from a webcam set up at a park near Neptune Beach. The hazy, low-quality footage was designed to show surfers the wave height. The camera was secured on a utility pole in the parking lot and caught just one lane of parking. The twelve-second clip they watched over and over showed a small woman climb into a vehicle, probably a van, next to a white Ford Escort in the lot.

Stallings said, "How'd we get onto this video?"

Mazzetti said, "The manager of a sports bar"—he flipped over a sheet of paper and read out—"the Fountain of Youth, called in a missing waitress."

"How long has she been gone? Usually a bar manager has employees going AWOL all the time."

"The guy seemed straight up and concerned. He said the waitress, Stacey Hines, was very reliable and they were like her family here in town. The manager and other employees checked on her all the time."

"That was enough to search for her?"

"They've been watching TV, and she's only five feet tall."

One of the other detectives mumbled, "Finally the media helps us out."

Mazzetti said, "The patrolman who took the missing persons report was on the ball. He ran her name and saw her car had been towed for overnight parking at Neptune Beach. He went to the lot and checked out the car and found her spark plugs had been pulled. We couldn't ignore it."

Stallings realized that they had a big break in the case. He just hoped it didn't cost a young girl her life.

Lieutenant Hester said, "What do you guys think?"

Mazzetti spoke right up. "We found her parents in Cincinnati, and they're sending us photos and are on the way themselves. The restaurant says she didn't have any stalkers that they noticed but that her car had broken down there before. One of the cooks said he thought the plugs were pulled but added he wasn't completely certain. I'd say we have this shitty video of the Bag Man's vehicle."

The lieutenant said, "The video only shows a door. Nothing else in the frame. So what do we do with it?"

Mazzetti said, "See about enhancing it. Maybe pick up a detail. Try and find anyone who was at the beach and saw the driver of the vehicle."

Someone asked, "How?"

Stallings blurted out. "We have to go public. Show the girl's photo. Ask for help."

Mazzetti immediately had an answer. "We're already flooded with leads."

"What else do you have in mind?"

Mazzetti thought about it, then sighed. "We don't need someone to leak it this time. I'll make the call."

They had another victim.

* * *

Stacey Hines felt her head clear but still couldn't move her arms or legs. The first time she'd awakened in this position she thought she was paralyzed for a minute until she was able to see the chains holding her in place. Each time she had woken up since then it took less time to remember what was happening to her. That also meant it took less time to think of what was going to happen to her.

She was still naked under a thin, wool blanket with a Thanksgiving motif. Pumpkins and Pilgrim hats now haunted her dreams. But she hadn't given up hope. So far William had taken great care to keep her clean, feed her, and make her comfortable. She tried not to think about what he did after he dosed her with the drugs that made her pass out. He also liked to tell her all the details of her own life. He talked about her brief stint at Youngstown State University, citing her 2.1 grade point average, and then saying, "Sounds like someone was a little immature for college." It was like he had been there.

She had no idea if it was night or day or how long she had been restrained in the little bed. The initial terror she'd felt was now more of a chronic fear. It must've been some psychological coping mechanism, because she would've gone crazy quickly the way she felt the first time she woke up in chains. The tiny room held no clues either. Just her bed, a lamp, and a small, hard plastic portable toilet he had slid under her twice a day. She didn't even shudder at him wiping her after each use of the toilet. It was so clinical and nonsexual on his part, and she was so terrified about other things that she barely resisted the action anymore.

The truly scary thing was that she knew that he was the Bag Man. He hadn't said it, and she hadn't asked, but she knew whatever he had planned for her she would end up crammed in a suitcase. She knew she had to do something to get away. He would never just let her go.

As she considered possible courses of action, William unlocked the door and walked in holding a tray of food, including the protein shake he required her to drink every day.

William smiled and said, "Good morning, sunshine. Time for nourishment."

This guy put a whole new meaning on the word "creepy."

Patty Levine looked up from her desk as she was closing up files for the night. Things had returned to normal in the days after the shooting—as normal as a giant serial homicide case could be. It was dark outside, and she hadn't eaten since mid-morning. The three Xanax she'd taken during the day had kept her calm as well as thirsty, and the water suppressed her appetite. Now she was ready to cut loose and eat. Preferably a buffet with lots of pasta and mashed potatoes. The way she felt right now the guy who wrote the *South Beach Diet* could kiss her ass.

Her stomach had felt like acid a few hours earlier, but some over-the-counter Zantac cleared it up. She wondered if that was something she needed to add to her prescription arsenal. Why not? She'd found relief in every other area of her life from some little pill.

As her computer cycled off she sensed Tony Mazzetti moving toward her. She'd noticed him at the far end of the squad bay for the last forty minutes. He always stayed late, but tonight she could tell that he was waiting until everyone else cleared out so he could talk to her. That was why she'd taken her time to pack up for the night.

The games people play for romance. They hadn't changed in centuries and hadn't changed for individuals since elementary school. Regardless, she smiled at his approach.

Without saying a word he slid a chair and plopped in it so that he was sitting and facing her from only a few feet away.

He looked at her and she remained silent until he said, "Hey."

"Hey."

"Got a minute?"

"Sure, Tony. I got all night." She didn't mean to make it sound like a crack about their attempt to make love, but that's how it came across.

He swallowed hard and said, "I wanted to talk about the other night."

"You'd have to be more specific." She liked the way he squirmed. It was cute.

He took a deep breath and said, "The other night when I was unable to perform in bed."

She kept quiet.

He looked off to gather his thoughts. "I've been thinking about the incident."

"The incident? That's what it was like for you? A homicide scene? It was an *incident*?" Her voice raised even though she wanted to cut the guy some slack.

"That's a poor choice of words. I'm sorry. What I've really been thinking of is you. You and me."

"Is there a you and me?"

"I-I don't know. What I was talking about was my problem."

"Couldn't it be *our* problem?"

He seemed to be concentrating on what he would say, not what she was saying.

Mazzetti said, "I don't think you understand. It's not you, it's me."

She let her anger seep away and smiled at the cute, nervous guy. "Relax Tony, I figured it out all by myself."

"You did? How?"

"I've been around a little, I'm not an idiot."

"What are you talking about, Patty?"

"I know you're gay, and your secret is safe with me."

"What? Gay? Me? No, wait a second, you really don't understand."

She held up a hand to shut him up. "Don't sweat it, Tony. I'm not judging you and know you think the guys in the bureau could be tough on you if they knew, so I won't say a word. But I think you're wrong. It's the new millennium. I doubt it'd make any difference at all to the detectives here. They already don't like you because you're an asshole."

He looked like he had more to say, but he started to hyperventilate, panting like a big dog on an August afternoon.

She watched him breathe faster and shallower until she got concerned. Then scared.

Thirty-one

John Stallings had let the analysts and Mazzetti scramble to find out all they could about the video from the beach cam. All it meant to him was another girl was missing and he'd failed in another pledge.

He'd been hitting the streets hard all day trying to find out who might've seen someone or something that could connect the dots in the investigation. He tried not to think of the anguish the family of the missing girl, Stacey Hines, was going through. He'd been there. Instead, he was out doing something. At this moment he was stopping in the Law and Order Pub to get some food into a young man he'd met off Bay Street who looked like he had not eaten in a week. He'd only give his first name—"Dan"—and not much else. Stallings could tell he was at least twenty, but something in his face told Stallings the young man needed a little help whether it was official or unofficial, so dinner sounded like a start.

As he was about to hold the door open for Dan, several uniformed cops came out of the pub, laughing.

The first two nodded to Stallings and gave Dan a cursory, dismissive glance.

The last cop out stopped and said, "Hey, Stall, who's your friend?"

Stallings looked up at Rick Ellis. "This is Dan, and we're going to grab a bite."

Ellis took a few seconds to reassess Dan but said nothing about the dirt caked on his neck and face, ripped T-shirt that used to be white, mismatched flip-flops, or hair frozen in place by grime. His face made it clear he'd caught the odor.

He looked back to Stallings and said, "Anything new on the big case?"

Stallings waited a second as Dan wandered a few feet away to look at a plant. "You heard about the video from the beach cam."

Ellis nodded.

"We're gonna release it tomorrow to see what we can stir up."

"Sounds like a plan. My bosses don't want me working with your task force again without clearing it through them first."

"Not surprised. Shootings make command staff nervous."

Ellis eyed Dan as he turned back toward them. "Gotta go. Keep in touch, Stall." The big sergeant was moving away from the smelly homeless man before Stallings could say good-bye.

William Dremmel checked the results of his drug trial so far. The detailed notes and a chart he'd made up showed that Stacey Hines slipped into a deep, unconscious state with a combination of Ambien and Nembutal. She'd do the same with Seconal but had a harder time waking up. Her mood had not stabilized yet even with Wellbutin included in her meals. The antidepressant hadn't had enough time to take hold, and she'd been distracted by her new surroundings. This was within the expected normal parameters of the trial.

Tonight he intended to ease her concerns, and the first way he'd do that was by giving her some time out of the chains. It would help her circulation. Maybe help her adjust. But he wasn't unprepared. In the rear pocket of his jeans he had a handheld stun gun he'd bought at a gun shop for $39.99. It looked like a pistol with no barrel—square and scary. The shock delivered through two electrodes at the end of it when he squeezed the trigger was guaranteed to incapacitate any human. If Stacey stepped out of line, he wanted to be able to act without leaving any serious marks on her perfect skin.

He moved to the locked room near the front of the house, checked to make sure his shirt covered the stun gun, smoothed his thinning hair, and taking a deep breath before using the single key to unlock the door, he entered. She was awake, but as usual didn't say anything when he first appeared.

He smiled, reassuring her that nothing would happen to her. At least nothing right now. After a few seconds he bent down to unlock first her feet, then the handcuffs holding her in place.

He said, "Thought you might like to walk around and maybe use the toilet by yourself."

She didn't say a word as she slowly sat up in bed, letting the blood flow stabilize, shaking her hands and wiggling her feet. He reached down to help her to her feet after more than a minute of sitting. She accepted and stood unsteadily for another minute, massaging her arms, then her legs. She stood straight, not hiding her nakedness. A defiance and elegance that he'd note on his report later.

She slowly stepped toward the toilet, leaned down like she was stretching, then, without preamble, turned with the hard plastic toilet in her hands, swinging the boxy solid commode, striking him in the head so hard he fell off his feet, slid across the terrazzo floor, and started to lose consciousness.

Tony Mazzetti's chest felt tight as he gasped for air. *It might be a coronary*, lashed through his mind. All he knew was that he didn't want to croak in the Land That Time Forgot, leaving the beautiful Patty Levine still believing he was gay.

He shook his head and could only repeat, "Not"—gasp, "Not"—gasp. "I'm not," This time he sucked in more air.

Patty squatted next to him with her small hand on his back. She leaned in to see his eyes and said, "Tony, I'm calling fire/rescue."

He shook his head violently and used what strength he had left to grasp her ankle as she stood up to rush to the phone. She paused at his grip and he gulped down some more air to finally spit out, "I'm not gay." He collapsed onto the thin carpet. Now that he had said it he was ready to die. At least that weight had been lifted off him. As he thought it, and lay on his back, he suddenly started to feel much better. Air flowed into his lungs, and his head cleared.

He sat up, which kept Patty in position near him and not springing up to call some dumb-ass paramedic. He faced her and said, "I'm not gay."

She didn't say anything, but the look told him he

better come clean and explain that she wasn't the reason he couldn't get an erection the other night.

He just dove right in. "I used supplements for a long time. Stuff like Andro, anything that would give me an edge in the gym. Sometimes I can't get it up easily."

She just stared at him.

"I mean I can sometimes, but not in a pressure situation."

"Was my bedroom really a pressure cooker?"

"No, not the room, the situation. I like you and didn't want things to go wrong. But when you think about what could go wrong, nothing goes right. Know what I mean?"

A smile spread across her pretty face, and she nodded. "I know exactly what you mean." She kept gazing into his eyes and said, "Why didn't you just tell me the other night?"

"I was scared. I just got caught up in the wrong atmosphere at the gym. I used to eat supplements by the carload, and it's embarrassing. You probably couldn't understand something like that."

She looked away and mumbled, "Yeah, I could understand."

Mazzetti said, "So that's my problem."

"And I know how to fix it."

"You do? How?"

She reached over and kissed him.

William Dremmel needed time to clear his aching head. But Stacey was advancing on him with the toilet now raised above her head for a vicious downward strike. He still admired the naked form of the woman before him now. With her arms raised, her breasts looked giant compared to her small body. He intended to pose her like this later after he regained control. Then the hard, heavy plastic toilet battered his arms that he held up to protect his head.

He reached for his stun gun, but a blow to his arms sent it skittering across the floor. He kept his arms up for protection. The blows hurt his right forearm but still didn't strike his head, and Stacey looked like she was having problems raising it again. Then she surprised him for the second time. A sharp, compact fist struck him across the chin.

He blinked hard and scrambled to one side as she abandoned the toilet and started pummeling him with her fists and elbows. This girl was a wild woman, and he'd never suspected it.

As he rolled onto his back she fell on top of him, still swinging. He knew exactly what he had to do to reverse this situation.

Thirty-two

John Stallings couldn't convince thin, dirty Dan to ride back to a homeless shelter with him. The skittish young man thanked him for dinner, then walked away down East Bay Street at a pretty good clip. If Stallings hadn't been watching him leave, he might not have noticed the head inside a parked car down the street. There was nothing unusual about someone behind the wheel of a car except the car was dark and didn't start while Stallings watched it.

He knew a surveillance when he saw one. Now the only question was if they were surveilling him. He made it a point to wave to Dan as he trudged away, making the occupant of the surveillance car think he was watching the young man and not the car. Sometimes cops who weren't used to surveillance believed that dark windows hid everything and they were virtually invisible while watching someone from inside their car.

He took his time opening his car and driving off. The suspicious vehicle never moved. As he pulled away from the curb, just before he turned left, away from the river, he glanced in the rearview mirror and saw the car, which he now knew was a Buick, headed down the street toward him. Stallings didn't speed up to lose them but instead slowed to give the Buick a chance to close the distance. They were on his turf, and he knew exactly where he'd lead them.

William Dremmel fended off most of Stacey's blows but still worried about the lucky punch that could knock him unconscious or leave an obvious mark. He shoved away from Stacey to one side and started to rise when she turned back at him like a crazy woman, all fists, feet, and fingernails. Jesus, he wouldn't have thought she was able to move like that.

He grunted, "Stacey, you need to calm down before you're sorry."

It was unfair, because he couldn't punch her back. First of all he didn't want to put one imperfection on that beautiful face; secondly he didn't want to have to treat a wound while running his experiments because he didn't know how the extra treatment might affect the drug trial. He also didn't know how the wound would heal while she was under the effects of the sedatives. For all these reasons he took her blows and didn't reply.

Then he glimpsed the stun gun off to one side. He could understand how they had fallen out of favor with police departments. The Taser created the same effect but from a distance. He wished he had some distance between him and Stacey now.

He threw her off him onto the mattress, then dove toward the stun gun lying in the corner on the floor. She followed him like a heat-seeking missile. She was no fool and knew this might be her only chance for escape. In some ways he admired her feistiness.

Dremmel had the stubby handle of the stun gun in his grasp as he felt the blow of Stacey's whole body on his back. He felt for the trigger, reached the gun across his chest, under his left arm until he felt it make contact with the bare skin of her side. Perfect.

He squeezed the trigger and immediately heard the electric chatter of the gun like the sound cartoon characters made when they hit high-voltage fences. Only this wasn't animated.

Stacey flipped off him onto the cold terrazzo floor, still convulsing. Her eyes rolled up in her head.

All Dremmel could do was stare in fascination as she twitched and gurgled. It almost looked like the orgasms he saw in the pornos he watched so often. He placed a hand on her shoulder to hold her down as she still convulsed, her breasts flopping from side to side. Then she went absolutely still.

"I told you to calm down. This is the kind of thing that happens when you misbehave." He wondered where he had gotten his disciplinarian attitude. His mother had never threatened him. Then, for some reason, he felt his dick move.

He put his ear to her chest and heard a strong, if fast, heartbeat. This was mesmerizing. He could study a reaction like this for months.

Stacey's eyes returned to normal as she tried to focus. She turned but made no effort to strike him again.

He felt a wave of disappointment, because he had enjoyed her reaction to the stun. Then he wondered how she'd ever allow him to resecure her to the shackles while conscious. It was more of a rationalization for what he did next. He looked her in the eye and said,

"This is for your own good. Anytime you act up, this is what will happen to you."

Without hesitation he stuck the small metal nodes of the stun gun on Stacey's inner thigh, brushing his hand against her soft pubic hair. He kept gazing into her eyes as he squeezed the trigger again, sending her back into a convulsive stupor.

Maybe the drugs weren't the only theory he could test on women over the coming years. There were definitely other fields in which he was interested.

Thirty-three

William Dremmel managed to secure the still trembling Stacey Hines before she regained her composure and fought him again. He'd gathered valuable information from his struggle and wouldn't make the same mistake again.

Her eyes focused on him with a look of anger, not fear, on her face.

He liked her naked body stretched out in front of him, the muscles on her inner arm straining as she tested the handcuffs once more. Her stomach had hard lines he had not noticed or was it that in the days she'd been here she'd already started losing the outer layer of baby fat? He'd adjust her calorie intake to make sure she didn't lose any more.

There were tiny burn marks where the stun gun had caught her on the side and inside thigh. It looked like a tiny vampire had attacked her in two places. The inner-thigh jolt had really affected her, and he wasn't sure if it was the location of the shock or the cumulative effect of the two jolts.

Dremmel said, "Did you learn your lesson?"

Stacey just glared at him.

"It'll be worse next time you act up. Once you learn that I just want a peaceful relationship, I think your life will be much more pleasant." He could tell by her look that if she got another chance it'd be worse on him too. Man, he thought, there's so much a good scientist could study if he only had the time and subjects. The idea of testing stun guns on naked women aroused him as much as his current lab work. He'd go through more test subjects, but it sure would be fun.

Stacey turned her head and said, "You know they're looking for me."

He'd seen her face on the TV, but there was no mention of what the police thought had happened to her. She was just a missing person.

"You said you lived alone, and your family was in Ohio."

"But they expect a call from me."

"Don't worry, you're safe here for a good long time."

"Why? What will happen in all that time?"

He was surprised at her precise questions without scorn or sarcasm. "You'll get plenty of rest."

"What will you get?"

"Who knows, maybe the perfect woman."

Stallings continued to drive at a reasonable speed to keep his tail near enough to continue the surveillance but not so close that the pursuer would realize Stallings was in control. There was no way he wanted to lead whoever this was to his house. That's all Maria and the kids needed now—Stallings shooting someone on their front yard. No, he had the perfect place. Quiet, confus-

ing, and isolated enough this time of night to allow him
to do whatever he had to.

He pulled the Impala onto the interstate and drove
north a few exits, then, after making sure the tail was
still on him, Stallings eased off the highway and took a
slow left into a shopping plaza and drove through the
first row of stores. This plaza had once been a mall, but
new designs had pushed the owner to break it up into
five individual strips of stores with three rows running in
one direction and two strips running perpendicular so
that from the air the strips looked like two Hs sharing the
middle building. If someone wasn't familiar with the
plaza's layout it was easy to become trapped in the lot.

Stallings turned into the middle of the plaza and
quickly pulled his Impala around and parked close to
the building. He shut off the lights, drew his Glock,
and waited, intentionally avoiding any speculation on
who his tail was or what he wanted. Now was not the
time for distraction.

The beam of a headlight passed over the lot as a car
slowly made the turn toward him. Stallings knew that
right about now the other driver was discovering he
had fucked up. Once the Buick had cleared the building and was just in front of Stallings he hit his lights,
threw the Impala into gear, and roared from his spot,
forcing the Buick to the side and pinning the car next
to a high curb.

As both cars came to a stop inches from each other,
Stallings popped out of the driver's side with his pistol
up and on the driver of the Buick.

Stallings said, "Let me see your hands, now." The
last word was a shout. He emphasized it by bringing up
the pistol slightly.

Inside the Buick a pair of hands rose and Stallings
kept the gun on the driver.

"Open the door slowly and step out. Do it now."

The door popped open and two hands immediately rose up. He could see a male's face as he focused past the front sight of his Glock.

He heard, "Okay, Stall, you win."

He recognized the would-be spook and still debated shooting him right where they stood.

The trauma of the evening rushed through Stacey Hines and she started to shake. Even under the wool blanket her naked body shuddered uncontrollably like she was laid out on ice. The bitter aftertaste of the water with several pills ground up and mixed in spread down her throat and up her nasal cavity. She knew what was in the cloudy glass of water. She'd even watched as William had pressed the pills under the bottom of a thick glass, then scooped the dust into a plastic cup with a few ounces of water.

After being shocked twice with that weird electric grip thing she decided she'd drink the water without complaint. Almost instantly she'd felt her system slowing down and then the shivering and shuddering started.

William leaned over her and stroked her hair as if he thought it would soothe her. "You'll sleep for a good long time, and tomorrow night I hope we don't have the kind of conflict we had tonight."

She didn't say anything but kept her eyes on him. She wanted to burn every detail of him into her memory so when the police finally saved her and needed information, she could give it to them. His thinning blond hair and pale blue eyes now made him look cold. His smile wasn't inviting like she'd thought before; it now appeared evil. Like the bogeyman her brothers used to tell her about to scare her. Somehow it was

William's mild good looks that made him scarier than if he had a hook for a hand or a horribly scarred face.

She started to drift off, wondering how soon her parents really would start looking for her. Stacey now wished she had more of a social life so someone did miss her. She didn't even know yet if anyone knew she was in trouble. Maybe someone at the Fountain of Youth would worry about her missing a few shifts. But would they be concerned enough to call the police?

The room went hazy and a calm, almost pleasant feeling drifted over her. William's face fell out of focus. Then she was dreaming about kissing her mom good morning back home as she smelled hotcakes and bacon on the griddle. She tried to hold on to the dream but snapped back to reality for just a moment and thought, *God, how did I get into this?*

John Stallings had his pistol holstered and his arms folded, and he leaned against the hood of his car as he stared across at Ronald Bell leaning against the hood of his Buick.

"Never did much dope work, huh, Ron?"

"Why do you say that?"

"Your surveillance skills are a little weak."

"We still follow people occasionally."

"We, as in I.A.?

"I've been in the unit a long time, so yes, when I say 'we,' I mean the professional conduct unit."

"No one calls it PC."

"I know, but that's the name of the unit."

"If you've been there that long without moving up that must mean you like it."

"Look, Stall, I know you think we exist to screw with good cops, but that's not the case."

"Then what are you doing following me around tonight?"

Bell sighed and wiped his handsome face down with his bare hand.

"C'mon, Ron, I got things to do. We gonna spend all night here or are you gonna spill it?"

"Two things have me looking at you. First of all there's Franklin Hall."

"Who?"

"The pimp you brought in for questioning."

"Oh, Jamais."

"Yeah, same guy. He claims you threatened him and damaged his Hummer with an ASP."

"He make a complaint?"

"No, I was looking at another issue when it came out."

"What else, Ron?"

"The media leak in the unit."

"You're shitting me. We're after a killer who's probably just grabbed his fourth victim and you're wasting time on who blabbed to a TV station?"

"I never said it was specifically TV." He leaned forward like he'd just made Stallings confess.

"No, you dumb-ass, but the reports are always on TV, then the *Times-Union* quotes them." He shook his head at this silliness. "And you think I'm the leak?"

"I have to investigate."

"And I have to catch a killer."

Bell said, "We each have a job to do."

"But mine has a fucking purpose."

Thirty-four

The photograph of Stacey Hines on the TV barely caught William Dremmel's attention as he walked past the break room in the rear of the pharmacy. In the photo she was smiling as if she'd just graduated or was the homecoming queen. The cute dimples on her cheeks and light in her eyes came through even on the cheap TV with sketchy reception. The image didn't startle him like the first time he'd seen it, because now the airwaves were flooded with her pretty face. His minor error was not looking for an Internet pole camera designed to show surfers the wave height and conditions. The grainy image from the webcam showed a petite woman, who the police said was Stacey, climbing into a vehicle. Even the police experts said it was probably a van, but no one could say it unequivocally. No one would notice him in his little tan Nissan Quest. Just like no one would see Stacey's face again in public. At least not outside a suitcase, and he hoped that wouldn't be for a long, long time. The story closed with the announcer saying that although there is no official comment it is believed the girl had been taken by the Bag Man.

Dremmel couldn't keep a smile from creeping across his face. He was the Bag Man. No one knew but him.

Then the announcer said that police have several leads that look promising. That made him freeze and a lump in his stomach rise to his throat. Did they really have a lead? Had he slipped up? Allowing his van to be filmed, even if only by a crude surf camera, was a mistake. How many others had he made?

As he considered this possibility he felt a quick sting on his butt and jumped, then turned to see Lori smiling.

"C'mon, Billy," she started. "You're not used to someone pinching your cute caboose?"

He forced a smile and mumbled he just didn't expect it. She followed him into the storeroom as he started to clean up old magazines. As he sorted through things to discard, Lori perched atop a case of baby formula and started chatting like she was on a class break in high school.

"How late do you work tonight, Billy?"

"I'm done here at six, but I have papers to grade after that."

"Wanna catch dinner?" Her white teeth almost glowed against her attractive dark skin.

"I can't tonight." He tried to say it firmly because he knew it might be a long time until he was free.

Lori continued to hang out with him for more than fifteen minutes, then followed him back into the break room. Just as they entered there was another news teaser on Channel Eleven with a photo of Stacey Hines.

Lori said, "Hey, isn't that the waitress you're sweet on?"

He turned as casually as he could make himself and looked at the small screen. "I'm not sweet on a waitress."

Lori pointed to the TV and said, "Isn't that the girl who served us lunch the other day?"

He looked again. "I guess it could be. That's a shame." He had no idea how to sound concerned or show any real emotion.

"I hope they find her before that goddamn Bag Man is done with her." Lori turned to leave, but Dremmel caught the sideways look she gave him.

He stood in the small break room alone, an uncontrollable shaking starting up one side of his body and down the other. He knew he couldn't have a link to Stacey. Lori would put two and two together soon enough. He had to act and act fast to keep his identity a secret.

Tony Mazzetti was exhausted from the events of the last few days and his responsibilities, but he wasn't in any kind of a bad mood. Hell, he felt pretty good. Patty had shown she was patient, and the pressure he normally felt with women had melted away. He'd considered Viagra but didn't want to talk to his own doctor about it. Not with his hot nurse, Darlene, right there and then having to face the doctor for every little thing after. He'd rather have extra rectal exams than admit he needed help with his own equipment.

But Patty seemed to be the only medicine he needed, and now all he wanted was an opportunity. That might be tough. Being the lead on a big case like this took up a lot of time and energy. Besides actually investigating the case he had to update bosses, talk to the media, dole out leads (making sure to keep the good ones for himself), and generally keep on everyone's ass to stay on top of things.

The video of Stacey Hines had motivated the detectives like nothing he'd ever seen before. Her photo was running on every channel and shown by the detectives to every cheap dope dealer or smart-ass pimp in an effort to scare up some information. The circumstances of the last deaths indicated that the Bag Man didn't kill victims immediately, and that gave everyone hope that they could still find the missing girl.

He assigned out a dozen shit leads. The kind of leads Stallings would be getting if not for his contacts in the homeless community and his protection from the L.T. He checked on Patty's assignment and saw she'd be hitting all the pharmacies on the South Side west of the river. He nodded to himself. That was a good and safe assignment. He couldn't wait until they both had a few minutes for each other.

Stallings looked over at the blond guy in the tan Nissan Quest trying to see his face. He was paranoid and suspected every jerk-off in a van of being the Bag Man. Ever since he had seen Trina Ester and not noticed the killer at the Wendy's, he had been careful to look closely at everyone. It was emotional and counterproductive; he needed to focus on real leads. The only thing he should be paranoid about was if he was still being followed by Internal Affairs. He had hoped his sincere, if not a little aggressive, chat with Ronald Bell would satisfy their concern that he was a leak to the media and now he could focus on finding the Bag Man.

The fucking case had started to eat him alive, and the video of Stacey Hines had only exacerbated his anxiety. He had barely been home while anyone was awake, skipped meals, forgot about any kind of exercise, and now found himself only thinking about leads and clues in the case.

He jumped every time his phone rang, fearing it was someone telling him they had found Stacey Hines in a suitcase somewhere. The entire situation was too similar to Jeanie's disappearance, and he knew that it had to be affecting Maria, but he wasn't home to support her. The story playing out on TV was gut-wrenching from Stacey's parents' arrival from Ohio to the volunteers searching aimlessly for her.

His experience told him that someone like the Bag Man wouldn't be caught by well-intentioned volunteers. Even if they found a decent lead, they probably wouldn't recognize its significance.

A detective like him was the best shot that girl had to live, and he wouldn't screw up any chances he found. It felt personal and direct since he had first seen Lee Ann Moffit's face. Now the desire to stop this guy burned even brighter inside him

He had a bullet with the Bag Man's name on it, and he needed to find him before it was too late. For Stacey Hines and his own family.

Thirty-five

William Dremmel felt as if he might be a little paranoid when he saw a man in a black Impala give his van a good long look as he pulled away from the intersection. But there was no reason to believe anyone suspected him of any crime. Even with the news stories and volunteers, no one was looking in Grove Park or anywhere close by.

His stomach growled as he headed for the pharmacy. He rarely ate as well as he wanted while at home feeding two separate but disabled women. His mother had been quiet the last few days, and he was pleased with Stacey's health too. She'd settled into the long periods of rest and didn't seem to be having any immediate health issues. His notes reflected that she had maintained her weight and had regular bowel movements, and her attitude, while still defiant, signified that she was not suffering strong psychological effects of the drugs.

He'd been very careful allowing her to move around since the night when she attacked him. He let her see the stun gun and once had even hit the trigger to see her flinch at the dreadful electronic chatter. Fear was a wonderful motivator.

He pulled into a Denny's for some good old-fashioned protein and fat. This Denny's generally serviced the string of independent hotels along U.S. 1 and out to the Interstate. He stopped, because all Denny's food was the same and there were no cars in the parking lot.

He hurried inside, sat at the counter, and was ready to order from memory when he was surprised by the pretty waitress who gave him a bright smile. She had clear, healthy skin and dark eyes that showed an open innocence that completely disarmed Dremmel.

"Hi, want some coffee?" She kept her perfect smile.

He eased onto the stool and shook his head. "Grand Slam, scrambled with O.J." He didn't take his eyes off her. She made him forget his worries about Lori, his issues with his mom, and even his status with Stacey.

The waitress said, "Need anything else?"

He glanced to each side of the empty counter and noticed the cook was busy on the far side of the kitchen.

Dremmel gave her his own smile. "Could you answer a question?"

"Sure, what's that?"

"How tall are you?"

Her smile stayed firm as she said, "Five feet even."

William Dremmel's mind started to race.

Patty Levine had been swept up in the concern for the missing girl like everyone on the task force. The main difference was that she didn't want to waste time on leads or investigative activities with little chance of success. She watched as other detectives rushed out the door to question random street people, surfers who might have been at the beach, even a sampling of sexual predators who lived on the east side of the county. These were all long shots to find the missing young woman. Patty intended to follow a deliberate investigative plan to catch the Bag Man. That way she would make her best effort to find Stacey Hines while she tried to identify the killer.

Today she had started a comprehensive canvass of pharmacies to see if any had been missing Oxy and if there were any insights pharmacists could give her. It was a duplicate of a quick check completed the first week of the investigation, but now the lieutenant wanted detectives checking out the whole pharmacy from employees to records. She had the southwest section of the city, and three other detectives were handling the other sections.

As she entered the fifth store of the day, feeling confident as a cop and as a woman for the first time in quite a while, she noted the traffic in the store. It looked like they catered to the free clinic and Medicare clients.

She'd already developed a shorthand for which pharmacies ran a tight ship and which ones didn't care what inventory looked like. If the manager was also the pharmacist and had to watch the cashiers up front too, the drug records were shitty. If the store hired a separate manager and had the pharmacist only worried about running the pharmacy section, then things were usually in order. The chain stores had a handle on things like this. It was the family-run stores that scared her.

Now she was in a family-run store that had several locations.

She identified herself and spoke to a cute thirty-year-old pharmacist who tried to make it clear this little store was just a blip on his career path.

He invited her back behind the counter, then into a small room with a TV, and scooted two chairs so they faced each other.

She eased into one chair as he plopped into another directly across from her. "When I graduated from UF, I had a lot of offers with the big chemical firms, but I wanted some experience in a neighborhood pharmacy like this."

Patty went right into her questions: Missing any Oxy? Ever hear anyone talk about mixing drugs? Ever overhear a customer talk about a source for Oxy outside the pharmacy? All the usual stuff.

The young pharmacist offered some professional advice. "From what you've explained to me and the type of drugs used by the killer, I'd say the Bag Man has a professional knowledge of drug interactions. He'd have to be someone trained in the area or else some kind of genius who can learn things on the fly."

Patty took notes furiously until the pharmacist said, "I bet you have some kind of big, badass cop husband." He smiled to show he was only half serious.

Patty shook her head. "No, I have a big badass cop boyfriend."

"And he could probably beat the shit out of me."

Patty let out a little laugh and said, "Honey, *I* could beat the shit out of you."

Twenty minutes later Patty was looking over records in the rear of the pharmacy amid discarded magazines and other trash.

She made a few notes; there didn't appear to be any problems with the inventory. The Florida Department of Business Regulation had been inside doing an audit in the last two months, but she didn't want that pharmacist to think she was just breezing through asking a few superficial questions.

Her metal notebook case sat on a stack of diaper boxes in the corner as she looked over the volume of inventory reports. She'd been on the move so much she had already left it at one pharmacy and had to return for it.

A blond man walked in the room, saw her, and froze. "I'm sorry, I didn't realize anyone was in here."

Patty knew the look of someone trying to ask who she was without actually asking.

She smiled and said, "I'm Detective Levine from JSO." She held out her hand, asking his name without really asking.

He took it and shook it briefly, keeping eye contact with her.

She had to say, "And you are?"

"Oh, sorry, William. William Dremmel."

"And what's your job around here?"

"I'm a stock . . . I do a little of everything. If you have any questions I can probably answer them."

"Notice any Oxycontin or other narcotics missing?"

"Not really."

"Anyone suspicious hanging around or asking questions about drug interactions."

He laughed and shook his head.

"Have you seen the photo of the missing girl on TV, Stacey Hines?"

He shrugged. "I guess."

"Have you seen her in here before?"

"I'll have to look at her photo again."

There was something about this guy that set off an alarm deep in Patty's head. It wasn't his answers so much as his demeanor. He looked like a nervous guy trying to act cool. She'd make a note of him and his name later.

The man said, "I have to get a few things in here,

then head back out to the floor. Do you need anything else?"

She shook her head and purposely returned her attention to the inventory sheets. She didn't want to telegraph that he had caught her professional interest. He rummaged around on the side of the room, grabbed a box of diapers, and left without another word.

She finished up, talked to the pharmacist for a moment, got on her phone to the office, then headed back out to her car. The clerk had just jumped onto her radar. She'd check him out and see if anything moved him up the ladder to a real "person of interest." Right now it was just a creepy feeling he gave her.

She didn't even have to write down his name. It was lodged in her memory: William Dremmel.

William Dremmel was as excited as he'd ever been in his entire life. He'd set up a second bed in his lab. Stacey's eyes followed him, but she never said a word as he laid a single mattress on the floor opposite her in the small room. He hastily installed eyebolts in studs in each wall, just like Stacey's restraints. He had a second set of cuffs in his own bedroom. He gave her a smile and wink but no explanation as he left the room.

At his computer in his bedroom he looked up everything he could on the little Denny's waitress who had said her name was Maggie Gilson. He found a Margaret Gilson with a criminal record, entered a hacker's site, and discovered Little Miss Innocent had a past for shoplifting, but all three cases had been dismissed. Retailers never followed through if the thief paid off the bill. She was twenty years old but didn't have any utilities in her name. He'd make her his next project. Just the idea of having someone new to learn about excited him. His erection threatened to rip his pants as he found little nuggets of information about the cute girl.

When he had searched databases enough he swiveled in his seat and picked up the three sheets of paper he had managed to slip from the battered gray metal case that Detective Patricia Levine had carried into the pharmacy. This was so easy he didn't need to look in the computer. Her schedule, in great detail, was on one page and phone numbers and notes on the others. An envelope with an unpaid water bill was stuck to the last page. It listed her address. Sweet.

Although he didn't have to dig too deep for information on Detective Patricia Levine, it was still exciting to learn about her without her knowledge. He'd noticed her look at him in a certain way that could mean problems. He had so much to do he wondered what to do first. Clearly he had to act if she started to investigate him. But Lori and her knowledge of Stacey Hines gave him a different worry. Either way he liked these kinds of challenges and knew he could stay one step ahead of the cops on this.

Thirty-six

John Stallings took several seconds to ease the front door of his home shut. The lock clicking sounded like a cymbal in the silent house. He didn't want to wake anyone, and he was so tired that just standing still at the door almost caused him to doze off. Not only was he exhausted by a day of following up leads and ideas that Peep Morans and Ernie had given him about narcotics dealers who specialized in prescription drugs, but he had a raging headache from lack of food and he was just too tired to eat.

He turned to head straight to his bedroom and noticed Charlie sound asleep on the living room couch. He snored lightly with his body twisted in an odd position that only a kid could sleep in.

Stallings felt a smile wash over his face despite his exhaustion as he bent to pick up the boy and carry him to his room. As he bent down he heard Lauren entering the living room from the kitchen.

"Hey Dad. Where've you been?"

"Work."

"I tried to call."

"My phone ran out of juice before me. Why? What's wrong?" He no longer had time to be eased into bad news.

"Just worried, that's all. Aunt Helen is here."

"Why, what's wrong?" It was a question he had asked too often.

"She came by and hung out this evening." Lauren looked over her shoulder toward the kitchen as if to prove she wasn't hallucinating about his sister visiting. Then she said, "Dad, you look really beat. Is the case going okay?"

He looked at his thirteen-year-old in a new light. In that moment, this beautiful young girl had done everything she could to assume many of Maria's roles. She showed interest in his life outside the house, she helped her brother with his homework, gave pep talks to Stallings, often cleaned the house, and always made sure she knew where everyone in the family was. The last thing Stallings wanted was to have another daughter robbed of her childhood. The simple question about the Bag Man case made him hesitate. He didn't want to suck his daughter into his obsession with this killer. He didn't even want her to know how far outside the law he'd already gone to gain any information possible. What the hell was he doing in homicide anyway when he had these wonderful kids at home worried about him? Then he thought about Lee Ann Moffit, Tawny Wallace, Trina Ester, and now Stacey Hines and knew why he was on the case. Jeanie. He blew it with his own daughter, but knew he might be able to help someone else's daughter or at least avenge them. That wasn't why he started police work, but he was wondering if that was how he'd end his career.

He stepped across the room without answering Lauren and scooped her up in a tight hug. Her spindly, awkward teenage arms wrapped around him as well. As he stood there holding his surprisingly tall daughter, Helen stepped into the room from the kitchen.

Stallings released Lauren. "What's up, Helen?"

"Just wanted to see the kids. Is that okay?"

His years on the street taught him to read people even though he tried not to use his unique abilities on his own family. Now the sense that there was more to his sister's visit was overwhelming.

He smiled to put her at ease, then said, "It's fine with me. Did you get to see Maria, too?"

The hesitation in his sister, her pretty face frozen as she formulated an answer, told him everything he needed to know. He turned abruptly and started quick-stepping for the master bedroom. Behind him he heard Helen call out, "Wait, Johnnie."

But he was on a mission to find out the truth, and as soon as he opened the bedroom door and Maria sluggishly turned in bed and gave him that familiar grin and sleepy-eyed look he knew what had happened to draw Helen to his house, where she had felt unwelcome since Jeanie disappeared.

Maria gave a breezy, "Well, hello there," as he moved to the bed and immediately noticed her dilated pupils even with the bright bed stand lamps both burning brightly.

He didn't need another complication in his life right now.

William Dremmel felt as if he was handling his business better than ever before. Instead of indecisiveness he was taking action, instead of quiet loneliness he was making efforts to never be alone again, and instead of fear he felt confidence. He knocked on the door lightly, knowing it was late and Lori would be the only one awake at this hour. She'd told him many times of her insomnia and habit of watching movies in the living room after her father and brothers went to bed.

Dremmel had a few things to say to Lori, but he also needed to gauge the threat she was to him and his experiments. Would she really continue to harp on his relationship with Stacey Hines, or was it a passing comment? He couldn't risk it. He also wanted to tell her how he really felt about her.

He tapped the door again and heard someone pad across the wooden floor of the slightly elevated house wedged in the neighborhood known as Durkeeville. Predominantly African American, the area had seen a renaissance in recent years, and Lori's family had always kept the little house and yard neat. He'd driven her home several times over the years and knew his way around the streets.

The old wooden door creaked open and Lori stood alone wearing simple shorts and a T-shirt. Her natural beauty didn't need cosmetics to make her stand out, but she usually wore them at work anyway. Now in the soft light from inside she looked like the girl next door if the girl was a modern dancer with dark smooth skin and a bone structure any Venetian artist would kill to paint.

"Billy, what are you doing here at this hour?"

He smiled and said, "I wanted to talk to you away from work. Is it too late?"

She looked over her shoulder into the house and shook her head. "No, my daddy's asleep." She stepped onto the wooden porch and shut the door quietly. "Now, what're you doin' over here at this time of night, Billy?"

He placed a hand on her arm and leaned in close. "I needed to talk to you."

" 'Bout what?"

"About how I feel. I don't want to scare you off or make you uncomfortable."

Her eyes reflected the streetlight, but he could also see her interest. She leaned in to kiss him.

He stepped back and said, "I really do think you're great. I care about you." That was absolutely true.

She stepped toward him again ready to show how she felt.

He said, "Let's walk around the side of the house so no one gets the wrong idea right out here on your porch." He turned and took the three wooden stairs to the ground and immediately turned down the pot-holed, cracked cement driveway. He didn't want to risk kissing her and then changing his mind over what had to happen.

She followed him eagerly in her simple bedroom ensemble and bare feet.

He stepped into the shadow of the house and kept moving, making Lori follow him without time to think.

Dremmel carefully stepped around a puddle of water in the deepest part of the shadow, quickly added two more steps to get farther away, then turned to face Lori and watch the spectacle he'd spent an hour setting up quietly earlier in the evening.

Lori didn't notice the puddle, which was really a pothole with more than six inches of water. She stepped into the small pool of water and froze, then convulsed onto the hard cement driveway, still shaking as her left leg dipped into the water.

Dremmel was fascinated by any form of death and this was a new challenge. He'd set an electric cord running from an outdoor socket into the water. He had jammed open the automatic GFI breaker in the utility room attached to the open carport. The juice running through her was just a powerful shock except that he allowed the shock to continue while she lay there for what was termed "low-level electrocution." This was more spectacular than the stun gun. The little device had given him the idea for this stunt. The current essentially caused her heart to drop into arrhythmia.

He stepped closer and looked into her twitching eyes. Was that her or the electricity? Stepping away from the water he unplugged the heavy cord.

Lori stopped moving. He rolled up the cord, stuck it in his pocket, then leaned down and placed two fingers along Lori's long, graceful neck. There was no pulse.

It took him only a minute to remove his block from the circuit breaker and pick up a CD player he'd seen in the carport. He plugged it in the wall and dropped it in the pool of water. The unit sparked, then shut off as the water on the line tripped the GFI breaker.

He surprised himself by feeling a lump in his throat for his lovely coworker, then squatted down and kissed her forehead gently.

Now there were no links whatsoever between him and Stacey Hines.

Thirty-seven

William Dremmel spent the early morning hours trying to chat with Stacey. He'd been so excited by his brilliant staging of Lori's accidental death that he couldn't even think about sleep. When she proved to be resolute in her silence, he spent the time feeding her part of her high-protein, low-carb diet. The food plan allowed her to maintain muscle and keep her from putting on extra pounds while she was stationary. It also tended to keep her energy more regular without the ups and downs of insulin coursing through her. He allowed her to sit on the portable toilet with her hands free but not her legs. It was awkward setting the toilet on top of her mattress, but it was safer than letting her go free.

Dremmel completed his favorite task, giving Stacey a loving sponge bath, just before dawn.

Finally she said, "What's the other mattress for?" She nodded her head toward the opposite side of the room.

"It might work out that you get a little company in here."

"Oh yeah, who?"

He just smiled. "There are several options open."

"You're never gonna let me go, are you?" Her voice was calm and matter of fact.

"Never is a long time."

She looked at him and said, "I'm never going to forgive you for what you've done to me."

That just gave him the idea for a different round of drug trials to see if he could soften her position. He'd see what he could pick up around the store today.

John Stallings had been distracted all day long. He had Maria's sponsor and his sister over at the house and felt confident she was in good hands, but the guilt of whether his long hours had contributed to her backsliding ate at him. Still he couldn't keep himself away from the case today. He'd spent the day talking to homeless men and showing around photos of the dead girls.

As soon as he burst through the office door he had a sense that something was wrong. The other detectives kept their heads down or gave him a quick nod hello. He didn't know if Tony Mazzetti had thrown a fit about something or if they were all just getting as worn down as him from the case and trying to maintain their own lives at the same time. God knows he felt as if he could just lie down and sleep for a few hours. But he had leads to follow and people to find.

As he approached his desk, near the old holding cell, he saw the door to the conference room open and Lieutenant Rita Hester lean out, look at him, then motion him into the room. He set down his notebook and hustled toward the room wondering what terrible thing had happened now.

At the doorway he paused, looking at the lieutenant, Tony Mazzetti, and I.A. weasel Ronald Bell all sitting around the long table.

"What's up, guys?" he asked as he slowly stepped inside.

The lieutenant said, "Shut the door, Detective Stallings."

Uh oh, he didn't like the sound of that. Stallings took a seat on the far side of the table so he had a table between him and Ronald Bell. It seemed like a simple precaution for the I.A. investigator's safety.

"What's this about? Looks a little like a lynch mob." Mazzetti didn't look at him.

The lieutenant said, "You wanna tell us again how you haven't been talking to the media about the case?"

"I can, but nothing's changed."

Now Mazzetti looked up. "Bullshit, Stall. I actually believed you. I was starting to think you might be worth a shit as a cop and then you do this."

"Tony, I have no idea what you're talking about."

Ronald Bell slapped a stack of paper onto the table. "Your county cell phone records."

Stallings picked up the first page and studied it, seeing his phone number and the Sheriff's Office name and address at the top. "Do I have to guess, or will you tell me what to look for?"

Bell leaned in, feigning the outrage that most I.A. investigators can turn on or off in a heartbeat. "You slipped up, smart guy. You made a call to a Channel Eleven extension from your cell phone." He pulled a page from the bottom of the stack and slid it across the table to Stallings.

Stallings picked it up and looked at the circled call

and thought about it for a minute. "That's the day Luis Martinez shot the pot grower with the underaged girl."

"Exactly, and Channel Eleven was there before anyone else, even the paramedics." Bell plopped back in his seat like an old-time defense attorney who had just made some major point.

Stallings shook his head. "I never called any TV station."

Bell's face was a deeper red than usual. He said, "Is it an error? Just chance that the number for Channel Eleven appeared on your bill?"

Mazzetti shook his head and said, "You're pathetic." Then he stood up and stomped out of the room.

Stallings was at a complete loss for words. Seeing Ronald Bell gloating across the table didn't help matters. Then the lieutenant stood up so she could look down at him and said the one thing he didn't want to hear.

"I'm sorry, Stall, but I'm taking you off the case. You're going back to the runaway roundup unless the sheriff wants to take more serious action."

Stallings swallowed hard, trying to lose the lump in his throat. This was the worst thing they could do to him right now. Didn't they realize it would crush him? When he looked across at the smug smile on Ronald Bell's face he realized that the I.A. investigator knew exactly what this would do to him.

Thirty-eight

John Stallings sat in his Impala looking at his sister Helen's car next to his in the driveway. He'd spent an hour just driving around Jacksonville trying to make sense of what had happened. He was trying not to hate Ronald Bell for jumping to conclusions because if Stallings had seen the same evidence he would've jumped to the same fucking conclusion. But he knew he hadn't called any TV stations. He had no reason to. The headache that had started to blossom hours ago pounded in his skull.

He wasn't certain why he'd sat in his car for twenty minutes. Everything had piled on him at once: work, Maria, and his feelings of failure made the walk from his car to the front door seem like the Green Mile.

His phone rang and he dug in his pocket. It was Patty Levine again, and like the last few calls, he let it go directly to voice mail. He didn't want to talk about the Sheriff's Office or what a prick Ronald Bell was. He didn't know exactly what he wanted to do right now, so he took in a deep breath and stepped out of his car, marched to his front door, and entered, feeling almost as much apprehension as if he was on search warrant.

Helen sat on the living room couch with a tearful Maria. His sister was patting her back and listening. She looked up and gave him a mild nod, then flicked her head to get him moving into another room.

Even with all the classes and counseling sessions he'd attended, it was still hard to imagine this sort of emotion without a specific cause. He knew a lot of it stemmed from Jeanie but why now, after more than three years? He didn't try to figure it out anymore. His job was to keep the kids safe and support Maria any way he could.

In a weird way it made his problems at work seem less severe, until he thought about the dead girls and the fact that he wouldn't be helping stop the Bag Man.

Patty called again. Another voice mail.

He walked into the family room to see Charlie and Lauren watching TV silently.

"What's up, guys?"

They both mumbled "Nothing."

Was this how he wanted to live? To let his family fade into immobility?

"Hey, I'm home a little early. Let's go do something."

Charlie brightened. "Like what?"

"Don't know, sport. Dinner out."

"Mom too?"

"We might need to give her some space."

His phone rang with a number he didn't recognize. He'd given the phone number out to so many people in the past weeks that it could be anyone. He still didn't want to talk. He didn't answer, then noticed a minute later whoever it was left no message.

He dismissed it. Tonight was about the kids.

* * *

Tony Mazzetti had a mountain of reports from the lab, other detectives, and even streamed video from city surveillance cameras. Someone on command staff had the bright idea that if the beach cam caught Stacey Hines, another camera might hold a clue. What they didn't reason out was the volume and randomness of the tape. Sure, he'd have a secretary or intern take a cursory look at the video, so he didn't have to tell some captain or major they were a dumb ass, but the idea was as useful as standing on the corner and looking for a girl being abducted.

The reports from the other detectives were mostly about clearing up leads that had come in and then not been relevant to the case. Citizens calling in about weird neighbors, stolen suitcases that could be big enough for a body, and sightings of Stacey Hines everywhere from downtown Jacksonville to upstate Georgia. It never ended and was part of any big case with media coverage.

The lab reports mainly confirmed what the medical examiner had said. The girls' bodies all contained large amounts of prescription drugs, including Ambien, Oxycontin, heavy sedatives, and assorted other narcotics. He kept wondering why the killer wanted the victims so doped up. What did he do to them? There was no sexual assault. No marks other than to show that they had been restrained. It made no sense in this world, but Mazzetti knew the world of a serial killer was vastly different and skewed. It was the difference between *Gone with the Wind* and a Bugs Bunny cartoon. What was rational in one world held no power in the other. He had to find the link between the two worlds and figure out what the killer was doing and why, in his own mind, it was important enough for him to kill people.

One report from the crime scene unit was on the orange thread found near Trina Ester's body. He remembered the long, heavy piece of string. They had determined it was a carpet thread. Someone in the unit had even gone above and beyond the call of duty and talked to a couple of carpet dealers. He appreciated that they didn't waste a detective's time on a task like that.

One of the carpet dealers said it was an industrial carpet thread probably sold in large quantity to an institution like a hospital or school.

Mazzetti filed it away in his computer brain as something that might come up later, but he had more important matters on his plate right now. He'd lost one of the best detectives, or at least luckiest, when John Stallings was sent home. He didn't miss the glory hound, but had to admit the guy got things done.

The other matter occupying his mind was of a more personal nature. When he looked up from his work and saw Patty Levine across the room he decided to handle that right now.

Stacey Hines woke up in the dark, silent room where she'd been held for a while. She didn't know how long, because it was hard to tell time in this place, and she had no idea how long she slept each time he gave her a dose of drugs. This was the first time she'd ever woken up quickly and without the overhead light battering her eyes. The dark was almost as terrifying as seeing William standing at the door with a tray of food and that spooky smile on his face.

She had no idea if anyone even knew she was in trouble and now realized the few restrictions her parents put on her were not enough to scare her away. If she got out of here, she was moving back home for good.

She didn't let herself cry; that didn't help anything. She sucked it up and tried to think if she could use this quiet, conscious time in the room to help her escape. She worked her hands in the cuffs, then tried her feet. Nothing. Then she heard footsteps outside the door and decided to play possum and not let William know the drug dosage wasn't enough to keep her asleep all night.

She had to try anything she could if she wanted to live.

Patty Levine closed her phone on the fourth time she got John Stallings's voice mail message. She knew he'd been relieved of duty just like she knew he'd never call a TV station. Why would he? All she wanted to do was make sure he was okay. He was tough. Tougher than anyone she'd ever met. With all that he'd been through she wasn't the least bit worried about him making it through something like this. But she still wanted to speak to her partner.

She glanced across the wide squad bay of the detective bureau, and Tony Mazzetti quietly caught her eye with a wink and a smile. She couldn't help but smile back. She watched as he carefully disguised a route across the busy room to her. He picked up a couple of file folders, then looked at them as he walked. He leaned down next to her, holding a folder open like he needed advice on something.

Patty hid her grin. "What was that wink for?"

"A hint at tonight."

Her smile broadened. "Pretty confident there, Detective Mazzetti."

"Actually, no I'm not. But you've given me hope that I won't freeze up."

She looked at the bags under his eyes and lines on his face. "Are you sure you're up to it? You look beat."

"I've waited long enough."

She considered her next comments. "I'd like to talk to John before I leave."

"That traitor, why?"

"He's no traitor. It's a mistake, and if you want me to look favorably on you, don't say another thing."

He shut his mouth.

She wanted to pat him on the head like a puppy and say, "Good boy." Instead, she said, "How about my condo tonight?"

Mazzetti said, "I'm gonna be late."

"Somehow I'll survive." She smiled, knowing he could take a joke.

The report of Lori's accidental electrocution was barely mentioned at the pharmacy. The manager told the employees first thing in the morning, then the store got busy. The only thing really bothering Dremmel about her death was the lack of sleep. He'd been up late with Lori, then gone home to Stacey. He'd dozed off for one hour at the house before coming into work and feigning surprise and chagrin at the news that Lori was dead.

The manager had even said, "It was just shitty electrical wiring in a shitty old house. All of Durkeeville should be bulldozed."

A help-wanted notice was on the Internet before lunch.

Dremmel felt pretty pleased with himself for the efficient and well-disguised job he'd done on Lori. On another level he didn't want to dwell on what he thought might be remorse. He'd made Lori part of his game, but she didn't deserve it. She'd been nice to him. She liked him. He already missed her smile around the pharmacy. But she knew too much. That's what he had to keep telling himself. She knew too much.

Luckily, he had other things to focus on. He'd spent part of the day researching other drugs and dosages for Stacey. She'd seemed hard to rouse this morning when he brought her breakfast and tried to spend time with her before work. Maybe he'd been going a little heavy on the sedatives. He could lighten it up for a few days to let her get back on a normal schedule. Stacey presented some challenges.

And she wasn't the only one. He already had a plan to deal with the pretty JSO detective. He knew where she lived and that she lived alone. His heart raced just at the thought of her lying in the little bed next to Stacey.

Life was sweet.

Tony Mazzetti had driven like a maniac, or, as they said here in Florida, driven like a New Yorker, to get to his house, shower, grab a protein shake, and change. He shaved and used Dolce & Gabbana balm on his face so there'd be no way he could give Patty a beard burn anywhere on her smokin' little body.

His house on a canal that led to the St. Johns River could've been the model of a bachelor pad from the seventies. It was clean, neat, and furnished with some of the funkiest furniture Mazzetti and his mother could find seven years ago when he bought the three-bedroom with a deck built to the edge of the water. He had visions of parties and an endless stream of women when he took out a loan that terrified him. But that was before he figured out that no one really liked him. It was tough to throw a party when only a couple of detectives spoke to you on a regular basis, and the guys you hung with at the gym didn't even know your name. He was pretty sure a couple of them had felony records, which meant he was supposed to steer clear of them or face questions about consorting with felons. It hardly ever happened, but was still a no-no for cops certified in Florida. He didn't want to hang out with shit-birds anyway.

He took an extra minute to dress casually, but well, for his big date with the first woman he could relax with in a long, long time. She'd like his odd taste in interior design. She appreciated his work ethic. She liked his smile. His fucking smile! No one had ever told him that before.

He made a quick check to make sure the house was perfect in case she wanted to come over here in the morning or even later tonight. There was so much he wanted to show her that it made him start grinning like a goddamn Patriots fan after Belichik cheated his way to another AFC championship.

He rifled through his nightstand to find the condoms he'd bought six years ago but had never used, sitting on the edge of the bed as he fumbled through reading lights, old issues of *Civil War Times,* and a cupful of change. The simple act of sitting and removing the pressure from his legs and back made him relax almost instantly. He'd been on full speed since early in the morning and missing sleep most nights. He laid back on the soft Posturepedic, feeling it support his back and neck as his lower legs dangled off the side of the bed. He shut his eyes for a moment and felt the world rush away, then saw a cloud with a monkey in the Union officer's uniform float by. His own snores didn't even wake him up.

Thirty-nine

John Stallings looked over his Sprite at Charlie and Lauren as they debated the virtues of PlayStation versus Wii game system. Next to them in the booth at Chili's were Maria and Helen, staring across at each other with the wall to their sides. Stallings intentionally jammed his wife against the wall, away from any possible egress. It was a risk bringing her along at all. His intention was to keep the kids' minds off the family problems, but Helen suggested they make it a family adventure and now he saw she was right. The kids liked as many adults around as possible and responded well to it. He wondered if it was a safety issue in the back of their minds.

He'd been very quiet, pretending to listen to the children. In fact, his mind kept playing out the events of the day and then back to that stupid phone bill and the call to the TV station. He'd done a little of his own checking and there was no doubt that a call to the station was made on his phone. That's what stumped him. He had no real recourse to appeal the decision because, as usual, Rita Hester had tried to take care of him. He hadn't been suspended or even technically punished. Just moved off a case. A case that was his lifeline, his chance to restore something inside himself. He couldn't explain exactly what had been pushing him so hard, but now that he could no longer work the case he felt the void even more acutely.

But the kids helped him. The tall waiter, who looked as if he lifted weights more hours a day than he slept, squeezed in next to the booth. Stallings had noticed Lauren stare at the handsome young man's smile, and he flashed it again.

He looked across at Helen and Maria and said, "Could I bring the ladies a couple of strawberry margaritas? They're two for one."

Helen shook her head and said, "No, thank you."

"C'mon, they're pretty good."

Helen shook her head again as Maria stared straight ahead, chanting some silent mantra.

"What if I bring out a little sample?"

Stallings tapped the man's arm, then motioned him to lean down. He whispered, "If you bring out a sampler I'll break that pretty nose of yours. She said no twice." He smiled and winked to disguise the threat from the kids. The waiter scrambled back to the kitchen on some unknown quest.

Stallings looked up as the kids resumed their game console debate and Helen stared at him with a look of horror. She knew him too well.

All he could do was shrug. Maybe Patty was right; he was a little on the aggressive side. He'd work on reining it in.

His phone rang and his first impulse was to just ignore it. Everyone in the world that he wanted to talk to was with him right now. That thought comforted and calmed him down. But the years of being tied to the phone forced him to at least look down to see who was calling. No number showed on the screen. Someone was calling from a blocked phone. He wanted to just shut it but he had to flip the phone open and see who it was.

The restaurant's thick roof and heavy walls blocked most of the signal.

"John Stallings," he answered in a professional tone. All he got was static with little bits of a man's voice.

"I'm sorry, I can't hear you."

More static and maybe someone calling out a name.

Stallings listened intently, blocking out the kids, terrified waiter, sullen wife, and spooky sister. Then he thought someone said "Ernie," but he wasn't sure as the line went dead.

He'd worry about it tomorrow when he tried to restart his life with his family and see if he really could walk away from the Bag Man.

William Dremmel still felt alert even after all this time without sleep. He cut out of work an hour early, but that had nothing to do with exhaustion. Now, as he slowly circled the neighborhood where Detective Patty Levine lived, looking for surveillance or security cameras, a parked police cruiser, or just an abnormal number of people on the street, he felt the excitement shoot through him. He'd had an erection since six o'clock thinking about the cute detective, but he guessed she had that effect on every man.

This was one of the few times he had no real plan and intended to make it up as opportunities presented themselves. He didn't have enough of her schedule to intercept her on the way to an appointment. But here, where she might be off guard, he thought he had a chance at surprise. He looked down at his container of homemade chloroform. That would do the trick if he could just get close enough.

Her condo was set off the road. Four stories high with three units on each floor. She had the bottom corner, which, with all the extra windows, he figured to be one of the nicer units. Her parking space was next to the walkway that led to her front door. A Jeep Wrangler, parked an aisle back, was her personal vehicle. He'd found it on a Web site site listing vehicles in Florida. It was backed into the slot, like a cop would do it, and covered by a corrugated aluminum roof that ran in each direction over the second parking space for each unit.

Just as he turned the corner again to drive past her building, Dremmel saw her unmarked police SUV pull into the spot in front of the condo.

She got out, walked around, and pulled bags of groceries from the passenger side, leaving the door open for her next trip back.

Dremmel beamed at the setup. This was just perfect.

Patty Levine struggled with just under half of the grocery bags in the car, tilting her small frame back to balance the load as her house key dangled from her right hand. She knew she should've given Tony Mazzetti a firm time of when to show up so she wouldn't rush like this, but she liked the thrill of just being surprised.

She'd given up trying to reach John Stallings. That was just like him, ignoring anyone who was concerned about him. In a way she was happy he had some time to see his family. She knew that tomorrow they'd have a long talk and work out whatever was going on with his supposed contact with the TV station. Tonight was about getting her own life on track.

She felt herself smiling, just thinking about the break from work and the chance to start a new romance. This was always the best time of a relationship. You had an idea where it was going, were attracted to the person, and you hadn't spent enough time with them for their little quirks to annoy the crap out of you. She wished she could freeze a moment like this. Simple, fun, and perfect.

Patty hurried back out to her Freestyle, grabbed the remaining bags, then started her awkward tilted walk back toward her condo's open door. It was cool enough out that she wasn't worried about mosquitoes or other flying pests invading the condo in the thirty seconds she left the door open.

She had made it though the doorway, kicked the heavy wooden door shut with her foot, and started toward the kitchen when she thought she heard something move behind her. Before she turned to see if it was her cat Cornelia, she noticed the plump feline on her regular perch next to her TV.

Then she froze as she felt someone step up behind her. Her heart skipped a beat as she prepared for Tony Mazzetti's muscular arms to envelop her. She didn't move to set down the bags as she briefly saw a hand reach around from behind her, then clamp down over her mouth and nose.

Instinctively she dropped the groceries and struggled to turn and face the person behind her, but her vision faded quickly as she became light-headed and unsteady. She vaguely heard a man say, "Don't worry, I've got you," as everything faded to black.

Forty

John Stallings's head pounded as soon as he opened his eyes to the rising sun peeping through the window nearest his side of the bed. Out of habit he reached over to feel Maria next to him. His hand brushed her naked thigh and a smile crept across his face not only because she was safe in bed with him but because she had the most beautiful legs he'd ever seen, and touching them was a thrill he didn't take for granted.

He had almost thirty minutes before getting the kids up and making breakfast. It was the rare quiet moments like this that he'd avoided over the last few years. Time to think about what he had lost and how he had staggered to this place in his life. Time to reason out how to protect Lauren and Charlie from the devastation of addiction. He had considered divorce, not because he didn't love Maria—he did—but for the sake of the kids and their sanity. Every family has hard choices to make at some point, but his seemed harder than most. Maybe his father did play a larger role in his life than he wanted to admit.

For now his quiet time was spent thinking about the Bag Man and what he could've done differently to stop him. This line of reflection also encompassed his transfer back to missing persons. His stomach turned at the thought of Ronald Bell. The I.A. weasel wouldn't fabricate evidence, so that left him back where he started until it hit him all at once: his friend Rick Ellis used his phone that day, purportedly to call his captain.

Stallings now knew his first task for the day.

Tony Mazzetti blinked hard a couple of times at the harsh light hitting him in the face and waking him up. Instantly he remembered Patty and sat up straight. How long had he been dozing? He looked over at his clock and saw it wasn't even eight yet. Plenty of time. He relaxed, surprised at how stiff he was from a ten-minute nap on the side of his bed. Then he realized what the light that had awakened him was—the sun. He grabbed the small alarm clock and looked closely. It was eight in the fucking morning. Oh shit.

He jumped up and rushed to the bathroom, brushing his teeth while he used the toilet. Then he washed his face furiously before he slowed his pace and then just stopped, staring down into the sink's basin. He was twelve hours late. She didn't want to see him now.

He padded back to his bedroom and checked his phone. No one had called since Lieutenant Hester the night before. He'd blown it, and he knew it. The condoms mocked him from the dresser.

He thought about calling her but didn't know what he'd say. He did know saying something was better than saying nothing. He listened as her phone rang, imagining her looking at the number, shaking her head, and throwing her phone across the room.

Then Patty's prerecorded sweet voice came on, telling him to leave a message.

"Hey, it's, um, me. Call me when you get this. I'm sorry. It was just a mistake. I'll explain when we talk." He cut off the call and plopped back onto the bed. For a guy who just slept twelve hours he didn't feel rested at all.

Patty felt her eyes open, but her vision wasn't clear. It felt as if she was wearing someone else's glasses and nothing was in focus. She had no idea what had happened. Maybe she fainted, or the exhaustion caught up with her.

When she tried to move she couldn't. She wasn't paralyzed. Someone had restrained her. Patty's first thought was that she'd had a seizure and this was some special hospital unit. Turning her head she saw a figure across the room in a bed, but her vision was still burry.

Panic rose in her throat as she considered how scared her mom must be or if anyone had even notified her yet. She tested the restraints and wiggled under the cover. She was naked, that much she could tell. The restraints were like handcuffs and her hands were suspended above her head. That wasn't like a hospital. Something was terribly wrong.

Patty struggled harder and croaked out a scream from her dry throat. "Hey. Anyone." She couldn't manage much more than that.

The door creaked open, letting in natural light. She then realized one floor lamp had provided all the light in the room. A man's figure waited at the door, looking at her. Then he said, "I'm not quite ready for you yet."

"Ready for what? Who are you? Where am I?" She

had more questions but lost them in the crackling dust of her throat.

The man moved toward her with something in his hand. As he got closer her eyes focused and she realized she knew the man from somewhere. He bent down and placed a soft cloth over her face.

Patty tried to bite him but also recognized him. This was the guy from the pharmacy. She had specific questions, but before she could ask, everything turned blurry, then dark again.

John Stallings sat in his Impala near the intersection of Atlantic Boulevard and South University just east of the St. Johns River. He knew where there'd been increasing complaints of speeders and media reports of needless accidents. He listened carefully to his handheld radio as the traffic unit called out speeders to other patrolmen down the road. It was an efficient net to slow people down and cost a few drivers points on their license as well as increased insurance premiums.

His phone had been quiet this morning. Patty had apparently taken the hint and the others had enough class not to call him. That was fine. He didn't want to talk to anyone until he had proof that he was owed an apology and got another chance to clear his conscience and catch the Bag Man.

Then he heard the call on the radio. This was his chance and they weren't too far away. He pulled out of the convenience store he'd been sitting in and drove east down Atlantic Boulevard. After a couple of miles he saw the two cruisers parked on the shoulder of the road. The ancient rite of the patrolman passing off paperwork to his sergeant.

Stallings eased in behind them, making sure they realized it was an unmarked police car. He gave his blue lights mounted at the top of his windshield a quick flash until he saw each man wave from inside. It was a courtesy and would keep him from being shot if he surprised them.

He walked alongside the supervisor's car as the door opened, then Stallings stopped near the trunk of the car.

Stallings said, "Rick, we gotta talk."

Sergeant Rick Ellis smiled and said, "Sure, what do you want to talk about?"

Stallings looked down at the ground, gathering his thoughts, then up into the big man's face. "First of all, we should talk about if you want me to kick your ass in front of your man. Then we'll decide how our chat will go after that."

Forty-one

John Stallings told himself to keep cool and not do anything stupid. There could be an explanation. Rick might not have anything to do with it, and this could be a waste of time. But something in the sergeant's face told Stallings that was all bullshit. He had his man. He acted as if Stallings's threat to kick his ass was just a joke.

Ellis stayed calm and casually strolled to the rear of the cruiser, cars on the road all slowing down as they approached, fearing a speed trap or rubbernecking to see the poor jerk who got stopped already. Once away from the road and between the cruisers, the big sergeant wrapped an arm around Stallings's shoulder and said, "What can I do for you, pal?"

Stallings gave him every chance. "I got removed from the Bag Man case."

"No shit? Why?"

"They claim I called Channel Eleven." He kept his eyes on Ellis's face, which didn't let out any hints.

"That's crazy, Stall. You wouldn't do that."

"I know that, and you know that, but they still believe it."

"Why? What's their evidence?"

"My cell phone. There's a call to the station from my phone." He noticed Ellis swallow hard, his Adam's apple bobbing.

"That can be a mistake. Shit, the cell companies keep records as accurately as a terrorist smoking pot." He wiped his forehead with his sleeve. "They're all riled up and clueless at the same time."

Stallings intensified his stare. "Rick, the call was made the day Luis Martinez capped the pot grower."

"There you go, it couldn't have been you. You were on the scene all day."

Stallings clenched his fist, ready to revert to his own ways of doing things. "Cut the shit, Rick."

Ellis stared at him then said, "Whaddya mean?"

Just the stare from Stallings made the big uniformed man wince.

The sergeant took a step back and held up his hands. "Don't rat me out, Stall, I'm in my last year." Then he started to cry.

Stallings released his fist, and all he could do was shake his head.

"Why?"

Now Ellis couldn't look at him. "It's a job for retirement. The company that owns Channel Eleven needs a director of security and this was my ticket."

Stallings just shook his head and turned around.

He had to find Patty and explain it to her.

William Dremmel caught himself humming while he used an electric griddle to cook scrambled eggs, ham, and pancakes. Although it was early afternoon he knew his two houseguests would be waking up soon, and he wanted them to feel like it was morning. Plus the meal he was making had plenty of protein in it.

His mother had surprised him early by rolling out of her room, across the walkway, and into the main section of the house. She had clear eyes, and her complexion gave her a healthy look he'd not seen in almost a year. She wore a bright yellow blouse that showed off her cleavage and nice form for an older woman. As always, she wore a long dress to hide her battered and unused legs. Even he hadn't seen her legs in a long time. Her smile and pleasant greeting made him feel a twinge of guilt for keeping her so heavily sedated. He'd thought she was fading and initially justified the heavy narcotics as a way to ease her pain, but that was rubbish. He needed his privacy, had thought about how his father had been pushed too far, and decided to take matters into his own hands. In his defense he had no plans to tranquilize her again today. She was safely down the steps in the family room watching the big-screen TV and enjoying the sun shining in through the rows of jalousie windows. Without his help she couldn't wheel herself up into the living room, then past his bedroom all the way to his darkroom/lab.

This was a day of firsts. His mother was alert and connected to reality, and he had not one, but two test subjects. He hoped to keep them in the trial for a very long and interesting time. And he had called in sick for the first time in his entire life. He let the manager at the pharmacy think he was upset by Lori's death and told the head of the science department at the community college that his back had gone out and hinted that it might be the result of teaching too many labs on the hard floors. Just the idea of a worker's comp issue made the professor encourage Dremmel to take off as long as he needed.

Now he was doing exactly what he wanted—running a serious experiment with two beautiful women and nothing connecting him to any of the recent crimes. He had slipped Patty Levine away from her complex after he put up her groceries, fed the cat, and moved her personal Jeep to a Walmart lot three blocks away. It was a risk to leave the unconscious detective for the few minutes it took to move the Jeep, but he thought it would pay dividends in confusing the cops when they tried to figure out where she was or what had happened. She didn't regain consciousness until she was secured. He used a lot less of his homemade chloroform a few hours ago when he dosed her again. He wanted her up and awake soon.

He looked at the clipboard that held the data sheets for both women. Stacey was becoming quite regular in her habits based on the dosages he had been administering. Patty's chart was blank, but he intended to start her on the heavy, powered Ambien with some hydrocodone this evening. He wanted both the women on different drugs to see the effects. He didn't have the time or resources to test each drug on each subject.

His mother appeared in the doorway but was unable to roll up the steps.

"What are you looking at, William?"

"Data on an experiment I'm running."

She beamed. "How interesting. You'll have to tell me all about it."

"I will, Mom, after we eat."

"You've made a lot of eggs and pancakes for just the two of us."

"I'm trying to bulk up a little, so I'm gonna eat all day long while I work in the darkroom. If I let you stay up and in the family room, will you promise to let me work?"

"I promise. Will you spend a little time with me later?"

"We can watch *Jeopardy!*"

She clasped her hands. "Just like we used to. That's great."

He smiled back at her, but something about her voice and her manner made an ancient memory flash through his brain. It felt like a faded image reflected in a mirror. It made no sense, but he felt its power over him.

His stomach turned as he stared at his mother, smiling contently in her chair.

John Stallings was a little worried about Patty when he couldn't get her on the cell phone and the secretary at the D-Bureau told him she hadn't been in yet. He didn't want to be seen in the office yet as he considered how best to explain what had happened. He had a couple of leads he could work without being officially back on the Bag Man case anyway. He hoped that Rick Ellis would come forward and explain everything himself.

Now Stallings was at Patty's little condo in the southeast part of the city, where a lot of the college students lived. The neighborhood had an arty vibe to it as he imagined Greenwich Village did or some sections of New Orleans. Her modern, plain condo building seemed out of place among the older, Southern-style houses with porches and tin roofs. As he pulled into the small lot he immediately noticed Patty's county-issued Freestyle in a spot closest to her door. He didn't see her Jeep anywhere.

Stallings slowly marched up the walkway, looking to see if there was any activity around any of the other condo units. He knocked on Patty's door and waited, then knocked again and called out, "Patty, it's John." Then he called her again, but the phone went directly to voice mail. That was odd for Patty, who always wanted to stay in contact and was too conscientious about work to just ignore calls.

He turned to leave, dialing the office again to see if the secretary could reach her. He couldn't think why she'd be ignoring his calls, but anything was possible. As he reached his car he stopped, looked up, and was surprised to see Tony Mazzetti getting out of his county Crown Vic.

Mazzetti said, "What's wrong, Stall, need another source of info for your TV pals?"

Then without consciously knowing he would do it, Stallings punched Tony Mazzetti in the face so hard it knocked the larger man off his feet and onto the sidewalk.

Forty-two

Tony Mazzetti held his eye with his left hand, even though it didn't ease the pain in any way. "What the fuck, Stall?"

"You run that mouth of yours and don't expect to get hit?"

"Not a sucker punch."

"I was standing in front of you and hit you in the face. That's not a sucker punch." Stallings offered a hand to help Mazzetti to his feet.

Mazzetti grunted as he took it and slowly rose. Blood pulsed through his head and seemed to circle his left eye, where the blow had struck hardest.

Stallings said, "What the hell are you doing here?"

"Looking for Patty."

"Why?"

"Whaddya mean 'why'? I just am."

Stallings looked him up and down, then said, "Are you two a couple?"

Mazzetti hesitated on his answer mainly because he had no idea how Patty felt about it.

Stallings turned away and said, "Aw shit. I think I'm gonna be sick."

"I was worried because I couldn't get ahold of her."

"I couldn't either."

"And the office hasn't heard from her, so I came over to check. We were supposed to see each other last night. But . . ."

Stallings looked at him like he expected him to finish his sentence.

"But I fell asleep."

"You stood up a girl like Patty. You really are an asshole."

"Should we call in that she's missing?"

Stallings thought about it, then said, "Is she missing or just avoiding us? It can cause a lot of shit to call in a missing person if she's not missing."

Mazzetti looked at Stallings and realized that was hard for him to say. For the first time he saw some of the dilemma Stallings faced the day his daughter went missing. He didn't want to overreact either. There was no indication that anything bad had happened to Patty. Then he felt his stomach turn. That was the same thing he had told dozens of worried parents over the years, and he knew it wasn't necessarily true.

Stallings's phone rang and he had it up to his ear in a flash. "Stallings. Yeah. Really? Where?" That was the only part of the short conversation that Mazzetti heard.

"Was that Patty?"

Stallings shook his head. "No. A dealer named Ernie who has some info on the Bag Man. I need to go talk to him."

"You're not even on the case anymore."

"Look, Tony, I didn't make the call to Channel Eleven. I know who did. He used my phone. But it wasn't me."

"Even if I believed you, the L.T. makes those decisions."

"She's not around, and I'm going to talk to this guy. Then I'm gonna find Patty."

Mazzetti was starting to see how this guy got so many things done.

William Dremmel was ready to enter the lion's den, or a least the small room where he had two wildcats chained up. He'd made sure his mother was completely involved in *The Quiet Man* with John Wayne and Maureen O'Hara before he prepared himself to enter his lab. He still had a butterfly in his stomach over the memory he'd been trying to pull up. He knew it had to do with his mother and him. And he knew it was wrong in some sense. But he couldn't nail it down. He had no models to compare his relationship with his mother with, so he had to go by his gut on many issues. His gut told him that she was not a typical mom. He felt certain the memory was more dysfunctional than drugging her most nights, but now he had a different emotion brewing in him, and he had no idea what it was or how to handle it.

He knew the old movie was one of his mother's favorites and would keep her occupied for another hour and a half. That would give him time to deal directly with his lovely test subjects.

At the door to the lab, he stood with his stun gun stashed in the front pocket of his baggy cargo shorts. On a tray he had two paper plates with plastic spoons. Each plate was piled high with eggs and finely chopped ham. He had two glasses of orange juice and a plastic bowl of strawberries in an effort to vary the subjects' diets and provide nutrients other than the vitamins in the supplements and shakes he fed them.

He unlocked the door with his single key, opened the door, then picked up the tray of food from the foyer table and entered the room casually, closing the door immediately behind him. He was shocked by the two sets of angry eyes meeting him. The detective's stare was even more venomous than Stacey's, and she had tried to kill him the first chance she got.

This whole situation might be trickier than he had calculated.

John Stallings was surprised when Mazzetti insisted on coming with him to talk to Ernie the dealer. Now, as Stallings craned his neck to locate the young man on a corner near the interstate, he had to contend with Mazzetti and his constant chatter. It had to be a New York thing.

Mazzetti said, "This guy is a good source, huh?"

"He knew Lee Ann Moffitt and spoke up. If he heard something else, I'm willing to listen." Stallings looked at him. "But you're going to have to not be you."

"Whaddya mean?"

"Just don't talk. He's a little skittish as it is."

"But it's my fucking case."

"That's what I mean. All I care about is stopping the killer. You can take credit any way you want."

Mazzetti sat mercifully quiet for a few minutes, then said, "Look, Stall, I'm sorry if I was out of line about anything I ever said about your daughter's disappearance."

Stallings didn't answer.

"I never realized, I mean I never saw things from the

victim's point of view. I'm sure Patty is off working things out and that's why she hasn't called, but it's still nerve-racking."

"You got the secretary figuring out what she was working on last?"

"Yeah, she's been canvassing drugstores in the southeast part of the city. I got Hoagie backtracking who she talked to. We knew she made it home last night."

"And you were too lazy to show her the respect she deserves."

Mazzetti just looked down at the dash.

Stallings saw Ernie and pulled into a Shell station on the corner. The young drug dealer hustled over to them, then hesitated when he saw Mazzetti sitting in the passenger seat.

Stallings got out of the Impala and motioned Mazzetti to stay put. He led the nervous young man away from the car.

Ernie said, "Who's that?"

"No one, just an idiot who jumped in my car. Ignore him." When they were under the shade of the canopy covering the gas pumps, he said, "Now, what do you got for me?"

"I met the guy who used to sell to Lee Ann."

"Where is he?"

"He left the city last night. Everyone's scared the way the cops are coming down on people. He needed cash, so he was going to Atlanta for a few weeks."

"What'd he say?"

"He said Lee Ann stopped buying from him right before she was found dead, because she'd met a guy who worked at a pharmacy and she thought he might become a good source for her and for the dealer. She never got back to him."

"Did she say anything about the pharmacy guy?"

"He's a blond guy. That's it. I asked him a lot of questions. Just like a cop."

"What's your dealer friend's name?"

Ernie just gave him a look. "He goes by the name 'Malachi,' but I don't use last names. You know that."

"If I get the Atlanta cops to find him you think he'll talk to me?"

"He didn't really know Lee Ann that well except he sold to her a few times. He said she worked at Kinko's."

"Yeah, that's right. Sounds like she had a connection with someone at a pharmacy too. I'll start checking the pharmacies near the Kinko's." He put his arm around Ernie. "You're a good kid. You need to try and find a real job."

"I just applied for one."

"Really. Doing what?"

He broke out in a broad smile. "I want to be a fireman."

Stallings laughed, slapped him on the back, and said, "Good for you."

At the PMB, in the Land That Time Forgot, Stallings and Mazzetti sat at the conference room table looking at a list of stores Patty had visited in the last few days. They had already talked to the stores she canvassed yesterday to see if there was any connection or any strange blond employee. Nothing.

Tony Mazzetti appreciated the odd looks everyone gave him when he walked in with Stallings. The lieutenant wasn't around, so he didn't have to explain himself to anyone. He believed Stallings now when he said he didn't call the media, but he wouldn't say who did.

Stallings obviously knew who had used his phone and said he handled it, but Mazzetti's curious nature made it hard to let go.

Stallings shook his head. "Beats me where she is. I say we call in the cavalry."

"Is this why it took so long for you to call in your daughter's disappearance? Not sure she was really missing?"

Stallings looked at him like he was trying to decide how trustworthy Mazzetti was. "Just between us, Tony?"

"I swear." He raised his right hand to emphasize his sincerity.

"I been over this with I.A. With that dickhead, Ronald Bell, specifically."

"What happened?" He was interested and concerned for the first time.

"The main delay in calling it in was that my wife was high at the time. I mean out of her mind on Oxy and Percocets. She couldn't have been more incoherent if she was mainlining heroin. I had to deal with her, thinking she knew where Jeanie was, keep the whole mess away from the other kids, then, by the time I knew something was wrong she was so unhinged that I couldn't let the detectives talk to her."

Mazzetti just stared, never realizing something like that could've happened but seeing it for the truth right off the bat. He felt like a shithead for the things he thought and the way he'd treated this poor guy. Jesus.

"To this day Maria is confused about the whole thing. Jeanie's disappearance nearly knocked her over the edge, but we've been bringing her back little by little."

"She doin' okay now?"

Stallings just looked at him but didn't answer. Then he said, "We gotta find Patty."

"Let's get to work."

Stallings said, "I'll go by the next set of pharmacies. You go through her notes and desk, talk to the other detectives, and let the L.T. know that we're concerned but not panicked." Then he added, "Yet."

William Dremmel had been staring at the information he'd found on Maggie Gilson and wondered if there was room for three in that little lab of his. Was he getting out of control? From one test subject every couple of weeks to two at once seemed bad enough but then to think that a third would make things even more interesting scared him a little. Maybe he was misguided on his research and treatment of his subjects. Maybe his mother had unbalanced him more than he thought.

It was easier to be abstract away from the test subjects, whom he had allowed to stay conscious as long as they were quiet. The only thing that Detective Levine had said to him was, "These cuffs are cutting off my circulation. You need to loosen them." It wasn't a question or request, it was an order. He hadn't been offended by it either. She was an expert in the use of handcuffs and she felt this set was too tight. He'd decided that after he dosed them and they were out cold, he'd loosen both sets of cuffs. It made sense. He didn't want unnecessary pain and medical issues that might infringe on his findings.

Now, sitting in the family room, watching *Casablanca* with his mother, Dremmel shifted uncomfortably on the sofa with his mother's wheelchair parked next to it.

"What's wrong, sweetheart? You can tell me." His mother put a small hand on his broad shoulder and started to knead the thick band of muscle. "C'mon, you used to share everything with me."

"I'm fine, Mom."

"I can see in your eyes that something is bothering you."

He shook his head. "I don't know, something is stuck in my head."

"What?"

"It's some kind of memory or nightmare from my childhood."

"Can you recall any details, dear?"

"It involves you and maybe a man."

She smiled as she looked off.

Dremmel said, "It's not a dream, is it?" It started to become clearer in his mind.

"What does the man look like?"

He hesitated. "A young black man?"

Now she was grinning. "Arthur. Such a sweet young man."

"It's true. You and him. In the . . ." He remembered it all and how it had ruined his life.

Forty-three

Tony Mazzetti had never experienced emotions like this. He was scared. Not the way he was scared of cockroaches or scared of the dentist; this feeling was on an entirely different level. Now, for the first time, he understood why families were so freaked out when someone was missing even if his experience told him they would turn up soon enough.

John Stallings had kept him calm when they were together, but now Stallings was out retracing her steps and Mazzetti was feeling the creep of panic rise in his throat with every phone call he made. He'd talked to Patty's mother and tried not to alarm her; he told her he was a coworker of Patty's. He doubted she'd been told of any real relationship between her daughter and him, but he sure as shit intended to start one up once he found her.

He focused on using his considerable experience and training to figure out who might know where Patty was. Whom she might have talked to. What she might have done. Somehow this was easier when he didn't know the missing person and had no personal stake.

Lieutenant Hester was calling up some help right now to see if more people looking for her would make a difference as the command staff weighed the value of going to the media.

His phone's ring made him jump as he racked his brain for ideas.

"Mazzetti, here."

"Tony, it's Hoagie."

"Whaddya got?"

"We found her car at a Walmart a couple of blocks from her house."

"Let's get crime scene over there right now to see what we can find."

"They're here. Once they learned it had to do with a missing cop they got off their asses and were here at the same time as me."

"Anything?" He wasn't sure he wanted to hear about blood or anything else that would indicate she was hurt.

"Nothing."

He relaxed, and, at the same time, was disappointed they didn't have a lead to find her.

Christina Hogrebe said, "Tony, I mean nothing at all. Someone wiped down the steering wheel and driver's door. There are no prints of value. We're checking the store video now, but so far it doesn't look as if she came inside."

"Any outside cameras?"

"Not in the area where her Jeep was left."

"Thanks, Hoagie. Keep on it."

"Tony, you okay? You sound funny."

"Just worried. We gotta find her."

"We'll break something open soon."

He hung up without another word, hoping the young homicide detective was right.

William Dremmel's head spun as the impact of what his mother had told him sunk in. He had seen her and the yardman's son, Arthur, having sex. Many times. He would hide in the wide closet and watch them through the slats in the door. Arthur's rock-hard, trim body and the way his mother would so carefully take him in her own small hands or how he would fondle her round breasts with pink nipples.

She was very pretty twenty-five years ago. She wore small, tight dresses and flirted with the neighbors. She even had her photo in the *Times-Union* once when they were all on Neptune Beach and she was in a bikini. The caption identified her as "Local beauty enjoying the sun at Neptune Beach." She had the clipping some-where in the house.

One Saturday in October, Dremmel remembered it was in the fall because he'd been teased by some kids for the Halloween costume he was previewing to everyone. It was a Wolf Man mask with hairy gloves he was supposed to wear with a long-sleeved shirt. Doug Cifers, from down the street, had called him a "were-dork" and made Dremmel cry as he ran back to his house, breathless and ready to tell his mom. He had vaguely noticed the old pickup truck with a hand-scrawled sign that said, "Whitley Yard Service," parked down the block and Mr. Whitley pruning some trees as the sun started to set.

He rushed in the house, then toward his parent's bed-room. The door was open just a crack and he froze, then peered around the door. His mother was on her knees, naked, and Arthur was standing in front of her.

He was fascinated. Arthur looked so happy as his mother's head bobbed up and down.

Then he heard a noise, turned, and his heart almost stopped. Standing behind him also watching the show was his father.

John Stallings impatiently flicked open his phone, not bothering to even glance at the number. "Stallings," he barked, keeping his pace on the sidewalk toward the front door to a family-run pharmacy.

"John, it's Helen."

He paused before asking what was wrong.

She added, "You know, your sister."

"Funny, what's up? I'm right in the middle of something."

"So am I, and it's called your fucked-up life."

"What?"

"Maria is still sort of catatonic, and I think you need to be here."

He sighed and stopped walking as he tried to think what to say and what to do.

"John, did you hear me? Your wife needs you here at home."

"Are the kids okay?"

"Yeah, I drove them over to Mom's under the guise that she needed help around the house for which they'd be paid a high hourly rate. But I could tell Lauren didn't buy it."

"Yeah, she's smart. Nothing gets by her."

"So let her see her father help her mother."

Stallings shifted his weight from foot to foot, taking

up the empty sidewalk with a nervous lateral shuffle. His mind raced through the responsibilities he had and the pressure of keeping it all together. He thought of Maria and how far she'd come. Then he imagined Patty in trouble, counting on him for a rescue. He needed a minute and took a deep breath, aware of the silence on the other end of the phone.

He almost told Helen he'd be right there, but he looked up at the pharmacy sign and thought of Patty. "Helen, I can't make it right now. Something's come up. We got a missing cop."

"John, this is your life here. There's always gonna be someone missing. You can't be the only one looking."

"No, but I am right now, and I need to be out here."

"That's one of the problems, John. You can't see the difference between what you need to do and what you want to do."

"I need to find this missing cop. Can you stay with Maria a little longer? Please, Sis."

"You have to make a choice, John. Work or family, because I don't think they can coexist any longer."

"Were you always a ball breaker, or did you develop this attitude recently?"

"I learned it on the street when I ran away. I just never had to use it on you. You turned out to be the opposite of Dad. At least I thought you did. You need to get your shit together, little brother."

"I appreciate you staying with her and helping. I swear I'll . . ." She'd hung up on him before he made a promise he couldn't keep.

Patty Levine had spent more than an hour breathing deeply and steadily, hoping to clear her mind so she could think her way out of the deep shit she was in. She had to stay calm not just for herself, but for the other prisoner, Stacey Hines. The younger woman, really just a girl, had talked nonstop after their captor had left, leaving them both conscious. Now Patty realized she wasn't sure how long he'd be away. It was hard to imagine what this girl had gone through at the hands of this creep. It made Patty angry.

Patty knew the effort going into finding the missing Stacey. She'd been unaware anyone knew she was gone and cried when Patty told her that her father had been on the news appealing for the return of the young woman. Now the detective wondered if anyone had noticed *she* was missing. She wished she had more of a social life, and that was the irony. She was finally starting to get a life together and met someone who may be special. Did Tony Mazzetti figure out she was gone? Who knew how men thought? She hadn't spoken to John Stallings, which was unusual, because for so long he had been the only person she spoke to every day.

She could only assume that between John and Tony someone had missed her and they were looking for her now. If John Stallings was on the case she had a better chance of being found. Once he got rolling there was no hope of stopping him. But she had learned over the years from both competition in gymnastics and police work that ultimately one could only depend on oneself. She had to act as if she were alone and had to do everything possible to protect Stacey and escape. Patty was no damsel in distress, and this creep would find that out when she got the chance.

She looked across the small room, taking in details. The terrazzo floor was clean but indicated an older home. The window had been bricked up by an amateur, displayed in the shoddy consistency and uneven nature of the mortar and crooked brick near the bottom left corner. The eyebolts in the wall were well secured, and Patty could tell she wouldn't be able to shake either her hands or feet loose by unseating the steel bolts.

Patty said, "Stacey, has he ever slept in here with you?"

"I don't think so. Once I'm out, I'm out."

"Do you know what drugs he gives you to sleep?"

"He changes them up. He said he intends to find the perfect drug cocktail to keep me happy but sedated and docile."

"Let's not give him a reason to stop that experiment. As long as we're in the experiment he won't hurt us."

"That's what I thought too."

"He's in some odd fantasy of conducting an experiment. We're part of that fantasy."

"He's so crazy he seems normal."

Patty agreed with that assessment, but it didn't make her happy. There would be no way to reason with Dremmel. She shuddered at the thought of him using a stun gun on her. She just had to find a path, a chance to surprise this son of a bitch.

Stacey turned her head and said, "I think one of the drugs he uses is Ambien. Do you know what that is?"

Patty said, "Oh yeah, I know it." And she saw a possible path to escape.

Forty-four

Thinking about his childhood had sapped William Dremmel of his energy. He could only flop on the couch next to his mother's wheelchair with another black-and-white movie on the TV. He thought he recognized Errol Flynn but couldn't be sure because his brain was on overload. Sweat poured from his face as he tried to suck in enough air to live but not be too obvious to his mother. He wiped his face with the tail of his untucked shirt, staining the bottom as if it had been dipped in a pool. He tried to clear his head as memories kept flooding back. His heart ticked along like a two-cylinder engine. Then he felt as if he had a grip. A tenuous one, but a grip on reality.

He turned away slightly from his mother and looked at the clean, off-white wall with the window set in it. His eye was drawn toward the floorboard where a floor lamp stood and he noticed a design. That was exactly what he needed. Something to focus on. Something to drawn his concentration.

The circle and lines meant something, but he couldn't

dig the meaning out of his confused thoughts. Then he realized what he was looking at: a blood spatter from the unfortunate incident with Trina. Somehow he'd missed a spot of blood that was obvious. Obvious enough to ruin everything and send him to jail for the rest of his life. How could this have happened? He was careful. He was smart. This opened a new line of questions in him. Has he made other mistakes? Did he take on too much by trying to keep the lovely Detective Levine for his experiments?

He made a quick decision. She had to go. He sat up on the couch, thinking where he had a suitcase large enough for her. She was taller than any of his previous subjects. Then he saw where he'd made his mistake. Pride. One of the sins. He didn't have to get rid of her in a suitcase. In fact, that would offer too much to the cops. Instead he'd find a place to leave her body where no one would ever find it. A Jimmy Hoffa, that's what he'd pull.

This would take a little planning and maybe a trip to scout out the location. He didn't want to frighten Stacey, so he'd use a strong dose of an Ambien-based cocktail tonight and by the time Stacey awoke tomorrow she'd be back in a single room.

He had started to push himself off of the couch, when his mother turned to him and said, "I don't want to go back to being drugged all the time."

John Stallings's conversation with his sister had shaken him. He wasn't being a good husband or father by working so much. The result wasn't much different than his father; they just arrived there by different routes. It killed him that Maria needed him at this very moment and so did Patty. This wasn't a normal investigation. His partner was missing. Now he'd made his choice and decided to go full throttle.

He had already hit three of the pharmacies that Patty had visited two days ago, spending almost no time at any of them. He asked a few questions, then moved on. He wasn't trying to build a case, he was trying to find another woman who had disappeared. No matter what he did it seemed like he spent a lot of time looking for people. This time he knew Patty wasn't the type to just run off. At first he suspected that she and Mazzetti had argued and she was just pissed off. Now, as the hours had passed and there was no sign of her, he suspected something more sinister. Had she crossed the killer somehow? He'd find out.

The pharmacy Stallings was in now had several locations all across the city. He quickstepped to the rear of the store, where the pharmacy counter was set into a solid frame behind glass to discourage robbers. He eyed each employee to see if any matched the description of the blond man given by Ernie the dealer. So far he hadn't come close to finding any employee that drew his interest except one pharmacist earlier in the day. He had looked at the blond man's personnel file and asked him a few questions about his personal life, but he didn't come close to the profile of the killer. He was married, owned a dog, not a cat, and had two teenage kids. Stallings could tell pretty quickly this wasn't the guy.

Now, in the back of the store, he noticed several customers waiting at the register and two more at the pickup line. Stallings stepped off to the side and waited until the young pharmacist in a white smock looked up. Stallings held up his credential holder so he saw the gold JSO detective shield on the outside of the holder.

The younger man looked around nervously and hesitated like he was considering making Stallings wait. To ensure that wouldn't happen he tapped the badge on the glass and signaled for the pharmacist to come over to him right now.

The man scampered up to the glass, then turned toward the rear wooden door entrance and opened the door a crack like he thought Stallings might be a robber. To satisfy the man he opened up the credentials to show the pharmacist his photo and name.

"What can I do for you, Detective?"

"First of all, you can open the door so we can talk in private."

"I'm sorry, but we're pretty busy now. Can it wait?"

"No."

"Look, I'm trying to be polite."

"So am I. Now let's go in back and talk." He pushed the door open and forced the younger man to back off, then turned and led him to a messy stockroom.

The pharmacist faced the detective, putting on his best arrogant, impatient act, when Stallings clearly read him as scared. He wore a University of Florida Alumni pin on his collar, his hair was neat with a little too much hair gel, and his smock and shirt underneath were pressed and clean. This guy wanted to project a certain image.

"Now, Detective, what's this all about?"

"Did a female JSO detective come by here yesterday?"

The smirk on the man's face told Stallings the answer was yes before he said a word.

"You her badass cop boyfriend?"

"What? No. Did she talk to anyone besides you?"

"Why?"

"Look, pal, I wish I had time to explain, but right

now I need to know if she talked to anyone beside you."

"Hey, I don't appreciate your tone."

Stallings grabbed his smock, wadding it in his hand and pulling him right next to his face. "This better?" He flicked the man back as he released his grip.

The pharmacist lost his arrogance as he carefully smoothed out his smock with both hands and tried to compose himself.

Stallings said in a low, calm voice, "Now, did she fucking talk to anyone else?"

"I, um, I don't know. She sat in here and looked over records for a while. When she left she said good-bye. When she first arrived we chatted about UF and her boyfriend."

Stallings knew that meant the pharmacist had hit on Patty. He looked him over, getting a sense of him. He had dark hair and seemed too button-down and strait-laced to ever sell drugs under the counter.

The pharmacist snapped his fingers. "I just remembered."

"Remembered what?"

"I think our clerk walked back here and stayed a few minutes."

"What's the clerk's name?"

"William Dremmel."

Forty-five

William Dremmel was shocked to learn his mother knew what he had been doing to keep her quiet for so long.

His mother said, "I know I made some mistakes as a mother, but I shouldn't have to have been in a coma the rest of my life. Just because I used some of my sleeping pills and muscle relaxers on you as a child doesn't mean you have to pay me back."

"What on earth do you mean, Mom?"

"To keep you quiet and give me some time I used to give you something to take a little nap once in a while."

"You drugged me?"

"Only a couple of days a week."

"Why?"

She leveled a stare at him. "Please, William. You know I had a few liaisons. I'm not perfect."

"More than just Arthur Whitley?"

"A few." She sounded almost proud.

"Wait a minute, you said I had mono one summer and had to sleep a lot. Did I really?"

She paused. "You were a growing boy and you needed your rest."

"You drugged me for a whole summer."

"Of course not, sweetheart. Only July and a few weeks in August."

He considered all this as the pieces of his life, his choices, his desires, all started to make sense. Perhaps the toughest thing was realizing his mom was a slut.

She still had a nice smile on her smooth, pretty face. Her blouse hung low, like she'd pulled it down, showing the pleasant curve of her breasts.

He looked at her. "Goddamn, Mom, you screwed me up bad."

"Nonsense. I had a young woman's healthy appetites. I attended to your needs as a child and never left your father unsatisfied. It wasn't my affairs that hurt you, it was your father's reaction to them."

Dremmel stared at her, not moving, not daring to move. He thought about his young, beautiful mom all those years ago caressing the handsome young black man

Then his father caught them and said in that even but terrifying tone of his, "William, go play next door at the Seikers'."

Dremmel, about eight years old at the time, watched as Arthur's head snapped up and he dove to one side, racing for the sliding glass door to the backyard. Dremmel scampered over to see what the Seiker girls were doing.

Then the story got murky for him. He'd heard a lot of speculation and stray comments from the police officers he had met over the following few days, but it was never crystal clear to him what had happened.

Officially his parents had been in a car accident that had killed his father and put his mother in a wheelchair for the rest of her life. But he knew the main flaw in the story was the accident part. His father wasn't the kind of man who had accidents. He had increased his speed on Emerson Street, running the year-old Buick into the concrete support of the I-95 overpass, destroying the car, killing himself, but tossing his mother out to the side and into the middle of the road.

Until now Dremmel had not thought about that day and what it meant. The other lesson he learned from hearing the cops talk quietly to each other: They weren't perfect either. They had no more idea of what had gone on and how the accident occurred than anyone else. William Dremmel learned that people could fool the police.

Tony Mazzetti scribbled furiously as he listened to Stallings on the phone, standing next to the squad's crime analyst. Stallings checked the pharmacies that Patty had canvassed the past two days and, lucky shit like he was, turned up something.

Stallings sounded like he was jogging as he said, "I may have a name."

Mazzetti finished writing down a list of tasks for the analyst and handed them to her. "I'm ready, what is it?"

"William Dremmel, D-r-e-m-m-e-l. White male with blond hair." He gave the date of birth and identifiers.

Mazzetti paused, then said, "I think I know that name."

"The pharmacist says he also works out at the community college teaching science."

Mazzetti sprang from his seat in excitement. "I talked to him. He's about five-seven and spends time in the gym. That means he could have known the first victim, Tawny Wallace."

"And the pharmacy has a branch near the Wendy's on Beaver where Trina Ester worked."

"This could be our guy, huh, Stall?"

"More importantly, he could have Patty."

Then Mazzetti remembered one of those little details that floats around in a cop's head for no reason and pops up without warning. "Stall, there may be some forensic evidence, too."

"What?"

"The orange string found near Trina Estler is industrial carpet."

"So?"

"I remember where I saw carpet like that."

"Where?"

"At the community college in the building where I spoke to this Dremmel character."

"No shit?"

"There's something else, Stall."

"What's that?"

"I saw him just after Trina Ester was found. She had a bruised knuckle like she'd punched someone."

"Yeah?"

"William Dremmel had a black eye when I talked to him."

William Dremmel carried a tray with vitamin supplements and several different narcotics on it. He had two separate, disposable cups of water to keep from cross-contaminating the subjects. He was trying to focus on the details of his delicate experiment, because his mother was in his head. Not just her but his whole, weird life seemed to have jammed itself into his conscious thought so that everything he saw reminded him of something else.

He was careful not to give any hint that sometime tonight Detective Patty Levine would be terminated from the experiment and moved out. He didn't want to spook Stacey or give Patty any reason to act up. Both the women were alert and their eyes were on him but not with the defiance of earlier in the day. Had they accepted their role in the experiment?

He sat the tray down on the small night table positioned exactly between the two beds and smiled at each woman. "How are we tonight?" He waited for the sarcastic remark.

Detective Levine said, "My fingers are numb. Could you loosen the cuffs?"

He thought about it, noticing the conciliatory tone. He knew she'd noticed the stun gun he made certain was visible in his pocket. She knew the consequences of misbehavior. Finally he said, "After you're out for the night, I'll loosen them. It makes sense to reduce possible problems before they begin."

"Thank you."

It sounded calculated, but at least she was responding directly to him. It made him rethink his plan to terminate her participation in the experiment. It was interesting having both of them here. Maybe he was just overreacting because of the things his mother said and the memories she had brought up.

He picked up the clipboard he kept hanging on the wall near the small table and turned to the detective. "So, are you allergic to anything?"

"What if I said I was allergic to everything?"

"Then I'd test that theory tonight."

She almost had a smirk on her face but relaxed and said, "No, no allergies."

"Do you take any prescription drugs?"

"Birth control pills."

"Nothing else?"

She shook her head.

"Excellent," he mumbled as he filled in some of the columns on her page. She did look like a good candidate. He'd hate to be rash and pass up a potential test subject. He set down the clipboard and took two Ambien and an Oxy, then mashed them into a fine powder with the bottom of the one glass he used to mix all the drugs.

"What's that?"

"Just a sleep aid. Don't worry, I'll change them up to be more effective and not build up a tolerance." Dremmel pulled off the wool blanket to look at her naked body. She made no movement and didn't try to turn or hide any part of her. "I have to make my best guess on the dosage based on your size and shape."

"You look as if you appreciate nice shapes."

He smiled at this woman's wit. He scooped the powdered pills into the paper cup of water and turned toward her. He thought, *she might make a good subject after all.* He probably could keep both of them safely.

He held up her head for her to drink the drugged water and caught the slightest look from her and then saw Stacey peek across the room at them. They had a plan. They were involved in a conspiracy against him.

Right then he realized the detective couldn't be part of the experiment.

This would be her only dosage.

It was dark by the time Mazzetti caught up to John Stallings at a deserted Chevron station a mile from William Dremmel's address. He still felt the sting of not identifying Dremmel after he talked to him at the community college. He'd fucked up and couldn't deny it or blame someone else. All the clues added up and he fit perfectly into them, but Mazzetti hadn't seen it. He needed a guy like Stallings to point him out.

Before Mazzetti was completely out of his car, Stallings said, "Where the hell you been? We gotta get moving."

"You gave me a lot of things to check, and I got 'em all right here." He held up a manila folder crammed with papers.

"Did you tell the L.T.?"

"We got to confirm a few things before we get all the troops out here."

"Tony, tell me this isn't a glory grab on your part. We're talking about Patty here."

"Don't pull that shit on me, Stall. You're the one who says too many cops slow things down. Now look at what I found." He laid the folder on the hood of his car and flipped through the first few pages. "This guy has never been arrested. Works part time at the community college and part time at this little drugstore chain."

"Yeah, I knew all that."

"Did you know one of his coworkers died the other night."

"How?"

"The chick that was electrocuted over in Durkeeville. We thought it was an accident but there were some suspicious circumstances."

"Like what?"

"She stepped in a puddle and supposedly pulled a CD player into the water at the same time."

"And you guys closed it out without investigation. Jesus, you and your clearance rates."

"Hold on, Stall. You've seen the squad. We got shit

going on. There hasn't been time to talk about murders when it looks like an accident."

Stallings held up a hand in surrender. "You're right, Tony. What else do we have on this guy?"

"Lives with his mother who gets disability. No police or fire service calls to the house or about the family."

"Nothing?"

"Not even a noise complaint."

"They're either the perfect neighbors or someone's keeping a low profile."

"You been by the house?"

"Yeah, there's a minivan in the carport and lights on in the main room."

"Could it be the vehicle from the beach cam?"

"Looks like a million other vans."

"You got any ideas?"

Stallings was a little surprised that the King of Homicide would ask for ideas. "It wouldn't hurt if we got a good look at the house quietly, then decide if we need to take action."

"Like get a warrant?"

"Tony, there won't be time for a warrant if we see something that tells us Patty's inside. We'll have to act."

"Didn't you learn your lesson the last time we did that?"

Stallings was about to just move forward without him, then realized the homicide detective might have a point. An image of Maria flashed in his head as he was trying to decide what he should do about a warrant. He'd lost his decisive edge and did the worst thing any cop could do. He just stood there.

Forty-six

Patty Levine had swallowed the water and realized how smart it was to put powdered pills in water and make someone drink it. That way they couldn't spit out the pills and the broken tablets acted faster with no time release. She recognized the familiar taste of the Ambien. The bitter stinging aftertaste on her tongue gave her confidence. This asshole had looked at her and thought two would knock the shit out of her. She wasn't sure what the Oxycontin added in might do, but the two Ambiens wouldn't beat the adrenaline pumping through her right now.

She lay perfectly still with her eyes closed as he heard Dremmel move around the room. He talked with Stacey for a few minutes longer. Patty listened but really didn't pick up much. It sounded like a checkup at the doctor's office.

Despite her heart starting to race at the prospect of her escape attempt, she forced herself to breathe normally, throwing in a little fake snore after a few minutes. It was so relaxing she almost made herself nod off for real; the Oxycontin apparently increased the effect of the sleeping pills. She fought the urge to give in to sleep, if not for herself, then for the girl across the room who was counting on her.

Then it happened. First she sensed her captor close to her. So close she felt his breath on her neck. He was checking to see how soundly she was under. She wanted to surprise him and take a bite out of his face as he leaned in close. She could imagine tearing his nose off or taking off part of his ear. But that wouldn't stop him. Instead she kept up the steady breathing and now closed her throat so there was also a slight snore.

Then she felt him stand up and start to fiddle with her handcuffs. He inserted a key and they notched open three clicks giving her wrist a wide birth.

She had a decision. Act now and use her hands while he was close or stay silent and try to slip out while he was out of the room.

Patience had never been one of her virtues.

John Stallings shushed Tony Mazzetti as they crouched in bushes on the side of a house directly across from the residence of William Dremmel. Mazzetti had kept blabbing about all the things that were wrong with this plan. Stallings had already explained that gathering intelligence on the house was the most important thing they could do right now. He didn't want to have to say it again.

Instead, Mazzetti said, "Stall, this is bullshit, slinking around like some kind of pervert. What do we do if someone catches us?"

Stallings just stared at him for a minute. "Tony, we badge 'em, you moron. Now shut up and let's see what's going on at the house."

The house was quiet as they sat in the bushes, a cool breeze kicking up from the east. Fifteen minutes of surveillance produced no information, but this was about Patty, and Stallings was prepared to stay all night if it meant saving her. The thought made him a little guilty as if he was choosing her over Maria, but he knew his wife was safe. He couldn't say the same for Patty.

Mazzetti leaned in and said, "We should let the L.T. know what the hell is going on."

"Go call her."

"You don't have to stay. There ain't shit going on. C'mon Stall, this is degrading."

"Welcome to police work, Tony."

Mazzetti grunted and started to move when Stallings grabbed him by his arm. "Take another look, Tony. You notice anything about the house we could throw in an affidavit for a search warrant?"

Mazzetti turned his eyes to the house and studied it. Concentrated hard on the older home. Then shook his head. "What do you see, Stall?"

"The path leading to the front door. Wouldn't you call that decorative sand on each side of the walkway?"

Mazzetti stared. "Son-of-a-bitch. Maybe you're not just lucky on cases."

It was the highest compliment Stallings could have ever expected from the homicide detective.

William Dremmel laid out the two, heavy-duty contractor bags in the living room while his mother continued her longest streak of consciousness in almost a year. He could hear the news from the other room. He'd finished with the girls for now, loosening Patty's cuffs mainly to let Stacey see him do it and keep her calm.

That's why she hadn't been put down for the night yet. He wanted the young woman to get used to a quiet room again while Detective Levine snoozed. He knew he should've just given her an overdose and be done with it, but he didn't want Stacey to freak out at the prospect of a dead woman in the room with her.

Later tonight he'd dose Stacey so she'd be asleep when he took the detective out for good. He'd end it quickly for her, probably with a simple asphyxiation either by strangulation or with a plastic bag over her head. He had no interest in either method for the purposes of his research and didn't want to try another knife attack because it was too messy.

There was a school being built just the other side of I-95 with the foundation about to be poured. He'd already scoped out how to peel back the metal mesh, bury Patty, and have the mesh back with virtually no chance of being seen from the road. In the next few days tons of concrete would seal his little foray into multiple test subjects and he could go back to maintaining one at a time. He already knew his next would be the waitress from Denny's, Maggie Gilson.

Now he had to go talk to his mother before he got her back on her medication schedule.

Patty Levine waited after she had heard the door click shut. There were no other sounds in the room. She used an old courtroom trick to stay awake silently by holding her breath for as long as she possibly could, then letting it out silently. The activity focused her hazy mind and made her heart rate soar, pumping adrenaline into her system to fight the effects of the drugs she'd been given.

She popped open one eye for an instant, then analyzed the scene she'd taken in like a flash photograph. There was only the smaller floor lamp on in the corner by Stacey. No one was in the room that she saw, and she couldn't tell if Stacey was awake or not.

Patty opened both eyes and scanned the room, then the door. She moved her head to check behind her toward the closed closet and caught Stacey's attention.

"I thought you were out for the night," said the young captive.

"That's what I wanted Dremmel to think."

"How'd you do that?"

"It's a long story."

"Special police training?"

"Yeah, sort of." For the first time in a couple of years she didn't feel the slightest twinge of guilt for her drug use. The two Ambiens were just her maintenance dose. Now she had some time to figure out what to do.

First, she moved her right hand but found it was secure even in the loosened cuffs. She just couldn't fold her hand enough to slip through the opening. She'd seen it from prisoners over the years where someone had thin hands or were some kind of crazy double jointed and slipped their cuffs. One woman just tossed the cuffs back to her but didn't try to escape from the patrol car. Another young man slipped the cuffs off, then managed to reach out the window, open his door, and sprint like a greyhound. He ran until he reached the next block and was hit by a city utilities truck. Patty had insisted on cuffing his broken arm despite his cries of pain.

Now she tried her left hand. This cuff was open a little wider. She touched her thumb to her pinkie and took a breath to ease out her hand. She felt pain shoot down her hand from the cuff scraping her thumb. But it was still moving, so she didn't stop. She pulled as if it wasn't her skin peeling away like cheese in a grater. It felt like someone had lubricated her hand when she realized it was her blood but it still slipped through the open cuff hole.

She let out the smallest squeak as pain overwhelmed the drugs in her system and her own natural toughness. She kept pulling until all at once her hand popped free. With no wasted motion she had the loose arm of the handcuff wiggled through the eyebolt in the wall and was sitting up working on her leg shackles. Using the open cuff arm that had swung free once her hand was out, she attacked the hinge of the leg shackles like it was a pry bar. When that didn't work she checked the chain itself. Handcuffs were relatively cheap but leg shackles could get expensive. Dremmel was apparently on a budget and bought cheaper shackles. The chain wasn't as solid as the handcuff's few lengths. She wedged the cuff arm through one of the chain lengths and popped it open with a few hard twists.

She was free.

Forty-seven

Dremmel acted as if he was watching *Jeopardy!* but, like most nights, there were no questions that could really stump him. *This country was once called Ceylon. What is Sri Lanka. This compound is present in all life on Earth. What is carbon.* The science questions tended to be downright insulting. His mother beamed with every right answer, justifying every act of parenting she had ever advocated. But he was only thinking about one right now.

Finally, at a commercial, he said, "Mom, we gotta talk."

"I'd love to chat with you, William."

"Mom, you really screwed me up with some of the things you did."

"You mean the drugs or fucking a teenage yard boy?"

He flinched and shifted on the couch. "Mom, don't talk like that, please." He shuddered.

"Whatever you want, dear."

"You don't understand what it did to me. What I've done because of it. I never had a normal girlfriend."

"I thought you had girlfriends. What about Lee Ann?"

He hesitated. "She wasn't really a girlfriend."

"Then what about the girl in the front room now? Isn't she a girlfriend?"

He stared at his mother, not sure what to say or how the hell she knew about Stacey. "Mom, um, how . . ."

She smiled, a light in her eyes he had not seen for years, then leaned up out of the chair, stood, supporting herself on the chair arms like it was a walker. "I can pull this thing over any of the stairs in the house. I have plenty of time during the day when you're out and about and you leave the key to the room in the front room cabinet."

Dremmel stared in shocked silence as his orderly world was shown to be a complete sham. "Did you talk to her?"

"Oh no. That's your business. I just checked in on her as she slept. She's very pretty."

The calculating, scientific part of his brain realized that his mom had grown tolerant to the Ambien he'd been feeding her like candy. He also didn't realize her desire to overcome her lonely existence and see the world. That gave him a pang of guilt too.

Finally, Dremmel had recovered enough to ask, "You get up in the middle of the day and cruise around the house?"

"Some days. Not too often."

"Do you want to hear about why there's a girl in my darkroom?"

She was about to answer when he heard a loud thump, then a crash near the front of the house. He sprang to his feet and reached for his stun gun in his pocket as he darted to the other room, his mother turning to follow him in walker mode.

Once she was up and around, Patty Levine immediately went to Stacey and broke her leg shackles the same way she broke her own. The handcuffs were a bigger problem until she let her engineering class she took her junior year come back to her. The professor drilled into them to think outside the normal parameters of a problem. Basically, think outside the box. Patty saw the answer almost immediately. She used the open cuff arm on her left wrist as a lever to start to twist the eye-bolt in the wall.

She looked back to Stacey and said, "Roll with the turn so I can get this thing out of the wall."

After two minutes they were both out of bed, naked, scared, and ready to kick some ass. Patty closed the open cuff so both of them were around her right wrist and not swinging awkwardly free. She had a separate shackle cuff with a short length of chain on each ankle.

Stacey still had her hands in cuffs in front of her, but they were ready to make their move.

Patty quietly tried the door handle. Locked. The door was thin, but sturdy. Now she had to decide if she should wait and try to surprise, then overpower Dremmel, or knock down the door and run. She wanted the confrontation, but wasn't sure what her reaction time was like because of the drugs and her depleted state. Her first responsibility was to ensure Stacey was safe and got away. Then she could worry about what she'd do to William Dremmel.

She looked at Stacey. "We'll be out of here in just a

minute. Once we're out, run for the front door. If you can't get to the front easily, just run to the rear of the house. No matter what happens don't stop."

"I'll follow you."

"No, you have to find the right door yourself."

"Why?"

"Because I'm staying." Then she turned and kicked the door as hard as she could.

Stacey was terrified as she stood behind Patty when she kicked the door once, twice, three times. It cracked, then she put her muscular shoulder into it and knocked the door all the way open. She followed the gutsy detective out the door but froze when William Dremmel stood right in front of the door with that scary electric shock thing in his hand.

Patty didn't hesitate to swing at him, connecting with his face. Then she heard the ugly chatter of the device and Patty yelped and jumped away from Dremmel.

Stacey kept her head down and turned toward the back of the house, ready to sprint. But two steps into it she almost fell over an old woman in a wheelchair.

The woman screeched, "William. William." Then she wrapped surprisingly strong arms around Stacey's legs. It was like being caught in quicksand. She struggled but it made no difference. The old lady held on tight and Stacey fell over, pulling her out of her wheelchair onto the floor.

Stacey started to break free of the screaming old lady when she heard another blast of the stun gun and then Patty was flopping around on the cold terrazzo floor.

The old lady's arms weakened and released as Stacey stood up into a crouch like a sprinter on starting blocks. She was going to make it.

Then she felt a strong hand on her ankle and looked back just as the stun gun made contact and the pain she'd felt before started crackling through her body.

John Stallings saw motion in the front room. There was a flash and he heard faint screams from inside the house. That was all he needed to push him into cold, calculated action. He looked over his shoulder to Tony Mazzetti at the other corner of the house attempting to make a phone call. "Tony, something's happening. We gotta move."

Mazzetti scurried up to Stallings for a look just as Stallings drew his Glock, stood up, and started sprinting across the empty street. He slowed as he approached the door but not much. He tried the front door handle. Locked. Now he could clearly hear yelling from inside as well as another sound that was familiar but he couldn't place. Then he heard it again and realized what it was: a stun gun.

Dremmel already had the detective flopping on the floor from a blast of the stun gun. Now he had the weapon firmly on Stacey's naked thigh, delivering 400,000 volts of incapacitating energy. The struggling girl immediately went limp under the power of the gun. But his mother was still screaming like an air raid siren.

"Get her, William, get her," she shrieked. Then she started yelling nonsense. The noise was so loud and shrill it disoriented him.

"Mom, quiet down." He doubted that he penetrated

the wall of noise. He raised his voice, "Mom, shut up." Still no effect.

Finally, trying to keep track of the two stunned, nude women, regain his own composure, and deal with his mother's wailing became too much. He put the nodes of the stun gun to her neck and let a charge of electricity fly.

Before he could appreciate the silence for a moment he heard someone at the front door. First trying the handle, then kicking it. Hard.

Dremmel stood, then raced toward the rear of the house, the stun gun still in his hand. He had no idea where to go.

Stallings was surprised how strong the door to the older house was, withstanding his first kick easily. He looked over his shoulder to see Mazzetti running toward the house, apparently not as sure hitting the front door was the right move. Stallings stepped back and delivered another kick just above the door handle and dead bolt. This time the door gave a little. Then, with all his power he splintered the door with a final kick.

Mazzetti timed it and ran through the open doorway without breaking his stride.

Stallings entered the house and froze at the sight of three bodies on the ground. Two naked women and an older women in a wheelchair were sprawled across the floor.

Then one of the naked women moved. Stallings kneeled to her and realized it was Patty. She let out a squeak and groan, then her whole body flexed.

He cradled her head. "Patty, can you hear me? Patty." He looked into her eyes and saw some recognition.

Mazzetti was helping the other woman on the floor. He turned and said, "How is she?"

"She's coming around. What about her? Is it Stacey Hines?"

"Yeah, and she's in shock."

"I think it was a stun gun or Taser."

Mazzetti joined him next to Patty and said, "I got her, Stall. Go get that son of a bitch."

Stallings saw that the woman in the wheelchair was stirring, so he turned and headed toward the back of the house, his gun up, ready to kill the first person he saw. He was a little surprised Mazzetti would give up the chance to catch the Bag Man himself. Maybe he wasn't the tool Stallings thought he was.

Patty Levine's head started to clear. She'd thought Stallings was with her. A blanket covered her on the soft couch, and she saw Stacey Hines sitting up in a chair across the room with a blanket wrapped around her. Tony Mazzetti gently patted an elderly woman sitting in a wheelchair.

She cleared her throat and croaked, "Tony."

He turned, then rushed to her side. He held her hand and smiled at her before she knew it. It felt natural. Mazzetti said, "Help is on the way."

"I'm okay. How's Stacey?"

"She's scared but all right. I think he didn't have time to hit her with the stun gun as long as you."

"Where is he? Tony, that's the Bag Man. Did you get him?" She felt her words rush out as her brain tried to catch up.

"Stall is after him."

"You need to go with him."

He smiled, patted her hand, and said, "I'm right where I'm supposed to be."

Forty-eight

William Dremmel was starting to calm down and think clearly as he drove the Honda Accord he had stolen two streets north of his house. He came out from between two houses and saw the Accord with the engine running and door open, then just jumped in. He needed to get away from the cops kicking in his door and then he'd decide where to go.

How had they found him? He hadn't even seen anything about Detective Levine on the TV yet. Somehow he'd left a clue pointing in his direction. It was maddening to think some flunky cop had figured out who he was and where he lived.

He fumbled with the radio dial but heard only music this time of night, no news. Traffic was light as he cruised the streets of Jacksonville keeping an eye out for police cars. He made an assessment of what resources he had with him. He had credit cards in his wallet, but using them would mean he could be traced. That left him with just over ninety dollars in cash. He might risk a stop at the ATM later, maybe throwing a misdirection at the cops by getting cash from a ATM machine south of the city, then driving north.

When he saw the sign for Denny's, the idea of some food and coffee to perk him up overwhelmed any instinct to just run blindly. The fact that the parking lot was empty and it might give him a chance to see the lovely little Maggie Gilson once more aided his decision.

As he walked into the restaurant, Maggie greeted him with a smile as he took one of the empty stools at the counter. There were no other customers.

Maggie smiled. "Hey there, where you been?"

"Just crazy at work. How are you Maggie?"

"Good." She studied him. "You okay? You look tired."

He thought about the question for a second and said, "A pipe broke in my house, so I have to spend the night out and see about it tomorrow."

"Hungry?"

"I am."

Maggie smiled and said, "Let's feed you, then we'll find a place for you to stay."

William Dremmel managed to smile at the young woman's pcrky attitude.

John Stallings felt his body sag as the events of the last few days caught up with him. William Dremmel's home was a beehive of activity as more cops arrived and neighbors came out on the street of the quiet neighborhood.

Patty Levine had insisted on staying while both Stacey Hines and Dremmel's mother were transported to the hospital. Patty wore her own clothes they'd found in the closet of the little dungeon. They were probably evidence, but at this point no one cared and it made Patty smile.

Outside the house, Lieutenant Rita Hester was already talking to a few reporters to get out the word about the man they were looking for and warn anyone else out there to steer clear of William Dremmel. The TV stations were going to flash both his driver's license photo and one found here at the house.

Stallings joined Patty and Mazzetti as the paramedics prepared to move her.

Mazzetti said, "Anything?"

He shook his head. "A kid a few blocks over reported a stolen Honda. It's out over the radio. Every cop in the city is looking to be a hero tonight." He turned to Patty. "How'r you feeling?"

"Like a truck hit me." Her smile told him all he needed to know about her chances for recovery.

Stallings said, "You're a real hero. Stacey is telling a great story."

She shook her head. "If you guys hadn't arrived . . ."

"You got out of his dungeon and made enough noise that we found you. You did great." He smiled.

She took his hand and gave him that motherly look she sometimes had. "Have you been at home enough? I know how important they are to you."

He looked down at the floor.

"John, I hope you didn't let this case distract you from the kids and Maria."

He shrugged, too embarrassed to answer. "Don't worry about it. You're safe now." Then he said, "It's almost over." He looked at Mazzetti. "C'mon, Tony, let's hit the street and see if we can find this creep."

A paramedic raised the gurney with Patty on it.

Mazzetti looked at Stallings. "No, I'm going to the hospital with Patty."

Stallings smiled and slapped Mazzetti on the back. "Good for you, Tony." He also felt a pang of guilt for not choosing Maria over the case.

Mazzetti said, "Be careful, Stall. Catch him, but don't do anything stupid."

Patty backed up that statement with a hard glare.

Maggie Gilson knew her manager didn't like any of the employees watching the little TV in the tiny rear office, but the manager wasn't here at eleven at night. No one was. That was why Maggie had Cesar, the night cook, watching the counter while she sat in the swivel chair in the rear room of the Denny's watching the twenty-inch TV.

She liked the *Friends* episode that always ran from ten-thirty to eleven, then sometimes she switched over to *Scrubs* for a few minutes. Tonight, right at eleven o'clock she started changing the channels and stopped at the local news when she saw a big banner in red letters that said, "Breaking News." Usually she cared little about what went on around her, but this caught her attention when she saw a photo on the screen. She thought she knew the man in the photo as the announcer said, "William Dremmel is the focus of a manhunt for questioning in the Bag Man serial killer investigation."

Maggie studied the photo and realized it was the guy who had been in the restaurant earlier in the evening and said a pipe broke in his house. That was bullshit. She'd told him about the J-Ville Inn.

She hurried to the employee lockers and grabbed her small Vera Bradley purse, then dug in it until she found her cell phone. Maggie scrolled through the numbers until she found the one person she knew she could trust. Cops could be tough, stupid, arrogant, and, occasionally helpful. But this guy understood people, and he'd know exactly what to do.

She dialed the phone and waited until after the third ring she heard a familiar voice say, "This is John Stallings."

Maggie knew he'd fix everything, just like he always did.

William Dremmel lay back on the hard bed in room 6 of the J-Ville Inn. The small hotel off U.S. 1 had twelve rooms with the office in the middle. Six rooms went off in one direction and six in the other. Dremmel had paid the scruffy clerk fifty bucks for the room on the end without paperwork or fuss. Dremmel promised to be out by six when the owner showed up.

He'd changed out the tag on the Honda he had stolen, then, as added security, parked the car three blocks away. The only things in the room with him were his stun gun and the clothes on his back.

At dawn he planned to get money from an ATM south of here, then double back and head north. He'd already screwed up his experiment and the life he had; there wasn't much else that could go wrong except getting caught. He planned to resist that as long as humanly possible.

With time and some ingenuity he hoped to start over again somewhere. Maybe out west or Canada. Now he just had to get away, no matter what.

John Stallings was almost to his house when his phone rang. He flirted with the idea of just letting it ring and checking the message in the morning, but he couldn't help himself and dug it out of his pocket. He flipped it open just as he slowed in front of his house. There was still a light on in the living room.

"This is John Stallings," he said as his usual greeting.

"Hey, Stall, it's Maggie Gilson."

He had to think for a moment to place the name and face. Then he remembered the cute little runaway who now worked at a Denny's. "Hey, Maggie. What's up?"

"I think I might know where the guy on TV, that William Dremmel, is."

He paused, then said carefully, "Where's that, Maggie?"

"He was in my Denny's earlier this evening, and I mentioned a motel on U.S. 1 called the J-Ville Inn."

"I know the place, just north of Edgewood Avenue."

"That's it."

"Thanks, Maggie, I'll go over and check myself."

"I knew you were the right person to call."

Forty-nine

The Shand's Jacksonville Medical Center was oddly slow tonight even with the reporters crowding the visitors' lounge hoping to get some kind of scoop from the survivors of the Bag Man. Tony Mazzetti had been here on a Saturday night when there was a full moon and the place looked more like a zoo than a hospital.

Now, in one of the small cubicles off the emergency room, he stood next to Patty Levine, holding her small hand while a nurse came in to check on her. They wanted to admit her for observation, but Patty insisted on spending the night in her own home. He couldn't blame her after what she'd been through.

Patty hadn't said much, but she didn't let go of his hand either, so he knew he was doing the right thing. He just followed wherever they wheeled her, and she seemed happy he was there. He still wondered what was happening with the search for William Dremmel, who he now knew was the Bag Man, and had given him the slip for longer than he cared to admit. Now some rookie road patrol guy would pull over the killer on a fucking traffic violation and be a hero. Shit.

Then his phone rang. He had ignored most calls tonight, because he knew it was just some stupid command staff member wanting an update. This time he saw it was Stallings on the line, so he answered.

Mazzetti said, "Whaddya got, Stall?"

"Tony, I have a reliable tip that he's out on U.S.1 at a hotel. Why don't you meet me there and we'll see if we can scoop this asshole up."

"You really think he's there?"

"One of my old runaways ran into him and gave him a motel that's safe to stay in."

Mazzetti's heart skipped as he considered his chance to really make a splash. If he could catch this guy after being the lead on the case, every news station in town would want to talk to him. A smile broke across his face as he considered the possibilities.

Stallings said, "I'm heading to the J-Ville Motel."

Mazzetti was about to say he'd be there, then he looked down at Patty and saw the fear in her eyes at the thought of his leaving. She squeezed his hand tighter, and that kept him from answering.

Over the phone Stallings said, "Tony, you gonna meet me?"

Then Mazzetti surprised himself. "No, Stall, Patty needs someone here."

There was a brief silence, then Stallings said, "Goddamn, Tony, you might be human after all."

For the first time Mazzetti smiled at something Stallings said.

Before he called in reinforcements, Stallings planned on checking out the small motel. He drove past it slowly twice but only saw an old Ford pickup and a semitractor with no trailer sitting in the lot of the J-Ville Inn. The motel had two wings jutting out from the office in the center.

Stallings drove past one last time and parked around the corner in the lot of a self-storage place. He pulled his shirt over his gun and badge, then approached from the road, walking along the covered walkway next to the first six rooms. He noticed a light on inside the farthest room marked with a number 6 as he crept toward the office. The rooms on either side of the office also had lights on. One had the pickup truck parked in front of it, and the other had the semitractor at a funny angle in front of it.

Stallings was in the glass door and standing quietly before the clerk looked up from an old TV with a half-blown speaker. Craig Ferguson's Scottish accent seemed to rattle the torn speaker fragment even more.

The clerk had the dark scowl of a pissed-off redneck. Longish greasy hair combed straight back with loose strands spiraling out around his ear. His dark eyes studied Stallings as he made him for a cop immediately.

The clerk said, "What are you doin' here?"

Stallings showed his badge just so there was no question who he was.

The clerk said, "I know, I could tell the second I looked up. What's the po-po need here in this shithole?"

Stallings held up a photo of William Dremmel. "You seen this guy tonight?"

The man didn't hesitate to shake his head. "Naw, been real slow here tonight."

"Let me see your registrations."

"You got a warrant?"

"No, but you'll have one on you if you don't show me your registrations right now."

The man was surprised at the aggression. He was apparently used to dealing with the younger, more polite police officers of the Jacksonville Sheriff's Office. Stallings stepped behind the half counter where the TV sat.

"Okay, okay, hang on." The clerk handed him a book with the list of occupants for the night.

Stallings snatched it from the man's hand, keeping his eyes on him as he set it on the counter and looked down to see two names, Bob Ura in room one and Dennis Bustle in room seven. Stallings flipped back a few pages to see how names had been entered the last few days. They had nine customers yesterday and six the day before. He looked up at the clerk, who still held a defiant look.

Stallings said, "You only have these two tonight?"

"Yep."

"So you have ten rooms empty?"

"That's right."

"Why was there a light on in room 6 at the end?"

The man hesitated and eyed the phone at the same time as Stallings.

Fifty

John Stallings was stuck. He knew he couldn't leave this asshole clerk alone or he'd warn Dremmel in room 6. He called the sheriff's office to send by a marked unit but knew he couldn't wait. He grabbed the ring with room keys and pulled the reluctant clerk from the office and had him follow down the walkway as they approached room 6.

Stallings turned and asked, "There's no back door?"

The sullen clerk shook his head.

"You wouldn't be screwin' with me again, would you?" He backed it up with a "no bullshit" look.

"Naw, no back door, and I think he's in there alone."

"Why didn't you tell me that when I asked in the office?"

"You're a cop. Never help the cops."

"I respect that kind of commitment. Now sit down right here and don't move."

The clerk sat in front of room 4 and crossed his legs. He coughed once, not bothering to cover his mouth. The smoker's hack sounded toxic already.

Stallings drew his pistol and continued on toward the last room.

William Dremmel was almost asleep when he heard a loud, hacking cough outside. The noise made his eyes pop open. He sat up quickly, reaching for the stun gun on the small night table next to the bed. Then he saw the shadow of someone crossing the window in front of his room. There was no back door. His head swiveled to each side, then up and down searching for an egress. His heartbeat picked up as he felt the walls close in. How had he been found? He clutched the stun gun, stood up, and moved toward the bathroom looking for any possible crevice in the bare room in which to hide.

He swallowed hard as he saw the door handle to the room jiggle.

John Stallings found the key marked "6" and slid it into the lock, while he said quietly, "Is this the day that changes my life?" He had his Glock in his right hand and turned his head every couple of seconds to make sure the clerk didn't move. His heart pounded in his chest as he considered what a bonehead move this was, but he had no choice. He couldn't risk losing Dremmel.

As soon as he felt the door lock click open, he shoved the door hard and ducked low, out of the doorway, where he knew he'd be silhouetted by the streetlights. He scanned the room once quickly with his pistol out in front of him, trying to control his breathing.

There was no one here. Stallings rose slowly with his Glock still out in front of him and crept toward the bathroom and closet at the far corner of the room, try-

ing not to give away his position. When he reached the
short wall that separated the bedroom from the closet
and bathroom he paused, took in a breath, and then
darted around the barrier, gun up and ready to fire.

Still nothing. The small closet was completely bare.

He could see into the open bathroom and it appeared empty. He stood to one side and used his left
hand to push open the door until it clinked with the
wall. He flipped on the single light and checked all the
way inside, letting his eyes sweep the tub, toilet, and
back wall.

Clear.

Where could this asshole be? Had Stallings's luck
just run out and he missed Dremmel? Had he gone to
eat?

He had turned to check on the clerk, when he noticed
the paneling inside the bare closet. Something didn't
look right.

William Dremmel had pulled the loose panel back
in place, covering him in the hole inside the closet just
as the door to the motel room swung open. It was tight
and dark, but he could stay in the narrow gap for a
while.

He waited, knowing someone was in the room, then,
after a few seconds, sensing the person move past the
closet into the bathroom. It had to be a cop.

He gripped the stun gun up close to his chest and
tried to breathe silently, which was harder than he expected when he concentrated on it. There was no hidden tunnel, just a gap in the wall where he pressed up
against the drywall of the main part of the motel room.
An insect scurried across his face, but he didn't move
or make a sound.

He heard the light and fan in the bathroom come on. Whoever it was, they were close. A tremor ran through his body as the events of the day caught up to him. He didn't think his shudder caused any noise as he continued to sulk in his cubbyhole.

Stallings paused, peering into the closet as well as listening for anything unusual. He could hear the light traffic trickle by on the street and the far-off sound of a boom box as the bass pounded off buildings. Then he noticed it. A slight dip in the design of the wall where the ancient paneling didn't match up just right.

Briefly he considered just unloading a few rounds into the wall. Instead, he reached in with his left hand and probed the panel. He stepped into the closet, pistol ready, and started to pull the panel when he saw some movement, heard a familiar clatter, then felt a tremendous jolt of electricity run though his arm.

The shock threw him back out of the closet as he lost his equilibrium.

Then he saw Dremmel burst out of the closet, leap over him, and dart toward the door.

Stallings rolled to one side, and, still disoriented, rose to his knees then onto wobbly legs.

He heard the buzz of the stun gun again and a scream, raised his pistol, and stumbled around the closet into the motel room.

Fifty-one

Dremmel got a partial shock on the arm of the guy in the closet, then didn't waste any time racing for freedom. He leaped the fallen, stunned man, zoomed through the room, and aimed for the open door. Without breaking stride he passed through the doorway, then slammed into someone coming inside, colliding with terrific force. He didn't hesitate and brought the stun gun up to the man's chest and squeezed the trigger.

The shock sent them in opposite directions. When he landed, Dremmel looked across the cement walkway and realized he had just sent the motel clerk into a violent convulsion on the ground.

Dremmel had started to rise to his feet when he heard someone from the motel doorway say, "Move and you're a dead man."

William Dremmel looked up into the barrel of a semiautomatic pistol held by a tough-looking man with a badge clipped to his belt.

Dremmel paused and said, "Who are you?"

"John Stallings, JSO."

Then Dremmel made his last pitch at freedom.

Stallings had this creep at gunpoint and he'd identified himself. But instead of considering the best way to
hold him until backup arrived he found himself assessing his chances of shooting this stinking pile of shit
and getting away with it. He edged closer, his pistol
still up.

Dremmel surprised him by driving up on powerful
legs like a nose tackle coming into the offensive line.
His arms up in front of his face, he struck Stallings
hard, shoving him back into the room, knocking the
pistol loose.

Stallings tumbled backward onto the hard floor with
Dremmel landing on top of him. He braced for another
jolt from the stun gun. Nothing. Just the younger man
trying to stabilize himself to land a punch.

Stallings drove his knee into Dremmel's groin. He
heard the gasp and yelp so familiar to any male ever hit
below the belt. He slid away from Dremmel and felt his
pistol on the floor as he did. He grabbed it and jumped
into a crouch, raising the gun at the same time.

He yelled, "Don't move."

Dremmel froze, gasping for air.

Slowly Stallings backed away, giving himself more
room and respecting Dremmel's athletic ability. He
stood and looked down at his prisoner.

Dremmel seemed to recover from the blow to his
groin and looked up at Stallings with defiance in his
eyes.

Stallings glanced out the door and saw the clerk was
still on the ground, virtually unconscious. This was the
exact situation he wanted. Just the two of them, iso-

lated, with no witnesses. He thought about Lee Ann Moffitt, Tawny Wallace, and Trina Ester. That old anger started welling up in him. He let himself wonder about his own daughter as he looked at this predator who had tried to claim two more victims, one of them his own partner, Patty. He thought about her in the hospital, then raised the pistol. He wished it was a revolver so he could cock it and let this asshole think about what was coming. It wasn't even murder. It was justice.

Dremmel stared up silently.

Maybe this is what he wanted? Then Stallings hesitated just long enough to think about Patty and her desire for him to think through his violent tendencies. Now was not the time to be indecisive. He kneeled down so he was the same height as Dremmel. He didn't want an ambitious crime scene tech to figure out the trajectory of the bullet made it look like an execution. He already had a stun gun burn on his arm and a lump on his head from being knocked back by Dremmel. No one would ask questions unless he got stupid.

Dremmel's expression never changed as Stallings went down on his left knee, keeping the front sights of the pistol in the center of the killer's face.

Stallings had to ask. "What pushed you to do it?"

Dremmel shrugged, showing no concern. "You tell me. Looks like we're not that different."

"Yes, we are."

Fifty-two

John Stallings dozed off on the hard wooden bench and instantly started dreaming about falling asleep while on patrol. It was a common dream among cops, but this time it was closer to the truth. He was still on duty even if he hadn't had a break in more than twenty-four hours. Now he felt the relative quiet of the room and the lack of constant motion catch up to him.

He'd avoided the crush of media, but he could hear the crowd of reporters in the outer room. He could imagine what the line of huge television cameras looked like ready to snatch any possible footage of him as he left. He just hoped none of them had managed to slide by his house and bother his family.

A hand on his back made him sit up straight and turn to see Rita Hester smiling. That wasn't a sight he was used to, at least not since she'd gone into management. She sat next to him, bumping him over on the bench without a word.

They sat in silence until she said, "You did a great thing, Stall."

"Woulda been better if we stopped him a few weeks ago."

"You could look at it like that, but we did the best we could. You need to lighten up on yourself. Not everything is your fault. But you're the one who stopped the Bag Man. That's something to be proud of."

He just nodded then asked, "Is Mazzetti coming?"

The lieutenant shook her head. "Detective Mazzetti has elected to stay at the hospital with Patty."

Stallings smiled for the first time. "Good for him."

"If it was Christmas, I'd call it a goddamn miracle."

"Mazzetti isn't so bad."

"Let me tell you something no lieutenant should ever admit about one of her troops."

"What's that?"

"I think Tony Mazzetti is a complete asshole."

"That's not a secret."

"He's also a top-notch detective, so as a boss I need him around. Just like I need you around."

"I wasn't planning on leaving."

"I mean in homicide."

Now John Stallings stared at his boss. "I don't know about that, Rita."

"Maybe in a coposition with missing persons. There are a lot of cases that overlap." She sat quietly for a minute and added, "Just think about it."

"All I can think about now is going home."

"You've earned it."

Someone walked past them. Stallings looked up and saw it was Ronald Bell.

Bell smiled, gave him a thumbs-up, and said, "I knew you'd do it."

Stallings didn't even bother with a response.

Rita Hester said, "No, you didn't, Ron. You told me three days ago he wouldn't be any help on the case."

He bowed his head and turned to walk away.

Rita was about to blast him verbally again when the rear door to the room opened. She snapped her head toward the back of the large room and she nudged Stallings, "There's your man."

He craned his neck to see William Dremmel, in an orange JSO prisoner jumpsuit, shackled at the ankle and handcuffed through a front waist chain, being led into the crowded courtroom with armed deputies on either side of him. Dremmel had no expression as a murmur rippled through the courtroom audience.

Stallings had made a lot of hard choices lately and figured he'd pay for some of them soon, but the choice to bring Dremmel in alive might pay off in positive karma in the long run. Thank God for Patty and her efforts to reform him.

He stayed just long enough to hear the judge say, "No bond." A sympathetic bailiff let Stallings slip out through a rear door to avoid the TV cameras.

The Bag Man was all done.

Fifty-three

It was light out when John Stallings finally woke up. He'd hit the sack after court about noon. The kids were in school, and Helen had taken Maria to a doctor's appointment. He figured it was late in the afternoon and was surprised he felt good enough to sit up and think about dinner with the family. He had no clock near his bed from his days as a patrolman. If he had to sleep during the day after a midnight shift he found he could only do it with no clock around.

He padded to the bathroom and started to clean up. After he'd washed his face and changed into shorts and a T-shirt the bedroom door opened and Maria walked in. She sat at the edge of the bed until he quietly joined her.

He said, "I guess you heard what happened." He held a secret hope she might be experiencing something like pride.

"You're a hero again."

"We stopped a killer."

She didn't respond.

"I was just coming down to see what was for dinner."

Maria looked at him and asked, "What time do you think it is?"

He looked to his dark alarm clock. Stallings shrugged, "Late afternoon, I guess."

"John, you've been asleep for twenty-two hours. It's ten in the morning."

"Holy crap, that's why I feel so good." He didn't think he had ever been in a bed that long, even when he was sick.

"We need to talk."

Stallings held up a hand. "I know I've been gone a lot, but now things will get back to normal."

"What's normal? Us not talking? You working weird hours? Working for days on end, then sleeping for days?"

He felt like this could be a result of her relapse and didn't want to argue.

Maria said, "I know I have issues, but I'm working on them. You have no idea that it's you too. You have issues." She started to cry softly then said, "We need a break. You need to leave."

"What are you talking about?" She sounded coherent, but the message didn't make sense.

"Helen is going to stay with us, and you're going to have to move out for a while. We have too much to work out right now."

"Maria, I think you're a little confused right now. Think about this." He felt his stomach tighten.

"I have thought about it, and you're the one who's confused. You've been detached from the family. Working all the time to save other kids has made you neglect us. You think I'm not involved. You're the one who's off trying to run from memories of Jeanie. You've been living in some kind of fantasy world. Helen tried to tell you, but you wouldn't listen." She placed her hand on his arm. "I love you, I really do, but I have to think about the kids. You have to move out and work on these problems."

He just stared at her; perhaps clearly for the first time. Was she right? Did he have it all turned around in his head?

John Stallings didn't answer as he considered what she had said and what she wanted. It hurt as bad as any punch he'd ever taken or any injury he'd ever suffered.

This really was the day that changed the rest of his life, and he never even saw it coming.

Fifty-four

The solitary holding tank at the Jacksonville Sheriff's Goode Pretrial Detention Facility kept some distance between William Dremmel and some of the street thugs swept up by patrol officers and narcotics stings. But he could hear the noise. Constant yelling and hooting. Off-key rappers and the ramblings of disturbed homeless men, shuffling around the wide cells that housed thirty prisoners each. The facility had a policy of no TV sets. Somehow Dremmel didn't think the reading material supplied by the Sheriff's Office was utilized by most of the inmates.

Dremmel was happy to be alone in a much smaller cell with its own toilet, even if it was exposed.

He had made it through his initial hearing and realized he was done. At least for now. Even his attorney wouldn't sit too close to him like he smelled or had lice that might jump onto the young, cocky public defender's cheap suit. At least they had told him that his mother was safe and comfortable at a facility near their house. She had of course been sedated, but he hoped she hadn't admitted to knowing about any of Dremmel's activities. He didn't want her charged as an accessory. He didn't want her to face anymore sorrow.

He looked down at the uneaten baloney sandwich and fruit juice sitting on the minuscule writing desk built into the wall and considered his plans. This was just a minor setback, which, with his superior intelligence, he could overcome given enough time. If he could direct the energy and focus he had been using on his drug trials, he might make himself feel a whole lot better.

He looked down at the thick scratches on his inner forearm. Blood dripped onto the cold cement floor of the cell. A single screw that projected out of the metal frame of his cot provided the sharpened edge he needed to draw blood. Not a lot of it but possibly enough to convince someone he was crazy. He'd admit to killing the girls if he could just be called mentally ill. That would give him time to find a way out of whatever jail they stuck him in. He didn't believe there was any building made that he couldn't, if he applied his intellect to it, find an escape from.

Then life would be sweet. He'd be free. In more ways than one. Of course he would literally be on the streets, but he also would no longer have to observe any constraint society wanted to put on him. Now he could kill without concern. It was all gravy. If he could just get out of prison.

He might find something else to study.

One thing he'd do is make sure that lucky cop, that John Stallings, regretted butting into his business. That was a goal he could look forward to.

He rubbed his arm hard across the bolt and felt it cut

into an artery near his elbow on his inner forearm. Blood spurted out and across the room, forming an instant dark puddle near the middle of the tiny cell.

In case that wasn't enough to show his mental state, Dremmel started to write his name in blood on the dingy wall. Then he wrote a short poem.

> *Sleep time, sleep time. All is well.*
> *Keep time, do time. See you in hell.*

He forced himself to keep grinning until one of the correctional officers noticed him and rushed to the cell door.

The muscular black man shook his head and said, "You're one crazy son of a bitch."

Dremmel kept smiling and thought, *thank you for noticing.*

John Stallings sat in the low early morning light from the solitary clean window in the Land That Time Forgot. He was wide awake after his odd sleeping pattern. He'd spent most of the day finding a place to live while Maria and he worked out their problems. He couldn't face moving in with his mother; in fact he hoped to resolve his marital issues before his mother even found out. But now, in the empty, silent Crimes/Persons squad bay he looked up at the nineteen-inch screen of the analyst's computer. It was the fastest machine in the unit, and he'd been viewing photographs and drawings posted by everyone from cops in Seattle to child advocates in Maine.

Three drawings had been of middle teens and from the time shortly after Jeanie's disappearance. They were all of bodies that had been discovered. He made

note of the investigating officers or tip line and knew
he'd have to wait a few hours before calling. He hated
these kinds of leads because they could only lead in
one direction.

He also had the number of a teen rescue house in
Dallas, where the woman who ran it, Rhonda Boyette,
kept a constant eye out for him. She was representative
of the kindhearted people Stallings had run across in
his endless search for his oldest daughter.

Working on this kept his mind off his most recent
problems and somehow made him feel like he had a
purpose. He just couldn't believe that he'd never see
her again. Something inside him, a hunch or sixth
sense, whatever it could be called, told him that this
chapter in his life was not over.

After a couple of minutes he clicked a Web address
that took him to a local TV station's Web site and read
a news blurb on William Dremmel. There was nothing
new in the short story. Just that the Bag Man was in
solitary at the Goode Pretrial Detention Facility on
East Adams Street. The judge had issued no bond and
ordered an array of psychiatric evaluations. All standard in a case of this nature. William Dremmel's
mother was at a hospital and resting comfortably.

Stallings read the rest but didn't worry about it.
William Dremmel's days of terrorizing Jacksonville
were over, and Stallings doubted he'd ever have to
worry too much about the killer again. The trial would
be simple, and Mazzetti would handle most of it.

Stallings felt a twinge of satisfaction that he had accomplished what he had set out to do.

He stood, stretched, and walked back over to his
own desk. He looked down at the seven framed photographs on his ancient wooden desk and picked up a
five-by-seven color shot of Jeanie posing with several

of the lacrosse players and her coach. Instead of focusing on Jeanie's smiling face like he usually did, he drifted over two girls to the smaller form of Lee Ann Moffit.

Somewhere, somehow, he knew there was a cop working just as hard for his Jeanie.